FALSE EVIDENCE

RACHEL GRANT

ISBN-13: 978-1-944571-90-0

Copyediting by Linda Ingmanson

Cover design by Jocelyn Grant/J. Grant Design

Books By Rachel Grant

Evidence: Under Fire

Into the Storm

Trust Me

Don't Look Back

Zero Hour

Evidence

Concrete Evidence

Body of Evidence

Withholding Evidence

Night Owl

Incriminating Evidence

Covert Evidence

Cold Evidence

Poison Evidence

Silent Evidence

Winter Hawk

Tainted Evidence

Broken Falcon

False Evidence

Fiona Carver

Dangerous Ground

Crash Site

Flashpoint

Tinderbox

Catalyst

Firestorm

Inferno

Romantic Mystery

Grave Danger

Paranormal Romance

Midnight Sun

Writing as R.S. Grant

The Buried Hours

This one is for Manda Collins.
Brilliant author. Fantastic alpha reader. Wonderful friend.

Prologue

Upper Marlborough, Maryland
December

Alexandra Vargas would give anything to find a way to fall out of love with JT Talon. Given the way he'd been treating her for the last several months, one would think it would be easy. But her heart made excuses for him.

He was grieving both the loss of his respect for his father, and now that Joseph Talon Sr. had entered hospice, he was grieving the man's impending death.

She paused and studied her reflection before she applied eyeliner. More than anything, she wanted to stay home tonight, drink spiked eggnog, and hate watch *Love Actually*. She disliked ninety percent of the story threads but still found the movie compellingly watchable.

But her annual holiday viewing wasn't in the cards tonight. No, she was JT's date for the Talon & Drake end-of-year party. It capped off a week in which the top employees from each branch had flown in for a summit, and now that the big meetings were done, it was time to play.

The problem was, engineers didn't know how to play, not to mention that JT was in a foul mood and had been for months. Still, she'd made the choice to stand beside him when his life imploded two and a half years ago. She and JT had officially broken up when she called off the wedding four years ago, but they'd been on the path to reconciliation when Joseph Talon Sr. was arrested, and it had been so easy to slide back into the role of girlfriend because JT had been hurting and needed her.

Tonight, she'd play her part as his date, dressed pretty and wearing the expensive necklace he'd given her as an early Christmas present. At least Erica and Lee would be there. Lee didn't work for the company, but he was one-third owner, having purchased Edward Drake's shares when he went to prison. Technically, the company name should be changed to Talon & Scott, but Lee didn't want his name on the letterhead. They were moving to just call it T&D as a soft rebrand.

In a lot of ways, tonight's party really mattered on that journey for the company. Two and a half years wasn't a lot of time for an engineering firm to shift direction, but JT had pulled it off and he deserved this celebration.

It was a shame he was too angry to enjoy it.

She finished applying makeup and pulled on the couture gown JT had insisted she get for this event. He and his father were too much alike in some ways. The women at their side must always be perfect and dressed in a manner suitable for the pages of *Vogue*. Joe had been a politician with his sights set on the presidency, and JT had intended to follow in all of his father's footsteps.

Alexandra had been a contender for the role of political wife, but she'd conceded a week before the wedding. Still, she dressed for the part to please JT, because the times he surfaced from the darkness and truly saw her were reminiscent of the early days, when falling in love with him had been as easy as breathing.

She looked with longing at her yoga pants and sweatshirt. Tomorrow night, she'd make a giant bowl of popcorn and binge-watch all the holiday movies. Maybe Erica would join her.

"What's taking so long?" JT shouted from the living room. "We need to go."

She growled under her breath. They had plenty of time.

After putting on the necklace, she sat on the bed and fastened the stilettos he insisted she wear. In the early days, once she'd gotten used to accepting his gifts, she'd loved this part. The shoes. The clothes. Even the jewels. It had made her feel beautiful and powerful, and JT had showered her with the best kind of attention.

But that magic was long gone, and none of it excited her anymore.

She wanted comfy clothes and an evening at home. She wanted to make love with him when the mood struck in whatever room they happened to be in. She wanted lazy weekend mornings.

But if she couldn't have any of that, she wanted a baby, which was the one thing JT would never give her.

It was one of the reasons she'd called off the wedding. But still, four years later, even though they'd broken up so she could find a man to love who also wanted children, she was still with him and only him.

Because she loved him and didn't know how to stop.

The problem was, ever since the fallout with his father, he was no longer emotionally available to her. She loved him but didn't *have* him. And she didn't have a baby. And as long as things continued on this trajectory, she'd never have either.

She placed her hand on her belly. She'd realized an hour

ago that her period was late—nearly two weeks—and had spent a frantic half hour searching the cabinet for a pregnancy test, but those would be at the apartment she shared with Kendall, not at the Talon Maryland estate.

She told herself it was just stress and resumed getting ready for the party.

If she were pregnant, JT would go through the roof.

She stood and twirled before the mirror, checking her appearance for flaws before leaving the bedroom to face the love of her life.

He wore a tailored suit and looked achingly handsome.

JT had celebrated his fortieth birthday in September, and the years looked great on him. Tall, with thick dark hair and brown, brooding eyes. He had his own dojo in DC where he worked out with Lee and Curt and a few other friends on a regular basis. He was even more fit than he'd been when they first met nine years ago.

He was brilliant, handsome, toned, and extremely wealthy. During the year after she called off the wedding, when they were truly broken up, tabloids had published photos of him with models and famous athletes by his side. He'd been auditioning high-profile women for the role of politician's wife, she'd presumed.

That was one thing Alexandra had lacked—her own platform. She'd earned her PhD a year after their breakup. Now she was teaching at a university, but her own research had stalled. She had applied for a research fellowship in theoretical physics at CERN but couldn't imagine leaving JT when he so clearly needed her.

Which was ridiculous. Her life and goals were just as important as his.

JT's eyes crinkled at the corners as he studied her. "You look beautiful."

His tone said he meant it, and she felt that old rush only he triggered. "Thank you. Worth the wait?"

He placed a hand around her waist and pulled her to him. He lightly brushed his lips over hers—careful not to muss her lipstick—and said, "Always."

She wanted this moment to continue. For them to throw caution to the wind and have a quickie right here and now. She could fix her hair and makeup and then she'd have a dirty secret all night as she watched him work the party.

She tugged at his lapels and pulled him to her. "We still have time, you know. Why don't I take off the dress but leave on the necklace and heels, and you can fuck me right here?"

"You like that, don't you? Getting fucked while wearing nothing but a thirty-thousand-dollar necklace."

She'd had no idea the necklace cost that much. It was outrageous to spend that much on jewelry. Later, she'd talk to him about selling it and donating the money to charity, but for tonight, she'd wear the precious gems that were perfectly displayed just above the dip of her cleavage.

"What I like is the way *you* look at me as you fuck me when I'm wearing nothing but your jewels." She needed to see that look. To feel like she mattered to him as much as he mattered to her. "Please, JT. I want you. Now."

He shook his head. "After the party. I promise."

"I'm going to hold you to it. I need you, JT."

His face flashed with emotion. Pain. Regret. Did he know how distant he'd been over the last several months?

"I'll do better, Lex."

Yes. He knew. And his words gave her a surge of hope. Maybe they could find their way back to each other. If she had JT, she could be content without a baby. What she couldn't tolerate was having neither.

Again, her thoughts flitted to her missing period. No. She

couldn't be pregnant. Her birth control was up to date. It was just stress.

"What's wrong?" JT asked.

She shrugged. She wouldn't tell him before she took a pregnancy test. No point in freaking him out unnecessarily. "Nothing. Let's get the party over with so we can come home and make love."

He gave her his killer smile that always melted her panties. "The things I'm going to do to you later tonight."

Hope shone bright. Lord, how she wanted JT back. Given that she hadn't found a way to fall out of love with him, getting *him* to love her again was her only option.

The party was being held in a DC hotel ballroom, a different venue from the first T&D holiday party Alexandra had attended nine years ago. That party—the night she met JT—had been held at the Menanichoch tribal casino.

She scanned the ballroom, searching for her roommate, Kendall, who worked for T&D's Bethesda office. She spotted Kendall in the back corner chatting with her boyfriend, Brent Forbes.

Brent was not Alexandra's favorite person. She'd been upset when the two reconciled again last year. Not that she could throw stones given her equally inconsistent relationship with JT. Still, Brent had earned her dislike, and she decided to put off greeting the roommate she hadn't seen in several weeks because she preferred JT's estate to their apartment now that Brent was back in the picture.

Her mood improved when Erica and Lee arrived. Erica had quit her job at Talon & Drake just months after everything went down with Joe, but she was still friends with her old boss, Janice. Erica, Janice, and Alexandra gathered at the edge of the room while JT and Lee worked the party filled with senior engineers and branch managers from all over the world.

Erica talked about her job as an underwater archaeologist for the US Navy, gesturing broadly as she told a tale about a navy airplane that was being raised from Lake Superior.

Janice frowned and reached for Erica's waving hand. "Did something happen to your ring?" She glanced toward Lee. "Is everything okay between you two?"

Erica sighed and mumbled, "I knew I should have worn it."

"What's wrong?" Alexandra said. She'd been so focused on her troubles with JT, she hadn't noticed that cracks had been forming in Erica and Lee's relationship.

"We're fine. I love him like crazy and he loves me. It's just that—he wants kids, and I don't know if I can be a good mom. It terrifies the hell out of me. I don't want to trap him in a marriage without kids. It feels selfish."

Alexandra sucked in a deep breath. She'd never shared with anyone—and was fairly certain JT hadn't either—why she'd called off the wedding.

Could she do so now? Would it make a difference to Erica —or even herself—to hear the other side of her conundrum from someone navigating the opposite situation?

But then, Erica and Lee were wildly in love. Which was *not* the situation with JT anymore. Sure, Alexandra loved him, but sometimes she wondered if he even liked her these days.

He was so moody and cold.

She remembered the look he'd given her earlier, and heat flooded her.

Nothing cold about that.

She cleared her throat. "JT and I have struggled with that question for years."

Erica's brows drew together. "Really?"

Janice gave a soft smile. "As a T&D employee, I think it's best if I leave you two to talk. Erica, know that I support you, always."

As Janice walked away, Erica murmured, "I really love that woman."

"I'm sorry if my confession drove her off."

Erica shrugged, "It's fine. You and I need to talk, and she's right. Lee might not be active in company management, but both he and JT are essentially her bosses. It's best to keep this stuff private. Especially given how much JT has been struggling."

"You know about that?"

"Honey, everyone knows. Lee's worried. He's been so grateful to you for sticking by him. I thought he'd told you that?"

"He has, but…I thought JT was doing a better job of hiding his struggle since then. Especially with Lee, given what Joe did to you both."

"Lee and JT went to see Joe in hospice yesterday."

Alexandra let out a gasp. "JT didn't tell me that. I mean, I knew JT went, but I didn't know Lee was there. Was it the first time Lee's seen him since the sentencing?"

Erica nodded. "I had to push him to go. Remind him he'd regret it when Joe is gone."

"How…how was it?"

Erica's gaze shifted to Lee as he stood twenty feet away, chatting with a small group of people. JT was nowhere to be seen.

"I think it went as well as could be expected. Joe cried and told Lee he's sorry again, that he loves him, and he asked for forgiveness."

"But Lee isn't there yet. He's not ready to forgive."

"No, he's not. I don't know if he ever will be. And

honestly, I think it's shitty to ask for forgiveness from your deathbed. Talk about a mind fuck. The pressure."

"But I get why he did it," Alexandra said.

"Yeah. Same." Erica bit her lip. "Sometimes I just want Lee to forgive Joe so we can put it behind us and move on, but who am I to talk? I can't forgive my dead mother, and because of her, I'm terrified of having kids with the man I love. That's why I told Lee we shouldn't say we're engaged anymore. It doesn't feel right until I know I can give him what he wants."

"But Erica, Lee loves you. And he obviously loves you enough to want to marry you even knowing you might not ever want kids. If he's saying that, he means it. Believe me, I know. Hold on tight and marry him."

"Is that what happened with you and JT, why you broke up?"

She gave a slow nod. "Except it went the other way. I want kids. He doesn't. There were other factors, but that was one of the biggest."

"But here you are, years later, still together."

"I can't seem to stop loving him. I tried dating, and…no one else made me feel like he did. The problem is, we never had a big fight or anything. Hell, even now, when he's being an absolute ass half the time and I'm not entirely certain he even likes me, I can't leave him. Believe me, I want to at times. But then, other times, he looks at me like he used to, and dammit, I just…melt."

It was clear when they sat down to dinner that JT had been drinking, which was odd because he usually limited himself at these kinds of events. They'd had champagne in the limousine on the way here, but usually, that was where his drinking stopped, with the exception of a glass of wine with dinner.

Still, she wouldn't judge. She'd had drinks while chatting with Erica, and it wasn't like either of them were driving. Plus, it was quite literally his party. He could drink all he wanted. It was just a shame that her plans for his body later might be hindered if he had too much to drink.

It wasn't until the second course was served that she started to worry. He wasn't slurring, but he was getting mean. JT wasn't a mean drunk, at least he hadn't been in the years they were officially together. But the last two years, everything had been different.

JT had a lot of anger inside him, and it was constantly searching for ways to break out. Alcohol opened a dangerous door.

Of course, as the boss and majority owner of the company, he could do what he wanted here without risking his career. And given the damage Joseph Talon had done, there was no harm he could do to his reputation that was on par with that. The owner getting drunk at his own holiday party wouldn't impact the company in a negative way.

Still, Alexandra was on edge. This wasn't the JT she loved. She'd had a brief glimpse of him tonight, but those glimpses were getting fewer and further between. Would that man disappear eventually?

An hour ago, Erica had asked her a question she'd never considered: if JT asked her to marry him again, what would she say?

She'd blurted out *yes* without thinking, shocking herself and making her wonder if that was what she'd been waiting for these last two years.

She thought of the man who'd smiled at her earlier and promised to do better. Who'd looked at her with heat in his eyes that dispelled the loneliness that too often filled the space between them.

That man she'd marry without regret.

But that man wasn't sitting next to her at this dinner table. No, that man had been left in the limousine.

She felt JT's gaze and turned to see him studying her cleavage with the strategically placed emerald surrounded by small diamonds. Then his gaze flicked across the round table to Calvin Moss, the Baltimore branch manager. "You checking out my date's tits or the jewels, Calvin?"

The man stiffened. "Neither, JT."

She hadn't noticed if Calvin had been looking, nor would she care if he had. The dress and jewels begged eyes to go there. Erica had joked about not being able to take her eyes off the display. *"And the big emerald isn't bad either."*

"Cool it, JT. Don't give me jewelry or ask me to wear dresses like this if you're going to be an ass when people look."

"But how will I get you to suck my dick if I don't give you diamonds?"

Erica gasped, and Alexandra bolted to her feet. She yanked at the necklace and would have dropped it on JT's plate, but naturally, something that valuable had a solid clasp, so all she did was risk a welt at the back of her neck.

She strode from the table as tears burned her eyes. If that was the kind of thing that came out of JT's mouth when he'd been drinking, what was going on in his head when he was sober?

She made it to the corridor that led to the ladies' room before JT caught up with her.

"Go away, JT." She didn't want to talk to him when he was like this.

"I'm not going to apologize."

"Naturally. You never do."

"We both know the only reason you've stuck around these last two years is for the money. The clothes. The gifts."

"If you believe that, you don't know me at all."

"You gambled I'd change my mind about kids when you called off the wedding, but you lost that bet. I heard what you said to Erica, that you want me to propose again. I get it. You miss having full access to my wallet. You expect me to believe kids are no longer a deal-breaker for you?" He shook his head. "Right."

He then smirked at her. "You should know, *Muffin,* you can't force my hand by getting pregnant. I took care of that last year when you were in Switzerland for two months. I got cut. So no matter how many holes you poke in your diaphragm, you aren't getting my sperm."

Hurt seared her. A sharp, hot pain right in the chest. Not that he'd gotten a vasectomy, but that he'd *hidden* it from her. Not only hadn't he trusted her, he viewed her as conniving.

She'd spent the last two and a half years trying to help this man get back on emotionally level ground. She'd pulled the entirety of the emotional weight of their relationship to *help him.* And he'd gotten a secret vasectomy so he could fuck her without fear of fatherhood.

"Well, that's a relief, then. When I was getting ready for tonight, I realized my period was late, and I was worried about how you'd react if I was pregnant."

"If you're pregnant, the kid isn't mine. Who else have you been fucking?"

"No one, asshole. I'm *relieved* because what you just told me means I can't be pregnant unless your vasectomy was botched or you're lying to me."

"If you're pregnant, you'll never get a dime of my money. All your scheming for nothing. Fucking around without birth control to better your odds of conceiving. Really stupid for a woman with a genius IQ."

She stared at him, shocked by everything he considered her capable of.

She held his gaze for a moment, then, without a word, turned and headed for the hotel lobby and the exit. She'd take a taxi to the apartment she shared with Kendall, grateful she'd made the choice to keep her own address after she'd essentially moved in with JT last year.

After years of wanting to fall out of love with JT, her wish had finally been granted.

Chapter One

Montgomery County, Maryland
Seven years later
December 21st

Alexandra was running late and would be charged a fine by the daycare. Again. But sorting through her deceased friend's belongings had been gut-wrenching. Kendall's suicide in late October was a heartache she hadn't yet begun to process.

Spending the day with Kendall's sister, Tanya, had opened the floodgates for the grief she'd been holding back as the fall term wound down. She'd had to get through her first semester teaching again after taking a yearlong maternity leave before she could let herself feel.

The mind was a strange, wonderful, and terrible thing in how it could pack stuff away until one had time to process it.

Today was that day, but as a result, she and Tanya had gotten less done than they'd hoped. They'd spent too long going through photo albums from college, back in the days before everything was digitized.

The digital photos that were taken in subsequent years could be viewed at her leisure, as she now had the hard drive of the computer they'd shared when she and Kendall had been roommates. It was bound to have hundreds of photos.

Her heart ached. Kendall had emailed her in October—days before her suicide—to ask Alexandra if she wanted the computer and other items Kendall had that belonged to her. They'd made plans to meet, but then Gemma had gotten sick and Alexandra had canceled.

The next day, Kendall was gone. Alexandra had missed her chance to reconnect with her friend and heal the rift that had widened again right before Alexandra moved to Switzerland.

Now all she had of the friend who'd meant so much to her since freshman year of college were the photos on the old hard drive and a box of trinkets in the cargo space of her SUV.

She wasn't ready to look at the photos from grad school, including the early years of her time with JT, but she was glad to have them. Maybe in another seven years or so, her brain would be ready to process that hurt and anger that she'd given so much of her life to JT, she'd nearly been too late to start living for herself.

But today had belonged to Kendall. The friend she'd loved. The friend who'd hurt her. The friend she'd left behind when she finally forged her own path.

She drove down a rural road, away from the farmhouse Kendall had moved into after she'd negotiated a part-time telework agreement with the Bethesda office of T&D, where she'd worked for the last nine years of her life.

Lee had been the one to hire Kendall, in one of his last acts as manager of the Bethesda office. At the time, Alexandra had been excited for Kendall to have landed on her feet after a difficult period, but then Brent had weaseled his way back into her bed, and the yo-yo started up again.

Kendall had lived alone in the house, only going to the office two days a week. No one had seen the signs that her ongoing battle with depression had taken a sharp turn.

Regret filled Alexandra. She'd been so busy as a single mom. Combined with returning to teaching, she hadn't been there for her friend in need. It didn't matter that they'd drifted apart. She should have gone to see her the moment Kendall reached out.

Gemma was sick with a stomach bug and fever. The mental reminder changed nothing. Guilt never gave way to logic. It joined the mountain of regret in her heart as she navigated the dark road.

Now that the semester was over, today had been the first opportunity to help Tanya sort through Kendall's belongings. Much as she'd ached at putting Gemma in daycare during winter break, Tanya needed help, and Kendall deserved her attention. Now, she was running late after a teary goodbye with Tanya, who was heading back to her home in Pennsylvania until after the New Year.

Alexandra's heart thrummed with a surge of happiness that poked through the grief. As soon as she picked up Gemma, their winter vacation would begin.

She was so eager for this time with her baby. It was her daughter's second Christmas, and this year, she was walking and talking and excited by the lights and sparkles that came with decorating. She wanted to savor this holiday. She'd been dreaming of these kinds of moments for more than a decade, and now, at last, they were upon her.

Blue lights flashed in the rearview, and she frowned as she glanced at the speedometer. Even though she was in a hurry, she hadn't been speeding. Maybe there was some sort of emergency, and the officer wanted to pass on the dark two-lane road?

She spotted reflectors marking a driveway on the left, and the opposite shoulder widened to accommodate a mailbox on the right. She braked quickly, stopping just in time to park on the widened shoulder.

The cruiser didn't pass by. Instead, it pulled up behind her fast, the officer likely forced to slam the brakes. The headlights hit the rearview, and the bright light blinded her.

Shit. The late pickup fee would double after thirty minutes. Quickly, she used a voice command to call Erica, who answered immediately. "Hey, Alexandra, what's up?"

"I'm running late to pick up Gemma, and I'm being pulled over—I don't know why. I wasn't speeding."

"You want me to pick her up?"

"Would you mind? I know it's a huge ask."

"No problem. Gracie will be thrilled with the company. I'll head out now."

"Thanks, Erica."

She disconnected and let out a relieved sigh as the cop climbed from the vehicle and approached. Thankfully, Erica was authorized to pick up Gemma anytime. The daycare was only a mile from Erica's house in Virginia, which made the arrangement extremely convenient. As a single mom, it was always good to have a backup mom at the ready. Erica was an absolute gift in that regard.

Erica was the one friend Alexandra had refused to give up when she and JT split for good, and the only time Alexandra had seen JT in the last seven years was at Erica and Lee's wedding.

She shouldn't have gone. After all, JT was best man. But she'd wanted to see Erica finally marry Lee after years of struggling with her own decision.

Not wanting to mar the happy day knowing JT could be a moody bastard, Alexandra had left right after the ceremony.

Now that she lived near Erica and Lee and their daughters played together, she was bound to cross paths with him, but so far, her luck had held.

The officer tapped on her window, and she rolled it down. The cold December air wafted into the car, making her hope this wouldn't take long. Her coat was in a heap on the passenger seat.

"Please step from the vehicle, ma'am."

The command startled her. "Don't you want to see my license and registration?"

"I said step from the vehicle."

She took a deep breath and tried to remember Maryland law on this. Could he compel her to leave the safety of her vehicle without offering any reason for why he'd pulled her over?

This didn't feel right.

"Why did you pull me over?"

He reached inside the window and hit the unlock button, then yanked the door open. "Out. Now."

She reached for her phone and hit the camera button on the lock screen, snapping his photo.

He yanked her phone from her hand, dropped it on the ground, and stomped on it.

Fear like she'd never felt before swept down her, leaving her dizzy.

This didn't make sense. He couldn't be a real cop, could he?

Was he some sort of serial killer who drove down back roads and pulled over women driving alone?

But how had he known she was alone? Her SUV had tinted windows. It was pure luck that Gemma wasn't in her car seat in the back.

Oh god. Her baby. Would she see her again?

In the midst of her panic, she had a moment of relief knowing Erica was on her way to pick up her baby girl. No matter what happened, Gemma was safe and would be with someone she knew and loved.

The cop tried to yank her from the car, but her seat belt was still buckled. He cursed and reached across her—she thought to unlatch the belt—but he twisted the key, shutting off the engine, then he yanked upward, snapping the plastic fob from the end of the key.

She shoved at him, trying to smash his head into the steering wheel. She might be assaulting a cop, but what he was doing couldn't be legal.

His elbow snapped back, hitting her in the face. Pain exploded along her cheekbone and radiated out to her jaw and ear.

Tears sprang to her eyes. She didn't know if they were from fear or pain.

He unlatched her seat belt as she grappled for her coat and the heavy metal hard drive it covered.

He yanked her from the vehicle. She landed on the icy-cold pavement; the hard drive made a crunching sound as it landed beneath her coat.

At this point, she didn't care if she'd broken it. She didn't care about the photos or the data it held. No. Now it was a brick. A weapon.

"Get up!" the man barked.

She moved slowly, her hand buried under her coat as she wrapped her fingers around the hard drive.

It contained so much more than photos. The computer had been a gift from JT in the early days of their relationship and was better, faster, with more storage than any computer she or Kendall could afford, so they both used it for the most important projects. It contained an archive of emails from the early 2000s, plus school and work files for Kendall, along with some of Alexandra's earliest research and theories about dark matter from her grad school days.

The files they'd saved on this brick added nothing to the weight, but the fact that they were there was the only reason she had this potential weapon now.

Dark matter to the rescue.

She wrapped her hand around the heavy brick that held information on neutron stars' relationship with free quarks along with dinosaur-killing matter and hoped it would have enough heft to save her.

Gemma needed her mom. The only parent she had.

She slowly rose to her feet, not faking the slight wobble as she reached her full height. "Why are you doing this?"

The cop said nothing. The headlights from the patrol car lit the dark road, and she could see his face now that he wasn't shining a light in her eyes.

He was a Maryland State Police officer. His uniform looked genuine. The patrol car was real enough. But no one could say anything about this stop was legal.

Surely a car would drive by and see what was happening. Maybe she could wave for help and someone would call 911 on her behalf. Or someone in the house she'd parked in front of would come out to see why police lights were flashing.

But a glance across the road showed only a long driveway. No house in sight. No lights.

"Who are you?" she asked. The bearded officer didn't look familiar.

The man smirked and said, "I need to search your vehicle. Do you consent to the search?"

At last, a nod to legal procedure. "Hell no."

"Then I'll just have to handcuff you while I do it. You have the right to remain silent—"

"What is your probable cause? What am I being arrested for?"

"You refused the search, and you assaulted an officer."

"I have the right to refuse, and you assaulted me first and never gave me a reason for pulling me over. You stole my phone and destroyed it, then you broke my car key."

"It's your word against mine, Dr. Vargas."

He knew her name. He could have gotten that information from running her plate, but somehow, she didn't think that was it.

"I'm a respected theoretical physicist. I don't have a credibility problem, while a cop who doesn't have his dashboard or body cam on during a traffic stop has something to hide."

"What makes you think my camera is off?"

"My genius IQ." She didn't usually make references to her Mensa status like this—IQ was a biased construct, after all—but right now, she'd do anything to hold the crushing fear at bay, and letting this guy know she was neither weak nor a dummy seemed like a good idea. Also, every second they stood here was another second in which car headlights might appear from around the bend.

The officer held up his handcuffs and stepped toward her. "Hands above your head."

She took a step backward. Her coat draped over her hand, hiding the brick she gripped so tightly, her fingers were going numb.

"Stop resisting, Dr. Vargas. I'll put you in the back of the patrol car while I search your vehicle, then we'll go to the station and book you."

"For what?"

"Assaulting an officer."

"Why did you pull me over? I wasn't speeding. My taillights aren't broken. I signaled for every turn and lane change." Truth was there hadn't been any. She was only a mile or so from Kendall's house.

The man took his baton and smashed her taillight. The quick violence of the action made her flinch.

She would point out that the bits of broken plastic now littered the roadside, much like her shattered phone, but she didn't need a genius IQ to know telling him what to do to conceal his actions would be a serious mistake.

He turned to her again and said, "Hands. Above. Your. Head."

He swung the baton so it hit his palm. His goal was definitely to terrify her, and she couldn't envision a scenario in which she walked away from this encounter.

She *knew* people. The former US Attorney General being one of them. She and Curt Dominick had known each other from the earliest days when she dated JT, before he was the US Attorney for the District of Columbia. They weren't close —not since things ended with JT—but she had no doubt he'd used his clout to make sure the investigation into this "traffic stop" was thorough.

But to get that investigation, Alexandra needed to make it to the police station alive...and she had a hard time thinking this officer really planned to arrest her for assaulting an officer. Not when everything he'd done since flashing his blue lights was blatantly illegal.

If she got in the back of that patrol car, she was a dead woman. She'd probably disappear from the face of the earth. Just her car and a broken phone and taillight to show she'd been here.

She thought of her daughter and the life she had now that she loved so desperately. Gemma. Erica. Colleagues she adored. Tanya, who she'd reconnected with just today. A career in a field she was passionate about.

He took another step toward her. Alexandra didn't hesitate.

All those years with JT, who'd given her lessons in his private dojo for more than a decade, had prepared her for this moment.

First, she landed a roundhouse kick to his chest, then batted away the baton with one hand as she dropped the coat that covered the other. He cursed and grappled for his gun, and she swung the hand that clutched the hard drive, hitting him in the head.

He dropped like a stone. She stood above him, breathing heavy, watching his hands.

When she was certain he was out, she reached for his gun and wrapped her hand around the grip but then spotted the Taser on his belt and grabbed it instead. She pointed the weapon at him while she checked his pulse.

He was breathing with a steady heartbeat.

She rose to her feet, trying to figure out what to do next. Could she get the SUV's engine to start with a broken key? It was still in the ignition.

It was that or steal the police car. She supposed she could cuff him and put him in the backseat. But the odds that other cops would shoot first and ask questions later were high if she were to take the wheel.

Her phone was destroyed. Could she use the police radio?

Headlights rounded the bend. The one thing she'd wanted desperately a few moments ago, but now…it would look to a passing motorist like she'd been the aggressor.

Against a cop.

She grabbed her coat and the hard drive—which had blood on it—and dove for the side of the road, jumping across the ditch behind the mailbox.

She'd hide until the car had passed. If they stopped, she'd decide if the driver was safe to approach.

She burrowed into the shrubs that lined the ditch and managed to pull on her coat as protection from the cool mid-December evening air. The temperature was supposed to drop tonight. Cold enough for snow if there was precipitation, but luckily, the forecast said the rain would hold off until tomorrow afternoon.

As she burrowed into her hidey hole, she shivered, not with cold but with the enormity of what she'd just experienced. Who was the officer? What was he up to?

She tucked the bloody hard disk into the coat's inside pocket, and now her hand was balled in a fist, but she could feel the sticky fluid.

She couldn't see the road from her hiding place and didn't dare raise her head to give herself away, but she could hear the car pull over. The crunch of footsteps on the gravel shoulder.

A low curse in a man's voice. Then the air cracked with the sharp bark of a gunshot that echoed down the long dark road.

Chapter Two

JT set the open suitcase on the bed and considered what he'd need for the cabin that wasn't already in the closet there. He hadn't been to the cabin since the summer and couldn't remember if he'd left any sweaters there. Might as well pack a few.

It would probably snow, so he added cold-weather hiking boots to the pile.

With each item he packed, he felt more settled in his decision to leave the DC area for the holidays. He usually enjoyed Christmas dinner at Lee and Erica's, but this year, they'd invited friends with children to join them: Curt and Mara and their son, and Alexandra and her daughter.

He couldn't avoid Alexandra if he wanted to spend time with the only family he had left, but it wouldn't be fair to any of them for him to bring his Grinchy Scrooge self to their holiday gatherings.

He hadn't enjoyed Christmas since the last one he'd shared with Alexandra anyway. This year, he'd go for a long walk in the woods around the cabin and pretend it was just another day. No tree. No lights. No gifts. No feast. And, most important, no family.

He'd miss Lee, who for nearly two decades had been his best friend in addition to being his former stepbrother. But Lee deserved to enjoy the holidays with his wife and daughter, and it was selfish of JT to resent how things had changed.

He could've had what Lee had. But he'd epically fucked up and driven away the only woman who could tolerate him.

The only woman he'd ever love.

He was happy for Lee. Erica might not believe it, but JT cared for her and was grateful for her role in Lee's life. She'd given him unwavering love and a child he adored. His brother had never been happier.

But then, JT's friendship with Erica—which had always been on shaky ground given how he'd treated her when they first met—had been strained since the night he insulted Alexandra in front of T&D's top executives.

The fact that he'd gotten the call his father was dead an hour before the nasty exchange had helped Erica to understand his mental state, but she was still right in asserting there was no excuse for his behavior toward a woman who had done nothing but love and support him when he was being his most unlovable.

No one knew the full truth: he'd done it intentionally to set Alexandra free. He'd known his insult would sever all hope for her. But that didn't mean he didn't regret his decision.

Still, there was no going back and undoing the damage. He'd briefly hoped they could find a way to reconcile when he saw her at Erica and Lee's wedding, but Alexandra had quashed that with her sheer and utter hatred of him.

He couldn't blame her.

She was better off without him.

Now, she had the child he'd refused to give her. He still

didn't know where the kid's father was, but it was none of his business. He wouldn't even know the kid's name if he hadn't set up a trust that would pay for Gemma Vargas's education and give her a large nest egg when she turned twenty-five. The age Alexandra had been when they'd met.

He owed her that much. Hell, he owed her so much more, but this was what he could do—and she couldn't stop him. The money would go to Gemma whether Alexandra liked it or not.

And when he sold T&D in a deal that would close on New Year's Eve, Gemma's trust fund would grow exponentially.

JT wasn't sure if it was irony or destiny that Calvin Moss —the executive whose gaze on Alexandra had been JT's excuse to pick a fight that last night—was CEO of the acquiring architect and engineering firm. Moss had been understandably uncomfortable working for JT after that and had launched his own firm just months later—taking several of T&D's biggest clients with him.

Now, JT was selling him the rest, and Lex's daughter would be rich because of it.

Gemma Vargas wasn't and would never be his kid, but there was nothing stopping him from making sure she and her mother had everything they'd ever need.

He'd stolen years from Alexandra. The least he could do was remove financial stress from parenthood and JT had more money than a single, childless, forty-seven-year-old man would ever need. Hell he had more money than a battalion of people with large families would ever need and he was about to get a lot richer.

He'd considered sending the documents to Lex as a Christmas present. He looked at the folder on his nightstand. He could drop them off at Lee's on his way out of town.

But no. Any intrusion by JT would probably ruin their Christmas, no matter how costly the gift.

He tossed the file into the suitcase. He'd stop at the DC office and leave a note for his administrative assistant to mail it to Lex after Christmas. Or maybe he'd mail it himself when he left the cabin to return to DC for the closing on New Year's Eve, because a stop by the office would add at least forty-five minutes to the drive.

He was tempted to leave tonight, as soon as he was packed, but he reminded himself that it could snow tonight on Catoctin Mountain, and the long driveway might not be clear of branches from previous storms. The last thing he wanted to do was remove debris in the middle of the night.

No, leaving tomorrow morning for the two-hour drive to the northern part of the state was his best option. Situated on the easternmost edge of the Blue Ridge Mountains, the cabin was high on the ridge, a twenty-minute drive down a rough road to get to the nearest grocery store.

His dad had purchased the land in the early '80s. It was a few miles from the Camp David presidential retreat, which was enough distance to offer privacy in the wilderness.

He'd loved going to Catoctin Mountain with his dad and Lee when they were boys. Lee was five years younger than him, and it was a novelty having a little brother after ten years as an only child. It didn't hurt that Lee had worshipped him.

He finished packing, then made himself a drink and settled onto the couch in front of the large TV and hit the power button.

"BREAKING NEWS" flashed across the screen with the chyron "Maryland State Police officer killed during roadside stop. Manhunt underway for suspect who fled the scene on foot."

He hit the Volume button just as the reporter said, "The police officer's identity is being withheld pending family notification, but Maryland State Police have just released the name and photo of the suspect."

A photo of a woman filled the box on the screen next to the reporter.

JT's stomach dropped as he looked at the face of the love of his life, while the reporter said, "Virginia resident Alexandra Vargas is a forty-one-year-old white female. Police urge caution as she may be armed."

Chapter Three

Alexandra had waited until the car drove away before moving. She'd spent precious seconds debating her options before deciding that she had no choice but to check on the officer. If he was still alive, she had to call an ambulance.

It didn't matter that she was sure to be the prime suspect in the shooting. If he died because she didn't do anything to save him, she would be complicit in his murder.

But she didn't have to touch the body to know he was dead.

He'd been shot in the face.

So she'd done the only thing she could and ran. She'd sprinted across farm fields and returned to Kendall's house, where there was a Volkswagen Jetta parked in the garage. An older model, it didn't have any new technology that would make the car trackable.

She had a key to the house—she'd been the last to leave and had planned to return after Christmas and continue sorting—and used it to enter and grab the car key hanging from the peg by the garage door. Before leaving the house, she'd picked up the receiver for the landline phone to confirm phone service had been cut off.

In the heartbeat before she knew the phone didn't work, she wondered who she'd call if it did. She couldn't call Erica. Erica would have picked up Gemma by now, and the police, once they confirmed Alexandra's identity, would try to track her down through her child, leading straight to Erica.

Would they take her baby and put her in foster care?

Surely that process would take a few days?

She was in unimaginable trouble and couldn't begin to understand why.

Thankfully, the Jetta's engine started and, even better, had a full tank of gas. She was on the road only twenty-five minutes after fleeing the crime scene.

Now, more than an hour after borrowing Kendall's car, she was driving north. She had no clue where she was going. All she knew was that she needed to put distance between herself and the dead cop and Kendall's house.

Had someone found the body already? How long would it take for them to trace her to Kendall?

A dog could follow her scent, but it would take time to get a dog to the scene. From there, how long would it take to figure out she'd taken a car from the garage?

There were so many variables. Right now, Tanya was driving to her home in Philadelphia, where she would stay until after Christmas. Would the police be able to track her down quickly?

Alexandra was on the main interstate heading north, trying to figure out where she could go and who she could call.

Erica and Lee had friends who worked for Raptor, a private security firm that would have the ability to help and protect her while an investigation was underway. But no one could hide her if there was a warrant out for her arrest. Harboring a fugitive would put the company in jeopardy.

Alexandra wasn't really friends with any of the key Raptor players. Those friendships had formed after she and JT broke up. That was his world, so she'd stayed away. She'd met Raptor's owner, Senator Alec Ravissant, and the CEO, Keith Hatcher, along with their wives at Erica and Lee's wedding a few years ago, but that was all.

Still, she felt certain they would help her, if she could find a way to contact them without going through Erica or Lee. She wouldn't risk her daughter's safety.

Gemma. What would happen to Gemma?

She was safe with Erica, a person who loved her, but she'd wonder where her mother was.

She was nearing the northern part of Maryland when she spotted a sign for Catoctin Mountain Park. It was a National Park and home to the Camp David presidential retreat. She'd spent many weeks with JT at his father's cabin—enclosed by a whopping ninety acres of Talon-owned land—which was nearby.

Her breath caught as she thought of the house, situated at the center of a vast, private wilderness. Isolated and quiet with only one road for access, it might as well be an island for the buffer it offered from the world.

Did JT still own the property? He would have inherited it when his father died.

The proximity of the cabin to the presidential retreat meant the Talons had installed a sturdy gate to keep out trespassers, and the house itself was near the top of a ridge, deep inside the property boundary.

Alexandra knew where the emergency gate key was hidden. Same with the house key.

If JT hadn't sold the place, she'd bet he still used the same hiding places.

She had no connection with JT anymore. Their breakup had been epic and painful. The cops might question him at some point, but he'd be far down the list. And JT would never in a million years guess that she'd flee to his cabin, the place where he broke her heart one week before their wedding.

Chapter Four

Alexandra thought she was going to puke as she approached the security gate. She wondered if JT had installed a camera. They'd never had one in the past—supposedly because of connectivity reasons, but she'd learned the truth in the days before she was to marry JT.

Joseph Talon Sr. regularly met with his mistress at the cabin and didn't want a camera capturing the other woman coming and going. He'd had both his marriage and his upcoming run for president to consider.

With Joe long gone, had JT installed a camera?

Lord, she hoped not, but she was about to find out.

The same solid metal gate greeted her. No sign of a camera.

If she couldn't find the key, she'd have to ditch the car and hike in. The problem was, it was only a matter of time before an all-points-bulletin was out on the Jetta, and she wasn't exactly dressed to hike up a mountain on a cold December night. Her flimsy sneakers would probably soak through before she found the key.

She climbed from the vehicle and approached the gate,

which was mounted to a rock wall on either side. The wall extended into the woods a hundred yards in both directions. It gave way to a ravine on one side—JT liked to call it the moat—and a cliff on the other. No car could enter the property from this access point without going through the gate.

She slipped under the high crossbar and walked along the wall to the right of the drive. The ground was uneven as forest abutted rock wall. She searched for the loose rock at the base of the wall.

It had been over ten years since she'd been here. She'd been overconfident in her ability to remember the location and hadn't taken weathering into consideration.

Desperate, she ran her bare hand over frozen stone after frozen stone, wondering if ice held the one loose rock secure and she'd missed the hiding place.

It was dark. Her cell phone was smashed by the side of the road near a murdered police officer who'd assaulted her, so she had no flashlight. Nor did she have a lighter or candle to thaw ice that might fill the crevices between stones. Maybe she could use the tire iron as a chisel. But she needed to find the right rock first.

Finally, her hand landed on a stone that wiggled. She pried at it with frozen fingers, tears burning her eyes as she tried to stave off panic. The rock came free, and she felt inside the crevice, her fingers feeling the bite of a metal key.

She burst into tears as she pulled it to her chest.

With scraped fingers that verged on numb, she unlocked the dead bolt and pulled the gate open. She then drove the Jetta inside and locked the gate behind her, tucking the key into her pocket as she climbed back behind the wheel. The driveaway was more than a mile long, twisting between trees as she wound her way up the mountain.

Thankfully, it hadn't started to snow yet. Still, the road

was slick, and she had to stop more than once to remove a tree branch. No one had been here in a while.

She gripped the steering wheel when the car slipped on a patch of ice. Her foot remained steady on the gas, and she slowly steered the car up the mountain road, well aware that if it snowed tomorrow, there was a reasonable chance she'd be stuck here.

Her heart ached at the thought of Gemma. All she could do was hope her baby was safe with Erica. Surely child protective services wouldn't be able to snatch her from a friend who was listed as an emergency caregiver with the daycare?

She had no clue how the law would treat her child if she was a fugitive wanted for murdering a cop. For some reason she'd never thought to plan for such a scenario.

She burst into tears again as the dark cabin came into view. The tears were relief that she had a place to hide as the temperatures dropped, but also triggered by shock and horror that this was necessary.

For the first time in her daughter's life, she hadn't been there to give Gemma her bedtime bottle, and tomorrow morning, she wouldn't be there to lift her from the crib.

Her sweet, darling girlie. She ached with fear and the need to hold her baby.

She'd give anything to be able to call Erica, but that would put Gemma's safety in danger and get Erica in legal trouble.

Finding the hidden key to the house was much easier than the gate key had been.

She held her breath as she unlocked the door and stepped inside, and let it out again in relief when there was no alarm keypad to be found.

If the house had an alarm, it was silent and managed through an app, but she suspected JT had never bothered to have one installed. The place was so remote, and the gate was an effective deterrent. Hikers could trespass, of course, but nothing of value was kept in the house, and hikers weren't going to steal a sixty-inch TV by carrying it down a mountain.

She grabbed the key to the side door of the enclosed garage—which was detached from the house—and returned outside to move the car so it would be hidden from drones or satellite images should anyone think to look for her here.

The three-bay structure was cold and dark, but the garage door buttons glowed orange, and she tapped the one for the empty middle bay.

She drove the car inside, then found the large canvas cover JT used to cover his Lotus and draped it over the Jetta. JT had purchased the Lotus immediately after Alexandra broke their engagement. Now she was glad for the purchase—which had in part been meant to hurt her—because the Jetta was completely concealed from a casual search.

She returned to the house and locked herself inside, then leaned back against the door and took a deep breath. She was far from the scene of the murder and, for the moment, safe.

But at what cost? By running, she'd made herself look even more guilty.

No one would believe that the officer had assaulted her. She'd hit him in the head and had been prepared to tase him, but she *hadn't* been the one to kill him.

She'd grabbed his gun before she spotted the Taser. When she returned to the road to check on him, his holster had been empty and a gun lay on the pavement, feet from his body.

Her fingerprints were on it and the Taser.

They had her car, purse, and phone. She rubbed her hands over her shoulders as a chill took her. She pushed off the door and went to the hall where the thermostat was mounted. A fire in the woodstove was the most efficient way to heat the main room, but she was too tired for that now.

The furnace must have been upgraded since she'd been here last, as there was a new control panel that divided the house into separate heating and cooling zones. She set the downstairs to sixty-eight degrees, then set off in search of a phone or computer, not expecting to find either but hoping nonetheless.

When her search proved fruitless, she grabbed a blanket from the guest bedroom she would sleep in and went to the living room, hoping the satellite dish was still connected.

She needed to see what was being said about her on the news.

Chapter Five

JT sat in the driveway in front of Lee's house and took several deep breaths. Lee was out of his mind for having suggested this. JT was the last person who should be responsible for anyone under the age of sixteen.

But the situation for Alexandra was dire, and Gemma could be used by the cops for leverage.

JT didn't really have a choice. He said yes before he could think it through.

Next thing he knew, Erica was on the phone, giving him a lengthy list of things he'd need. He'd then gone to a twenty-four-hour mega store and practically cleaned out the baby section.

There could be no waiting for morning. He had to get Alexandra's daughter out of town before CPS showed up. That could take days or even weeks, but no one wanted to take the chance it would be later rather than sooner.

Not when Gemma could be moved like a pawn. A gambit to draw out her mother.

Right now, the police might not even know Erica had

picked up the girl from daycare, and they weren't breaking any laws in passing the child off to JT, except that Alexandra would probably question Erica's judgment in choosing him, of all people.

Still, he was the only logical choice. His and Lex's breakup was well known to anyone familiar with him or T&D. It wasn't often a CEO melted down so publicly.

Calvin Moss had quit not long after and started his own firm that had become T&D's top competitor in the DC area. At one point, he'd thanked JT for the impetus to find a way to control his own destiny. By *impetus*, he'd clearly meant discovering how volatile T&D's CEO was, which had inspired him to make the leap.

Now, his and Alexandra's history worked in their favor. Days would probably pass before Maryland State Police came knocking on his door, and when that happened, he'd be up at the cabin on Catoctin Mountain enjoying an unplugged Christmas holiday, just as he'd told his staff he would. No one expected him back in the city until New Year's Eve, at which point he was selling the company that had consumed his life.

His assistant was tasked with arranging the New Year's Eve closing celebration, to be held after the papers were signed, a big party to end not just the year but an era. JT would be free.

If police questioned his employees while he was away, no one would even think to suggest he was playing nanny to Lex's kid. His discomfort with children was as legendary as the breakup.

Truth was, for about fifteen seconds, he considered hiring an actual nanny, but there was no time, and that was bound to give him away.

Shit.

There was no helping it. He was going to have to take care of the kid. He had a big box of Huggies, a mega-pack of diaper wipes, and a thing called Butt Paste in the back of his Lexus SUV next to a travel crib, a random assortment of toys, clothes, and a thousand other baby items he'd paid cash for in the middle of the night.

Then he'd gone to the grocery department and purchased ten days' worth of food—the maximum amount of time he could spend at the cabin before returning to complete the sale. The idea that he might have Gemma Vargas in his care for that long terrified him. He feared for Gemma. For himself. But most of all for Lex.

In front of him, Lee's garage door opened. He took a deep breath to brace himself and drove into the empty bay. They'd agreed he wouldn't collect Gemma on the street where anyone could see. Weird enough that he was showing up at Lee's house at one in the morning.

He shut off the engine, and Lee hit the button inside the garage to lower the door. Once it was down, JT climbed out of the SUV as Lee circled around to the driver's side.

Lee's expression was tense. No surprise there, but still, JT's heart squeezed at the idea there might be news he didn't want to hear.

He raised a brow, and Lee gave a sharp shake of his head. "Alexandra knows better than to call us. As soon as the cops figure out we've got Gemma, they'll have us under surveillance."

"Your phones are unhackable."

Lee gave a slight nod of acknowledgment. He was a computer and cell phone security expert and used encryption that spy agencies envied.

"Alexandra doesn't have my burner number. She has the same one the cops will track down, and half the battle of protecting a phone is keeping the number secret. They might not be able to listen in on my calls, but they can subpoena my call log."

"You got a burner you can give me?"

Lee reached into his pocket and handed over the phone. "Already configured. Password is six digits. Month, day, year your dad married my mom."

JT nodded and unlocked the phone, seeing Lee's burner number was programmed in.

"I won't keep my burner handy," Lee said. "I don't want the cops to find it if they manage to get a warrant to search here. Leave a generic voice message, and I'll call you as soon as I can."

JT tucked the phone in his pocket as the door to the house opened and Erica stepped out. She looked even more worried than Lee.

His friendship with Erica had been strained for the last seven years, but for the most part, they got along. He had no doubt the woman held a grudge, but she loved Lee too much to let her feelings toward JT interfere with Lee and JT's relationship.

She really was an excellent person and a wonderful partner for Lee.

Tonight, she surprised him by giving him a fierce hug, and as he held her, he wasn't sure if the hug was for her or for him, but either way, he needed it.

When she released him and stepped back, she swiped at her eyes.

Erica didn't cry. At least, she never had in front of him. And sure as hell, he'd given her cause to cry more than once.

But then, he wasn't a crier either, and his eyes had burned from the moment Lex's situation sank in.

"Thank you for taking Gemma."

"Of course," he said, as if he didn't believe it was a terrible solution.

He wanted to ask her again what Lex had said on the phone about the cop, but he knew she'd been going over every moment in her mind ever since the BOLO went out. She'd told him what she knew already.

"Let's make sure the car seat is properly installed." She opened the rear side door and then turned to him in surprise. "You already installed it."

"Check the latches. I'm not sure if I did it right." He'd used the built-in anchors. Not something he'd ever thought he'd need when he bought the Lexus last year.

He preferred driving the Lotus, but it lacked a backseat. Alexandra had asked him if he bought the car after she'd canceled the wedding because it was a car that would never, ever transport a child, and he'd admitted that was part of it.

"So, Gemma is big enough that she can face forward in the seat, which is good because then you'll be able to check on her with the rearview mirror."

"Won't it freak her out to see some strange man driving the car?"

"Hopefully, she'll sleep for most of the drive. But also, she'll freak out no matter what. Strange car. No mom. And she's used to facing front."

Erica reached in and unclipped the seat, then flipped it around, locking down the three tethers. Once she was done, she said, "Okay, do you know how to set up the portable crib?"

He nodded. "They had one on display in the store, so I played with it until I got it figured out."

What he really needed was diaper-changing lessons, but he'd have to learn on the job there. No way would he wake a baby just to practice wiping her bottom.

Erica returned to the house to grab a diaper bag. She placed it in the back and inspected the baby food he'd purchased. He'd even gotten a baby-food grinder, because Erica said Gemma only had her front teeth and all solid food needed to be turned to mush. Cheerios were allowed, but that was as solid as it could get.

"This looks good. She has milk in a bottle at bedtime. The rest of the time, she drinks from a sippy cup. For the new ones you bought, you'll need to sterilize them, but I've put the bottle she used tonight in the diaper bag; that will get you started. Keep it in the front seat. If she wakes and is fussy, you can give it to her. It's mostly water with a small amount of apple juice."

The idea of Gemma waking while he drove was nothing short of terrifying. Still, he nodded and said, "Got it."

She gave him a look that said she knew he got nothing.

"Have you ever changed a diaper before?"

"The only baby I've ever been near is Gracie. Have you seen me change her?"

Lee chuckled. "Bet you're wishing you'd done it when you had the chance."

"Not really." He loved Grace, but he was waiting for her to be old enough to go fishing or play baseball. Once she was a real person.

He figured the fact that he didn't see a baby as a real person had a lot to do with his lack of desire to be a father.

But how interesting could babies be?

"Okay, one thing you need to know with girls," Erica said, "is wipe from front to back. That way you decrease the chance of an infection caused by getting fecal matter in the urinary tract or vagina."

He knew this was necessary advice, but damn, it was a wakeup call for what he was in for.

He was so screwed.

Alexandra took inventory of the pantry, glad to find a large bag of rice, another large bag of dried beans, along with a decent amount of canned goods. The freezer held bricks of cheese, several pounds of butter, and frozen meats and vegetables.

She pulled out a two-pack of pork tenderloins and placed it in the refrigerator so it would start to thaw, then set a pound of beans to soak in a pan. Tomorrow, she'd make enough beans and rice with shredded pork to last a few days.

Right now, she was probably hungry, but she was too tired and anxious to eat anything. Her brain buzzed with what she'd seen on the news. They had her name and address. Her driver's license photo had been on the local and national news.

She was at large and presumed dangerous.

No one bothered to ask *why* a college professor would kill a cop at a traffic stop.

With each news segment came the plea for anyone who knew Alexandra to call the network. It was implied that they just wanted to help her.

Bullshit. They wanted a scoop. A frenemy to inform on her.

She figured now would be the time to find out if she had any enemies. A fellow professor who harbored resentment over her tenure-track position. An ex-lover she did wrong.

Their best shot there was JT. But even if he still hated her, calling a reporter wasn't his style. He knew all about scandal, and there remained a chance that he would follow in his father's political footsteps now that Joseph Talon's crimes were history.

She left the kitchen, turned off all the downstairs lights, and checked all the doors and windows, making sure they were locked tight.

By the time she ascended the stairs, it was after three a.m. She was wound tight, scared, and she missed her baby.

She settled into the guest bed wearing a T-shirt she'd found in one of JT's closet drawers. She shivered as she wrapped the cool sheets around her and waited for the bedding to warm against her skin.

She closed her eyes and saw the blue lights flashing in her rearview. The cop's arm as he reached through the window and broke her car key.

She'd been so busy running and trying to figure out what to do, she hadn't had a chance to ask why. Why pull her over? Was it a random stop? Was he a predator on the hunt and any woman would do?

Or had she been targeted specifically?

Why her?

She'd had to finance her own maternity leave after returning from CERN because the year she took off fell between her fellowship ending and starting her new job at the University of Maryland. Thanks to JT, she'd had the money to get by until she returned to teaching at the start of the fall term, which had ended last week. She had a handful of eager graduate students, and the undergrads had been typical—testing the waters of an extremely difficult subject.

No one *accidentally* took theoretical physics, nor did they take it for an easy A. She generally had a good rapport with students and faculty.

Sure, there was misogyny and academic rivalries, but she'd been checked out of that during her maternity leave.

She'd weaned Gemma before the start of the fall semester and, for the last two months, had slowly ceased milk production, but now her breasts ached with letdown. A physical pain to have her baby with her. Her body was ready to provide nourishment.

Gemma's safe. She's with Erica.

She lay in the pitch-dark room of the quiet house, breasts aching, nipples anticipating a latch that wouldn't come. Wind rattled the windows softly, but it was an otherwise calm night. She shivered as she saw in her mind the cop lying on the pavement with a gunshot to his face and a pool of blood beneath his head.

He'd already been lying on the ground when he'd been shot.

Straight-up cold-blooded murder.

But who had done it? And why?

Chapter Six

JT's first glimpse of Gemma Vargas came when Erica carried the sleeping baby into the garage to tuck her into the car seat. The lights had been dimmed for ease of transition, but he got a glimpse of short tufts of pale hair as the child slumbered against Erica's chest just before she leaned into the open car door and deposited Gemma into her seat.

The girl made a sound, and Erica soothed her in a gentle voice he'd heard her use with Grace. "You're going for a car ride with one of Mommy's friends."

"Mommy?"

"She's not here yet, baby. JT will take good care of you while Mommy is gone."

"Panny?"

Erica extracted herself from the vehicle and turned expectantly to Lee. He handed over a tattered stuffed toy that looked panda-ish. Erica handed the stufty to Gemma, and the girl grasped it tight, leaning her cheek on it as she settled in the seat.

Erica leaned in and kissed the girl and whispered, "Love you, Gemmy."

The girl made a soft sound, then whispered, "Lovey." Her eyes closed, and she appeared to nod off.

JT could barely breathe after watching the exchange.

He didn't even know *why* it got to him. He'd seen Erica's love for Grace every time they were together. He'd just never imagined a similar affection between her and a baby who wasn't even her child. Especially given that the one thing he'd had in common with Erica was her ambivalence over having children.

Erica closed the door as quietly as possible, then turned to JT. "Panny is her comfort toy. Goes with her to daycare every day, and she sleeps with it every night. Lose the panda at your own peril."

"Got it." He would duct tape the thing to Gemma if needed.

Erica looked back inside the car and swiped at a tear. "It's probably good you're taking her. I won't be able to hide my fear from her much longer."

Surely a baby couldn't pick up on worry for Lex? Eat, sleep, play. That was a baby's job.

Lee put his arm around Erica. "Keith is calling in the team, and Curt has influence with the FBI. There *will* be a proper investigation."

"A proper investigation means nothing if vigilante cops shoot Alexandra on sight."

And that right there was JT's top fear. The news had all but painted a target on Lex. They'd said the officer had a head wound and was already lying on the ground when he was shot.

There was no way in hell Alexandra Vargas had pulled that trigger.

After more than two hours of driving—that included a lengthy surveillance detection route as insisted upon by the CEO of Raptor—a loud shriek from the backseat made JT jump and nearly swerve on the dark highway.

The screaming continued, making JT wonder how such a small child had the lung capacity and decibel range.

"Hey there. Uh. Gemma…I'm…Uncle JT." Should he call himself uncle? That was what Grace called him, but he actually *was* her uncle. Sort of.

The screaming continued, only pausing when she drew air into what must be magic lungs. Between screams, she hiccupped and cried, "Mommy! Mommy!"

"I'm your mommy's friend." Not really, but once upon a time, they'd been the center of each other's world.

"Remember when Auntie Erica told you about me?"

Of course she didn't. She'd been half-asleep. And she was only what…a year old? Wait, he knew her birthdate. He'd needed it for the trust. She was born in September of last year, making her a year and three months old now.

Was she still a baby or was that a toddler? He'd forgotten to ask Erica if she could walk. Felt like something he ought to know.

He tried to remember the soft tone Lee used with Grace. Was that how he should talk to Gemma?

Did he even know how to make his voice sound like that?

"So…ugh…" He pitched his voice higher. "Sweetie. You need to stop crying."

The sound she made… Were his ears bleeding?

He debated pulling over, but a car parked on the side of the highway at nearly five in the morning…it would get attention sooner rather than later.

He steeled himself against the onslaught to his ears and took the next exit. He followed the signs to the nearest gas station, then pulled up to a pump.

He didn't need gas, but he didn't want to look suspicious. He twisted in his seat and faced the child who was strapped in the middle of the backseat.

"Hey, kid," he said softly. "You're okay. I'm going to take care of you for a few days."

Tears dripped down pudgy baby cheeks. He'd thought she was cute when she was sleeping. His heart had done a weird kind of twist when he saw her hair was blonde like her mom's.

This was Alexandra's baby daughter.

He thought of the woman who would always have his heart and took a deep breath. He thought of the quiet moments when they'd snuggled on the couch and he'd held her and known paradise. With thoughts of Lex in his mind, he found a softer register and said, "Hey, cutie pie. I'm sorry your mommy isn't here, but Uncle JT is going to take good care of you."

She paused in her shrieking, but her chin still quivered. "Mommy?"

"She's going to come home as soon as she can. Promise, honey."

"Panny?"

JT scanned the backseat and didn't see the stuffed bear. He unbuckled his seat belt, climbed from the SUV, and opened the rear door.

Panny had escaped to the floor. He scooped up the bear and handed it to her. She sniffled as she held it to her chest and...nibbled on an ear, which might have made him shudder a bit.

His car was clean, but what if she dropped the toy on the Metro? Or in on a station platform?

Gross.

How had humans survived as a species?

"Hungy," she said.

He had baby food, but he couldn't exactly sit in the gas station parking lot and feed the kid orange goo.

This was a Lexus with leather seats. But more important, he supposed, was the fact that someone might spot them. Thanks to the surveillance detection route, they were still more than an hour from the gate to the Catoctin cabin.

It was still dark. Surely, Alexandra didn't feed the girl at five in the morning. She drank milk, not formula... That meant she'd been weaned, right?

He paused, wondering if Lex had nursed her daughter. Erica had nursed Grace, but Mara hadn't been able to nurse her son, if he remembered correctly. He'd tried to avoid those conversations, but once two couples in a friend circle had kids, it was baby, baby, baby all the time.

Now Isabel was pregnant, he'd lose Alec to the proud-dad club in the spring. He gave thanks that Keith and Trina had no plans to procreate.

They were his people.

Except, he felt uncomfortable with all the happy couples, whether they had kids or not.

He returned his focus to the living nightmare in a car seat. "We need to drive a bit more. Then we'll have breakfast." And a nap. JT had been up all night, and he was too old to pull all-nighters, especially when sex wasn't involved.

They'd get to the cabin. He'd feed the kid, and then he'd put her in the portable crib, and they'd both sleep for six hours. Easy-peasy.

But no sooner was he pulling away from the gas pump after putting in a token amount of gas than Gemma was screaming again.

Now she was chanting, "Hungy! Hungy! Mommy!"

He was screwed. He couldn't drive an hour with her catlike high-pitched yowls. He couldn't drive five minutes.

He saw a sign for a motel across the highway and took the overpass.

Shit. How would he get a room with the kid screaming? Would the clerk think he'd abducted a child?

He pulled out his phone and downloaded the app for the motel and gave thanks that he could book a room—and get a key—with his phone.

Five minutes after pulling into the lot, he was checked in. Now, he just had to convince the girl to be quiet while they made their way to their second-floor room.

He climbed from the driver's seat and moved to the back. She quieted as he took the seat next to her and closed the door. It didn't feel right to just reach in and grab her when he'd never so much as touched her before. He would take this slowly. Let her get used to him.

He found the soft tone to his voice that Lee used with Grace and said, "You want to eat, honey?"

Her wet cheeks glistened in the dome light as she nodded. "Hungy."

"I got us a room here." He pointed to the motel and wondered if he was being ridiculous. Would she understand any of this? But he figured it couldn't hurt and might help win her trust.

Huh. He'd never figured someone so young could have complex emotions like trust. Grace had just accepted him, but then, he'd been present in her life from the get-go, while Gemma hadn't seen his face until he handed her Panny several minutes ago.

"I'm going to unbuckle you and carry you inside. Then you'll get breakfast. 'Kay?"

"Mommy?"

"No, baby. Your mommy isn't here."

Her face crumpled, and she let out a keening sort of sound. But at least it was quiet.

He studied the car seat. She was strapped in like a racecar driver.

As an engineer, he was impressed by all the baby gadgets he'd looked at in the store. The portable crib was an engineering marvel. It had to be, given it was essentially a safe-baby jail.

It wasn't easy to unbuckle the safety harness, but finally, he got the button to release. He moved the straps off her shoulders and said, "Can I pick you up?"

She gave a small nod. He scooped her up, then sat back, holding her so she faced him.

He stared into her eyes, seeing they were the same blue as Alexandra's, and said, "I love your mommy more than anyone in the world, Gemma. I won't let anything happen to you." He pulled her to his chest, and she shocked him by leaning against him and popping her thumb in her mouth.

He found it hard to breathe as his eyes burned.

This was *nothing* like the first time he'd held Grace. But then, that moment hadn't been fraught like this one was.

He was terrified for Lex, and according to Erica, he couldn't let Gemma pick up on that.

He placed a hand behind her small head, his fingers touching her soft hair, and he just breathed, taking in this moment. Holding Lex's precious baby for the very first time.

His heart ached, but it was also filling in the weirdest way.

These emotions were uncharted territory. He'd grown used to being without Alexandra, but now that he'd opened the part of him he'd walled off for his own survival, he felt this small girl slipping inside.

When all this was over—and he was determined that this would end happily for everyone involved—there was no way he'd be able to return to a life that didn't include Alexandra.

She would never love him again, but maybe they could find a way to be friends.

He reached for the door handle and slid from the vehicle, being careful not to dislodge the finally quiet baby.

It was chilly outside, and neither he nor Gemma were wearing a coat, but she was snug against him, so only her backside would be cold. He'd closed and locked the door and was heading to the hotel room when he realized he couldn't just leave the baby in the room while he returned to the car to get her stuff. At the very least, he'd need the portable baby jail.

He returned to the SUV and used the kick sensor to open the back. The crib was still in the box—and there was no handle. Impossible to carry while carrying Gemma.

He set her down on the pile of supplies, and she squawked.

"This will only take a minute," he said, hoping it was true. He managed to rip open the box and was thankful to see the crib was inside a nylon bag with a handle. He set it on the ground, then scooped up Gemma again.

He was feeling like a pro when he locked the car, picked up the bag, and was heading for the side door, until he came face-to-face with the RFID sensor. He felt like a juggler as he set down the bag and fished his phone out of his pocket, scanned the lock with his phone, pocketed the phone again, and opened the door—it took three tries for him to do this in the moment before the green light on the door pad turned red, but finally, he had the door open and had picked up the crib and was heading up the stairs to their room.

The process was repeated at the motel room door, but this time, he got the timing right on the first try.

Inside the standard room with a king bed, he let out a sigh of relief as he deposited the baby on the bed.

He looked at her and said, "I need to set up the crib so I can go back to the car and get the rest of your stuff."

Gemma let out a shriek.

He panicked and put his fingers over her mouth, which, of course, only made her cry louder. He quickly removed his hand and scooped her up. "Shhh. Sorry."

She stopped screaming, but she definitely wasn't happy. "You want to come back to the car with me?"

"Hungy."

Yeah, there was no way she was going to wait patiently in the crib while he unloaded the SUV.

And if the smell was any indication, she needed a diaper change, so he needed the bag Erica had packed too,

Resigned, he headed back to the car with her in his arms.

He took two more trips, grabbing his own bag in addition to baby supplies. The groceries would be fine in the back of the SUV—it was only a few degrees above freezing, after all—and he figured they'd be stuck in the motel for several hours.

He needed to sleep. There was no way they'd leave before the eleven a.m. checkout time. He would book a second night as soon as they were settled. Late afternoon, they'd head to the cabin.

Back in the room with the last of what they needed to get through most of a day, he wanted to collapse on the bed and sleep, but the kid seemed to think he should feed her.

Was she really this hungry at six in the morning?

But then, she was tiny, and all that screaming had to burn a lot of calories.

He looked at her and said, "Diaper or food?"

"Hungy!"

Well, at least she was consistent.

He found the baby spoons in one of the shopping bags and washed one in the bathroom sink. It was too bad this motel didn't have suites with kitchenettes, but at least it had a fridge, microwave, and coffee maker. He'd survive.

Erica had told him to get a portable, clip-on feeding chair, and he'd gotten absolutely everything on her list, but the chair was in the back of the SUV. No way was he making another trip, so it was sit on the bed or floor for mealtime.

No sooner was he seated in front of her with a spoonful of mashed peas than she'd yanked the spoon from his hand and spilled the contents on the bedspread on the way to her open mouth.

It didn't get much better from there, mess-wise. But more food ended up in her mouth than on the bedspread, so that was a win.

Finally, she dropped the spoon and said, "Pow."

He had no clue what that meant. He offered her another bite, and she pushed it away, splattering more green goop. "Pow!"

Pow?

He held up the spoon again.

"No! Pow!"

Then he remembered "pau" in Hawaiian meant "finished" or "done." He had a house on Kauai, and he and Lex had spent many happy weeks there. Together, they'd attended many pau hana—finished with work—cocktail parties and happy hours.

Gemma was *pau. Done.*

He wished he'd thought to ask Erica for a baby dictionary, but at least he'd managed to work that one out on his own.

"Got it," he said, removing the food jar and spoon from her reach. Now he needed to change her diaper and then, blessed sleep.

His first diaper change went about as well as expected. Thankfully, the bulging diaper was full of urine and nothing else.

He wasn't ready for the big league. He needed a few rounds in the minors first.

She squirmed, and he didn't fasten the diaper tight enough, as evidenced by the fact that it fell off her the minute she started crawling toward the edge of the bed.

He dragged her back to the changing pad by a heel. "Where do you think you're going, little missy?"

She squealed, and he stopped, but then she rolled over, and he saw her smile. He felt a strange flutter in his belly as he realized the squeal was a giggle and the smile…damn. It warmed his chest in a way he'd never felt before.

Who knew baby smiles triggered endorphins?

Probably everyone but him.

He smiled back at her and said, "Sorry, but motel rules require all non-potty-trained individuals to wear diapers at all times."

She twisted and started crawling away again.

He pulled her back and said, "Diaper time."

She giggled. *Giggled.* "Nakey baby! Nakey baby!"

He laughed. Apparently, this was a thing for her, because she had a two-word response.

She was kind of adorable. But no way was she running—or crawling; he still didn't know if she could walk—around the motel room without a diaper.

He finally got her butt covered, and then he set her on the floor to see what she would do.

She held on to the bedspread and pulled herself to her feet and then…she started walking. And immediately bumped her head on the edge of the round table and started to cry.

It was then that JT accepted he wasn't going to get to sleep anytime soon.

Chapter Seven

Alexandra managed a few hours of fitful sleep. But whenever she dropped into slumber, her mind filled with horrific images as the evening's events played out in nightmare form. Or she dreamed about Gemma, always crying, in danger. Out of reach.

Waking wasn't a respite from these fears.

She finally rose just after eight in the morning and forced herself to eat plain oatmeal in spite of having no appetite. After breakfast, she searched the house from top to bottom, hoping to find a cell phone or other communication device, but came up empty.

She tried an internet browser built into the TV, but stopped short of logging in to any of her email addresses using the web interface. Surely the police were monitoring all her email addresses by now, and she didn't have a secret address that didn't appear on her laptop's mail app. She could create a new account, but who would she reach out to? The satellite dish didn't have a virtual private network, which meant her messages would be traceable.

She paced the house. In a few days, she'd either have to

bite the bullet and send a message from the TV or drive to town in Kendall's Jetta.

She searched the cabinets for something she could use to color her hair. Being blonde, her hair took color easily. She could cut it, dye it. Or maybe she should just wear a hat and a scarf. It was cold enough outside to warrant that. Sunglasses would complete the disguise.

If she waited a few days, maybe people wouldn't be so vigilant. Already the news was pulling back from the story, given the lack of updates.

It was late afternoon when a statement was released by Gemma's daycare stating that an authorized individual had picked up Alexandra's unnamed daughter and they wouldn't share the name with the press due to confidentiality laws. She had no doubt they had given Erica's name and address to the police, though. They likely had a warrant.

Again, her stomach twisted. What if Erica was forced to surrender Gemma to social services?

She wanted to google that question using the TV internet, but was afraid somehow the search could be traced to her. Who knew what kind of spyware was available these days? Plus, it wasn't only the police she feared. It was entirely possible the person who killed Officer Corey Williams was looking for her too.

She spent the day with her brain spinning in circles, every idea that sparked hope instantly shot down by the realities of what she didn't know.

She had devoted her adult life to studying the particles that made up the universe, aiming to understand the very nature of existence—not simply human existence, but, to borrow a phrase from *The Hitchhiker's Guide to the Galaxy*, she wanted to understand life, the universe, and everything. Her focus was really on the everything part. But to understand something so big, first one needed to understand the smallest of the small.

Her focus had been intensely singular. Nothing in her world could have prepared her for this. She'd lived in a bubble that included the privilege of never fearing a traffic stop could change her life on a dime.

But here she was. Wanted for murdering a cop.

Her brain was no help. It was caught in attempting to calculate danger and what her next steps should be, but she had zero experience in these areas and no way to research it.

Research was her best coping mechanism and she didn't even have that.

Her arms ached to hold Gemma. Her heart ached with fear. Her breasts ached with milk no one needed. Once again she felt tears burning, but held them back. If she gave in, she might never stop.

She needed a clear, rational mind if she was going to find a way out of this nightmare.

She breathed through the press of tears until they were locked down tight, then she straightened her shoulders, grabbed her coat, and stepped outside. She needed to take a walk. If nothing else, she could find a quiet place in this private forest to scream until she lost her voice.

Gemma finally drifted off to sleep just before noon. Naturally, she was lying on JT's chest when it happened, and he didn't dare move lest he wake her. So that was how they slept. Her deeply. Him fitfully.

Toddler and forty-seven-year-old man who'd only rarely and reluctantly held a child until six hours before.

He knew now that the brief times he'd held Lee and

Erica's kid didn't count. He'd passed Gracie off at the first sign of discomfort—on either of their parts.

No, being stuck with a kid who didn't want you was entirely different. It brought back memories of Christmas past when a blonde elf had swooped in and saved his day.

But Gemma kept him grounded in the here and now. She was a trooper. Once she accepted that JT could not and would not pull her mother from the ether, she made a resolute face that reminded him oh-so-much of Lex.

He was truly dumbfounded by the depths of a fifteen-month-old. Maybe she was extra smart thanks to the genes of her brilliant mother, but he had a feeling he'd also underestimated the entire human species below the age of two.

Alexandra's daughter was at once a charmer and a devil. Even now, as he lay with her snuggled to his chest, exhausted beyond belief after chasing the little tornado around a tiny motel room for hours, his brain refused to slip into a deep sleep as he listened to the sounds she made as she slumbered, which, he had to admit, were sort of cute.

Witchcraft. It was the only possible explanation. The same sorcery that had trapped him in Alexandra's snare extended to her daughter.

He was destined to worship all Vargas women for the rest of his days.

There were, in fact, worse fates.

Like living in a world without Lex. Without Gemma.

He had to get this two-and-a-half-foot-tall tornado back to her mother.

But how would he find her before the police did?

Chapter Eight

Dawn broke the sky after a second night of fitful sleep for Alexandra. She gave in to the tears at some point in the wee hours. After a long cry, she managed to sleep a bit, dreaming of Gemma, crying furiously and just out of reach.

She woke with a headache and heartache. She should go to town today. Call…someone. Curt Dominick?

He was her best bet. She'd known him for years, long before he was a US attorney, let alone Attorney General of the United States.

Curt was a straight arrow. He would do everything by the book, but he'd also believe her. Help her. She just needed to figure out how she could get his private phone number or a message to him.

Erica was best friends with his wife, Mara. But calling Erica was out.

JT had his number, certainly. But was it safe to call JT?

Her gut said he was safe, but her heart said something different.

She let out a heavy sigh and tossed aside the covers. She

would take a shower and then go for another hike. She had miles upon miles of forest to explore. It was her prison, but it was also her salvation.

There'd been a light dusting of snow in the night. It would melt quickly in the morning sun, but a real storm was forecast for this afternoon. If Alexandra wanted to go to the nearest town and find a phone, she would need to do it before noon, as the storm was expected in the midafternoon.

She was terrified of showing her face in public, but also scared of getting snowed in without reaching out. Maybe Curt could stop CPS from taking Gemma away—if that was something the police would try to do for leverage to get her to turn herself in.

But what if she was recognized and arrested? Or, more likely, shot on sight by an angry officer?

She should have left Maryland. Not that cops in other states would like her any more than they did in Maryland, but at least in West Virginia or Pennsylvania, they might be less vigilant?

She set out for her walk. Mindful of her footprints in the snow, she stepped in bare dirt or in patches where the snow was thinnest or most likely to melt in the sun.

She wouldn't take any chances.

She walked uphill to the top of the ridge, remembering romantic walks with JT in this same forest. The first time she'd had sex against a tree was on this property. The last time too, come to think of it.

They hadn't visited this property after the time they'd been here and JT's father had shown up with his mistress. It had been eight days before their planned New Year's Eve wedding, exactly eleven years ago.

She hadn't known about the senator's many affairs and had been more than a little shocked that JT knew and condoned his father's actions.

It had been a critical time in their relationship, with the wedding so close. JT had made his views on children clear, and she'd been prepared to accept that. After all, she respected his views—she would never force fatherhood on him any more than she believed motherhood should be forced upon a woman. Nor did he need to give a reason he wished to remain childless. People who wanted children were never asked to explain themselves. Everyone's choices were valid.

So she'd had to make the decision for herself. Would she be content with JT and only JT?

Then she learned the love of her life was complicit in covering up his father's cheating.

Alexandra had grown close to Lisa ever since the Christmas Eve when they first met. JT had seemed close to her too. If he was fine with his father cheating, it was easy to assume he had a similar moral compass when it came to his own relationships.

But the tipping point came when she discovered—on the very same day—JT's political plans were not in the distant future. No. He intended to run for Congress in a matter of weeks.

She'd known from the start—she'd been the *only* person who knew aside from Joseph Talon—that JT intended to follow his father into politics. She'd stared at the big diamond on her finger, the countdown of days until the wedding in single digits, and saw a bleak future for herself. Second to JT's political ambitions. Probably even, eventually, to a mistress.

It was easy to see herself in the same role as Lisa Talon,

childless, loveless, second fiddle to everything that was important to JT.

Still, Alexandra loved JT enough that she might have accepted that fate if he'd agreed to having a child together. But he'd refused. He hadn't understood how his father's affairs and his own looming ambition had chilled her to the core. He'd thought she was reneging on their agreement—on the prenup she'd signed without hesitation.

She'd tried to make him understand how his father's affairs and his decision to run without telling her his plans had changed their agreement. But he'd accused her of using his father's secrets to turn the screws for more money.

She'd seen a new side to JT, one she'd never imagined existed, and in Lisa Talon, Alexandra saw her future and felt sick.

She made her decision on Christmas Eve, after they'd returned to the city because their pre-wedding getaway at the mountain cabin had been spoiled by Joe and his mistress. In the DC hotel where they were supposed to marry a week later, she'd removed the two-carat diamond from her finger and set it on the table. *"You think this is all I want from you? Fine. You can have it. Enjoy the honeymoon without me."*

She then turned and walked out the door. That night, she drove to Kendall's apartment in Bethesda, where she cried on her friend's shoulders for a month.

Kendall had been the best friend imaginable, holding her while she cried. For a year, Alexandra had stayed strong, seeing JT only long enough to get her belongings back from the townhouse he'd bought for them to share in DC while she was in school.

He lived in New York most of the time anyway, so not much beyond her address had changed. Letting JT back in after the broken engagement had been a slippery slope. Soft and smooth, like the snowflakes that drifted gently down as she walked through the woods.

The problem was—and for years it continued to be—that Alexandra hadn't called off the wedding because she didn't love him. It had been so easy to slip back into bed with him. To be broken up but still sleep together.

They had incompatible goals. She had grad school to finish. Then postdoc. Her life would never be in New York, and while he talked about moving his base of operations to the DC area, he never made the change.

Kendall had tolerated her fickle friend. After all, she had her own problematic boyfriend.

They'd been quite a pair.

Now the senator whose infidelities had widened the cracks in their relationship was long dead. JT's loathing of Alexandra was a known fact in certain social circles, Kendall had committed suicide, and Alexandra was wanted for killing a cop.

She finally had the child she'd always wanted, but her daughter might end up being raised by someone else. If Alexandra was arrested and convicted, she'd give up parental rights and ask Erica and Lee to adopt her.

She took a deep breath of the crisp, cold air. A puff of white vapor released with her breath as she moved uphill. She usually avoided thinking about her breakup with JT, but being here on the very property where their relationship had first shattered, she couldn't escape the thoughts.

She should focus on her situation, but now she knew she'd yet to process the pain she'd ignored for years. Hell, she'd never found another man to love because she couldn't get over the pain of loving JT.

She would never forgive him. Never love him again. But she probably also would never get over him.

Thank god for vibrators. She didn't need him.

There are no vibrators in prison.

She let out a laugh-cry. That was literally the least of her problems.

She reached the top of the ridge and looked down the hillside toward the house, not for the first time wondering what it felt like for JT, or his father before him, to look over this vast wilderness and know that all the land he could see was his.

Alexandra hadn't wanted to marry JT for his money, but the security of it had certainly been appealing. Until the end, when his wealth was his primary reason for distrusting her.

Just the thought of JT's words that last night caused her anger to spike.

Wait until he found out what she'd done with his jewels.

Family jewels indeed.

She had something a million times more precious.

She stood for a long moment on the top of the world, breathing deeply, disappointed to discover that answers didn't await her on this peak.

Movement on the hillside below caught her eye, and she gasped as she stepped behind a tree, instinctively taking cover as she watched an SUV navigate the long, winding driveway to the house.

Oh shit. Oh shit. Oh *shit!*

Someone was here.

Was it JT?

His girlfriend?

Someone else?

She thought about the house. She'd cleaned up after herself in every room. Dishes washed after eating. Bed made. Leftover beans and pork were in the fridge, but that might not be noticed right away.

Only someone paying sharp attention would know she'd

been there at first glance. Unless, of course, they spotted her car in the garage bay.

The dark SUV disappeared into the trees. Was it JT's vehicle? Or had someone figured out where she was? Could it be police here to arrest her?

She debated her options, finally deciding to retreat into the woods and wait. If someone had come for her, they'd find the car and search the woods. She needed to be ready to bolt.

But if it was JT...maybe he would help her? If he didn't still believe she was a gold-digging bitch. Erica had assured her he no longer believed that, but his complete and utter failure to acknowledge how out of line he'd been in the seven years since their final split spoke volumes.

There wasn't any vantage point from which she could see the driveway and front of the house, so she had no way of knowing who it was as long as she remained on the ridge.

She had no choice but to hide until after dark. If she waited until JT was asleep, maybe she could steal his phone and slip out without him ever knowing she was there.

Chapter Nine

It was a relief when JT reached the gate to the driveway at last. After spending well over a day with him in a motel room, Gemma no longer feared him and hadn't fussed much during the drive, especially after he found the kids music streaming channel.

Of course, after an hour of songs sung by Muppets, *he* was ready to cry.

Well, except for "Rainbow Connection." That song brought back memories of six-year-old Lee's adoration of his new big brother. At eleven, JT had loved the attention.

He parked in front of the steps to the porch and met Gemma's gaze in the rearview mirror. "Ready to see the cabin I've been telling you about?"

"Hungy!"

He smiled. Of course she was hungry. She hadn't eaten in ninety whole minutes. "Sure thing. Right after I unload the SUV."

Her face scrunched up, but he wouldn't give in this time. She could scream all she wanted, there was no one for miles.

Today, the dynamic between them would change.

Stripped of the ability to disturb other motel guests, the fifteen-month-old no longer held all the cards.

He carried her into the house and deposited her in the living room, taking off her shoes so she wouldn't track mud on the cream-colored carpet and couch. "Wait here while I unload the car. Got it?"

Her eyes were big and round as she stuck her thumb in her mouth and leaned back against the plush couch cushion.

He left her and was grabbing the portable crib when he looked up to see her walking barefoot in the patchy snow on the front steps.

She slipped, and his heart leapt into his throat as she tumbled down the last step with a loud shriek.

He dropped the crib and scooped her up. He scanned her for injury before pulling her to his chest as she sobbed.

He needed to clean the fresh scrape on her forehead.

Shit. What was he doing? He was utterly incompetent. Of course she'd follow him outside. Barefoot. *In the snow.*

"I'm sorry, baby," he crooned in the pitch he no longer had to work to find when talking to Gemma. "Uncle JT shouldn't have left you like that."

He glanced at the portable crib, thinking he could place her in it while he unloaded the SUV. That's when he realized he'd dropped it in a slushy mud puddle next to the path.

Crap.

He resigned himself to once again unloading the car with only one arm free to haul the bags.

He'd finish unloading *after* he cleaned her scrape and made sure her feet were warm. And fed her a snack.

An hour later, the car was unloaded, and he moved his SUV into the carport next to the garage. He put Gemma back in her car seat for the drive twenty yards across the driveway. He'd forgotten to grab the garage door opener in his haste the other night, so he'd need the side door key to get inside and hit the button. The carport would do for now.

He carried Gemma back into the house and let out a heavy sigh as he set her down, then leaned against the closed door.

He wondered what the odds were he could get her to nap, then remembered the soaking wet crib.

Next chore: clean up the crib.

Gemma was running in circles in the living room—she appeared to be a big fan of the open floor plan—and he realized how not baby-proof the room was.

For the next hour, he rearranged furniture, used masking tape to cover all power outlets, and moved all the breakables from low shelves and tables on the main floor of the house. He placed the breakables and cleaning supplies in the laundry room and drilled a hole in the door and frame and screwed in eyebolts in both holes, then threaded a scrap of electrical wire through the holes and twisted it together for a make-shift lock.

He surveyed the downstairs and mentally declared it Gemma-proof. His gaze landed again on the dirty crib, which he'd left on the slate floor in the foyer, and sighed.

He then scooped up Gemma, who was singing while sitting in a laundry basket he'd set out for her to play in. Who knew toddlers were so much like cats?

"What do you think of showers?"

She grabbed his ear with a pudgy hand and said, "Ower?"

"C'mon. We'll all get clean."

He grabbed her diaper bag and the crib and headed up the stairs.

He wore boxers in the shower. It was silly, he knew, but at the same time, he wasn't comfortable stripping bare, not without Lex's permission, even if it was just a shower for kid and crib.

It was clear that Gemma had never taken a shower before, but no way would he try to give her a bath—he didn't have a safety chair and had no clue how to bathe a kid. As it was, he had a large two-headed shower stall that fit him and the fully setup crib, with Gemma giggling in the corner whenever he sprayed her with the shower wand, in between washing the mud from the baby jail.

He was feeling like a pro by the time he secured a fresh diaper and clean onesie on the smiling girl, who now smelled like baby shampoo.

It was late afternoon, and she'd skipped the nap Erica had promised. What were the odds that would translate to an early bedtime?

He dressed her in a pink set of footed pajamas he'd purchased in the middle of the night a day and a half ago, marveling at the elasticity of time.

On one level, that shopping trip had been a lifetime ago. It had happened in a world where he didn't know Gemma Vargas. And now he couldn't imagine a world without her in it.

Thirty-eight hours.

"Hungry?" he asked. As if he didn't know the answer.

"Hungy! Hungy!"

He smiled. "We need to teach you some new words. Can you say 'yes'?"

"No."

He laughed, then enunciated clearly, drawing out the word, "*Yeessss.*"

"No."

"No?"

"Yesss." She smiled, an eight-tooth grin, and giggled.

Holy shit. She had made a *joke.*

"Silly," he said.

"Knock-knock."

Wait, she told knock-knock jokes? "Who's there?"

She stuck her tongue between her lips and made a raspberry sound.

He laughed. "That might be the cutest and funniest knock-knock joke I've ever heard."

She made another raspberry sound.

This kid. He might be in love.

All at once, he thought of how much danger Lex was in, how much she must be missing her daughter, and he squeezed Gemma tight to his chest as he fought the burn of tears.

Gemma pushed at his chest. "Hungy."

He loosened his grip and swiped at his eyes. "Let's get you some food, kid."

He left the crib to drip dry in the shower. Gemma wouldn't be able to sleep in it tonight anyway. Once again, his chest would be her mattress.

Chapter Ten

Alexandra studied the SUV in the carport. Was it JT's car? It had to be.

She turned with a bit of dread and faced the house, which might not be her safe haven anymore. Whoever was here would have their phone with them in the house.

Oh, what she'd give for the car phones of her childhood. She remembered her dad's excitement as he'd shown her five-year-old self the latest in cellular technology. He'd joked that he would need to get an answering machine for his car. Now, car phones and answering machines were a thing of the ancient past.

She took a deep breath and tried to mentally prepare herself to peek in the windows of the house. If JT had arrived and brought a girlfriend, there was a reasonable chance she'd get an eyeful of something she absolutely did not want to see.

JT had been a big fan of the privacy that ninety-plus acres provided. She'd lost count of the number of times she and JT had sex in the living room, curtains wide open for any Peeping Tom to see.

She shivered. The sun had set an hour ago, and the snow had begun to fall again. She'd spent the day burrowed into a shelter she'd made with branches, but she was chilled to her core. She needed to get inside and warm up, or grab her car and go.

After scouting through the windows, if the coast was clear, she'd use the hidden key to enter the house. Once inside, she'd steal JT's phone if she could, then bolt. She had little doubt he still used the same six-digit password.

Easy-peasy, as long as JT was alone and upstairs.

If he wasn't, she'd have to wait.

Silently, she stepped up onto the deck that lined the back of the house. She dropped to all fours and crawled to the window and peered inside. A light was on in the corner, but it was dim. She could barely see into the room, and she didn't see anything but the back of the couch.

No JT. No other woman.

Thank god no one was having sex.

She took a slow, silent breath and crawled along the icy-cold treated wood planks. The dining room was dark, only a faint glow from the single lamp in the living room giving the outline of the table and ten chairs. Beyond it, the kitchen was completely dark. A blank, black wall.

She crawled to the edge of the deck and slowly rose to a crouch so she could skirt around the house to the front porch, where there was a window into the kitchen.

Snowflakes kissed her cheeks as she made her way around. She gave thanks for JT's abhorrence of light pollution, which meant the porch lights were off.

Soon, the night would be nothing but inky darkness, even with the falling white snow.

One of the porch steps creaked under her feet, and she froze, waiting to see if anyone had heard the sound and knew what it meant. But no lights came on. No movement sounded.

The kitchen was as dark from this side as it had been from the back of the house.

There was no more putting it off. She had to go inside. If JT was alone and she couldn't find his phone, she'd ask for his help. But if his phone was easily grabbable, she'd take it and run.

She toed off her shoes so she wouldn't make a sound on the slate floor of the entryway or the hardwood in the living room and kitchen, then squared her shoulders and slipped the key into the dead bolt and turned. The door opened without so much as a squeak. She stepped inside and closed it silently behind her.

She went for the kitchen first. JT usually dropped his phone on the counter as he made a beeline for the fridge.

The counter was empty.

She turned for the living room. If she was lucky, he'd have left it on the coffee table.

She stepped softly into the living room. The L-shaped couch was at an angle, but she could see a male hand draped on the back cushion. Then she heard a loud snore.

JT. He must be sleeping on the couch. She'd bet anything the phone would be on the coffee table or end table closest to his head. He wasn't the type to sleep with it in his pocket.

She held her breath to keep from making a sound as she tiptoed around the end of the couch. She didn't look at the man, afraid even her gaze would wake him.

She spotted the phone and pressed her hand to her mouth to silence the gust of relieved breath. Her hands shook as she stepped closer and reached for it. Her heart pounded so loud, she was sure it would wake him.

She grabbed the phone, but it slipped from her shaking fingers and hit the table with a soft thunk.

Her gaze jerked to the man on the couch. His eyes popped open and widened in shock. His hand moved from the back of the couch and pressed to the bundle on his chest.

Her gaze dropped to his hand and took in the dark shape.

She let out a soft cry, and tears burst forth as what she was seeing in the dim room became clear.

Her daughter was sound asleep, snuggled in a ball against JT's bare chest.

Chapter Eleven

JT couldn't believe his eyes. He had to be dreaming. A fantasy his conscious mind didn't dare offer up, but which slipped around the barriers when he finally got the little hellion to settle down and sleep.

He held Lex's gaze, not even daring to breathe lest he wake the tiny, volatile Mr. Hyde who rested on his heart.

"Gemma?" Lex's voice was a choked whisper.

She reached out a hand, as if to touch her daughter's soft hair, but then pulled back. Was she also afraid to break this magic and wake the demon?

Gemma let out a soft snuffling sound, her body completely relaxed on his chest. As if this was the most normal thing in the world.

He cupped the back of Gemma's head and then scooted to lean against the armrest so he was no longer flat on his back.

The movement broke the spell, and Alexandra let out a sob and dropped to her knees next to the couch. She rained kisses all over Gemma's blonde hair, some landing on JT's fingers. She straightened and kissed JT's cheek, then burrowed her head into his neck and let out a muffled sob.

He wrapped an arm around her and scooped her up. She shifted, pressing herself to his side on the extra-wide lounge seat. She snuggled against him, her hand cupping the back of her daughter's head as she silently sobbed.

JT's tears fell too, rolling down his cheek and soaking her hair. He could burst with the amount of emotion he was holding inside.

Finally, Lex let out a shuddering breath and whispered, "How did you know I was here?"

He shook his head slightly. "I didn't. We didn't. I'd planned to come here for the holiday anyway, and Lee figured it would be safest for Gemma if she wasn't with them."

Tears spilled down her cheeks. "Thank you. For protecting my baby."

His tears also fell as he choked out his response. "Of course."

He had a thousand questions for her, starting with what happened on that deserted Maryland road, but right now, he just wanted to hold her. Hold her daughter. Breathe.

Get his emotions under control.

She burrowed against him, and he realized how cold her body was. He grabbed the throw that was draped over the back of the couch and did his best to drape it over her without shifting too much to wake the kid.

"You're freezing."

"I saw your car on the driveway when you first drove up. I wasn't sure if it was you or someone looking for me, so I hid in the woods, waiting for darkness, so I could sneak in and see who was here."

"When did you get here?"

"Late the night...everything happened. I would have told you—or Lee—but no phone. No computer."

Had she been here before he picked up Gemma? If he'd come straight here instead of stopping at the motel... But he couldn't regret that. It had been the best choice he could make at the time.

"It's good that you didn't call Lee. The cops are likely watching his house. I wouldn't be surprised if they got a warrant to tap his landline. No way could they listen in on his cell, but that doesn't mean they won't try. I haven't checked in with him since I got Gemma."

The child shifted, and he realized he was creeping toward speaking in a normal voice. He'd said her name, which could be one of her wake words.

Alexandra's gaze had been fixed on her daughter since she'd snuggled to his side. Now, she sat up and stroked her daughter's soft blonde hair. More tears fell as she said, "I've been terrified I'd never get to hold her again." She then lifted her sleeping daughter from his chest and shifted her to her own.

Cold seeped in at the loss of the bundle of heat against his heart, but a different warmth flooded him as he watched the love of his life sob as she cuddled her daughter.

Gemma smelled of baby shampoo and Cheerios, and Alexandra couldn't hold back the cry that erupted from her as she held her baby tight.

Her baby. Her everything. Safe in her arms.

For now.

It was that *for now* uncertainty of what would happen to her that triggered the sob. Joy and pain all at once.

Strangely reminiscent of the two years when she and JT

were back together—she had the man she loved—but his volatile emotions had kept her on edge, knowing it would never last. Even though she shared his bed, the meaningful part of their relationship was over.

But there was no end to the meaningful part of her relationship with Gemma. She would always be her mother, even if she was in prison.

Prison.

She could go to prison for a crime she didn't commit.

Gemma woke. *Of course* she did. Her mother was sobbing loudly and squeezing her tight.

She didn't cry, though, and Alexandra figured she'd known from her scent that she was in her mother's arms before she even opened her eyes.

But she did push back against Alexandra's tight grip. Tiny hands pressed to Alexandra's chest and arms extended their full short length, she tilted her head up and said, "Mommy!"

Her chin quivered, and the anger she must have harbored at her mother's disappearance rose to the surface. She smacked Alexandra's collarbone, then grabbed her jaw with both hands. Her nails hadn't been clipped in days, and the sharp little edges scraped Alexandra's skin. "Mommy *gone*."

The outrage she managed to put in the second word made up for her limited vocabulary.

"I'm sorry, baby. So sorry. I didn't know I'd be gone."

Gemma's precious face crumpled, and she burst into tears. Alexandra held her and cried with her, not trying to stop either of them from shedding the well-earned tears.

JT's arms surrounded them both, and that just made her cry harder.

Who was this man who'd taken care of her child, protecting her when it could put him in legal trouble?

Every minute they spent together added to his risk. JT had political aspirations that had been destroyed once already. Helping her could crush his renewed hopes, if he had them.

The thought brought an end to her crying. She pulled back. "Gemma and I need to leave, or you'll be arrested for harboring a fugitive."

"I don't give a fu—" He cleared his throat and continued in a softer tone. "Fig. You aren't going anywhere without me. I have resources and can help you. You take Gemma and run, and you're both in far more danger."

Gemma's tears subsided. True to her daughter's cyclone nature, she wiggled from Alexandra's arms and said, "Tee-Tee!"

Alexandra frowned. "Tee-Tee?"

JT tapped the switch on the end table light, and the room filled with a soft glow.

Gemma twisted so she was on her belly as she slid off the couch in new footy pajamas. She ran to the diaper bag. Alexandra hadn't spotted it in the dark corner when she first entered the room.

Gemma grabbed her favorite tattered stuffed panda and a brand-new plush dinosaur. She ran across the room, waving the green plushy. "Tee-Tee."

Alexandra looked to JT, raising a brow. "Tee-Tee? Because it's a T-Rex?"

"I think? She calls me Tee, so she also might have named it after me."

Her daughter had a name for JT. All at once, she was reminded of her private name for him. *Jay.* And only Jay called her Lex.

Her Jay.

But Gemma had Tee.

She might swoon.

Gemma held out the new toy for inspection, and

Alexandra kissed it on the snout and welcomed Tee-Tee to the family.

"We need to talk," JT said.

She nodded as she rose from the couch. Tears and introductions were over. She needed to know what was going on and share her story with Jay. "I think we need to get Raptor involved. Will they help me?"

He stood and cupped her cheek, then kissed her forehead. "They already are. If you're anything like your daughter, you must be starving. Food first, then you can tell me everything."

Alexandra was impressed with the supplies Jay had managed to get in the middle of the night. Enough groceries for him and a baby for several days, plus all the accessories a toddler needed.

Erica had given him a detailed list, and he'd gone above and beyond, right down to picking up a stuffed T-Rex that Gemma had fallen in love with.

And given the way her little girl looked at him, she figured Gemma was equally enamored of Uncle Tee.

It was wild. JT didn't even like kids.

But damn, he'd come to Gemma's rescue without hesitation.

Her heart squeezed. Never in a million years had she imagined JT spending a minute with her daughter, let alone changing diapers, feeding, and bathing her.

Now he cooked dinner while Alexandra moved the portable crib out of the shower and into the sauna attached to the primary bath for a quick dry. The thin mattress hadn't gotten dirty in the mud, nor had it gone into the shower. It was clean and dry.

Gemma would be able to sleep in the crib tonight,

although Alexandra was just as likely to pull her into bed with her. It was hard to imagine letting the girl be more than an arm's reach away.

She adjusted the temperature of the sauna, then pulled the door tightly closed.

"Okay, squirt. Let's go help Uncle Tee make dinner."

Gemma picked up her dinosaur and panda, who had been having a gibberish conversation on the bathroom floor.

They left the bedroom and crossed the landing to the top of the stairs. One thing JT hadn't gotten was a gate to block off the stairs. Gemma had only recently learned how to navigate stairs, and Alexandra was glad the upstairs of this house, built in the seventies, had wall-to-wall carpeting, including carpeted stairs and landing.

She considered carrying her down, but she needed to know if Gemma could do this. So she watched, ready to grab her if she stumbled as the girl turned and presented her backside to the world as she descended on all fours, one stuffed animal clutched in each hand while she pressed dino and panda into the carpet one slow step at a time.

When she reached the bottom, Gemma grinned with her achievement and praised her toys. "Good job, Panny Tee-Tee!"

Every moment felt extra intense as she watched the things her daughter could do after the constant fear and horror of the last days. The horror wasn't gone. The fear might never leave her.

Her joy and relief in this moment was mixed with a huge dose of dread at the uncertainty of what faced her.

She'd do whatever it took to protect Gemma.

Raptor would help her.

Jay would help her.

She'd been prepared to surrender if it was the only way

to keep her girl safe, but knowing she had backup, she vowed to go down fighting.

Chapter Twelve

"We need to get word to Erica and Lee that you're safe, but we can't let them know you're with me. It will be easier for them to face questioning if they're telling the truth when they say they don't know where you are."

"How do we do that? If you call them, they'll figure it out. Lee knows I've been here before. He could easily guess I know where the keys are hidden. We also don't want any direct phone calls between you and them in case the police are monitoring Lee's cell phone."

JT couldn't help but smile. "If there's one person whose phone can't be hacked, it's Lee. But still, we need to be careful. Whoever killed Officer Williams might also be searching for you. I'm sure they hope you'll be taken care of by an angry cop, but they won't leave it to fate, because they can't know if you saw them or not."

"I didn't, though. I don't know if it was a man or woman, or even what kind of car they drove. I was too scared to take a chance at being seen. They had a deep voice, which made me think the person is male, but that's hardly definitive."

"I'm pretty sure Lee will dig into the dead officer's background. Maybe he'll find some connection between you and him that will make this make sense."

"I wish I knew if he targeted me specifically or if he was trolling for women driving alone."

"He didn't look familiar?"

She shook her head. "He blinded me with a flashlight at first, so I didn't really see his face until I was out of the car. Honestly, by then I was so panicked, I wasn't seeing straight, but what I saw didn't ring any bells at the time."

"Did you see his official portrait on the news?"

"No. The only photo they showed when I watched was mine."

Her words brought back the kick to the solar plexus he'd received when he saw her photo on the news. But much as he hated that moment, without it, he wouldn't have brought Gemma here.

"I think our best bet is Keith Hatcher—CEO of Raptor. I can hire them to investigate what happened in Maryland, and Keith can help you retain an attorney so you'll be protected by attorney-client privilege. If you have an attorney negotiating with Maryland State Police for you to present yourself for questioning—on neutral ground, preferably Raptor's Virginia compound—maybe we can get them to call off the manhunt."

"You can't tell Keith I'm with you—"

"I'll say I'm hiring them on my own initiative. He knows…" He paused and closed his eyes, then continued. "He knows I'll do anything for you. He might guess you're here, but he's too smart to ask the question."

Alexandra glanced at the clock on the stove. "It's after business hours and tomorrow is Christmas Eve. Raptor—and any potential attorney for me—will charge a fortune, and that's only if they'll take your call."

"I don't care what it costs. I can afford it."

She flinched, and he knew why. He'd always been generous with her, but in the end, he'd held even that against her, unable to believe there was any reason she'd stand by him except his wealth. "I'm going to do this for you. I don't care about the money. I'm not letting you go to prison for a crime you didn't commit."

"My fingerprints are on the gun."

"You didn't pull the trigger."

"I know I need outside help, but I'm scared. If MSP figures out where I am…with a warrant, not even these ninety acres will protect me. And I'm sure they have a warrant by now."

"I trust Keith with my life."

"We aren't talking about your life. We're talking about mine. And Gemma's."

Her voice had taken on a hard edge. He had it coming. For years, he'd allowed her to believe he didn't care about her at all.

He could still see the look on her face when he said the words that ended their relationship for good. He'd been vicious. At the time, he'd told himself it was the right thing to do. While it was true that setting her free was necessary, there was no justifying his method.

He'd wanted her to hurt, for no reason other than he was an asshole and it gutted him that he'd never be enough for her. He'd wanted her to feel the same misery he lived in.

It wasn't until later, when he broke it down with a therapist, that he could see how much he'd held himself back from Alexandra. *Of course* he wasn't enough for her.

"I'm sorry, Lex. I was a total prick, and you never deserved it. You have no reason to believe me, but I've never stopped loving you."

She scoffed. "Listen, JT, I'm grateful for your help, but

you don't need to lie to me. I'm not here hoping to work things out. That ship sailed long ago. You killed my love for you with one brutal blow, so save your apologies that are seven—no nine years too late."

Nine years. The number was specific. Nine years ago, they were together, ostensibly trying to make their relationship work. It was also when he got a vasectomy and hid it from her.

The shit of it was, he knew he could have told her. She respected his bodily autonomy as much as he respected hers. But he hadn't told her because he was afraid it would be the final straw that made her give up on him when he was in a terrible mental space and wasn't giving even a fraction of what he was taking from her for emotional support.

And she was right; now wasn't the time to discuss any of this. She was in a desperate situation and needed help. From him.

He'd do whatever she needed, no question. Not because of their past relationship. No, it was because she would always be the love of his life, and the only thing he wanted for her was that she get her happily ever after, even if it didn't include him.

He gave a sharp nod. "Fine. I would trust Keith with Lee's life." It was a well-known fact that he loved his little brother, who was his closest friend in the world. It was only thanks to Lee that he had other friends like Keith, Curt, and Alec.

Left to his own devices, he'd have run everyone off the same way he'd shoved Lex away.

If it weren't for Lee, he'd never have shared his private gym in DC with the others. Hell, he'd bought the place because his, Lee's, and Curt's sensei had retired and he couldn't deal with the idea of finding a new dojo, nor did he want to lose the connection with Lee that had been forged when the kid was a twelve-year-old hacker who needed a hobby that wouldn't land him in prison.

"Okay, then. I'll trust Keith too. He seemed nice when I met him at the wedding, and I liked Trina a lot. How do we get in touch with him?"

As the head of a private security and paramilitary training organization that was owned by a sitting US senator, Keith had connections and wildly good security.

"Lee gave me a burner phone. I'll use it to tell Keith you contacted me, but not that you're here. He'll be able to set up a consultation between you and an attorney."

"Thank you." Lex rose from her seat at the dining table and cleared their plates.

"I can do the dishes."

"No. You cooked. And babysat for a day and a half. I can wash up."

It was weird to be relegated to the role of babysitter, but he supposed that was what he had been. He wasn't even Uncle Tee. It was a courtesy title for a caretaker.

He looked over to where Gemma sat on the carpet, playing with her stuffed toys and the wooden blocks he'd gotten her, which she was stacking. Building houses for Panny and Tee-Tee?

He gave a half smile. Engineer in the making already.

He and his father had both been engineers. His dad had always wanted JT to have kids to pass on T&D. Keep the engineering dynasty going. Instead, JT was selling it in a week and would be glad to be free from the business that had consumed his life since he first started working there when he was all of fourteen years old.

He looked at Alexandra's daughter, building towers for a panda and dinosaur, and wondered once again about Gemma's father.

He knew her last name was Vargas, but that meant nothing. Alexandra hadn't planned to take the name Talon when they married, and it was her right to give her child her name, no matter who the father was.

Hell, JT's last name, Talon, wasn't even his. If Joseph Talon Sr. hadn't been cheated out of being raised by his birth mother, his name would have been Ricky Guerrero. JT would be Ricky Junior, maybe. But then, JT probably wouldn't exist. Ricky Guerrero would have had a vastly different life.

Better or worse in adulthood, no one could know, but definitely better than a childhood of being raised in an Indian boarding school, run by a white headmaster who hated the Indigenous children forced to live in his school.

The Carleton School for Indian Boys was one of many Indian boarding schools that was under scrutiny now, especially because it had operated longer than most of the schools that started in the late 1800s with the purpose of erasing Indigenous culture from all tribal children. The graveyard behind the school was vast and dated back to when children had been removed from their homes at gunpoint.

JT wasn't a tribal member by blood, as he'd thought until he was thirty-seven. He'd been raised within the tribal community, everyone believing he was one-quarter Menanichoch. One of their own. In the end, that was good enough for the tribe, and after processing the rift that undermined his very foundation, he realized it was good enough for him too. They were his family in a way even Lee wasn't, even though he shared exactly the same amount of blood with the tribe as he shared with his stepbrother. He'd grown up with the tribe's traditions, straddling Indigenous and white man's world as his father's wealth grew.

Now JT was an extremely wealthy man. He was also a registered member of the Menanichoch tribe—accepted in before he was born. In reality, his grandfather had been a dark-skinned Cuban man, his grandmother a pale French-

Canadian woman. JT resembled his father, whose ambiguous ethnicity had worked in the favor of the kidnapper who dumped four-year-old Ricky at the boarding school and gave him the name Joseph Talon, along with identifying him as a Menanichoch tribal member.

Alexandra's daughter was blonde and blue-eyed, like her mother. She'd been born in Switzerland, while her mother was there on a research fellowship.

Did she have a Swiss father?

Staring at the happy toddler, he asked the question he'd never dared to ask Lee. "Where is Gemma's father?"

"Lee didn't tell you?"

"I…didn't want to know." For the longest time, he'd resisted even finding out if she had a boy or a girl. It wasn't until he decided to set up the trust fund for her that he'd needed to know her name and birthdate. But now wasn't the time to tell Lex about the trust.

"Her bio dad is a popsicle. Frozen sperm."

That surprised him. "You said you'd never do that. You wanted a family."

"I never found anyone I wanted to have a kid with, and my biological clock was shutting the door. I changed my mind." She cleared her throat. "It's a good thing I made the decision when I did. I ended up having trouble conceiving and had to go through fertility treatment in addition to artificial insemination. It took me nearly two years to conceive, and several expensive rounds of treatment." She looked at her daughter. "She's my precious Gem."

Alexandra descended the stairs, baby monitor speaker in hand, walking softly in hopes that Gemma would stay asleep in the portable crib. She could hear JT on the phone and didn't make a sound as she entered the study, where he sat in a large office chair, facing the dark window with his back to the desk and doorway. She silently settled into the love seat in the corner of the large office and listened to his side of the conversation.

"We need to get word to Lee and Erica that Alexandra is safe without connecting the info to me. I'm sure they're being questioned daily, so best to keep them in the dark."

He was silent for a moment, then said, "I appreciate it, Keith. I'll pay whatever it takes."

Alexandra silently vowed to pay him back. This was her problem, not his. She'd gratefully take his help now, but wouldn't be beholden to him in the long run.

It was a relief that Erica and Lee would know she was safe. She hated the stress they must be feeling. In three hours, it would be Christmas Eve. They all deserved peace this holiday.

Alexandra and Gemma had been invited to Erica and Lee's for Christmas dinner. She had initially declined until Erica assured her that JT wouldn't be there because everyone attending would have kids. Curt and Mara would be there with their son. Alec and Isabel's baby wasn't due until March, but they planned to join the fun.

She'd been so looking forward to it. Once upon a time, she'd been friends with Curt and wanted to get to know Mara, who was close to Erica. The women were tight in a way Alexandra and Erica had been for a time.

The way Alexandra and Kendall had once been. Before Brent. And, to be fair, before JT.

Now Kendall was gone and Alexandra's future was in serious doubt. Would she ever have a chance to forge new friendships that had felt so promising a week ago?

She wanted Gemma to have the feeling of an extended family, even though she was the only child of a single mother who had also been an only child. Alexandra's parents were still alive, but both had dementia and lived in a care facility in Delaware.

Like Gemma, Alexandra had been born to a woman of advanced maternal age, and her parents were now in their mid-eighties. Her mother's mind was sharper than her father's, but she was only sporadically lucid.

She shuddered at the idea the press might find a way to invade her parents' peace in their memory care facility, but security was extremely tight to protect the patients, so it was unlikely.

JT said goodbye to Keith, then spun around in his chair to face her. "I'm pretty sure Keith didn't believe me when I said I didn't know where you were, but like I figured, he didn't probe."

"I'm going to pay you back. I know Raptor doesn't come cheap."

JT rose from his seat and circled the desk to stand in front of her. He reached out a hand. She took it, and he gently pulled her to her feet.

His arms enfolded her. He'd held her on the couch, but this was the first time they'd embraced without Gemma between them.

He held her tight. She'd never in her wildest dreams imagined being in his arms again. His embrace was both familiar and foreign.

His grip loosened, and he raised his head. She did the same and met his gaze. "Let me do this for you, Lex."

She studied his eyes. Deep brown and beautiful. His hair was going gray, and the salt and pepper looked damn good on him. "You don't understand. I can't let you, JT. You put your money between us in the past. I don't trust you not to hold this against me too."

"I was a complete ass, looking for a reason why you'd

stayed with me. I figured it had to be the money because it was never my winning personality."

His words were shockingly self-aware for a man who'd never exhibited such insight before. "I was with you because I loved you."

Past tense. Now she was with him because she needed him. And right now, what she needed was his money.

"I wasn't worthy of your love then. So I was certain you only tolerated me because I was rich."

"That's because you're a dumb fuck. But yeah, you're right. You didn't deserve me." She'd put up with him far longer than she should have. And it was that tolerance that had made him disrespect her more.

It had been a vicious cycle.

"I've done a lot of work. I'm not the man I was then. I was working up my courage to reach out to you, to make amends. When I heard you'd had a kid, I knew I'd waited too long to get my shit together, and I didn't want to intrude on your happiness, even if only to give you closure."

She pushed away from him, stepping back and pacing away. His words were nice, but even now, it was all about him. He couldn't *bestow* closure on her. She'd had to find that for herself. No. He'd wanted to reach out to make himself feel better. Closure for *him*.

"This isn't the time to talk about this. I need your help, and I don't want to fight."

"I'm making it worse, aren't I?"

"Not worse, but not better either. You're still centering *you*."

He smiled. "I love that you aren't hesitating to call out my shit even now."

"I've learned it's better than stewing in silence."

"You used to do that. When we were first together. When

we were engaged. Even when we were on again, off again. It wasn't until my life fell apart that you held back."

"Will it make you happy to know it's because you were fragile as a wasps' nest?"

He frowned, his brow furrowed in question.

She spelled it out for him. "Paper thin, brittle, and if you tap it, you get stung. Several times."

He nodded. "Accurate."

No man likes to be told he's fragile, but JT took it in stride. Maybe he really had changed.

But something about his words and manner brought to mind the man she'd fallen in love with once upon a time. Maybe, instead of changing into something new, he'd gone back to being the man who'd swept her off her feet when they first met.

Chapter Thirteen

Menanichoch, Maryland
December 17th
Sixteen years ago

Alexandra took a seat on a barstool and let out a sigh as she lifted her stiletto-shod feet from the floor. The heels were gorgeous, but she couldn't imagine wearing four-inch spikes on a regular basis. They *hurt.* And her date was bothered that she was as tall as he was when wearing them. He should have told her there was a height code and she'd have saved money on the shoes.

As a broke, twenty-five-year-old grad student, she wasn't cut out for being the plus one at company holiday parties for professional men in their thirties, but Kendall had begged her to make it a double date, and the guy was handsome and had promised a gourmet meal, good wine, and dancing.

The food was good, and she'd enjoyed the wine served with dinner, but once the complimentary wine was gone, Russ had opted to skip the dancing in favor of gambling.

Alexandra had watched him at the blackjack table for a

half hour before sheer boredom took over. She'd returned to the ballroom where the private party was being held, thinking she'd join in on the dancing, but it was a slow song, and Kendall was pressed tight to her date with a dreamy expression on her face.

Kendall had been dating the engineer for two months, and she was certain he was *the one*. Kendall was Alexandra's sister in all but blood, which meant she had been on the Kendall- coaster too many times to count and had little faith Brent Forbes was really *the one*, but Kendall was happy right now, and that was all that mattered.

Deciding to leave the couple alone, Alexandra had gone to the quieter of the two bars that served the private party and was relieved to get off her feet.

The bartender was young—closer to Alexandra's age than her date was—and had darker coloring and features that hinted at Native American heritage, which made sense given this was a tribal casino.

The casino was the venue for the holiday party because the majority owner of the engineering firm her date worked for was a Menanichoch tribal member. Joseph Talon was now a US senator, but someone in the family was CEO.

Or at least she thought that was what Kendall had said when she began her campaign to get Alexandra to play wing woman tonight. She hadn't really paid attention because she'd been deep in the throes of a research paper that would make or break her first semester of graduate school.

Really, it should be illegal to talk to someone during the last weeks of any semester of graduate school, with fines doubled for theoretical physics students.

No. *Tripled.*

She'd said yes because the party was the day after her last paper was due and a free meal sounded about right for her budget. Plus, Russ had been fun when he came to their apartment for movie night with Brent a few weeks ago.

It hadn't been meant to be a setup—after all, Alexandra had only joined them for pizza as a study break—but Russ had told Brent he was interested, and the idea of her joining the three of them at the holiday party had been launched.

She didn't have time to date. She wouldn't for the next several years. But she'd decided she could spare one evening over winter break.

So now here she was, alone at the bar, her date more interested in cards than dancing. Of course, that hadn't stopped him from giving her a key for the hotel room he'd booked at the casino's resort.

Not just no, but *hell no*.

"What can I get you?" the bartender asked as he set a beverage napkin in front of her.

She frowned. This was a cash bar, and she was broke to the point where she'd be snitching drink garnishes for a fruit salad if she hadn't just had a four-course meal. "Club soda?"

"Is that a question?"

"How much?"

"Depends on if you want it with lime juice, mint, and white rum."

"A mojito would be amazing, but out of my budget. Club soda with a lime wedge, please?"

"You're with Talon & Drake?"

She shook her head. "My date is, though."

He winked at her. "I'll put it on the company tab, then."

She smiled. "Better yet, put it on my date's room." She gave him the room number, not even feeling slightly bad about it. He'd abandoned her without a second thought. She'd charge a taxi to his room if she could.

The bartender muddled the mint with a flourish and proceeded to assemble an excellent mojito. She added a hefty tip and signed the bill, then turned on her stool and sipped her drink as she watched the dancers.

The slow song had ended, and a current hit by Green Day had her considering joining the dancers, but one look at her shoes changed her mind. Sure, she could dance barefoot, but then when Russ returned, he'd be happy she was shorter than him again, and she was feeling just pissy enough to want to avoid that.

A man in a tailored suit approached the bar. His gaze swept over her as he neared, and she felt a zing of attraction fill the space between them.

He was utterly gorgeous. Thick, dark hair, light brown skin. Thirtyish. He moved with confidence. Like an adult. A handsome, successful *man*.

This wasn't a boy. Nor was he a student.

She spent most of her time with students. Undergrad and grad, they ranged in age from teenage geniuses to men years older than her, but sometimes it felt like the academic environment trapped them all in a state that was out of sync with the rest of the world. There were students and there were professors, and only the latter group were the adults in the room.

Which was ridiculous.

It probably stemmed from her own insecurity due to the judgments people made based on her looks. She was tall, blonde, and stacked, which meant she had to fight to be taken seriously in the real world. In grad school, students and professors alike knew there was no way she'd be in the program if she didn't have the brain for it. So it was a safe zone of sorts, but she'd still spent her first semester doing everything she could to prove she belonged.

Deep down, she'd known Russ had only invited her to this party because of the aforementioned hair color and oversized breasts, which would, she presumed, impress certain coworkers. For her part, she'd agreed for the free dinner, not because she was eager to get to know him, so she couldn't really complain. They both had superficial reasons for being on this date.

But she didn't know what was worse, that he'd been so confident she'd jump into bed with him that he'd reserved a hotel room, or that he was still thinking he'd get laid after abandoning her for a blackjack table. He was probably bragging to the other players about bagging the blonde right now.

She wasn't a person to him. She was a trophy, like catching a really big tuna and posing for pictures to show the world what a great fisherman he was. And he probably thought she was too young and silly to pick up on that.

Anger burned all over again.

She fixed her gaze on the handsome man who now stood one barstool away and ordered a drink. This complete stranger had better odds of getting her into bed tonight than her date, and she never screwed around with strangers.

While he waited for his drink, he turned and caught her stare. He gave her an easy smile. "You work for Talon & Drake?" He scanned her again, and his thick, dark brows furrowed with skepticism.

Okay, so maybe not. She rolled her eyes and shook her head. "No, I'm afraid my blonde hair makes it impossible for me to math. No engineering for little me."

He snickered. "Huh. I'm told that having a penis makes it impossible to detect sarcasm, but still, I'm hearing notes of something in your very logical statement about the correlation between hair color and the ability to compute."

"Maybe you don't have a penis, then."

He grinned, turned to the side, and made a show of pulling on his waistband and looking down. "Whew. Still there." He turned back to her. "I was asking because I haven't seen you before, and I feel certain I'd have noticed you in the office."

"There are several East Coast branches at this party. Maybe I work at one you aren't familiar with."

"Nope."

"Nope? You know everyone at every office?"

"Not by name. But again, I'd have noticed *you*."

"Maybe I'm new."

"Nah. You see, you've given yourself away because *you* don't recognize *me*. So, are you crashing the party, or is your date the dumbest man on the planet to leave you alone?"

He sure had a high opinion of himself. He couldn't be much older than thirty. How important could he be in a company like Talon & Drake? It was an engineering firm, not a tech startup. "My date could be a woman."

"Still dumb to leave you alone."

"You think I need a babysitter?"

"No, I think you're bored and maybe a little pissed."

"Honestly? More than a little."

"Who's your date?"

"Russ Spaulding."

The man grunted but said nothing. Probably not a good idea to diss on a coworker. For all she knew, Russ could be this guy's boss.

She sipped her drink to prevent herself from saying something she'd regret. It wouldn't be fair to either man.

She was the trophy date who got a free meal. Kendall was having fun. Classes were done, and she didn't even need to fret that she wasn't studying right now.

Plus, she had a free drink. "You work for Talon & Drake long?"

He shrugged. "Long enough."

That was a nonanswer. "You like it?"

"Sure."

"You ever meet the senator who owns it?"

"I have."

"You vote for him?"

He looked at her askance. "Secret ballots are a constitutional right."

"Ah. So that's a no."

He laughed. "I can't vote in Maryland."

"Ahh. Convicted felon. I get it. Don't worry. I'll keep your secret."

The man tilted his head back and let out a full laugh. It was warm, and she felt a buzz at having triggered it. "No. I live in New York most of the time. That's where I vote."

"Most of the time? You have multiple houses?"

"I stay with family when I'm in the area." He nodded toward a *very* tall man who was approaching the bar. "Speaking of, I should get back."

The tall man had dark hair, but his skin was several shades lighter. The two men didn't look related, but that didn't mean anything.

"It was nice meeting you," the man said as he picked up two drinks from the bar. "Find me if Spaulding loses his shirt. I'll see to it you get home safe."

She sipped her drink as she watched him walk away. Nice ass. And the tall guy was fine too. He looked to be closer to Alexandra's age. His gaze landed on her, and he smiled, but not with interest. Not like the man she'd just been chatting with.

His look was simple curiosity.

She wanted to ask the bartender if he knew who the men were, but it would be ridiculous. There were over three hundred guests at this party, employees of Talon & Drake and plus ones like her. The odds that the bartender would know anyone was slim.

She finished her drink and set the empty glass on the bar. It was magically refilled, but she hesitated before taking it.

"On the house. Don't tell anyone."

She drew a line across her closed lips, then added, "Thank you."

She sipped her fresh drink and tried to decide what to do. Wait for Kendall to tire of dancing and get a ride home with her? Or take the stranger up on his offer and see if he'd spring for a cab?

She would *never* go out on a date this far from home without cash for a cab again. It had never occurred to her she could be stranded in Menanichoch, a forty-minute drive from the apartment she shared with Kendall.

Just when she was working up the courage to interrupt Kendall's fun, Russ reentered the room. She watched him as he stood in the doorway, scanning the crowd. Finally, he spotted her and made a beeline in her direction.

He was only a few feet away when he said, "Hey, gorgeous. I was wondering where you went off to."

"Oh. Did you notice I was gone?" She'd left him at the card table over thirty minutes ago.

"Sure. I didn't have my good luck charm."

"And yet you still kept playing."

"Well, sure. Had to try to win it all back. I knew you'd be having fun in here with Kendall and Brent."

"Yeah, because couples really love it when a third person moves in on their slow dance."

Russ's brow furrowed. "Cranky, are we, babe?"

Lord, now he was treating her like she was a toddler without a nap. "I'm not cranky. I'm *angry*. And bored. I want to go home."

"What's the rush? It's still early."

"No. It's not. We finished dinner an hour ago, then you

played cards and expected me to watch like some sort of groupie."

Russ turned to the bartender and ordered a drink.

She gritted her teeth. "Russ, you're driving. You can't have another drink. I want to go home."

"You know I got us a hotel room, sweetheart."

Did he even remember her name? Sweetheart. Gorgeous. Babe. She wouldn't mind the terms if she believed he knew her actual name.

"I'm not staying here tonight. Give me money for a cab."

"C'mon. Let's have a drink. Maybe dance a little and discuss it."

She huffed out a sigh. "I'm too tired to dance." She nodded toward an empty table at the edge of the crowd. "Let's sit. I'll finish my drink, then you can get me a cab, or Kendall and Brent can give me a ride home."

She had a free drink to finish and wanted to get the kiss-off conversation over with here, so he would *never* come back to the apartment with Brent again.

Before they sat down, however, she decided to visit the ladies' room. Let him stew by himself for a little bit and see how it felt.

Chapter Fourteen

The blonde at the bar was breathtaking. And funny. And she didn't put up with bullshit. JT was a huge fan of that exact combination in a woman.

He would've asked her name, but learning she was there with Spaulding changed things. He had no problem moving in on another man's obviously miserable date, but if he did it to Spaulding, he'd have a problem with HR. And Ed Drake.

"So, what's the deal?" Lee asked. "Who's she here with?"

"Fucking Spaulding."

"Well, damn. That complicates things."

Lee knew about JT's issues with Ed Drake. As his former stepbrother, he knew all the players but had nothing to do with the company, which made him the perfect confidant. He hadn't attended the formal dinner part of the evening because he said engineers gave him hives, but he'd shown up for the after-party to keep JT company.

Six years in, and JT was still working to earn the respect of the company's top executives, who'd balked at him taking over as CEO when his dad was elected to the Senate, but in a privately held company, they didn't have the votes to oust him. Not when Joseph Talon Sr. anointed him and forced his partner and minority share owner, Edward Drake, to support the decision.

Drake wasn't happy, but he was a team player—when Senator Talon demanded it. Now he just worked to sabotage JT from the inside.

He was counting the days until the man retired. Unfortunately, it wouldn't be anytime soon.

He watched the blonde as she sipped her drink. Stunning didn't begin to describe her. Blonde, blue-eyed, tall, and busty, she was a centerfold come to life. And from their short conversation at the bar, he knew there was more to her than gorgeous face and body.

Of course, her taste in dates wasn't a ringing endorsement of her intelligence, but he was the guy who'd hired the prick four years ago, so he couldn't judge. Spaulding made a good first impression.

The foolish but lucky man stepped into the arched doorway for the private party, and JT leaned toward Lee. "That's him. Spaulding."

Russ Spaulding scanned the dance floor, probably looking for his date. There were only a half dozen couples dancing, making it easy to see that the tall blonde was not among them. Finally, Spaulding spotted her on the far side of the room and made his way toward her.

JT had hoped to give the woman a ride home, but it looked like she wouldn't have to rely on the kindness of strangers.

He should have given her his card, but he'd been stupidly hesitant to be so heavy-handed. Plus, he'd liked the idea that she had no clue who he was.

These days, everyone wanted a piece of him—either because he was a senator's son, or because he was CEO of an international engineering firm with a net income of over 200 million dollars for the previous fiscal year. And he was only thirty-one years old.

Sure, nepotism got him on the fast track, but he had an engineering degree, and it was under his management that the number of active projects had increased by forty-six percent in the last six years, and the average budgets for those projects had increased by twenty-seven percent.

Spaulding and the blonde spoke by the bar. JT was pretty sure she was asking for a ride home, but the guy ordered a cocktail, and they moved to a table ten feet from where JT and Lee sat. The blonde placed her drink on the table and headed for the casino floor.

For a moment, he thought she was leaving, but then she turned toward the corridor for the restrooms. She'd be back. Maybe he'd have a chance to get her number after she ditched her dumbass date.

He turned his focus to the engineer whose gaze also followed the blonde. The moment she was out of sight, he picked up her drink and took a sip.

JT had a view of his profile and saw Spaulding smile as he set it down, then reached into the inside of his suit jacket. JT couldn't see anything in his hand, but he definitely saw the guy's hand hover over her drink for a second. Then he put the drink back in the spot where she'd left it. His hand disappeared into his pocket again.

"Motherfucker," Lee whispered.

"He's so fucking fired. Right after he gets arrested." JT kept his gaze on the drugged drink as he spoke to Lee. "There should be a plainclothes security guard at the edge of the casino floor by the entrance to the steakhouse. If he's not there, get one in uniform."

Lee rose. "On it."

JT was grateful to have Lee here. This way, he could keep

an eye on Russ Spaulding and the drink, ready to move should the blonde return.

Internally, he seethed. He wanted to take the bastard out with violence, not the law.

Minutes ticked by. Lee returned with the plainclothes guard before the woman reappeared. He and the guard took a position on the far side of the table, appearing to be chatting casually as they watched the couples on the dance floor, keeping an eye on Spaulding with peripheral vision.

For his part, Spaulding appeared oblivious to the attention he was getting.

Lee typed a message on his BlackBerry, and JT pulled his out to see what Lee had to say.

Received: Tribal police are in the hall, ready to move in. They have a digital camera and will record when the blonde returns.

This was about to get ugly. JT felt sweat dot his brow. He'd seen hand motions, nothing more. What if the drink wasn't drugged?

No. He knew what he saw.

At last, the blonde returned. JT's stomach clenched at what would've happened next if he and Lee hadn't seen Spaulding slip the drug into the drink.

She didn't smile as she took her seat next to the prick. JT rose and took a step toward them, ready to stop her from taking a sip, but he knew they needed to let the scene play for a moment if they wanted more evidence for prosecution.

The song that was playing ended and a short break was announced. Security must have talked to the DJ. He hoped that meant the camera wouldn't have a problem recording Spaulding and the blonde's conversation.

"Bummer," Spaulding said. "I was looking forward to dancing with you."

"And I said I'm too tired to dance."

"Ah. Don't be that way, babe. We can still have fun tonight."

"I want to go home. I need to study."

"It's winter break. Relax."

"I need to start in on next semester's reading."

"I hardly think there's going to be a major development in theoretical physics in the next few weeks."

She was studying theoretical physics? The woman must be wildly smart. And this prick intended to drug that beautiful brain? His hand curled into a fist. Bringing the cops in was the right thing to do, but JT sure wished he could break Spaulding's face first.

He pulled out the BlackBerry again and moved slowly, as if he were heading to the bar while reading. He was a mere three feet away when Spaulding picked up his drink and held it out to the blonde in a toast. "To second chances."

"I don't give second chances." Her voice was silky smooth. Not intentionally sexy, but alluring, nonetheless.

JT stopped and stared at the BlackBerry as if he'd just gotten a long email he needed to read.

"Fine. I'll take you home after you finish your drink."

"You aren't taking me home."

"So you're staying at the hotel with me tonight?"

"Not a light wave's chance in a supermassive black hole."

"Oh. It's sexy when you talk about things being supermassive."

She snorted. "Just give me money for a cab, Russ."

Spaulding took a drink as he nodded to hers, which she hadn't touched. She let out a sigh of impatience and raised the glass.

JT stepped forward and touched her wrist, stopping the

glass's trajectory to her mouth. "What are you drinking?" he asked.

She startled, looking at him like he was nuts. She pointed to the sprig of fresh mint. "A mojito." Her tone conveyed the unsaid word, *dumbass*.

He smiled. "The Cuban drink? Is it any good?"

Spaulding frowned but didn't appear fazed. "I'm sure the bartender can make you your own."

"But I want to try this one first."

Spaulding's eyes widened. The blonde looked confused.

JT gave Russ Spaulding a feral grin. "Or better yet, why don't you drink it, Russ? I'll get the lady a fresh drink."

Spaulding bolted to his feet, causing his chair to tip over. His hand swiped toward the drink, but JT was faster. He took the drink from the blonde's hand, spilling only a little before he had the glass pressed to Spaulding's lips, his hand at the back of his head. "Drink up, Russ."

Spaulding kept his mouth tightly shut as first the security guard, then the cops moved in. Spaulding managed to spill a bit more of the liquid, right before his hands were cuffed behind his back, but JT figured there was enough residue in the glass and the container the cops pulled from his inside pocket to convince a prosecutor to file charges.

With what they got here, it should be easy to get a search warrant for Spaulding's home, where, odds were, more drugs would be found.

"What does it look like?" JT asked the cop who'd searched Russ Spaulding, then read him his rights.

"My guess? GHB," the cop said. He turned toward the blonde. "You're lucky these two spotted your drink being spiked. We need you to make a statement."

The blonde, who'd watched everything unfold with shock on her face, turned to her date. "You put fucking *gamma-*

Hydroxybutyric acid in my *drink*? So you could drag me to your hotel room and *RAPE ME*?"

The last two words were a full shout that garnered the attention of anyone in the room who hadn't noticed the bust going down.

"They're full of shit! I'm going to sue! The tribe. The casino. And Talon & Drake! This was a setup!"

"Then why wouldn't you take a sip, Russ?" JT asked in a low voice. "Why was there a vial in your pocket? And why did you work so hard to pressure her to drink?"

The woman was magnificent, cheeks bright red, towering over Spaulding as he cowered. She pulled back a fist as if she were going to throw a punch, but as he braced for the blow, she kneed him in the balls.

He doubled over, unable to speak. Every officer looked away, calling out instructions for taking statements, making a show of not seeing a damn thing.

Chapter Fifteen

Rage didn't begin to describe the emotion that coursed through Alexandra. She turned to Kendall and Brent, who'd come running at some point after the cops swarmed Russ. "Did you know about this?" she asked Brent.

His eyes widened and he shook his head. "No! Of course not!"

She turned her gaze on her best friend. "You spent two weeks hounding me to be his date."

Kendall let out a shocked breath and took a step back. "I had no idea! I swear."

Of the two denials, Kendall's was the only one she believed. She turned to Brent. "You are not welcome in our apartment ever again."

"No!" Kendall said, then she turned and must've seen something in Brent's gaze because she took a step away from him.

"It's him or me, Kendall." She pulled the hotel room key that Russ had given her earlier and turned to one of the police officers. "He'll be in jail tonight?"

The man nodded. "We can hold him while we test the

drink and vial. It's Friday night, so he won't go before a judge until Monday morning. A prosecutor will file charges if the tests come out as we suspect they will."

She turned back to Kendall. "Brent can take you home tonight. Pack up anything he left at our place. You can come back in the morning and pick me up. Alone."

Kendall nodded.

The officers ushered people around so they could be questioned separately, Alexandra was escorted to a private corner of the ballroom. She saw Kendall and Brent leave while she was still being questioned.

As she spoke to the officers, she met the gaze of the hot man who'd been her rescuer. His eyes were intense as he watched her. She felt a strange burn in her belly.

She was thankful, angry, and attracted. A dangerous combination.

She still didn't know his name, but now, she didn't want to know. She liked the mystery of it. Did it matter who he was? Or who she was?

She spent her days studying the latest theories about the matter that made up the universe and the power of black holes. She knew exactly how insignificant she was on a cosmologic scale. But she mattered. To herself. To her parents and friends. And tonight, this man had cared enough about a stranger to protect her.

For all she knew, Russ was his boss. She wasn't foolish enough to think prosecuting a man for a crime that had been prevented would result in much more than a slap on the wrist, even if it had been premeditated rape.

Everything would hinge on what they found in Russ's home. It would be awful to discover he'd done this before, but at the same time, if they found evidence of other such assaults, he'd do serious time.

Finally, her interview was over. She scanned the room,

seeing her rescuer in deep conversation with the tall man he'd indicated was family earlier.

The party had ended with the arrest, and the room was being broken down, but the dessert table still held a few treats. Alexandra crossed to the table. The fancier desserts had been consumed or cleared, but there was a tray of assorted muffins: cranberry, pumpkin chocolate chip, apple cinnamon, lemon blueberry.

There was nothing humble about these muffins. She felt bad for them that they'd been left behind. As if they couldn't hold their own against a tart.

She grabbed a plate and loaded up, then headed for the door. She paused as she passed the two men who'd been instrumental in her rescue. The cop had told her that the tall man had gotten security and police involved while the shorter man kept an eye on Russ and the drink.

She felt all fluttery again.

She crossed to the two men. "Thank you. For everything."

Both men nodded, faces solemn. "I'm sorry it was necessary," the tall one said. "But glad we were there." He then stepped back.

She was alone—sort of—with her savior. He studied her face, his brown eyes probing but warm. Heat shot through her. She held up the plate she'd loaded with desserts. "Do you like muffins?"

His mouth shifted in the slightest of smiles while his eyes lit with humor. "Yes. Some more than others."

"Room 2204. Fifteen minutes. Don't be late, or you'll turn into a pumpkin."

His smile deepened, and the sparks in her belly turned to a flame. "Yes, ma'am."

She started to walk away, then turned. "One more thing. If you haven't learned my name from the police…don't."

His face showed surprise, but he nodded. "Do you know mine?"

"No. And I intend to keep it that way." She turned and headed to the hotel room that Russ Spaulding would pay for. Her first order of business was to place a room service order for the most expensive bottle of champagne she could get.

"She invited you to her room." Lee gave JT a wry smile.

JT grimaced in response even though the invitation had pleased him. "I'd be thrilled, but it's messed up how it came about. She's got to be wrecked right now. And technically, it's Spaulding's room."

"It's the room where he would have raped her."

"Yep."

"Offer to take her home instead. Ask her out. Take her to dinner next week when she isn't reeling from an assault."

"I'll offer, but from what she said earlier, Spaulding's buddy Brent Forbes might be at her place tonight. She can't go there."

"There's always the family home."

He shook his head. "No way am I taking her to the senator's estate. Or his townhouse." JT's dad was weeks from completing his first term as a US senator. He'd been referring to his father by his title or first name in work situations for years—it came with the territory of working for the family business—but this might be the first time he'd done it when speaking to his brother.

Former stepbrother, really, but it wasn't just the brother bond that had lasted far longer than the marriage between JT's dad and Lee's mom. The paternal bond had remained as well. But ever since Joe entered politics, Lee had stepped back, wanting no part of living on the fringe of the spotlight that followed Senator Joseph Talon wherever he went.

Unlike Lee, JT had no choice. He was the senator's only biological child and he'd taken the reins of the old man's company, ensuring management caused no ethics violations for the junior senator from Maryland.

JT didn't mind because he had his own political ambitions and was content in the reflective glow. He'd put in his time at Talon & Drake, an engineering firm that had contracts all over the world. He cut deals with governments and sometimes even royalty, literally building bridges that would secure international support when he made his own move.

Not that anyone outside the US could vote, but it never hurt to show you were an international player. His dad had used the springboard to great effect and intended to throw his hat in the primaries for the 2008 or 2012 presidential elections if he had enough support—financial and political—to be viable.

And if Dad didn't make it to the Oval Office, his work would just be paving the way for JT, who, at thirty-one, had more than enough time to build his team.

The fact that Talon & Drake had a sexual predator on staff was not publicity he needed, however. At least if the arrest made local news, he could show it had been dealt with swiftly in cooperation with police and the guy would be fired the moment the tests on the drink were official.

He'd fire Brent Forbes too if he was linked to the crime.

"Be careful, my friend," Lee said. "She's had a rough night." The kid was five years younger than JT, but he no longer saw him as a little brother or even protégé. He was one of the few men JT could really be himself with, who understood what it meant to exist in the senator's orbit.

It was probably why JT had never told Lee about his own

political ambitions. Lee might want to distance himself from JT, just as he had from Joe, and JT couldn't afford that.

JT's world was a lonely one. He didn't socialize with employees. He was younger than the executives who worked beneath him, and way too far up the ladder for the employees who were of similar age. It was easier to keep himself separate because the executives wanted to put him in his place, while the midlevel biologists and engineers who would be his peers were intimidated.

Events like this one were a job requirement, but not one he would bring a date to. This was work. Lee, knowing how miserable JT would be after the formalities were over, had shown up so JT wouldn't be alone with executives who despised him, or worse, be the recipient of awkward attempts at small talk from employees looking to become drinking buddies, or the women who weren't afraid to make a pass at the young, rich CEO.

He'd been ready to call it a night when the blonde returned to the party, alone and mad as hell, and JT was absolutely certain she did not work for Talon & Drake, making her a party guest he could spend time with.

So he'd approached her and was surprised to discover she had no clue who he was.

Even better.

Now she'd invited him to her room for muffins. And that wasn't even a euphemism.

"She needs a friend and a shoulder," he said to Lee. "That's all I'll be." He glanced at his BlackBerry. Nine minutes until he turned into a pumpkin. Better get going, because the hotel was a walk from the casino, and she was on a high floor. "Thanks for coming. I know you hate this stuff."

"Glad I came. See you Christmas Eve?"

"Not if I can get out of it."

"You know you can't. It wouldn't be Christmas without you."

If only it was just JT's presence he was referring to. "I better get a kickass present from you."

"One anatomically correct blow-up doll coming up," Lee said as he headed for the casino floor.

"Damn, I hate it when we get each other the same thing," JT called after him. "Ruins the surprise."

Lee laughed and disappeared into the crowd on his way to the exit.

JT headed for the covered walkway to the hotel. His gut clenched as he crossed the parking lot that separated hotel from casino. A chill wind blew off the Chesapeake, and he shivered.

Emotions swirled through him as he rode the elevator. Anticipation and anxiety warred for supremacy.

From the moment he'd spotted her and realized she wasn't an employee, he'd felt a kick in the gut. It had been completely superficial. The woman was stunningly beautiful. Flawless pale cream skin, loads of platinum-blonde hair, heavily lashed big blue eyes. An hourglass figure atop long legs made even longer with sexy stilettos.

His attraction had grown exponentially after speaking with her.

He reached her room and paused before knocking, feeling nervous. She might well have fallen apart in the fifteen minutes since she'd left the ballroom. He might be the last person she wanted to see now.

He took a deep breath, then raised his fist and hit the door, his heart pounding with a matching thud.

The door swung open. She met him with a wicked smile. "You're late, *Pumpkin.*"

He couldn't help but grin at seeing her in the fluffy white hotel robe. Was she wearing anything underneath?

He stepped into the room, backing her up against the small foyer wall. He planted an arm beside her head and leaned in. "I'm pretty sure I made it just under the wire." He pulled out his BlackBerry, just as the appointment reminder went off. "See?"

She yanked the device from his hand. "Is this one of those new smartphone thingies that can send and receive emails?"

He grinned. "Yes. And as you can see, I'm right on time."

She studied the screen. "You set the meeting for fifteen minutes from now, which would make you *very* late."

"It's a reminder that goes off fifteen minutes before the meeting, so I had to fudge it a bit to set it quickly. BlackBerry says that in future models, you'll be able to set timers and alarms without tying them to a meeting."

"So you admit you're late."

"Does that mean I don't get any muffins? That's what you invited me here for, right?"

She slipped under his arm, still holding his phone. He followed her into the king suite. The plate of muffins sat on the coffee table in front of the couch. She waved to the plate. "You can have the pumpkin one."

"My favorite." He picked up the indicated muffin and took a bite from the center of the top. He chewed then said, "Moist and delicious."

She rolled her eyes, even as she laughed.

There was a knock at the door.

"You expecting someone else?"

"Room service."

He followed her to the door, pulling out his wallet.

"Don't worry. I've got this." Then her eyes flared. "Well, Russ does. And tonight, he's a big tipper."

She opened the door to reveal a man in hotel uniform holding a silver ice bucket containing a bottle of sparkling wine in one hand and two champagne flutes in the other. JT accepted the wine and glasses, while she signed the check.

JT set the bucket on the small dining table and pulled out the bottle. He let out a low whistle.

"I asked for the most expensive bottle of champagne they have. I figure Russ owes me."

"Revenge is a dish best served in an ice bucket."

She laughed. "Something like that." She took the bottle from his hands and inspected the foil that covered the wire hood, then handed it back to him. "Sealed tight. Open it for us?"

He imagined she would be vigilant about her drinks from now on and couldn't blame her. Hell, he was glad she'd be wary.

But still, what kind of prick drugged his date's drink at a company party? Wasn't it the kind of thing guys only got away with if it was a stranger who couldn't identify them later?

Did he really believe she'd stay silent after being raped?

But then, GHB was a club drug because for some it caused arousal. Maybe Spaulding had intended to claim she'd brought the drug and taken it herself. Then it would be he said/she said. And there were more than a few people in the legal system who would be happy to blame a woman dressed as sexily as the blonde was tonight.

He removed the foil and began untwisting the wire hood. "You sure you don't want to know my name?"

She stepped forward and placed a finger over his lips. "No. The cops have your name. I could find out if I need to. And I'm pretty sure your tall friend heard me invite you to the room."

He pulled the cover off. "And why am I here? For muffins and champagne?"

"I think you know what I want."

"You're going to have to be explicit. I assume nothing."

"Do you have a wife, girlfriend, boyfriend, or any kind of significant other who would object to your spending time with me?"

"No. But my stepbrother expressed concern that you're vulnerable and pointed out this room"—he glanced around the deluxe suite—"is the very room where Spaulding intended to rape you."

She flinched, but quickly recovered. "The tall guy is your stepbrother?"

He nodded. "He suggested I take you home. Get your phone number. Take you out to dinner later this week."

"He sounds like a nice guy. You can tell him I said thank you for his concern, but I can't go home tonight, and I'm not interested in you for dinner. I'm not hungry." She smiled. "Or at least, not hungry for food."

Heat surged to JT's groin. He moved toward the sliding door to the enclosed balcony and slid it open. The cold December air would do him good. She followed him outside and stood beside him as he worked the cork with his thumbs. It made a satisfying *pop* as the plug launched into the air, arching, then dropping into the closed pool area below.

She took the bottle from his hand and licked the dribble of foam from the lip before taking a drink.

The sight of her tongue on the rim sent yet another round of heat to his balls. So much for the cool December air.

Back inside, she sat on the couch and poured champagne into both glasses. He gave thanks that she didn't intend to continue drinking from the bottle.

He settled on the couch next to her. "I need a name for you. I can't just think of you as the hot blonde I met at the bar."

She smiled and reached for his muffin. "Call me whatever

you want, Pumpkin." She took a bite and closed her eyes with pleasure. "These are really good. I've always liked muffins more than cupcakes, which really are just a vessel for frosting. A good muffin doesn't need decoration to do the heavy lifting for flavor."

He studied her. She'd taken down her hair, removed the four-inch fuck-me heels, and now wore a fluffy white robe that covered her from wrist to neck to ankle.

He grinned. "I couldn't agree more, *Muffin*."

She burst out laughing, set his muffin back on the plate, then raised her champagne flute. "So what do you say, Pumpkin?"

"To what?"

"Will you fuck me, here, now? I can't…put into words what it means to me to take this kind of control after what could have happened. I just know I want this. Want you."

JT picked up his champagne flute and downed it in one long gulp. He set the glass aside, stood, then reached out a hand, pulling her to her feet.

With a finger beneath her chin, he turned her face up to his. Barefoot, she was a few inches shorter than his six feet. He held her gaze for a long moment, seeing desire, hope, and, hidden beneath the more obvious emotions, he saw fear.

Fear of what almost happened, or fear he would reject her?

He would never reject her. But he also couldn't take her up on her offer, not if he ever hoped for more with this woman.

He lowered his mouth to hers. He licked at the seam of her lips, and she opened for him. She tasted of pumpkin and chocolate and champagne. Even if he never saw her again, he'd bet he would always associate those flavors with her.

He left her mouth to run his tongue over her collarbone. Up her neck. Below her ear.

She whimpered and pulled him close. His arm around her waist tightened. His heavy erection pressed into her belly. He moved his arm lower, scooping her up so his cock met her center as the robe split and she wrapped her legs around his hips.

"Damn, Muffin. I want to be inside you."

"I have condoms. I bought them in the lobby on my way to the room."

Shit. He couldn't do this. His plan to kiss her to show it wasn't a rejection had backfired. He hadn't guessed how quickly things could get out of hand.

"Tell me one thing. If I fuck you tonight, am I ever going to see you again?"

She stiffened against him, then wriggled until he shifted, lowering her feet to the ground. They stood chest to chest. She tucked her face in his neck.

"Fuck," she whispered.

"I take it that's a no."

She raised her head but didn't meet his gaze. "I—I can't. I don't have time to date. I don't *want* to date. Just fuck me. Let me feel in control. Then we'll part ways with good memories to drown out what could have happened."

"I won't be satisfied with a nameless, shameless fuck. Don't get me wrong. I would love every minute of it and would make sure you did too. But that's not what I want. I want *you*."

"How could you? You don't know me."

"No. But I want to know you. And if we do this now, tonight, I'll be part of your processing trauma and putting it behind you. But then you'll need to put *me* behind you too."

She stepped back from him, pulled the sides of her robe back together, and cinched the belt. "I'm *not* traumatized."

"Muffin." The name felt awkward, but it was all he had. "Your date booked a hotel room, slipped something into your drink, and then cajoled you into taking a drink, which you would have done if we hadn't been there to stop you. He would have then taken you to this very room and assaulted you.

"Even though it didn't happen, it's a fucking nightmare scenario that was aided by your roommate and her date, who convinced you to go to the party with Russ Spaulding. Physically, you're fine, but you can't tell me you don't feel the pain in your gut. The fear. The what-ifs. *I* feel it. I want to go to the hotel gym and punch the fuck out of the heavy bags. And the adrenaline of it all means I want to fuck you. Desperately. But if I let you use *me* as your punching bag, or your fuck-and-forget friend, then I can't be part of your healing later."

Her face crumpled then, and she let out a shriek.

He stepped forward and wrapped his arms around her. Her fists thumped on his chest, but not with a force meant to hurt. "Damn you. I was *fine*. I was going to get laid by this hot man who saved me from a monster. And then I was going to leave this hotel room whole."

He rubbed her back as she wound down and slumped against him.

He stroked her hair, marveling at the soft feel of it between his fingers. "It's not that simple, sweetheart. You'll have to face him in a courtroom. His attorneys will claim you wanted the drug, that you use it as an aphrodisiac. They'll get his friend who set you up to confirm that you asked for it. This is only the beginning. I'd rather be there for you down the line than do something now that will make me part of the nightmare."

She pulled back and met his gaze. Her eyes were damp. "Have you considered I might not want you with me later?"

"Of course. But I hope you give me a chance." He stroked her cheek. "Dinner, Sunday?"

"I told you. I don't have time to date."

"What I overheard indicated you're a student. Grad school?"

She nodded.

"Do you have the next few weeks off?"

She nodded again. "Until the ninth, actually."

"I'm in town until New Year's Day."

She shook her head. "I can't…I… Please. Don't ask me for anything. Not when I don't know what I have to give."

He brushed his lips over her forehead. "Then just know I'm here, when you're ready or if you need me."

"I don't see how that's possible because I meant it when I said I don't want to know your name. I don't want your number. And I won't give you mine. Don't get my name from the police. Or, if you find out accidentally, don't use it to find me. I wanted to feel in control here. That's what this… tonight…was going to be about."

"You are absolutely in control. If you want me to leave, I'll go."

"What if I want you to stay?"

"I'll stay. But I won't have sex with you."

"Even if I say pretty please?" She batted those thick, long eyelashes.

He chuckled. "Oh. Well. That changes everything."

She tucked her head against his chest and let out a pained laugh.

"Do you want me to leave?" he asked.

The arms around his waist tightened. "No. I…I don't want to be alone here. In this room." He felt her shiver against him. She raised her head and met his gaze. "Please. Will you at least hold me until I fall asleep?"

The pain in her blue eyes gutted him. "Of course. I'll hold you all night if you want."

"I want." She loosened her hold and stepped back.

"Thank you. I'll uh…get ready. For bed." Then she rose on her toes and kissed his cheek, right next to his lips.

He was so tempted to turn his head and make it a real kiss, but he wouldn't toy with her that way. He was here for comfort, not sex. But damn, she was hard to resist.

"You're a good man, whoever you are." She whispered the words as she kissed his neck just above the collarbone.

He touched her cheek. "You're a strong woman." *I hope you'll give me a chance to get to know you.*

She slipped from his arms and readied herself for bed in the bathroom while he removed his shoes, socks, belt, tie, and dress shirt. He had a T-shirt underneath; his suit pants would just have to be slept in. He actually had a hotel suite on the other end of this floor and considered going there to grab his toothbrush and a pair of sweatpants to sleep in, but he remembered the shiver that ran through her when she said she didn't want to be alone.

She crawled into bed, and he took his turn in the bathroom. He didn't have toothpaste or a toothbrush, but there was a hotel bottle of mouthwash on the counter, which he swished around after rinsing with water.

He turned off the lights, then crawled into the king-sized bed beside her. He reached for her, and she curled up on his lap. He held her in the dark, taking in her scent and enjoying the feel of her in his arms.

After a while, they shifted positions until they lay spooned together, and at last, her body relaxed. He had no clue how much time passed before her breathing evened out and he was certain she was asleep.

He lay with his arm around her waist, knees tucked up behind hers, and marveled at the events that had led to this moment. He'd known her for less than four hours and still didn't know her name, but still, he felt certain this woman would change his life. Maybe she already had.

Chapter Sixteen

Catoctin Mountain, Maryland
Present

Alexandra hadn't intended to fall asleep in JT's arms. She didn't plan on falling asleep at all. But it happened anyway. It had been so natural to lie next to him on the couch, accepting the comfort she so desperately needed.

So much like the night they met. Complete strangers then, but she'd been through a traumatic experience, and he hadn't hesitated to comfort her. That night, she'd had no intention of ever seeing him again.

Here she was, sixteen years later, and once again sleeping in his arms. She shifted, rising on her elbow to study him in the dark. They lay side by side on the wide lounge seat on the end of the plush sofa.

In sleep, JT's face was free of the lines he'd earned in the twenty-two years he'd been CEO of a multimillion-dollar international engineering firm. She'd met him six years into his tenure, back when he had his own dreams of entering politics.

The man she'd first met at a Talon & Drake holiday party sixteen years ago had been so very different from the one she'd said goodbye to at the same event nine years later.

Who had he become in the last seven years?

Was he more like his former incarnation or the latter?

Honestly, it was hard to imagine either version of him willingly babysitting a toddler for any length of time, let alone agreeing to care for Gemma indefinitely.

Yet he had. And he'd done a good job of it.

A few hours ago, after the dinner dishes were done and they settled in the living room. Gemma had grabbed her tattered *Goodnight Moon* board book from the diaper bag and climbed onto JT's lap, demanding he read it to her.

Alexandra's eyes had burned with tears as he read with gusto and Gemma giggled wildly. It was decidedly *not* a bedtime story the way Uncle Tee read it.

Her eyes burned again just thinking about it. She let out a soft sniff. She would not cry.

"Hey, sweetheart." JT's voice was soft and sleepy. His arm tightened around her. "It's okay. You're safe. Gemma's safe."

She wanted to protest that that wasn't why she was fighting tears, but she also didn't want to admit what *had* triggered them.

She did the cowardly thing and buried her face in his side and let him hold her.

"Your daughter is really amazing, Lex. A genius, just like her mom. You know she told me a knock-knock joke?"

She swiped at her eyes and said, "Did she make a raspberry sound?"

"Yep."

"She started doing that last week. It will never not be funny."

"I had no idea kids her age could…have so much personality."

"What about Grace?"

"I guess I wasn't paying attention."

She could believe that. "I should go check on her."

His arm tightened. "I haven't heard a peep from the baby monitor. Stay a little longer? Holding you like this…it reminds me of the night we met. I held you all night, sleeping in my slacks even though I had more comfortable clothes down the hall. But I didn't dare leave you."

She let out a soft laugh. He was right. They both were still dressed. They'd settled on the couch to brainstorm ways to prove her innocence, and she'd slowly inched toward him until she was snug against his side.

Sliding into sleep had been inevitable from there. It was the first time she'd truly relaxed in days.

"I needed this as much as I needed you then."

He kissed her forehead. "I will always be here for you, Lex."

He'd made that promise before. That first night, in fact. It had taken him a lot of years, but he did eventually break it.

But it wasn't really fair to hold a man to a promise he made to a total stranger and think it would mean the same thing after she'd called off their wedding years later.

She'd been the first to break a promise.

"I appreciate that, but someday, you're going to meet the woman I could never be for you, and she won't be thrilled with me coming around for emotional support."

"Impossible. You're the only one for me. I've known that from the day we met."

"Right." She pulled away from him. He'd read too much into the comfort she'd accepted from him.

He sat up, moving to the corner of the couch. She

grabbed the throw blanket that had covered them both and pulled it around her, using it as a barrier.

"I won't ever love anyone like I love you, but I understand why you don't believe me. I was far too lost when we were last together. We can open those wounds later. Right now, I just want you to know I will move heaven and earth to help you and Gemma, and I have the engineering skills and tools to do it."

"Earth is your zone as an engineer. I'm the one with the knowledge of the heavens, and I can say with authority you won't be able to get the cosmos to budge on my behalf."

He chuckled. "Ah. Literal Lex is in the building."

She felt a pang at the name. Kendall too had called her that. "Just sayin'. I don't think your money or your company can save me."

"I'm selling the company. Then I'll have a crap ton more money."

"You are? Does Lee know? Of course. He must know but...he hasn't said anything." But then, Lee and Erica didn't talk about JT with her, at her request.

He shrugged. "The closing is New Year's Eve. Big party to follow where fat bonuses will be handed out."

"Was the sale something Kendall was working on?"

He frowned and cocked his head as he considered the question. "Probably. Her numbers as a cost estimator would have been part of the due diligence. Why?"

"She said something about an issue with her job she wanted to talk to me about."

He frowned. "Have you considered that what happened to you could be related to her?"

"I have. But I haven't a clue how it might connect."

"You were only about a mile from her house. The cop could have followed you."

"But why?"

"What all did you get from Kendall's house?"

"I left most everything there—I planned to go back next week with a rental van to pick up the couch and boxes that I wanted to take my time sorting through. Many of my school papers had been mixed with hers. I filled one archive box with framed photos, my mom's cookbooks, and a few knick-knacks we'd purchased for our various apartments together.

"It was all I'd planned to take, but when I loaded the box in my SUV, I remembered she'd mentioned the old PC you gave me for school that first winter semester. She'd said the motherboard had burned out, but she was certain the files were intact. Rescuing old files from dead computers had been on her to-do list for years, but she was admitting defeat and wanted me to take the computer off her hands, or she'd throw it away. One less thing to worry about."

She grimaced, remembering that moment when she'd considered tossing the computer and being done. She'd lived without the photos and files this long. She wouldn't know what she was losing, so did it matter?

But Kendall was gone. There would be no new photos of her, and she'd just spent hours crying over long-forgotten photographs with Kendall's sister, Tanya. There could be some treasures on that hard drive.

So she'd given Tanya a big hug in the driveway, and the woman drove off.

"Tanya left, and I went back inside. I gave myself twenty minutes to find the old computer before I hit the road to pick up Gemma. It took me about ten to find the tan console box with the old Talon & Drake logo on it in the CPU graveyard in the office closet. Knowing that all the other electronic components in Kendall's house would be recycled, I decided not to grab the whole console box. I opened it up and pulled the hard drive.

"I was in a hurry when I left, which is why it wasn't in the box with the other items. I tossed it on the front seat with my coat. I was mad at myself for not just grabbing the console, when I was already on limited time."

She'd gotten lost in memories in the closet. The damn computer had represented so much. JT had wanted to help her with school, but she didn't want to feel indebted to him, so the compromise had been to accept a used but upgraded work computer that was no longer needed.

She'd known even then it was a lie. The Talon & Drake logo had been slapped on it to make it look used.

That was why she didn't want the console box. She didn't want the reminder of those wonderful early days, when she was falling head over heels for JT Talon and trying her hardest to demonstrate to them both it was the man she wanted, not the stuff.

And so she'd wasted precious minutes pulling the hard drive.

"In the end, it's a good thing I didn't take the whole console and that I had it in the front seat with me. It's what I hit the cop with."

"Where is it now?"

"In Kendall's Jetta. In the glove box. It has the cop's blood on it."

JT rose from the couch. "I'll grab it. Is the car locked?"

She nodded and rose to get the keys from her coat pocket.

Minutes later, he was back with the hard drive. He set it on the marble countertop, and Alexandra felt sick at seeing the dried blood on the sharp edge of the rectangular metal box. There were a few hairs caught in a seam.

She covered her mouth with her hand and tried not to gag.

She hadn't killed him, and she'd fought in self-defense.

But still, knowing that the head injury she'd caused had led to his cold-blooded murder made her ill.

JT's arms surrounded her again, and again, she remembered the night they met. When another man had intended to hurt her, but JT had stopped him.

She thought about their first kiss. She'd been so angry and wanted mindless sex to claim her bodily autonomy. This was different.

She wanted to kiss him tonight too, but this time, it was to escape the horror. Forget the nightmare.

Still, anger was there too. Why had the cop—Corey Williams—pulled her over and assaulted her? Was she one of many such victims? Would investigators discover he was a serial killer? That wouldn't clear her name, but it would go far to show hitting him with the hard drive had been done in self-defense.

She didn't want to think about those moments by the side of the road when she wondered if Williams intended to rape and kill her.

No, she wanted to think about JT's hand on the small of her back. His scent was oh so familiar. This man, who she'd loved since she was twenty-five and a struggling grad student.

Her hands moved up, sliding around his neck. She tilted her head back and met his gaze.

"Lex," he said. His voice almost pained. His erection was a familiar pressure against her belly.

"Kiss me."

He looked like he was going to refuse her, but then he lowered his head until his lips met hers.

It was like a thousand kisses they'd shared before, yet it was also totally different. His tongue explored, stroking hers. Deep and slow. Thorough, like he was making up for lost time. Lost kisses.

She responded in kind. This was exactly what she needed. To get lost. To escape.

This would be like the times they'd slept together after she'd called off the wedding. No commitment. Just sex. Wonderful, hot sex.

She reached for his belt buckle.

JT ended the kiss. His hand covered hers as she worked the leather free. "Lex. We can't."

"Please, Jay. I need this."

"Sweetheart. You know this would be a mistake."

"It's just sex. Don't worry. I won't expect a ring afterward and I don't want your money. I know Gemma is the ultimate JT repellant. I just want you to fuck me. So I can forget."

He flinched. "I know I had that coming."

"I didn't mean it as an insult. It was meant to be reassuring."

"And once again, I don't want to be your fuck-and-forget buddy."

"You wouldn't be taking advantage of me. We're not strangers this time."

"Yeah. But *you* would be taking advantage of *me*."

She took a step back. He was serious. "You don't want me. I've got a kid. She's not optional anymore. There is no other dad she can be shipped off to, like Lee was when his mom found him inconvenient. I would think you'd be thrilled to get laid again without worry that I want more than you can give."

"Well then, you'd be wrong." He pointed to the hard disk on the counter. "I'm going to check and see if I've got an old console to plug this into in the attic. Get some sleep. Night, Lex."

He left the kitchen without looking back.

She'd hurt him. She hadn't intended to throw his words

back at him like that, but still, she wondered if some subconscious part of her had done it on purpose.

Things had been so much simpler when they hadn't even known each other's names. Before they had a world of hurt built up between them. Back when their biggest problem was Brent Forbes and Russ Spaulding.

Chapter Seventeen

Menanichoch, Maryland
December 18th
Sixteen years ago

Alexandra woke up to find herself alone in the suite and asked herself if she was disappointed. If he were here, would she relent and tell him her name? Give him her phone number?

She honestly didn't know.

She'd meant it when she said she didn't have time to date. But that didn't mean she wasn't interested in a man who would turn down a no strings screw because he didn't want to make it impossible to be with her later.

Should she make an effort to learn his name?

No. If he was smart, he wouldn't be interested in the light of day. After all, she'd been all over the map last night, demanding sex from a stranger. Mad when he wouldn't give it to her.

She'd fallen apart and pummeled his chest, all because he

reminded her she'd been through an ordeal she needed to process.

Was it trauma?

Maybe. It was nothing like what her friends who'd been raped had gone through, but she didn't need to put it on a scale and measure it to know last night had affected her.

She would never leave a drink unguarded again—even on a date that absolutely should have been safe. That, of course, brought to mind Kendall and Brent.

She never, ever wanted to see Brent again. Even if he really hadn't known, the association would always be there. Brent Forbes was best buds with a predator.

He'd set her up on a date with that predator.

What would that do to her relationship with Kendall? Her best friend. Her roommate. Friends since freshman year of college, when they'd been randomly assigned to share a dorm room.

Kendall was in love with Brent. This could destroy their friendship.

The hotel room phone rang. Alexandra jolted at the sharp sound.

Who knew she was here besides Pumpkin?

She snickered. She'd really called the hottest man she'd ever kissed, the man who saved her from being raped, *Pumpkin*.

But damn, it had been fun messing with him.

The phone rang again. She hoped it wasn't her date calling. Could he be out already? Was it possible charges weren't going to be filed?

A shiver ran through her, and she wished Pumpkin were here.

She picked up the handset, squeezing it tight as she pressed it to her ear. "Hello?"

"Oh, thank god," Kendall said. "We need to get you a cell phone."

"You know I can't afford one. Besides, you found me. I don't need one."

"Are you ready for me to come get you?"

"Sure. I'll meet you out front."

"I'll be there in forty-five."

Alexandra slipped off the robe she'd slept in and put her bra and party dress back on while the in-room coffeemaker brewed. She then sat at the small dining table and ate the apple cinnamon muffin while she drank coffee. Given her lack of change of clothes, this would look like a walk of shame, but all she'd gotten was a hot kiss and a little grinding.

She was disappointed. But also, she wasn't.

The kiss had been everything she wanted. But the man, he was so much more. Gentle with her feelings even as he turned her down. Understanding why she needed to feel empowered.

She checked the clock and tried to remember what time Kendall had called. Was it time to head down? She would love to have one of those BlackBerry thingies so she could set reminders. Plus, it would solve her cell phone problem.

But if she couldn't afford a cell phone, she definitely couldn't afford a five-hundred-dollar next-level pager.

Someday. When she had her PhD and was teaching or got a research fellowship at CERN, she'd get a phone. And a better computer. As it was, she had to rely on the computers in the department, which meant a lot of long hours at school.

She *really* didn't have time to date. Not when she had to spend nearly every waking hour at the university.

She grabbed the mostly full bottle of champagne. It was warm and probably flat, but it would be a shame to waste it. She'd mix it with orange juice. She also grabbed the remaining muffins, noting the half-eaten pumpkin chocolate chip one was gone.

She slipped on her coat before leaving the hotel room and paused when she felt the weight of something in the right pocket. She reached inside and pulled out not just the BlackBerry device, but also a charging cord and headset, along with a handwritten note.

Muffin,

You'll find the user's manual online. You're stuck with my phone number, but I'll contact everyone and give them my new number asap.

Yours truly,
Pumpkin

She let out a bark of laughter.

She didn't think she ever wanted to learn his name. He would forever be Pumpkin. Only for her.

The BlackBerry buzzed with a message late that evening while Alexandra was reading a thriller she'd gotten from the library. She set aside the hardcover book and picked up the device from the nightstand.

She'd spent an hour playing with it after finding the user's manual online earlier in the day. It had been a good distraction as she avoided discussing with Kendall what had happened last night.

Now she read her first message.

Received: Finally got my new

BlackBerry set up. New model is a phone no headset needed, so thank you for the excuse to upgrade. How was your day, Muffin?

She smiled, feeling strangely warm. He really had given her his smartphone and now she had no reason to return it. Well, except she couldn't afford the monthly usage fees.

Sent: Thank you for the phone, but whenever your current contract for it expires, you'll have to take it back. I don't have the budget for it.
Received: It will stay on my business account. Talon & Drake can pay your bill.
Sent: No! That's theft. I don't want to get you in trouble!
Received: It's fine. Cleared it with my boss. Least T&D can do.

She frowned. That was a little too glib. But she supposed he'd had to explain to someone why he needed a replacement phone, and as far as she knew, BlackBerrys weren't widely available to consumers—just professionals.

Sent: I don't feel right about this, Pumpkin.
Received: I promise. It's not an issue. You can ask my boss.
Sent: To ask your boss, I'd need to know your name.

Received: That's your call, Muffin. I'll tell you. Even give you my boss's number. Or better yet, his work email, so you'll know it's legit.
Sent: I'll think about it.
Received: In the meantime, use it. It's paid for through the end of the year.

She had ten days to decide if her conscience could handle it. She wouldn't set up email on it or do anything that would make it hard to give up.

Received: I want to see you. Can I buy you dinner tomorrow?
Sent: Depends. Are you going to put out?
Received: If I do, are you going to bolt right after?
Sent: That's really a performance question.
Received: That won't be a problem.

She smiled, remembering the feel of him against her last night. She suspected he was right.

Received: Dinner at seven, then?

She stared at the device and the little cursor that flashed, waiting for her to reply. She'd thought about him all day.

Sent: You had your chance with me last night.

Received: I didn't want to become something you regret.

It had been twenty-four hours since the assault that didn't happen, and she'd spent most of her waking ones today wondering if she'd have regrets if she'd had sex with her rescuer last night.

She didn't think so, but she also knew she definitely wouldn't want to see him again, regrets or not. He *would* be so entwined with the bad part of the night that thoughts of him would be tainted.

But now, she remembered the way he'd kissed her and then held her as she fell asleep. He'd cared for her mental state more than she had.

Because he didn't want to be something—someone—she put behind her.

Plus, he was incredibly hot. His mouth had set her on fire. And she'd spent far too much time today itching to open *Yahoo!* and see if she could figure out who he was.

But that would violate her own rules. Not that he'd care. But she would.

Sent: Do you like to dance?
Received: Depends on what kind. My ballroom is rusty.
Sent: Maybe I should change your name to Rusty Ballroom. Sounds dirty.
Received: But not in a good way. I promise you my balls are fine. How is your ballroom?
Sent: Nonexistent.
Received: I meant dancing.
Sent: So did I.

Received: You like dancing?
Sent: I don't know. It's been so long since I've gone out and just had fun. I was looking forward to dancing last night.
Received: We'll go dancing on our second date, then.
Sent: You're so certain you're getting a second date? I haven't even agreed to the first.
Received: Muffin, I'm already planning date number 6.
Sent: Yeah? Where are you taking me?
Received: I don't want to spoil the surprise. You might want to skip dates 2-5.
Sent: But not date 1?
Received: No, sweetheart, you definitely don't want to miss that. Tomorrow. 7 p.m.
Sent: Where are we meeting?
Received: Are you in DC?

She didn't live in the city, but close enough.

Sent: Yes.
Received: I'll leave a note for Muffin at the Mayflower concierge desk.

She scrolled back up, rereading the full conversation. So

many emotions swirled through her, but they all held a buzz of excitement. Joy.

Sent: What should I wear?
Received: Whatever makes you happy. But I wouldn't object to the killer heels.
Sent: See you tomorrow, Pumpkin.

Chapter Eighteen

The concierge gave her an envelope with "Muffin" written on the front in a neat, blocky script. She crossed the lobby to a couch outside the restaurant, sat down, and slid her finger under the flap to open the envelope.

She pulled out a single folded piece of paper.

Muffin, take the stairs to the right of the reception desk to the mezzanine level. I'm at a small table in a corner overlooking the lobby.

She glanced up, scanning the railing that wrapped around the mezzanine level. She spotted him almost immediately, watching her. He raised a hand in a subtle wave.

Her stomach tightened with anticipation. She'd considered canceling multiple times. But she couldn't get him out of her mind—in a good way.

So here she was, wearing the fuck-me heels and a sexy emerald-green cocktail dress she'd dug out from the back of her closet. She'd worn it to a bachelorette party two years ago.

She felt his gaze as she rose from the couch, so she turned in a circle, allowing him to admire the dress that showed a lot of cleavage and stopped mid-thigh. She paused before heading to the stairs and caught his appreciative grin.

He'd no doubt be watching her ass as she crossed to the stairwell, so she made an effort to add a seductive sway, but she was very much out of practice walking in heels, so she didn't overdo it for fear of stumbling.

The carpeting on the mezzanine level made circling around to meet him slightly less of a slipping hazard. He stood in front of a table that held a sealed bottle of wine in an ice bucket along with two white wine glasses.

She wondered how to greet him—*handshake, hug, wave?*—when he placed a hand on her waist and dropped a soft kiss to her lips before stepping back and indicating a plush chair.

"You look beautiful," he said as she lowered herself into the seat.

"Thank you."

He pushed the chair forward, then took the seat next to her. "Wine?"

She pulled the bottle from the silver bucket and checked the wrap around the cork. She nodded and handed the bottle to him to open.

"Why here and not in the restaurant?" she asked as he performed the chore.

"My family does a lot of business here. I'm known in the restaurant. Someone might slip."

He was respecting her wishes to keep his identity secret. She appreciated that. Still, that raised more questions. "So why not choose a place where you can be anonymous?"

"Because we do so much business here, I was able to get

our usual suite. I've decided to stay here instead of with family until after the New Year."

The Mayflower was high-end, and he said his room was a suite. She'd figured he was in a good financial position, but there was comfortable, and there was ten-days-at-the-Mayflower-when-you-could-stay-elsewhere-for-free level of wealth.

If his family did business here, he must come from money. She brushed aside the thoughts. She didn't want to know who he was. This was just meant to be fun. An escape.

She didn't want to know who he was because it didn't matter in the long run. After the holidays, he'd return to New York—assuming he lived where he voted—and she'd be back in school, sleeping, eating, living, and breathing nothing but theoretical physics.

He filled her glass and his, then raised it in toast. "Thank you for joining me."

They clinked glasses, and she took a sip. She didn't begin to know wine—she purchased based on price, in general—but liked the taste of whatever he'd selected. "So what's the plan for tonight?"

"It's up to you. There are any number of restaurants within walking distance. Or"—his eyes lit with heat—"there's always room service."

She flushed, instantly aroused. She'd been the one to proposition him on Friday night, and yesterday, she'd asked if he'd put out, but the idea that they'd skip the whole dinner in a public restaurant dance and go straight to his suite was… deliciously wicked.

And maybe a little scary.

She hadn't told Kendall where she was going, and definitely hadn't said who she was meeting. Kendall could very well know who her date was, and she did *not* want to think about Kendall telling Brent she was seeing someone she'd met at the party.

She didn't want to think about Brent or his buddy ever again.

She took another sip of wine, studying him above the rim of the glass. "Does this mean you've decided to put out?"

He grinned. "Not at all. It means I want to spend time with you. Get to know you as much as you'll allow. I'm not opposed to fooling around a little bit. But I'm going to make it clear right now, sex is not on the menu. I'm not that easy." He leaned forward his eyes lit with humor as he tapped his chest. "You want this cow, you're going to pay for the milk."

She laughed. "I'm afraid I can't afford your milk."

"All it costs is your time."

"I don't have an abundance of time, either."

"But you're on winter break."

"I'm supposed to pick up shifts at a coffee shop I worked for over the summer." Although, the shop was overstaffed with other former employees on break from school and looking for hours.

"How much are you likely to make over break? A grand? Two? I could help you out there."

"I can't take your money. What would that make me?"

"Sweetheart, I'm the one who's refusing to put out unless you pay me with your time."

She chuckled and shook her head. "I think you're breaking my brain."

"I highly doubt that. I understand you have an exceptional brain."

She usually believed that about herself, but right now, she was spinning. She liked this guy. He liked her. He was fun and funny and sexy as hell. All he wanted was to spend time with her, and she trusted him.

And in ten days, he'd be gone. No messy long-term entanglement.

She rose to her feet and picked up her glass and the bottle of wine. "What's your room number?"

JT followed his gorgeous date into the suite, enjoying both the sway of her ass and her oohs and ahhs as she took in the luxurious room that had an office area, living room, dining room, and separate bedroom.

She set the wine bottle on the table and then drifted from one area in the suite to another, her hand lightly touching the various items that decorated the space.

Much as he'd hoped the evening would go this direction, he hadn't really expected she'd take the leap. He'd have been content with dinner out and a goodnight kiss at the Metro station, but this was so much better.

She picked up the cordless phone from the desk and quickly dialed a number. "Hey. It's me. I won't be home tonight. If there's an emergency and you absolutely must reach me, you can call this number." She then read the number printed on the phone, gave the room number, and hung up.

"I like how you made it clear you didn't want to be disturbed unless it's an emergency."

"She's been known to call because she can't find her sunglasses."

"And did you know where her sunglasses were?"

"Well, yeah. I'd put them in the case by the front door where they belong."

"Have you lived with her for a while?"

She nodded. "My roommate in the dorm freshman year. We've lived together ever since."

He wanted to ask how they were getting along since Friday night, but was certain she didn't want to touch that topic tonight. This was their fresh start. He wouldn't blow it.

He stepped in front of her and touched her chin. She lifted her face to his. He stared into those gorgeous blue eyes framed by thick, dark lashes, waiting for permission.

Her lips curved, and she gave the slightest of nods. He lowered his mouth to hers. He started easy and gentle, and she responded in kind.

It was a sweet exploration. Slow meeting of lips and tongues. He could kiss her like this for hours. Which was good, because he intended to only use his mouth to pleasure her tonight. Well, mouth and hands.

Oh, what he hoped to get to do with his mouth and hands.

He raised his head and enjoyed her dreamy expression as she kept her eyes closed. Her lips were open and wet, and he wanted to explore again, but there was plenty of time for that.

"Want to see the room service menu?"

"Do we have to waste time eating?"

He chuckled. "Making sure I get food is part of the cow price."

Her body shook with laughter. Rubbing against him in all the best ways. "Five magic beans should do it, then."

He nipped at her neck. "Did you bring magic beans?"

"Sadly, no. I guess we're stuck with room service."

"We'll just have to suffer through it." He released her and went to the settee to grab the menu.

She made her selection for a main course and nothing else, leaving him to choose appetizers, salads, and desserts. "You okay with something other than a muffin?"

"Of course. But we don't need so much food."

"Indulge me."

She leaned into him and kissed his cheek. "Thank you. I think this date is going really well so far."

He caught her around the waist and kissed her collarbone. "I think so too." He cupped her butt. "After I place the order, we're going to dance." He stepped back and nudged her away. "Now scoot. I need to place the order, and they'll probably need me to confirm my name."

She took off for the bedroom, leaving him alone to make the call. It was strangely hot that she didn't care to know who he was. He was so used to women only being interested in him for *who* he was. This was a novelty. He was even blatantly showing her his wealth, and while she might enjoy it tonight, it wasn't changing her attitude.

He made the call, then went to the living room and set up his iPod in the speaker dock as he called out, "It's safe to come out, Muffin."

When she stepped into the room, she wore the complimentary hotel robe, just as she had the other night, but this time, she still had the fuck-me heels on. The robe wasn't plush like before. It was a soft cotton that molded to her. The cocktail dress had been hot as hell, but this was sexy in a different way.

"What kind of music do you like to dance to?"

"What have you got?"

"Everything."

Her brow furrowed skeptically. "Everything?"

He pointed to the white iPod 2 that was about the size and thickness of a deck of cards. "Pretty much."

He ran his finger over the touch wheel and selected the seduction standby, "The Way You Look Tonight," sung by Frank Sinatra, and held out a hand in invitation.

She laughed and took his hand, and then they were dancing. More of a slow sway than any actual dance moves, but it was just his speed when all he wanted was an excuse to hold this woman close and make her smile.

The feel of his hard body against hers as they swayed to one romantic song after another was pure magic. Time folded in on itself, each moment a mix of bliss and anticipation, with the pull of gravity and the momentum of a rocket.

New math would need to be invented to understand how a single moment in time could feel infinite.

They were probably on the third song when their mouths followed the pull of gravity and came together. It was so natural, so gradual, it felt like a tide coming in. A slow rise of the waterline without the drama of crashing waves. His mouth was hot earth that baked in the afternoon sun, while she was the cool sea that heated the instant water met land.

They swayed as they kissed, the music the only reminder that time moved forward as she floated in the moment. After an endless—or maybe it was only an instant—interval, he raised his head, releasing her mouth.

She opened her eyes to meet his hot gaze. Her arms were around his neck as he held her at the waist. Their eyes were level, thanks to her heels.

A slow smile spread across his face, lighting yet another fire in her belly.

"Tell me your name," he whispered. "Lie. Make up a nickname. Just give me something that is more *you* than Muffin."

She understood. She wanted something more *him* than Pumpkin also.

"Please?"

She considered the question. What name could she give him? She always insisted her fellow students call her Alexandra, while Alex was her barista and informal work name. Friends like Kendall called her Alex. But Alex was too close to who she was. It wasn't a name just for him.

She ran a hand along his neck and up, cupping his cheek, then she leaned forward, pressed a kiss to his lips, and said, "Lex. You can call me Lex."

His brown eyes lit, and he grinned. "Lex." He touched her forehead, tucking a loose lock of hair behind her ear. "Lex," he repeated. "I like it. It suits you. Does anyone else call you that?"

"Not really."

His voice was a low, sexy rumble. "I like that even more. It's my name for you. Just mine."

"You have to give me a name too, then."

He ran a calloused finger across her cheekbone, along her jaw, over her chin, his toughened skin tracing her features with a gentle touch.

She shivered at the thought of how that rough finger would feel elsewhere, and he must've felt her reaction because his eyes flared with heat.

"Okay, Lex. You can call me Jay."

"Does anyone else call you that?"

"No. Say it. I want to hear it from your lips."

She ran her hands down his chest as she said in a husky voice, "Jay." She kissed him, whispering the name against his lips. "Jay. Admit it. You like that we're keeping this mostly anonymous."

"A little. It's hot as fuck. But I know it's not going to be enough for me. I like you, Lex. I think this could be something special."

"But if it's not…if *this*…doesn't live up to the anticipation, you can disappear without apologies. Same for me."

"When it exceeds expectations, what then? Are you still going to vanish?"

"I don't know. I've worked my whole life to get where I am. I'm not going to screw it up with distractions."

He stepped back and took her hand, leading her to the table where their half-full wineglasses waited. "We have now. Tonight." He nodded toward the couch. "Let's relax. Enjoy the wine. Room service will be here in another twenty minutes."

Alexandra had never actually had room service. She grew up in a comfortable middle-class household, and her parents indulged in some areas, but even when they stayed in hotels with room service, the surcharge was never deemed worth the convenience. She understood. Her parents were smart and responsible. They'd raised her to be the same.

Ordering the bottle of champagne on Friday had been a wild rebellion—but not one aimed at her parents. Far from it.

Now, she anticipated her first *real* room service meal, and she had a feeling it would ruin her for all time. In the same way Jay might ruin her for other men.

Dinner arrived, and she was right to think that no other room service would compare. They ate a slow, lingering meal, laughing and talking as they enjoyed eating in no particular order, given that everything had arrived at once.

Alexandra ate a little of each dish but not too much of anything, even though it was delicious and so tempting to eat until her belly ached.

She hoped to convince him to change his mind about not having sex and wouldn't ruin it by overindulging in food or wine.

They sat at the table, lingering after they'd both finished eating. She rose and picked up the wine bottle. "Shall we move to the couch?"

He grabbed both their glasses and led the way. She waited

for him to sit, then set the bottle on the coffee table and joined him on the couch by straddling him.

His arms went around her as he let out an amused laugh that cut off when the robe split open and her center settled on his growing erection.

It was a shame she wore underwear. A bigger shame he wore slacks.

His hands slid around her waist inside the robe, those rough fingers warm on her bare skin. "This is sudden."

"Not really."

"No. I suppose not. But still a surprise. I thought I'd have to work a little harder."

She rocked against him. "Getting there." She let out a soft moan. "You lied about your rusty ballroom."

He laughed again, rocking his hips in a perfectly wonderful way. "Don't get too excited, Lex. This is all the attention you'll get from my cock tonight."

His mouth explored her neck as his hands slid up, over her ribs, then he cupped her breasts, which were unfortunately covered with a satin-and-lace bra. She knew she should have stripped down to nothing but the heels and robe.

His thumb brushed over her nipple as he licked and sucked along her throat and collarbone. He spoke between kisses. "You…can have…my mouth…my hands. I give you free rein to use me for your pleasure… But my cock is not joining in the fun. Not tonight."

She whimpered at the feel of the one body part he was denying her. She wanted him inside her. *Now.*

One large, rough hand slipped inside her bra and pushed the cup aside, freeing the full, large mound to his gaze and touch. He licked her breast as his hand cupped her and squeezed. "Fucking magnificent," he murmured as her nipple peaked. He licked again, then sucked her into his warm mouth.

As he teased one breast, he freed the other, then his mouth moved, giving attention to the newly bared breast as his thumb took over teasing her abandoned nipple.

She groaned against him as his play caused a tightening in her pelvis. “Please. Fuck me.”

“I will. With my tongue. Now, promise to abide by my rules, or I’ll stop.”

She clamped her mouth tight against more begging. If he stopped now, she might implode.

His mouth left her breasts and moved up her neck until he found her lips. The kiss was deep and carnal. His tongue made promises as his hands moved down to cup her ass. He rose from the couch, lifting her as he did so.

She was no featherweight, and the smooth action turned her on even more. He carried her to the bed, raised a knee to the mattress, and leaned over her as he set her down. He then released her and stood, gazing at her with smoldering eyes.

“You look so fucking amazing on my bed. Tits out and legs spread, waiting for me.”

The belt of the robe had loosened. It was open but still tied. She reached for it as she said, “Don’t make me wait long.”

He held her gaze as he unbuttoned his shirt, a slow striptease as she slipped her arms from the robe so she could unhook her bra. When she sat up and reached behind her back, he stopped her. “Let me.”

She lowered her arms, and he was against her again, arms going around her. He smelled so good. A musky scent mixed with cologne.

She was hit by a wave of emotions. They were just fooling around, she knew, but this was—or it could be—so much more.

It struck her for the first time that she could fall in love with this man.

Another reason to keep names out of it until she knew him better.

He unhooked her bra, but before he could move back, she placed a hand behind his neck. "You're pretty fucking amazing yourself."

He grinned. "Sweetheart, I haven't even gotten started."

She laughed and flopped back, now naked except for panties and heels, and watched him finish removing his shirt and the T-shirt he wore beneath. Next, he removed his shoes and socks. Then his watch, which he tossed on the floor with his clothes.

Slacks and belt remained.

"At least remove the belt. For comfort."

He shook his head. "Consider it a chastity belt."

She snickered. "Pretty sure your slacks have a fly."

"Maybe I sewed it shut."

She didn't believe that for a second, but she knew the rules, and she would not blow it by pressuring him again. "Come here and kiss me."

"Where do you want me to kiss you?"

Her pelvis clenched. "Everywhere."

He reached for her hips and pulled her to the edge of the bed. "You need to lose the panties, then." He tugged them down.

She braced herself for the inevitable comment about her being a natural blonde. She understood why men said it, but still, it sometimes felt like finding out if the carpet matched the drapes was the point. Like fucking a natural blonde was on some secret bingo card and they'd just won a round.

So when Jay said nothing, she was…surprised.

His gaze ran all over her, from head to full breasts that relaxed to her sides without the bra for support, to her belly and downward. Through it all, his eyes lit with appreciation.

When he got to her hips, she spread her legs slightly in invitation.

"Oh, Lex, the things I'm going to do to your body. The way I'm going to make you feel."

The way he was *already* making her feel. She was on fire for him.

She opened her legs wider.

He leaned down and licked her. His hot tongue stroked across her clit, and she let out a gasp and sigh at the glorious attention.

He leaned in and licked harder, and she bucked against him. *So good. So very, very good.*

He pulled her to the edge of the bed and dropped to his knees. "So this is how fast you want it? I was going to explore every part of you first."

"Start here. Explore later."

"Dessert first? That's not how you ate dinner, even though you could have."

"If I'd had my way, we'd have done this before dinner."

He nodded. "True enough." He leaned down and licked her again.

She cupped a hand behind his head and held him there, crying out as every touch elicited pleasure. His hands ran along the inside of her thighs, then those wonderfully rough fingers joined the play. He ran his thumb over her clit while his tongue found her opening and dipped inside her swollen sex.

"You taste amazing." He fucked her with his tongue while his thumb worked magic on her clit.

Just when she was getting close, he slowed down. His touches and teasing tongue moved more lightly along her folds.

She would complain, but she didn't want to come that

quickly. Not when she knew she wouldn't get to play with his cock in the same way. She wanted this feeling to go on and on forever.

She ran her fingers through his hair as his tongue returned to her clit, stroking more leisurely now. Like she was a lollipop, and he was in no hurry to get to the candy center.

A finger slid inside her with the same savoring pace. Her entire body focused on what he was doing to her with finger and mouth, and she relaxed into the sensual touches. He kissed. He sucked. He teased.

He raised his head. She met his gaze through slitted eyes, lost in the sensation of him.

"I could do this to you for hours."

"Please do."

"Okay, then." He returned to her wet center and took her clit into his mouth and sucked.

She jolted. A pure flash of electric current pulsed from her center. He then returned to the licking and stroking, but now she was winding up again. Needed more. Harder. Her fingers curled in his hair, and she surged, pressing herself to his face.

He laughed. "So not hours, then?"

"Minutes. Maybe only seconds."

"Is that what you want, Lex? You want to come now?"

"Yes, please."

"Well, since you said please." He slid two fingers inside her as his tongue again found her clit, pressing harder this time, giving just the right friction.

Still, he kept her on edge, giving just enough to keep her on the brink.

She loved every moment. Every lick. Every stroke.

"Please. Jay. Please."

He increased the speed and pressure. She tipped over the

edge. Pleasure rippled outward in wave after wave as his tongue pressed her clit.

Finally, spent, she pulled back, gasping as she caught her breath. She'd been very vocal as she came. Her voice might even be hoarse after that. When she could speak again, she said, "I really hope these walls are soundproof."

"Pretty sure we're fine in a room this large. And I loved every gasp and scream."

She flopped back on the bed, wishing desperately for him to let her take him into her mouth. But instead of voicing her desires, she tugged at his shoulders. "Lie down with me?"

He nodded, and she scooted up on the bed. He settled beside her, and she kissed his chest and neck, and finally ran her hands over his bare skin.

She kissed, and he kissed her back. A slow, easy caress that wouldn't work either of them up, although, from the feel of him against her hip, he was plenty aroused.

"Will you stay the night with me?" he asked.

She nodded. "I won't use you and run."

"So my plan is working."

"Was there ever any doubt?"

"You have me questioning everything, Lex."

"I do? How so?"

"Like I wonder how I can be so crazy about a woman I barely know. Who won't even tell me her name. How can I be so certain you're going to wreck me?"

Her heart squeezed. "Wreck in a good way?"

He shrugged. "All I know is I'm too far gone already. I have ten days to convince you I'm worth taking a chance on."

She'd assumed this was just a game for him. Entertainment while he was in town. His interest would only last as long as she kept secrets and distance.

She studied his face now, and what she saw made her

believe this could truly be more for him. He was doing everything he could to win her over, all while complying with and respecting her rules.

She owed it to him to open herself to the possibility this could be more for her too.

Chapter Nineteen

JT slipped out of bed and went to the living room to answer the call from his father on his BlackBerry. "Hey, Dad. What's wrong?"

"Your stepmother said you aren't coming to the Christmas Eve event."

"You called at six a.m. for that?"

"You can't skip the event, and you know it. You're Santa. It's tradition."

And that's why I canceled, Dad. "Lee can play Santa."

"Where are we going to get a Santa costume to fit a six-foot-five-inch man?"

Damn Lee and his extra inches.

"Sorry, Dad. I've got a date that night."

"You're seeing someone? Bring her along. She can be an elf."

"She's too tall to be an elf."

"Then she can be Mrs. Claus."

"You're assuming she celebrates Christmas."

"Does she?"

"I have no idea."

"Ask her, then. And bring her. You know how important these events are for our PR. If you want to get into politics, you need to start building your following now."

He wasn't wrong. It wasn't enough to be Joseph Talon's son, and he couldn't get by on his business dealings alone. But he was uncomfortable around children. Always had been. Even when he was one. Hell, *especially* when he was one. Lee had been the only kid younger than him that he'd tolerated, but that probably had more to do with the five-year-old worshipping ten-year-old JT from the first moment they met.

"Who is this woman, anyway? Why am I first hearing about her now?"

JT smiled as he said, "It's new. Too new to want to talk about. Certainly too new to put her on display at a political event."

"It's our annual Christmas Eve fundraiser. It's a dinner party."

"At a community center with wealthy donors and a few dozen families in transitional housing. It's a photo op."

"It's a photo op that happens to be one of my favorite projects—helping homeless families transition to permanent housing. And I know what the gift-giving part means to you, or you wouldn't donate so much every Christmas. Not to mention, Talon & Drake built that community center, and having the CEO show up and be Santa is a win all around."

His father was right. It was a damn good program and a lot to be proud of. He huffed out a breath. "Fine. I'll do the Santa thing. But this is the last time. And I can't promise to stay for dinner this year."

He was really hoping to convince Lex to spend Christmas Eve with him. She hadn't mentioned anything about having family in the area, and if her roommate was still dating Brent Forbes, he doubted she'd be spending the holiday with them.

"Bring her. I want to meet her."

That was the last thing he could do. *I know you don't want to know my name, but please meet my father, who I happen to be named after.*

"We'll see."

His father hung up, and JT sat in the quiet living room, thinking about the woman sleeping in the bed twenty feet away. Would his father approve?

And why did Joe's approval matter?

Ever since JT entered politics, Joe was hard to please when it came to the women JT dated, more concerned with whether she would be an asset or detriment to his—and JT's—ambition.

Joe was the only person who knew JT intended to follow in all of his father's footsteps. Joe was, on the surface, happily married, but he'd chosen his third wife with an eye to the political role she'd play. This Christmas Eve gathering was the perfect example. Lisa Talon knew how to raise money for charities and network for her husband.

She was beautiful and kind and had her own ambition: to be First Lady.

JT had no intention of consigning himself—or anyone else—to a marriage built on ambition, which was another reason he kept his political aspirations a secret. It was also a reason he was glad Lex had no idea who he was.

She wanted him for his body. Not his money or potential political power.

Alexandra was in a happy haze as she stepped into the Metro car for the ride home. Jay had been gone when she woke in his hotel suite, and that was fine with her.

She wasn't ready to have a morning-after discussion with him when she'd yet to decide if she would see him again at all, but there was no denying the more time she spent with him, the more likely she was to want more than this wild, anonymous fling.

She disembarked the train in Bethesda and walked the five blocks in the biting December wind to the apartment she shared with Kendall. Today was the first day in forever that she didn't have anything planned.

No school. No work. Today or tomorrow, Kendall would head north to spend the holiday with her sister and wouldn't be back until Sunday.

Knowing Alexandra's newly retired parents were on a monthlong cruise for the holiday, Kendall had invited her to join her at her sister's. She'd initially said yes. But after Friday, she figured she needed some time alone.

She could dance in her underwear in the living room if she wanted. She smiled, thinking of Jay and his rusty ballroom that turned out not to be rusty at all. Dancing with him in the hotel had been unimaginably sexy.

Did he have plans for the holiday?

He must. That was why he was in DC until the New Year. To spend time with family. She felt a ripple of disappointment that he'd be too busy to spend those days with her, but she was the one who'd made the rules.

A Christmas alone would be good for her. She would go to Blockbuster and load up on DVDs. Maybe she'd finally start watching *Sex and the City* and find out what the fuss was about.

She was making a mental list of movies to rent when she slipped her key into the dead bolt on her apartment door and pushed it open.

She paused by the entryway closet and pulled off her long wool coat, revealing the cocktail dress she'd donned yesterday evening. Another day, another walk of shame.

She smiled, feeling absolutely zero shame.

She was definitely going to see him again. No way would this end without getting him naked and inside her.

It was with this dreamy thought that she left the front hall and came face-to-face with the man who'd intended to rape her three nights ago.

Chapter Twenty

"Get out!" Alexandra's gaze flew from Russ to Brent. "Both of you."

"Relax, Alexandra," Brent said. "We just want to talk."

"Get out of my home. Now."

"It's not your home. It's Kendall's. Her name is the only one on the lease."

Her face drained of color. That he would use that excuse meant Kendall had shared that detail with him—to justify letting him in after Alexandra had banned him from the apartment? Betrayal cut deep.

"It's my legal residence. On my driver's license. I'm calling the police."

Russ smirked and held up the cordless handset. "How are you going to do that without a phone?"

She reached into her purse and pulled out the BlackBerry. Her fingers shook as she jammed the headset plug into the jack and dialed 9-1-1.

"Where did you get that?" Brent asked.

"None of your fucking business. Now get out before the police get here and throw your ass back in jail."

Russ yanked the headphone cord, pulling it from the jack. "Fuck you, bitch. Who did you drink champagne with and screw in my hotel room? The same prick you were with last night? Or is this a new john? Your slutty behavior will just back up my statement that you spiked the drink yourself because you wanted to play."

Her whole body shook as he loomed over her. The call had gone through, but without the headset plugged in, the operator wouldn't hear a damn thing.

She took a step back, but the four-inch heels got the best of her and she tripped, falling backward. She landed on her ass, slamming her head into the wall behind her.

Russ gave her a nasty grin. "You little cunt. You've fucked everything up with my work. Making a fool of me in front of my bosses."

"That was *your* doing. You shouldn't have put GHB in my drink."

"How do you know it was me? It could have been the bartender. Or some other guy you met."

"They found the vial in your pocket."

"It was planted on me by the cop."

For a moment, the thought flashed in her mind that Jay could have spiked her drink while they were at the bar. But no. She'd finished that drink. The bartender made her a second one, on the house.

How twisted was it that Russ made her second-guess what she knew to be true?

Shit. Would a jury believe her? Would they believe Jay?

Russ was the older of the two men. Probably senior in the company hierarchy. Would he be more convincing?

"See, sweetheart? You fucked up, and now I'm going to make you pay."

All at once, she remembered how thin the walls were in the apartment and let out a shrill scream. She banged her elbow on the wall at her back and shouted, "Call nine-one—"

Russ grabbed the front of her dress, yanked her to her feet, and slapped a hand over her mouth. He shoved her backward. Head and shoulders slammed into the wall. Pain radiated from the base of her skull.

"Fuck, Russ. You said you wouldn't touch her. We need to go."

She kicked at Russ's shins and scratched at his face.

Brent shoved Russ in the shoulder, pushing him toward the door. "Out. We can't be here when the cops arrive."

Once her mouth was freed, she screamed again. Louder, using all the air in her lungs to push out as much noise as possible.

Russ gave up and followed Brent out the door.

Tears spilled down Alexandra's cheek as she lunged for the cordless phone and again dialed 9-1-1.

Twenty minutes later, police arrived to take her statement. She learned no one else had called—her next-door neighbor wasn't home, and knocks on the door across the hall also went unanswered.

They dusted for prints—the only proof the two men had been there, but it was Brent who'd held the phone, and he'd spent many hours in the apartment prior to today.

The only things she knew for certain Russ had touched were her and the cord to the BlackBerry headset. The cord was too thin to hold a fingerprint.

"He was here," she whispered to the police officer. "They both were."

"How did they get in?"

"Either my roommate gave Brent a key, or he had one copied from her keychain."

The officer's gaze swept down her body, taking in the cocktail dress and heels. "You got home at 10:15 a.m.?"

She nodded. They'd gone over that already.

"Who were you with last night?"

"What does that have to do with the men who invaded my apartment and assaulted me?"

"Can anyone confirm the time you arrived home?"

"I don't see what that has to do with anything."

"How about we go to the hospital and get you checked out?"

"My head hit the wall, but not hard enough to warrant a trip to the hospital."

The other officer spoke. "Still, it's a good idea. Make sure everything is fine. For our report. If this guy just got out on bail as you say he did, it will work in your favor for getting a restraining order. You can get a blood draw too while you're there. To show you aren't using GHB recreationally."

She felt the blood drain from her face and wobbled on her feet at the implication. They didn't want her to go to the hospital out of concern for *her*. They took one look at her morning-after dress and pegged her as someone deserving sexual assault and were suspicious of her claim against Russ.

"Do you treat all women like this, Officer Lindberg, or am I just lucky?"

"Like what?"

"Like I'm the one who needs to prove my innocence when I'm the victim here."

"We're just crossing our Ts here, Miss Vargas."

"No, you're not. You're looking for ways to paint me as the villain. A man who intended to rape me was in my home, right after getting out of jail. He cut off my call to nine-one-one and shoved me into the wall. But *I* need to give you a blood sample?"

"I don't see why it's a problem if you don't use drugs."

"I don't, but that's neither here nor there when it comes to the man who assaulted *me*."

"I think we're done here," Officer Williams said.

She followed both men to the door and locked it behind them—fat lot of good that would do if Russ now had a key—and leaned against it. She slowly slid down to the floor and let tears fall.

This was far from over, and if Russ Spaulding was going to face prosecution, it was clear she was the one who would be on trial.

Kendall arrived home thirty minutes after the locksmith arrived. He was still changing the dead bolt when she entered the living room with a flushed face. She cast a worried glance toward the entry hall where the locksmith worked. "What's going on, Alex?"

"Your boyfriend and his buddy were in the apartment when I got home. They threatened and assaulted me."

"Brent wouldn't—"

"He *did*, Kendall. When I said I was calling the police, Brent withheld the cordless handset from me." She nodded to the phone, which still sat on the kitchen table. "I told you I never wanted him in our apartment again, and you gave him a fucking *key*?"

"I didn't! He never had a key."

"Then how did he get in? Did you leave the door unlocked?"

"Of course not!"

"Then he had a copy made without telling you at some point."

"Brent wouldn't do that."

"And yet he was *here*. With Russ. He held onto our only phone and watched Russ shove me into the wall."

"What happened?"

As emotionlessly as she could, Alexandra gave a rundown of everything that happened, leaving out the cops' implied accusations. Russ would have a field day if Kendall shared that tidbit with Brent.

"You let cops search my room? Not cool."

"You know what's also not cool? Being assaulted in my own home by a man who'd planned to drug and rape me."

"It must've been Russ who copied my key. At Brent's place, he could have gotten it from my purse. He was over often enough."

"It doesn't matter who made the key. Brent was here, with Russ, who threatened me. So I'm having the locks changed, and *you* are paying for it.

"I can't afford that."

"Then make Brent pay for it, because it sure as fuck isn't my fault, but I need to be safe in my own home." Her voice dropped. "Brent was here with him. They probably came here right from the arraignment. Are you really going to stay with a man who's aiding and abetting the man who planned to rape me?"

"Brent doesn't believe Russ did it. People at work, they have it out for Russ because he's running some big project. Drake—one of the company owners—insisted on Russ as the project manager even over Talon's objections. Talon has been trying to find a reason to get rid of him. This could be it."

The words were a blow to the gut. "Listen to yourself making excuses for a guy you've only been dating for two months. We've been best friends and roommates for six years. This isn't about an engineering project. It's about sexual assault. My *body*. And you're going to believe some bullshit conspiracy theory? Explain why he had a hotel room. And why he pressured me to take a drink."

Tears spilled down Kendall's face. "I don't know, Alex. I just—oh my god. Russ really was going to rape you? And Brent was *here*? With Russ?"

It appeared her words had finally sunk in.

Alexandra nodded. "I'm going to get a restraining order against Russ. Brent too, if I can. He will not be allowed anywhere near this apartment as long as I live here. Even if I can't get the restraining order, I'm afraid it's me or him, Kendall."

Kendall didn't say anything.

"When are you going to Tanya's?"

"Tomorrow."

"Is Brent going with you?"

"He was, but…I don't know."

"You have until the day after Christmas to decide. If you choose him, that'll give me a week to find a place. I'll move out New Year's Day."

It really hurt that Kendall just nodded. No objections. No saying of course she'd choose her best friend of six years.

No. She needed to think about it.

Maybe Alexandra should move out no matter what Kendall decided.

Chapter Twenty-One

The last thing JT wanted to do on the Tuesday before Christmas was drive north to New York City for a meeting with Edward Drake, but his dad's business partner was avoiding his calls and emails, and there was nothing left to be done but confront the man who owned one-third of Talon & Drake in person.

Russ Spaulding was done. No severance package. No reference. There was nothing Drake could do to protect his pet this time.

His phone rang as he was nearing the Jersey Turnpike. Caller ID said it was Lee, so he hit the answer button, then reached for the mic he'd clipped to his collar at the start of the drive and slipped the attached headphone in his ear. "What's up?"

"I did as you asked and got an update from the prosecutor who filed charges against Spaulding."

JT had asked Lee to get the update, as he needed the information to back up his decision with Drake. Lee had promised to keep Lex's real name to himself. JT would use her name only if absolutely necessary.

It would probably be impossible to avoid, but JT was trying to respect her wishes. "I assume he's out on bail?"

"Yes. First thing Monday morning. Fifty-thousand-dollar bond. He put down the required five grand and got a bondsman to cover the rest. Next court date is set for six weeks from now. Prosecutor feels confident she'll have enough to go to trial. We all will be needed to testify, so you can't keep your identity secret for long."

He'd known that. He was going to be integral to the prosecution. There was no way Lex wouldn't learn he was Spaulding's ultimate boss. All he could do was put off the inevitable as long as possible.

He'd been in talks with HR about the firing, and he was on solid ground. If the guy hadn't been at a company party and JT hadn't witnessed the drugging of the drink himself, there could be issues with firing someone who hadn't been convicted of anything yet, but his contract had a morality clause, and JT would see that it was enforced.

"Thanks, Lee. Hopefully, she'll decide to tell me her name sooner rather than later."

"There's another thing you need to know. Spaulding went to her place yesterday."

JT only just managed to stop himself from causing an accident at that news. He scanned the highway for an exit and moved to the right in anticipation of pulling off or over. A sign indicated a service plaza was a mile ahead. "Hold on. I'm going to pull off and call you back."

He clicked off the call and, two minutes later, was pulling into a parking space at a busy truck stop. He left the engine running as he called Lee back.

"What happened?"

Lee relayed the story, which he'd gotten from the police report, not the prosecutor, who had only just been informed of the incident minutes before Lee's conversation with her.

"I'm going to call Curt Dominick—remember him? From karate?—he's an assistant US attorney in the DC office, which is also the DC District Attorney's office. I want to know what he thinks about the Bethesda cops failing to contact the county prosecutor handling the case about the assault at the apartment. Especially because she specifically told them he must've just gotten out on bail."

"Motherfucker. So the cops took the report yesterday morning and didn't notify the prosecutor until today?"

"Yep. And the police report goes into great detail noting she was still dressed in clothing from the night before, and her refusal to submit to a drug test."

JT was glad he'd pulled over because he could no longer see the convenience store in front of him. No way could he drive as rage rushed through him.

"She refused to tell them the name of the person she was with prior to returning home."

He snorted at that. Not that she could, but she had to know he'd back her until the end of time. Wait until the cops learned he was Senator Talon's son. Because they would learn.

He'd make sure of it.

Alexandra put the DVD of *Bridget Jones's Diary* in the player and settled on the couch with a bag of cheese puffs and a big box of wine. Kendall had just left an hour ago, and finally, she could relax and let herself fall apart.

The BlackBerry on the coffee table next to the bowl of puffs signaled a text, and she hit the Pause button on the DVD.

Received: Hey. I just heard what happened yesterday. You okay?

She stared at the screen. She should have realized he'd hear about it. He was a witness for the prosecution. Of course he'd be in the loop. Or insert himself in the loop.

Did he know her name?

Did it really matter?

She took a sip of wine. Honestly, it was Kendall's potential betrayal that took priority now. If she didn't have Kendall, she had no one.

She held her breath to prevent tears. She did not want to cry about something that might not happen, but in a way, it felt like it already had.

She stared at the BlackBerry and typed a reply before she could think it through.

Sent: I want to see you. Tonight.

A minute passed before the response came.

Received: Shit. I wish I could, sweetheart, but I'm not in DC.

Was he lying? Making up an excuse?

Sent: I thought you said you were here until the New Year?

Received: A work thing came up.

Did she believe him? For all she knew, he had a date tonight, and it wasn't as if she could blame him. She wouldn't even tell him her name.

She set the BlackBerry aside and hit Play on the DVD. He

could do what he wanted. Maybe she'd screwed up in keeping her distance, or maybe it was the right thing to do because he was already moving on.

Another message came in.

Received: I want to see you. I just can't tonight. If I'd known about yesterday… Shit. I'm already halfway to New York, but I can turn around.

Her heart twisted. She'd always considered Kendall as the one whose emotions moved with the drops and rises of a roller coaster, but now here she was, unable to hold on to one feeling for longer than it took to hit the next curve.

She needed to get her head together. If he came back to DC just for her tonight, she'd be indebted in a way she wasn't ready for, and she might fall harder than was healthy.

Sent: No. Do your business thing. When will you be back?

Received: Friday.

Christmas Eve. Of course, he was coming back to be with his family for the holiday.

She wished she could afford to go somewhere. Suddenly, it didn't sound so great to be alone, even if she had scored DVDs of BBC's *Pride and Prejudice* and Season One of *Sex and the City*.

Received: I need to play Santa at a Christmas Eve event for kids in transitional housing, but after that, I'm free if you want to go out.

She sat up straighter.

Sent: You as Santa? I'd kind of like to see that.
Received: Technically, you've been invited to play Mrs. Claus.

She snickered.

Sent: Pass, thanks.
Received: Figured. Meet me at the Mayflower after? I could get there by nine.

She considered the question. If she spent Christmas Eve with him, she'd have to come up with a gift for him. Maybe she could make something?

All she knew was she really didn't want to spend the holiday alone.

She agreed and signed off. He had a drive to finish, and the cheese puffs weren't going to eat themselves. Plus, she needed to figure out what she could possibly give her mystery man for Christmas.

Chapter Twenty-Two

Catoctin Mountain, Maryland
Present

The attic was a bust as far as computers went. He found two thirteen-inch cathode-ray-tube monitors from the '90s that weighed a ton, too many outdated cords, floppy disk drives in multiple sizes, a Zip drive, and even an old Apple IIc. Nothing that could run a pre-2010 PC hard disk. The laptop he had with him was a MacBook.

Tomorrow, he could drive to town and see if the thrift store had something that would work, but the odds were against success. Lee could crack it in a heartbeat. Or Raptor could ship a computer to him. He and Lex and Gemma could stay here forever.

But that would be its own kind of torture.

Next to the tech graveyard, he spotted red and green plastic boxes. His heart squeezed as he remembered packing up those boxes and moving them up here the day after the wedding that wasn't.

He and Alexandra had come up here for Christmas, planning a quiet holiday, just the two of them, before their New Year's Eve wedding in DC. JT had surprised her with a fully decorated Christmas tree in the living room. He'd hired a decorator and paid a woman to knit stockings with their names. He'd bought Christmas dishes, the whole works.

But they didn't get their cozy, pre-wedding holiday because Joe showed up with his mistress.

Lex had been horrified to learn JT knew about Joe's affairs and had kept the secret from Lisa. In retrospect, JT could understand her reaction better now. At the time, he hadn't understood why Joe's infidelities had any bearing on his and Lex's relationship.

Joe didn't help the situation when Alexandra overheard him lecturing JT about keeping her in line so she didn't ruin both his and JT's political prospects.

He knew now that he'd already been withdrawing from her. He'd grown more distant the closer they got to the wedding. He'd known she had trouble accepting that he didn't want kids. And he hadn't told her about the open congressional seat in New York.

All this came together like a hurricane gathers wind, and next thing he knew, she'd called off the wedding and moved back in with Kendall.

Two days later, he'd purchased the Lotus because it only had two seats. No children allowed.

He'd then driven it north to this cabin, where he proceeded to get drunk by himself on New Year's Eve and spent a very hungover New Year's Day packing up all the Christmas decorations in these boxes, determined never to look at them again.

He'd packed up part of his heart that day. Four years later, when Lex was back in his life, back in his bed, trying to help him heal from yet another blow, he'd been too incomplete to be able to open himself back up to her. He'd sabotaged their relationship before she could hurt him again.

Now she was back in his life again. In this very cabin. She needed his help. Needed his money. And she wanted to use him for a cold, convenient screw.

He was thrilled with the first point. He would do anything, spend anything to help her. But the last… It somehow hurt as much as being dumped days before the wedding.

He flicked open the plastic clasps on the nearest storage box and caught his breath when he saw what was inside.

Shit. He was too raw for this.

He reached into the box and pulled out the Santa hat and beard, revealing the wool elf costume beneath. Green tunic. Red leggings. Even the shoes were here.

He closed his eyes and remembered the first time he saw her in costume and what it had meant at the time.

His Lex. He'd known in that moment she was his. Would always be his. This was the relationship that would define his life.

He'd loved her as best he could. But his best hadn't been nearly good enough.

For the first time since he packed this box away, tears slid down his cheeks. He held his palm to his lips, but there was no stifling his gut-wrenching sob.

Chapter Twenty-Three

Bethesda, Maryland
December 23rd
Sixteen years ago

Thursday morning, a text arrived, and Alexandra's heart thumped with a new rhythm as she picked up the phone to see what Jay—who'd been silent since Tuesday—had to say.

But the message wasn't from Jay. It was *for* him. Someone, apparently, didn't know he had a new number.

> **Received:** I'm having the Santa suit delivered to the Mayflower tomorrow at noon. Your father said your new lady friend might be Mrs. Claus. I need her size.

She stared at the screen. He'd been serious about her playing Mrs. Claus? She'd been sure it was a joke.

Her heart pounded as she stared at the screen. How would Jay react if she showed up in costume?

There would be no hiding his identity after that, and he'd insist on knowing her name. It was only fair.

This could be just what she needed. If she was going to lose Kendall, at least she'd get to enjoy a week with Jay before he returned to New York and she had to find a new place to live.

One week of fun. No secrets. It wouldn't just be a Christmas gift for Jay, it would be one for herself.

Her fingers trembled as she responded.

Sent: No on Mrs. Claus. She would prefer an elf costume. Size 8 with a 36DD top. Five nine height. Shoe size 10-11.

She figured elf shoes would be more shoe covers anyway.

Received: That's a custom size. We'll have to buy, not rent.

Guilt tugged at her. But she didn't think Jay would balk if he knew.

Sent: I'll pay for it. What time do I need to tell her to be there?
Received: As usual, the kids will arrive at 6:30.

She pondered how she could get the address without sounding like she wasn't Jay. She took a deep breath and typed, hoping this wouldn't give her away.

Sent: I'm busy and don't have the address handy. Can you type it here so I can forward to her so she can find it with MapQuest?

There was a long pause, and she wondered if she'd blown it. Was the party at the Mayflower?

Received: She can't look up the Dalia Davis Community Hall on her own? And didn't T&D build the complex? You should know the address by now.

She wanted to point out that Jay didn't work for the Bethesda office of Talon & Drake, he worked in New York. Why would he be expected to know the address of every construction project? But given that she didn't actually know what his job was, that could make things worse.

Sent: Sorry. Wasn't thinking. I'm in the middle of something. See you tomorrow.

She set the phone down, her heart racing as she hoped whoever she was texting with would be there tomorrow, or she'd really blown it.

Received: See you tomorrow. Love you, kiddo.

She read through the messages again. Could it be his mother? Grandmother or aunt?

She didn't even know why she thought it was a woman,

but she did. Definitely a family member, given the reference to Jay's father.

Now she had to make a decision. Was she really going to do this? She had a key to the suite at the Mayflower. She could pick up the costume right after it was delivered, before Jay got back from New York. If he returned early, so be it, but if not, it would be fun to surprise him.

She wouldn't decide now. She had twenty-four hours to make up her mind.

It took an hour and a half to take the Metro to the Mayflower and back to her apartment in Bethesda, but now she was home with a green elf costume that looked a lot like the ones the elves wore in the Will Ferrell movie. It was quality wool felt. Even the shoes were real and not shoe covers.

She'd checked out the Santa costume in the hotel room, and it was also well made. Nothing but the best for Jay and his helper. Would the kids be getting generic toys donated to organizations like Toys for Tots, or was this a charity that specifically catered to the individual children's Christmas wishes?

Either way, she felt her first rush of Christmas spirit this season as she tried on the costume. Even without the fun of surprising Jay, she'd want to be part of this. The idea of seeing kids bright with excitement as they met Santa and received even a small gift was enough to put a bounce in her step as she tugged on the comfy pointy-toed slippers.

The elf tunic was a perfect fit at the bustline. This had definitely been custom-made by a skilled seamstress. It was tasteful while still showing off her curves. Sexy but not inappropriate, thank goodness. After all, this was a party for children, not an adult Halloween party.

She twirled in front of the mirror and made up her mind. The costume fit. She wanted to grab this holiday spirit and hold on tight.

But most important, she wanted to see Jay's face when he realized she was ready for the next step.

She was going to buy the milk.

JT was disappointed to see the Santa suit hanging in the entry closet of the Mayflower suite. He'd hoped that when Lisa hadn't gotten back to him with instructions for picking up the costume, she'd found some other fool to play Santa.

No such luck.

Still, it wasn't like his stepmother to forget to tell him such an important detail—what if he'd been running late and went straight to the hall?

Luckily—or unluckily—traffic had been smooth on the drive south and stopping at the Mayflower was no problem. He'd rather hoped he'd find Lex here early, but the room was sadly empty with no sign she'd been here during his absence, even though he'd told her she could use the suite as much as she liked.

Would she meet him after he performed his Santa duties, or would she back out? He knew he'd been asking a lot when he invited her to spend Christmas Eve with him. They barely knew each other.

He crossed to the bedroom and set his suitcase on the rack. He'd unpack later. Right now, he needed to put Lex's Christmas present in the safe and get ready for the party. He pulled the blue Tiffany box from his briefcase and lifted the lid, pulling out the jewelry case. He opened it to reveal the diamond earrings and matching necklace.

He couldn't look at the stones without imagining what she'd look like in the necklace and nothing else. Well, nothing except those four-inch heels that brought them eye to eye.

Never in his life had he spent this kind of money on a gift for a woman he'd only just met, but something about her made him want to shower her with gifts, treat her to all the things his money could give her.

As fun as the fantasy was, he had to get moving. He needed to shower and shave so the damn beard would adhere to his face.

He deposited the jewels in the safe, stripped, entered the shower, and tried not to think about the woman who'd been the center of his fantasies for the last week.

Two hours later, JT was in the chair. The beard itched. The suit was hot. And he had not learned how to talk to children in the 366 days since the last time he did this.

The first kid was cute. Big smile, no front teeth. He wanted a baseball bat, gloves, and ball, and Lee stepped in to assist one of the hall's overworked volunteers in locating the boy's present, which included cleats in his size and a baseball uniform signed by his favorite Baltimore Orioles player.

Like kids the world over, the boy would open his presents tomorrow morning. For tonight, he had no idea that he was getting far more than he'd asked for. Only Santa and his elves knew.

"I thought you were going to have an elf to help you?" the harried volunteer said as the kid slipped from JT's lap and headed for his mother. "Mrs. Talon said you were bringing a helper this year."

"She probably meant me," Lee said.

"I had you down for helping with the party games."

"Must be a mistake, then. Where am I needed most?"

The man glanced at the line of kids. "Here. Move the kids from the line to the lap."

That was all JT was tonight. A lap.

Lee nodded and turned to the kid at the front of the line, taking the slip of paper from another volunteer in charge of ensuring all the kids had the number that corresponded with their name and gift.

JT let out a hearty "Ho! Ho! Ho!" as the girl approached. All at once, she stopped in front of him and let out an ear-piercing shriek.

It was going to be a long night.

Chapter Twenty-Four

Alexandra slipped through a side door and found herself in a service corridor. She moved deeper into the building, following the sounds of clanging of plates and squealing children. On one side of her was the kitchen; on the other was the service entrance to the main hall, where the party was in full swing.

Across the hall, she spotted Santa's throne. The gilded seat was up on a stage surrounded by white cotton batting and a red carpet lined with candy-cane-striped poles topped with poinsettias. Gold glitter ornaments and white twinkle lights decorated fake evergreen trees that flanked the seat of power.

On the throne sat an alarmed-looking Santa with an angry child on his lap.

Alexandra stepped deeper into the room, drawn to the spectacle. She passed men and women who shook with silent laughter as they hid their mouths behind hands.

One woman whispered to another, "This is my favorite part of Christmas every year. He has no clue how to talk to children who are afraid of Santa."

"You're late," a young man in a service uniform stepped up beside her.

"Sorry. There was an accident on GW Parkway."

The man reached for her bag. "I'll put it in a locker and bring you the key. Santa needs help. He's got a crier, but Mom isn't giving up on getting a photo."

Poor kid being forced to sit on a stranger's lap for a photo that would only come out terrible. And poor Jay was little more than a prop in the sad photo.

She pulled on her elf cap and hurried forward, her eyes on Santa and the child on his lap. She noted he didn't hold on to the girl—she was free to escape—but the mother was shouting encouragement that kept the child rooted in place.

"Smile, then you'll get your presents, and we can all have ice cream!"

Jay's tall stepbrother stood to the side, a bag of gifts in hand. "Are those for her?" she asked.

He nodded, then startled as he recognized her.

She pressed a finger to her lips, then took the bag and entered the stage. She grinned as Jay spotted her, jolting so hard, the girl wobbled and nearly fell from his lap.

Alexandra dropped to one knee and supported the girl, then pulled a wrapped gift from the bag and presented it to her. "Hey, princess, Santa wanted me to give this to you now because he knows you've been extra good this year."

The girl's face lit up as she grasped the sparkly pink package. "Fo me?"

"Yes, honey. Just for you. Now let's smile for your mommy so Santa can give the other kids their presents."

Alexandra tried to scoot out of the shot, but the girl grabbed her hand. There was nothing to be done but turn toward the camera and smile.

The girl's face was tear-streaked, but her gap-toothed smile was big. Hopefully, her mom would be satisfied.

Alexandra stood and scooped the girl off Jay's lap, then walked her and the bag of presents to Mom before going to collect the next child destined for Jay's lap.

She felt his eyes on her with each step, and when she faced him, he wore a happy and somewhat smug smile, visible even through the beard. He let out a very cheery "Ho, ho, ho!" and beckoned the child by name. He must have a cheat sheet on each child.

Impressive.

The next gifting ceremony went smoothly, as did the third. When she took the bag of toys from Tall Man for the fourth child, he whispered, "He's happy you're here, and it shows with the kids. Thank you."

"I'm a sucker for kids."

Tall Man smirked. "Sadly, our current Santa is not."

She laughed and took the bag. "I noticed."

The next child viewed Santa with trepidation. He couldn't be older than four. He stopped short of Jay, just out of his reach, looked to Alexandra, and asked in a loud whisper, "Does being bad today count?"

She dropped down to a knee and whispered equally loud, "No. The naughty list isn't updated until eleven p.m. daily. And even then, so long as you're sorry and try to do better, Santa is very forgiving."

The boy's face brightened. "I didn't mean to do it. It was an accident."

He turned to Jay, who again greeted the child by name. They went through the routine, and Alexandra presented him with the bag of toys, which, according to the tag she removed before handing it off, contained a collection of wooden Thomas the Tank Engine toys, including several yards of track.

As far as she could tell, each child here was receiving specific items from a wish list. The toys weren't cheap either.

For children living in transitional housing, this had to be a Christmas miracle. She found herself tearing up along with some of the parents as the evening wore on.

There were at least fifty kids present. It must've been an enormous task to get the wish lists and collect and wrap the presents. Someday, when she wasn't so broke herself, she would make a donation to whichever charity organized this event.

It took more than an hour to work through the line, which was limited to five kids at a time to prevent toddlers from losing their minds at the long wait.

They'd had two more criers, but no more screamers by the time Alexandra escorted the last child to their dad. The curtain that enclosed Santaland dropped as Jay let out one last hearty "Ho! Ho! Ho! Merry Christmas and to all a good night!"

Alexandra slipped through the curtain and faced Jay. They were alone. Sort of. "Ready for a break, Santa?"

"Not quite. I've got one more person to interrogate." His gloved hand circled her wrist, and he pulled her to his lap. "Tell me what you want for Christmas, Lex."

She laughed softly, well aware the curtain wasn't much of a sound barrier. "But Santa," she whispered, "I've been *very* naughty this year."

The fake beard tickled her ear as he whispered, "As long as you're sorry and try to do better, I hear I'm lenient."

"But I'm not even a little bit sorry and intend to be naughty again." She tugged at the beard and would have removed it, but he must've used some kind of adhesive to secure it, because it didn't budge. She leaned back. "You're going to have to remove the beard, because it's not doing it for me."

"Aww, come on. Just one kiss?"

She leaned in and kissed the tip of his nose.

He laughed softly. "Tell me what you want for Christmas."

The padding that enlarged his belly hung over his lap, or she'd have wiggled her butt to get a physical response as she whispered, "You know what I want." She ran a thumb over his cheekbone. "I missed you this week."

"I missed you too."

Tall Man slipped behind the curtain, took one look at them, and shook his head. "Do you have any idea of the trauma you'd cause if a kid saw Santa cheating on Mrs. Claus with an elf?"

Jay's belly shook with silent laughter, and it really did feel like a bowl full of jelly against Alexandra's hip. Must be gel padding, not foam.

"We're totally innocent," she said softly. "He just wanted to know what I want for Christmas. Mrs. Claus will understand."

"Innocent. Right." He met Jay's gaze. "Your stepmom wants to know if your elf friend here is staying for the dinner and what name to put on the place card."

Jay looked at her. "If you haven't figured out who I am yet, there'll be no avoiding it if you stay."

She nodded and took a deep breath, then slid from his lap and spoke to Tall Man. "Alexandra Vargas."

The man smiled and held out his hand. "Lee Scott. It's nice to meet you, Alexandra."

She ran a hand down the wool costume. "I need to change if I'm going to stay."

Lee nodded. "Follow me. Your bag was placed in an employee locker. We'll retrieve it, and I'll show you to a room where you can change."

He led her through the back. She didn't turn to look at Jay as she left. She didn't know why she felt so nervous. It wasn't like her name would mean anything. Well, anything more than she wanted to get in his pants, which he most definitely knew already. But still, it felt like she was taking a huge step, even though this remained a silly fling.

After collecting her bag from the break room that had a row of lockers, Lee showed her to a restroom that had lounge area. She quickly changed into a deep green knit dress, glad that the yarn withstood wrinkles after being rolled up and stored for a few hours.

It wasn't fancy, but it was Christmassy, and it hugged her curves in a flattering way. She put on low black heels and a necklace with red and gold beads, then secured her hair up with a clip.

Her shoes were scuffed and the necklace obviously cheap. She would *not* fit in with the women she'd spotted who must be donors to this fundraiser and wondered if Jay would be embarrassed by her.

It was a ridiculous thought. This was a charity event for kids who had next to nothing. The parents hadn't been dressed to impress. If Jay was a snob, it was his problem, not hers.

But at the same time, it had never occurred to her how uncomfortable she'd feel stepping into his world, when she had no clue what his world was other than he came from money.

He might not be the one who was rich, though. He'd said the suite at the hotel was paid for by his family. And the BlackBerry he'd given her was being paid for by his employer.

She really should have searched for him online before coming tonight, but that wouldn't have been fair, given that she'd expressly told him not to try to find her. She had her flaws, but she tried not to be a hypocrite.

Now she was wildly nervous as she faced stepping into the unknown of Jay's world. This was a case of ignorance not being anywhere close to bliss.

She took one last look in the mirror and decided to reapply lipstick before leaving the safety of the ladies' lounge. She placed the elf costume and her bag back in the locker, securing it with the key, which she tucked into the small cocktail bag that didn't match her dress, but was the only one she had.

She returned to the main room, which was full of the buzz of conversation as people mingled near the cash bar—all purchases would go to charity—on one side of the massive room, while kids and their families played games and did crafts on the other.

She spotted Tall Man—Lee Scott—near the bar and headed in his direction. She expected it would take some time for Jay to remove the beard. She would need to circulate without him. Lee was a safe person to start with.

But before she made it to Lee, she was intercepted by a woman who Alexandra guessed was in her sixties. Beautiful and polished, she looked intimidating, but had a kind smile. "Alexandra, my dear! I need to thank you for assisting my stepson. You performed an absolute miracle in getting him to interact with the kids."

She smiled and said, "I'm glad I could help."

"How long have you known JT?" the woman asked.

She needed to call him JT. She mentally practiced saying his name. "Not long, really." *Exactly one week.* But she didn't want to admit to that. She didn't want to say a single word about how they met.

Lee approached and placed a drink in her hand. She would hesitate to accept, but he was one person she knew she could trust. The mint garnish told her it was a mojito. "You, uh, might want this," he whispered. Then he raised his voice and spoke to JT's stepmom. "JT just texted that he'll be out in a few minutes."

"Oh, good. His father wants to talk to him before dinner is served and he makes his speech."

Alexandra took a sip of the drink as her nerves bubbled up again. Dinner involved speeches? Was JT making a speech, or was the speaker his father?

A handsome older man who bore a slight resemblance to JT approached. His skin was a tad darker and his hair streaked with gray, but the jawline was similar.

But that wasn't what caused her to jolt, sloshing her drink. No, it was that she *recognized* him. The senator from Maryland. The one who owned Talon & Drake.

Her mystery man was Senator Joseph Talon's son.

And now she remembered Brent complaining about the CEO, who was far too young to run the company but had gotten the job because he was the senator's only child.

Chapter Twenty-Five

JT knew the exact moment the truth became clear to Alexandra. It wasn't when she nearly spilled her drink; it was a moment after, when the pieces must've come together in her mind.

Was she thinking about that first night, when she asked him if he'd met the senator? Or when he'd told her he knew she didn't work for Talon & Drake because *she* hadn't recognized *him*.

She'd probably thought he had a big ego, but he'd been stating a basic fact.

He stepped up behind her and placed a hand on her waist. "Alexandra, darling. I see you've met my dad and stepmom."

Her smile was overly bright, but she'd recovered well enough. "We were just getting to that. It's an honor to meet you, Senator Talon." She held out a hand. "Alexandra Vargas."

"A pleasure," Joe said as he shook her hand. "JT has told us very little about you."

"That's my fault, really. I wasn't sure if I could join you tonight, and I didn't want him saying anything in case I failed to show."

Smooth. Very smooth.

"We so appreciate you helping, but I hope we haven't pulled you away from family this evening," Lisa said.

"My parents are on a cruise celebrating my dad's retirement. I was going to spend the holiday with my best friend, but that fell through, so here I am."

Her best friend. The roommate who was dating Forbes. He was glad she'd made the decision to spend the holiday with him instead.

A server passed by with a tray of hors d'oeuvres, and Lex took a cracker topped with veggies and cheese. "I didn't realize it would take so long to do the gift-giving, or I'd have eaten earlier."

"Dinner will be served shortly," Lisa said. "And really, JT should have warned you." She gave him a look that conveyed her disappointment at his failure.

He slid his hand lower and cupped Lex's hip, just shy of an ass grab. He'd have warned her if she'd told him she was coming. He would make her pay for throwing him under the bus later. They would both enjoy her punishment.

She turned to face him, licking crumbs from her lips with a wicked smile. Holy hell. She was here to play.

How many minutes until he could get her alone in his hotel room?

But first, Dad wanted to talk.

He kissed Lex's cheek, then followed his father to the manager's office. Once they were alone, Joe said, "I had an interesting call from Ed Drake tonight."

"We both know if this is about Talon & Drake, we can't be having this conversation."

"No one will know."

"*I* know. We agreed that when I was named CEO, you would not interfere. We could lose our government contracts if you're found to be in violation of Senate Ethics Rules. Either that or you can be impeached."

"We both know ethics rules are only as strong as the willingness to enforce them."

"I don't care. And I don't care what Drake has to say. He already told me his thoughts, and when that failed, he ran to you like a child trying to turn Dad against Mom."

"He's also been my business partner since you were in diapers, and he owns a third of the company."

"He's wrong on this, Dad. Firing Spaulding was justified. He's facing charges for attempting to drug a woman with the intention of raping her."

"Being charged doesn't mean he'll be convicted. And he didn't actually commit the crime. Attempted means something very different. If he's found not guilty, he could sue us."

"He did it at the company holiday party, meaning the *victim* could sue us."

He had no clue if Alexandra could make a claim when, as Dad had said, she hadn't actually been drugged. But it didn't matter. He wasn't backing down on this.

"But the victim doesn't work for Talon & Drake, does she? She's done a fine job manipulating you. You even moved her into the Mayflower. Got her so-called attacker fired."

How did his father know Alexandra was the victim? All at once, he realized Drake would have probably sent him the police report.

She'd told Lee her name. Lee told Lisa. It wouldn't have taken long for his father to connect the dots.

He wanted to point out that Lex hadn't known who *he* was, so it could hardly be manipulation, but Joe would never believe that, and the last thing JT wanted to do was explain the finer details of his yet-to-be-fully-consummated relationship with a woman he was increasingly certain would be central to his future.

"She's not manipulating anyone. And you must not have been informed of the part where Lee and I were the witnesses who watched Spaulding spike her drink. He's a scumbag who no longer works for Talon & Drake. That's final."

"We might lose the Lewiston contract."

"Spaulding was fucking it up anyway. He wasn't ready to manage a job that big, and it was bullshit that Lewiston and Drake insisted on making him the project manager. I've got seven other PMs who can step in and do better. I'm in talks with bringing Pamela Morrison up from Miami."

He saw his dad flinch at the woman's name, and that was why it was good that neither he nor Drake were in charge now. It wasn't that either man believed women couldn't manage a hundred-million-dollar build like the bridge replacement and neighborhood revitalization contract, it was that they worried the client would balk at having a woman at the helm.

The boys club was alive and well and determined to use any excuse to exclude women from power. If JT did nothing else as CEO of Talon & Drake, it would be to ensure all the top hires and promotions would be fair.

Edward Drake hated it.

"I've increased revenue by thirty-nine percent in six years. I've more than proven myself."

JT had done little but work for the last six years for this exact reason. He knew much of the business world had thought Joe was a fool for appointing JT CEO when he was just twenty-five years old. Political rivals claimed JT was a puppet.

Two years in, JT had done an extensive interview with *TIME Magazine* that resulted in his face on the cover and a story that laid out JT's—not his father's—vision for the company and the strides he'd taken to make it come true.

"Drake doesn't like it, he can suck it up. We aren't beholden to stockholders." This was the key point that put JT in the driver's seat. Company employees came first, not a stock price. "Waiting for a sexual predator to be convicted before firing him is not an option. My word is final."

"I'll admit, the woman is gorgeous, but you need to be certain she's on the up-and-up. We made it through reelection, and now I need to start looking at a presidential run in 2008. If that were to happen, you need to be positioning yourself for your own senate run to fill my seat in 2010. Part of that is getting serious about finding a woman who can fulfill the duties of a politician's wife."

The idea of choosing a partner based on what she could bring to a campaign was repugnant, but at the same time, his father wasn't wrong.

Tonight's event had been planned, as it had been every year for the last several, by Lisa, Joe's third wife and the first one suited to the role of political spouse. Lisa had her eyes on being First Lady, and there was a decent chance Joe could give that to her.

But that was four—or more likely eight—years away. "I don't need relationship advice, Dad."

"Don't you, though? She's pretty, and she helped out plenty tonight, but she needs more polish if she's going to stick around. A cheap dress and makeup get a pass at a charity event for transitional housing families, but they won't fly at a political fundraiser. And she better not be a twit."

JT cringed at his father's words. Alexandra looked beautiful just as she was. But his father had always been obsessed with having a wife who looked perfect at all times and wore couture clothing whenever she left the house. He suspected it was one way he sought to show the world how far he'd come after being raised in an Indian boarding school in which the headmaster spent every day telling the students how worthless they were.

"Pretty sure she's smarter than both of us. She's working on a PhD in theoretical physics."

"Oh. That's good. But possibly too intimidating."

JT rolled his eyes. "I'm not having this conversation with you."

"When Drake finds out you're screwing her, he's going to flip."

"It's none of Drake's damn business who I'm involved with." JT crossed to the door.

Behind him, his father's voice rose. "It's awfully convenient that she glommed on to you. Hire an investigator. She needs to be vetted."

Oh, hell no.

"And for god's sake, wear a fucking condom. I don't care if she says she's on the pill. Women lie."

The last words were practically a shout. JT yanked open the door and came face-to-face with Alexandra, whose hand was frozen in the air, as if she were about to knock.

Her face was deathly pale. She cleared her throat. "Y-your stepmother asked me to get you and the senator. Dinner is about to be served."

"Thank you." He had no doubt the final words had been loud and clear in the hall, but how much more had she overheard?

"I…I um…I think I'll get going. I'm not hungry, and I promised my parents I'd call."

"Lex—"

"Enjoy your evening." She ran her hand over her dress. "I—I wasn't sure what the dress code would be. Better that I go."

Shit. She'd heard *everything*.

She headed down the hall and he followed her into the break room with the line of lockers.

"Lex. My dad is an asshole."

"Better not let the people in the main room hear you say that."

"Half of them know it too. He's a good senator. And usually a good man, but he's…got plans for me and forgets that I have my own mind."

She unlocked a locker and pulled out her purse. "Tell your stepmom the elf costume is here."

She tossed him the key. It bounced off his chest and hit the floor.

She headed for the door.

"Lex. Wait."

"I'm not sitting at a table and eating with him and smiling like I didn't hear him spew some awful things. Does his wife know his thoughts on women and lies?" She hiked her purse onto her shoulder and stepped into the hall. "You're better off without an unpolished, too smart, gold digger like me. I might make you look bad. Or intimidate people who aren't put off by my cheap clothes and bad makeup."

He followed her into the corridor. "Why are you mad at *me?* I didn't say any of that shit."

"Listen. I just came here to get laid. I didn't know that would require a private investigator to dig into my life. Or that I'd have to take a pee test to prove I'm on birth control. For the record, I hardly ever try to entrap wealthy men whose names I don't even know."

Her voice carried in the corridor, and JT had no doubt the caterers were getting an earful, which made him smile. He was years out from throwing his hat in the political ring, and even if he weren't, there was no scandal here. His dad had been an ass, but this was a family matter.

She exited the building and crossed the parking lot. "Stop following me."

"Then stop walking away from me."

She neared a Honda Civic that was made in the mid-eighties, with a paint job that had seen better days. "Don't bother giving me your father's opinion of my car. I can guess exactly what he'd say." She swiped at an eye, then unlocked the driver's door. Under her breath, she said, "I can't believe I wasted my gas budget on this."

She pulled on the door handle, but his hand pressed on the window and roof, holding it closed as his body pressed to her back. "Lex. I am not my father. Please. Give me a chance."

"Why does he hate me? What did I do to him?"

"He's mad because I fired Spaulding over his and Drake's objections. That's why he wanted to talk to me alone."

"You *what*?"

"That's why I went to New York. To tell Drake I was firing his pet for cause. It wasn't something I could do on the phone. I needed my team in the office so we could reconfigure the management structure for our biggest project. Calling everyone in for a meeting two days before Christmas wasn't my most popular move as CEO, but I got their support. Spaulding is out as of last night."

"Does…does he know?"

He nodded. "Please. Come home with me tonight. You shouldn't be alone at your place. Spaulding might show up again."

"I don't know, Jay. This has all gotten so ugly."

"I'm sorry my dad was a dick. I was caught off guard. Didn't know he knew anything, but I should have guessed. He and I—we aren't supposed to talk about the company at all. And it's my call all the way. He has no say. So he was lashing out like a child because he recognized your name. Drake must've told him or sent him the police report."

"Will he tell Drake about you and me?"

"I don't think so. But I'm hoping Drake will find out because you'll be my date at the next company event."

"We aren't going to start dating, JT. You live in New York, and I have zero time for dating, let alone long distance."

"But don't you see? Long distance is perfect for our busy schedules. Instead of wasting time with dinner dates and movies, we'll just have phone sex."

She laughed at that.

He leaned down and brushed his lips over hers. "Please, Lex. Give me a chance."

She tucked her head against his sternum. "I can't believe you fired him. I was worried that he was *your* boss."

"I'd have fired him on the spot that night, but we needed the investigation to move unhindered and having charges filed gave me more ammunition to do it properly. He was in a vital position for the company, so I needed to be careful."

"I can't believe I demanded anonymous one-time-only sex from a billionaire just a few hours after meeting him."

He had to work to hide his smile. "I'm not a billionaire. But I do okay. And it killed me to say no to your offer. But if I'd taken it, we wouldn't be here right now. And I want to see where this can go more than I wanted a single orgasm."

"Oh, I'd have made you come more than once."

He laughed. "Sounds like a testable hypothesis."

"I can't go back in there, Jay. Go have dinner and perform your official duties to the Talon family, or campaign, or whatever this was."

"It's a charity my stepmother helped create. Talon & Drake built the community center. My dad sees to it that it gets the funding it needs."

"Who funds the Christmas gifts for the kids?"

"I do. It's one reason my stepmom insists I play Santa. She wants me to see the kids' faces. But honestly, I'd rather be a secret Santa. I don't need to meet them to know what it means. My family wasn't always rich."

She rose on her toes and pressed her mouth to his, then whispered, "But still, you do it. Which makes me think part of you does want to see the joy your gifts can bring."

She might be hitting a little too close to home there. He nodded toward the passenger side of the car. "Do you mind letting me drive?"

Her brows furrowed. "Yes, I mind. Also, you need to go back inside."

He pulled out his BlackBerry. "I'll send a text to Lee."

He held the screen so she could read as he typed.

Sent: Sorry, bro. Joe upset Lex, so I'm taking her home.

"There. Lee will make excuses for me. Let's go."

"You aren't driving my car."

He leaned down and kissed her. "Fine. Unlock the passenger door."

His phone pinged.

Received: No fair. He upsets me all the time, but you always tell me I have to stay.

He smiled and typed a reply.

Sent: She's cuter than you, and you know how to handle Joe.

His phone pinged again as he tucked it away.

"Wait. What else did he say?"

He knew he was still winning her trust, so he showed her the phone.

Received: Have fun. I'm glad she's giving you a chance. Don't blow it.

She smiled after reading. "He seems like a good guy."

"He's my best friend. I mean, also my only friend, but whatever."

She laughed.

He circled the car while she climbed into the driver's seat, then leaned across and pulled up the lock from the inside. The old Honda didn't have power locks or windows. He seriously hoped it had heat, but he wasn't about to diss on her vehicle.

They were on the road before she asked, "Where are we going?"

"Are we spending the night together? Or do you have plans for Christmas morning?"

"No plans. You?"

They came to a stop at a light. He lifted her hand from the stick shift and kissed her knuckles. "I was hoping to spend it with you."

She slipped her hand from his just before the light changed and they were moving again. "Okay. So your place or mine?"

"My place has room service."

"Sold."

They were thirty minutes from the hotel. She turned on Christmas music.

"Tell me about Lee."

"He was my stepbrother for several years when we were

kids. He's five years younger than me and was five when my dad married his mom. The marriage didn't last, but the little brother stuck."

"That's sweet. Especially given your age difference. So Lee is my age? Twenty-five?"

"Twenty-six. I'm thirty-one."

"And when you were my age, you were taking over Talon & Drake. That's a little wild."

"It was, but I'd been working for the company since I was fourteen. Started with internships. All through college, I was working for the company on the side."

"Was that your dad's idea?"

"To be honest, I don't really know anymore. I mean, I remember how it came about. I remember asking for the jobs, but I don't know if Dad planted the idea, the drive. It was just always understood that I would take over someday and needed to be ready. It just happened far sooner than I expected when he decided to go into politics—and then won. He never would have stepped aside if it wasn't for ethics rules. Dad loves that company, probably even more than he loves me and Lee."

"That doesn't bother you?"

"Not anymore. It feels different at thirty-one than it did at twelve. Plus, he basically gave me the company, so I guess that means I'm important to him. Joe has lots of loves. He loves the tribe. He loves being a senator. He loves Lisa."

"In that order?"

"I honestly don't know. I'd put the tribe above politics, I think."

"You're going to want me to meet him again, aren't you?"

"If this thing between us goes anywhere—which is what I want—then yes. But we don't need to worry about that now. Honestly, it's one of the reasons I was content to keep my identity secret. I liked being just Jay. No distraction of my family. No politics. No company to consume all my time."

"But then you had to leave town for an emergency meeting at that company because of me."

"Not because of you. Because of Spaulding and what he did. He's responsible for his actions. Not you."

He caught her half smile. "I think I like you, JT Talon."

"And I'm thrilled to finally meet you, Alexandra Vargas."

Chapter Twenty-Six

Catoctin Mountain, Maryland
Present

Gemma was sound asleep in the portable crib when Alexandra tiptoed into the primary bedroom, which JT had insisted mother and daughter share. She was so tempted to pull her daughter into the king-sized bed so they could sleep snuggled together, but she knew she'd have regrets later. It had taken months to get her daughter to sleep well in her own bed.

Still, she wanted to hold her. Instead, she just studied the sweet, sleeping face. She would never tire of looking at this little human, who had filled the hole in her heart that first appeared when she called off the wedding.

She had never known it was possible to love someone with every fiber of her being, and yet also know that giving all of herself—and what was marriage other than going all in on a person?—would be a huge mistake.

If she'd married JT when she was thirty, she would have

been trading her dreams for his. All of her dreams. At the time, he'd even suggested she drop out of the PhD program.

Why finish her studies when she wouldn't work or continue her research once she moved to New York full time? She didn't need school. As JT Talon's wife, she'd be wealthy beyond imagination, and she'd be busy running charities like Lisa, supporting JT as he threw his hat in the ring and followed in his father's footsteps (again) and entered politics.

Alexandra had overheard JT and Joe discussing JT's plans to run for Congress in New York. He intended to announce his run in early January—ten days after the wedding. She'd realized in that moment that the reason he'd been so desperate to marry her on New Year's Eve was because he needed her installed as his wife for his campaign.

And he hadn't even mentioned it, let alone discussed it with her.

He played dumb when she confronted him. Claimed he was just considering a run. But he'd flinched in a way that told her he had decided. It was a done deal.

Would their whole marriage be a series of unilateral decisions?

Of course it would. It was his money. His house. His car. His business. His sperm.

And no, he wouldn't revisit the no-children decision he'd made. That was nonnegotiable.

She'd known then she'd always be a second-class citizen in her own marriage. No voting rights. Not when he brought everything to the union and all she brought was a womb he didn't want to use and a vagina he did.

She loved him. He loved her. She'd never doubted that.

But she would never truly have him, not when he wouldn't surrender any part of himself to her, but he expected her to surrender everything.

She readied herself for bed, again sleeping in a borrowed T-shirt, then slid under the covers. It was just after one a.m.

She'd had that nap earlier in JT's arms and had no idea if she'd be able to sleep now, but she was beyond exhausted. Emotionally drained. She had spent so much energy these last years holding on to her anger at JT because that anger was her shield against loving him.

She couldn't be angry at him now. Not when he'd protected her daughter. And being in his arms again had been the homecoming she hadn't known she needed.

She'd hurt him tonight, which was a little shocking because in all their years together, he'd been impervious.

A JT who reacted with hurt instead of cruelty was dangerous to her heart. But more important than her was Gemma. Gemma didn't have a father and could easily get attached to Uncle Tee. But he would never stick around for the long haul. Not when Gemma was everything he didn't want.

Her baby girl would be hurt when Uncle Tee disappeared from her life. Hopefully, this arrangement would only last a few days, and then she and her baby could both move on from the heartbreak of letting JT in, even if it had been just a crack.

It was officially Christmas Eve. In the morning, she'd figure out how to make the holiday special for Gemma, all while feeling thankful that at fifteen months, she was too young to remember this.

This would be a holiday to get through, not one to remember.

The boxes were much as JT remembered, overloaded with ornaments, lights, garlands. The decorations were generic, purchased by a decorator who'd specialized in store displays. Impersonal, but pretty.

It was better than nothing and could be a bridge between him and Alexandra. A piece of normalcy in a topsy-turvy world.

The last box in the stack threw him for another loop. It was full of unopened gifts. Not the store display variety—shiny boxes full of air. No. These were the gifts he and Alexandra had gotten for each other that last Christmas before the wedding that wasn't.

It had been a Christmas that wasn't too.

He wondered what gifts he'd gotten her. He had no clue. But then, with the exception of jewelry—which he'd loved buying for her, always imagining making love to her when she wore nothing but gemstones—he never picked out the gifts he gave her himself. He had assistants and personal shoppers who could do that.

He looked at the boxes and felt like an ass. No wonder his gifts had always meant nothing to her. They'd meant nothing to *him*.

Well, this year, they'd open these gifts and find out what his assistant had picked out for Lex eleven years ago. It was too bad there wouldn't be any toys for Gemma in the mix, but there were a few things he'd purchased for her the other night that he hadn't given her yet. What toddler didn't want a onesie and a tube of Butt Paste?

But then he remembered he did have a gift for Gemma. A rather large one. How would Lex react when he gave it to her?

But it wasn't Lex he wanted to please with presents, and what he had for her wasn't a toy to play with. He thought about Gemma's immediate attachment to the T-Rex stuffed animal and how she'd made a place for it in her world as a new best friend.

JT wanted to be part of Gemma's world. And he didn't think he'd be satisfied with being a distant, occasional uncle. Still, Gemma wasn't one he'd have to convince to accept him. It was the woman he'd spent the last sixteen years convincing he wanted nothing to do with being a parent.

Everything JT had ever believed he wanted had shifted in the time he spent with Gemma. He'd always known he wanted Alexandra. That was never in question. What he hadn't realized was that he could—and would—love any child of hers. Maybe it was because he could love anything that brought Lex the joy he'd failed to give her.

But Gemma didn't exist merely as an extension of her mother. No. She was a fully formed human who'd managed to steal his heart the first night they'd met, just like her mother had all those years ago.

Chapter Twenty-Seven

Gemma was up at six a.m., which wasn't bad considering all the major upheaval of these last few days. Still, Alexandra could have used another hour of sleep. Exhausted but grateful to have this morning at all, she carried her toddler down the stairs on her hip, not having the patience to let Gemma descend on her own when coffee waited at the bottom of the staircase.

She noticed red and green plastic boxes stacked in the corner of the living room as she passed through to the kitchen. They must be full of Christmas decorations JT had found in the attic.

She wondered if he'd had any luck with the computer hard drive, but didn't see an old desktop console among the boxes. But then, they didn't need a working PC, just a SATA —Serial Advance Technology Attachment—cord with USB. She'd been too tired to remember that last night when JT suggested searching the attic for an old PC. She had that kind of cord at home—she'd needed it to rescue files after a computer crash more than once. One could probably be ordered from Amazon, but they didn't have same-day delivery on the mountain, especially with the forecasted snowstorm, and since tomorrow was Christmas, most, if not all, businesses in this area would be closed.

In the kitchen, she put the coffee on to brew as Gemma demanded breakfast. Alexandra set her up in the clip-on travel high chair and gave her dry Cheerios to start with, then scrambled eggs for both of them.

JT entered the kitchen just as Alexandra was sitting down to eat, and she jumped up to make his breakfast. "Sorry! I thought you'd sleep in. I can make you eggs too."

He shooed her back into her seat. "Sit. Eat. I can cook for myself."

She dropped back into her chair, glad to eat while her food was warm. But still, she felt guilty. After all he'd done for her and Gemma, the least she could do was fry some eggs for him.

The coffee was starting to kick in by the time JT sat at the table. She took a sip from her mug and nodded to the boxes in the corner. "You were busy last night."

"Today, we'll set up a Christmas tree. We've got ornaments and lights."

"But no actual tree."

He waved toward the woods beyond the window. "You can't see the trees for the forest."

She laughed. "Aren't they a little big?"

"Smaller trees grow by the pond. I'm sure we can find one that will work."

"Do you have a tree stand?"

He nodded. "In one of the Christmas boxes."

"A saw or an axe?"

"Both are in the garage."

She felt a little fluttery as she looked out the window. "It's starting to snow again."

He grinned. "Then we should go sooner rather than later. The hill will get slippery with accumulation."

It sounded magical, but they had another problem. "Carrying Gemma uphill in snow won't be easy, and I don't have boots for her. Even if I did, she wouldn't have the energy."

"They had those baby backpack thingies at the store where I got the crib and all the other paraphernalia. I figured walks in the woods would be fun, so I got one."

That fluttery feeling intensified. A walk in the woods in the snow on Christmas Eve with her daughter and the love of her life for the purpose of cutting down a Christmas tree? It was the stuff her fantasies had been made of, once upon a time.

She leaned sideways and kissed him on the cheek. "That sounds amazing."

He kissed her back, but instead of going for the cheek, his lips brushed over hers. Then he tilted his head toward Gemma. "Your kid deserves a real Christmas."

"Holy shit." JT stared at his phone, his heart pounding as he reread the text.

"So, you know I'm not anti-swearing in any way," Lex said, "but hearing a toddler swear isn't cute to me, so I try to watch my words now that she's talking."

"Oh. Fu—I mean da—I mean…" He grimaced. "Gosh. Sorry." He glanced at the toddler and was glad to see she was absorbed with watching some kids' show on PBS that Lex had put on while they checked in with Raptor before heading out to cut down a tree.

"It's fine. Just a reminder. I make mistakes all the time. But I'm trying. So what did you read that's swear-worthy?"

"I sent a message to my contact at Raptor asking them to

look into Kendall's suicide, given that you were pulled over after leaving Kendall's house. I was wondering if Officer Corey Williams was part of the investigation into her death. He wasn't, but they found a different connection between Williams and Kendall. And you."

He held up the phone so Lex could see the screen. "Williams was one of the two Montgomery County police officers who responded to your 9-1-1 call when you lived with Kendall. The ones who didn't report that Russ Spaulding assaulted you right after being released from jail."

Alexandra's face paled. "Holy shit."

JT raised a brow and glanced toward Gemma.

She shrugged. "It's appropriate." She stared at the text on his phone. "It can't be a coincidence. But I honestly haven't thought about him in years. I don't remember his face at all. Pretty sure I never heard either man's first name, and I completely forgot their last names. I never spoke to them again after that day."

The text had included both names: Corey Williams and Tom Lindberg.

"I'll ask Raptor to look into Lindberg, find out where he is now. Now I have to wonder if it was Williams who made the evidence against Spaulding disappear. The prosecution was handled by Anne Arundel County, while Williams worked in Bethesda for Montgomery County. But as a cop, he could have gotten access to the evidence room. It was easier back then."

JT felt sick as he considered the possibility. Russ Spaulding had escaped prosecution because the evidence against him disappeared before the case went to trial. Drake had then pushed for JT to rehire the prick, claiming Alexandra had set the whole thing up to land herself a rich boyfriend.

If JT could have fired Edward Drake, he would have then, but no, the man remained a thorn in his side until seven and a half years later, when he was arrested for murdering JT's grandmother along with smuggling and money laundering.

The man had died in prison a few years ago.

JT had not felt an iota of grief, but now he wished Drake were alive to answer questions. He'd never connected Edward Drake to Russ Spaulding's attempt to drug Alexandra, but that was because the man's corruption hadn't been revealed until years later.

Drake had been livid at Spaulding's firing. Brent Forbes had escaped the same fate only because Drake protected him and there had been no proof Forbes knew what Spaulding had planned for Lex.

Forbes still worked for the company, but he'd never been promoted above midlevel. That he was bitter was an understatement. JT's response when HR passed on his grievances was always the same. *"He's welcome to quit."*

But he hadn't, and JT made certain he never moved up in the ranks. He didn't balk if a supervisor wanted to throw him a bonus, but those were capped.

JT had never trusted Forbes after the holiday party sixteen years ago, but his animosity had deepened when he learned Kendall hadn't broken up with him as she'd claimed. She'd secretly continued seeing him after he'd brought the man who'd intended to rape Alexandra into their shared apartment. Lex had been so busy with school and seeing JT when she could that she didn't find out until a weekend when she was supposed to take the train north to NYC, but JT had to cancel at the last minute due to a work emergency. She returned from the train station to find Kendall and Brent having sex on the couch.

JT had purchased the townhouse in Georgetown after that. Lex had stayed with Lee for several weeks until the house closed. She then lived in the townhouse for three years, moving out when she called off the wedding. She and Kendall had slowly rebuilt their friendship in those intervening years, and she'd moved from JT's place back to Kendall's.

After the breakup, JT had sold the townhouse, no longer able to bear being in the place where he and Lex had planned a future that wouldn't be. When he'd visited DC, he stayed with Lee at the Watergate.

Kendall and Brent had been on again/off again, and Lex had been forced to tolerate the man when she moved back in with Kendall.

After Drake and his father were arrested, JT took possession of the family's Maryland estate. Lisa had divorced his dad and moved to Florida to be with her sister. JT moved home, relocating to the DC area permanently. Lex had lived with him but continued paying rent on a room in Kendall's home, maintaining a place to land when JT inevitably destroyed the relationship that had become a shell of what it had once been.

"Was Kendall with Brent in the end?" he asked.

"No. They broke up for good about two years after we did."

"Were they still in touch?"

"I don't really know. Kendall and I…we had our own falling out. She and Brent threw a party—at our place—and Brent invited Russ."

"I'm so sorry Lex. That must have hurt."

"Almost as much as the night you ripped my heart out."

He swallowed. "I will never be able to convey how sorry I am. I hate myself for what I did to you." He took a deep breath. "And I know this sounds like an excuse, but I did it on purpose. I needed you to give up on me. For both our sakes."

She shrugged, and he understood. He'd gone too far that night. There was no excuse.

She cleared her throat. "She never really believed Russ or Brent were guilty of anything. She hated you for holding Brent back at work."

"I was protecting you."

She raised a brow. "Don't put it on me. Your vendetta against Brent outlasted any feelings you had for me by several years."

"That's not true. But I get your point. I know I was a prick, but I won't ever understand why Kendall believed Brent over you."

"For her, there was no proof. He fed her a lot of lies about you having it out for Russ, even before that night at the holiday party. She didn't trust *you* and believed you'd set him up."

"But you and I were dating."

"She and Brent were dating. She thought I was as blinded by you and your money as I thought she was blinded by her feelings for Brent." She gave him a piercing stare. "She wasn't the only person who accused me of being more interested in your money than you."

"I will regret that to my dying day."

She sighed. "So, what now? Williams is dead, but it can't be a coincidence that he was involved both then and now."

"It changes everything. We have a place to start looking now. This all connects back to what happened then. Kendall's death looks pretty damn suspicious now."

Lex nodded. "She'd always battled depression, but as far as I know, she'd never been suicidal. And from what Tanya said, she'd been doing really well. She'd found meds that worked for her and had been working with a great therapist for nearly three years. She had a new guy and was happy. Tanya was stunned when she got the call that Kendall killed herself."

"What did the boyfriend say?"

"He told Tanya that Kendall had broken up with him a month before she died. She cut him out completely."

"How did…how did she do it—supposedly?"

"Carbon monoxide poisoning. Car left running in an enclosed space. She was in the garage, but not in the car."

"The car being the Jetta?"

She nodded.

"Okay. I'll get Raptor to look into her death. Look for more connections with Williams."

"The problem with the Williams connection—it does give me motive for murder. Especially if he's behind the evidence against Russ being lost."

"You didn't recognize him, remember his name, or have contact with him in sixteen years."

"But he could have told me who he was."

"Did he?"

"No! Of course not."

"You didn't shoot him. That's what matters. And if Russ Spaulding is involved, he's just made a big mistake. Because he's back on my radar now, and he won't get away with fucking with you this time."

Lex's gaze flicked to Gemma, and he added, "Sorry."

"It's fine. The only person I hate more than Brent Forbes is Russ Spaulding."

He was damn glad he wasn't on that list.

"No one is going to get much done today. I'll call Raptor, and then it's time to go get a Christmas tree."

She smiled. "I want that. Desperately."

He put an arm around her waist and pulled her to him,

giving her a light hug. "Go get Gemma ready while I make the call."

She leaned her head against his chest. "Thank you."

He placed a finger beneath her chin and raised her face to meet his gaze. He smiled, then brushed his lips over hers. "Christmas begins now."

Chapter Twenty-Eight

Clinton, Maryland
Christmas Eve
Fourteen years ago

The last of the kids had received their presents, and the curtain closed. JT pulled Alexandra to his lap and kissed her neck. The white beard tickled her skin. "Christmas starts now." The words were a whisper against her skin.

She shivered with anticipation. This would be the third Christmas Eve in a row in which they skipped out on the dinner and returned to DC for their own celebration, but this year, they were returning to JT's newly purchased townhouse in Georgetown. Alexandra had spent the last few days moving into the three-story, four-bedroom home.

The first time she and JT had made love, it was Christmas Eve. This year, it would be the first time they made love in a home they shared. The start of this next phase of their lives together.

She didn't think she'd ever been so happy in her life.

It was weird to think that she had Russ and Brent to thank for her current happiness. First because she'd never have met JT if it wasn't for them and certainly wouldn't have propositioned him that first night if not for what Russ tried to do.

And now, she had made the decision to move in with him because six weeks ago, she'd discovered Kendall was still dating Brent. He'd had free access to their apartment when Alexandra wasn't home.

It explained why things had been moved in her room. Files deleted from her computer. The prick had a vendetta against Alexandra, and Kendall had looked the other way.

She shook off the painful thought as she slid from Santa's lap and adjusted her tunic. "I've been very naughty again this year."

JT grinned as he stood. He cupped her ass. "I know. If we hurry home, we can be naughty together one more time before midnight."

"Only *one* more time?"

"I intend to take my time now that we have plenty of it."

JT had been begging her to move in with him since about six months into the relationship, but she'd resisted because she didn't want to be dependent on him financially. But she also didn't want Brent and Russ to have access to her living quarters ever again, and so she'd finally agreed.

The townhouse had closed three days ago. JT had driven down to DC to sign the papers, but then he'd had to return to New York because of another crisis caused by Drake. She'd busted her butt to get moved in and unpacked and accept furniture deliveries. The only room that was completely set up was their bedroom, but the living room at least had a couch and TV.

If they were lucky, they'd have a dining room table in a week. A finish carpenter had been hired to build custom shelving for the living room and Alexandra's home office after the New Year.

JT had returned late this morning, and the first thing they did was go out and buy a Christmas tree, which was now set up but not decorated in the living room. They'd been on a tight schedule to make it to the fundraiser to play Santa and elf once again.

Now she took JT's hand, and they slipped out the back so they could remove their costumes. They'd agreed to stay for one drink to appease Joe and Lisa, and then they would leave.

Alexandra helped JT remove the beard, not wanting to spend a minute more than she had to mingling without him. She and Senator Talon had gotten off to a bumpy start, but after two years, the tension between them had eased. She was genuinely fond of him when they weren't at political or charitable events, where he viewed her as a prop—an extension of JT.

At private family gatherings, he relaxed and was genuine. He was warm to his wife and sons. She got along well with Lisa, who'd told her this evening how excited she was that she and JT were finally moving in together.

But by far Alexandra's favorite member of the Talon family—outside of JT—wasn't a Talon at all. Lee Scott was the brother she'd always wanted. They were just a year apart in age, and he had a wicked, dry sense of humor. She'd tried to fix him up with Kendall—before she knew she was secretly still seeing Brent—and had been so disappointed when it didn't work out.

He was a fine man who would make some woman very lucky one of these days.

In the last two years, he'd started his own consulting business providing computer and cell phone security. In DC, businesses and individuals who needed tight security from hackers were in abundance, and a few months ago, he'd purchased a three-bedroom condo at the Watergate.

The night Alexandra arrived home to find her roommate screwing her enemy on the couch, JT had been sent on a last-minute business trip to Brazil. Alexandra had called Lee, who arrived thirty minutes later to help her pack up and vacate the apartment she'd lived in for four years.

She'd moved into the guest bedroom in Lee's condo until JT signed the papers and she was given keys to the townhouse.

Lee had her eternal gratitude. She couldn't believe how lucky she was to have met two amazing men the night she would need them most.

Fate was looking out for her.

She'd donned a designer dress for the cocktail reception, having accepted in the months after she and JT started dating that dressing the part of a politically ambitious millionaire's girlfriend was nonnegotiable. So while she wouldn't let him subsidize her living expenses when she lived with Kendall, she did let him buy her clothes.

She now had quite a wardrobe and an even bigger jewelry collection. JT loved buying her jewels. That first Christmas, he'd given her an emerald necklace and earrings that had to cost more than her car.

She hadn't been able to afford a gift for him that year, so she'd baked him a pie. She'd made the crust from scratch and the pumpkin puree had been homemade, but still, it was a small gift.

He'd loved the pie and assured her it was a perfect present for a man who could buy himself whatever he wanted, the one exception being her time and attention.

And so that was how their gift giving continued. He bought her jewelry, and she gave him treats made with love.

The first item she'd baked in the townhouse had been the chocolate cheesecake she would give him tonight.

And then she'd go down on him in front of the Christmas tree, wearing nothing but whatever jewelry he planned to give her tonight.

She smiled as she fixed his tie, making sure it had the perfect dimple. "Are you sure we have to mingle before we can go home?"

"God, I love the sound of *home* coming from your lips. But yeah. One drink."

She huffed out a sigh. "I suppose it's a good cause." The kids had been adorable tonight, and this time, the only tears had been happy ones. One nine-year-old got an adorable rescue puppy and would receive lessons on how to train it because they were finally moving into an apartment that allowed pets.

There wasn't a dry eye in the house when the boy met his new dog and immediately got a face bath from the puppy.

"You love this event," JT said.

"I love the kids. I wish they could all have puppies."

"I do too. But that was a special case. The bicycles were fun this year."

Two kids had gotten bicycles, a gift that, like a puppy, was hard to disguise so they couldn't wait for morning. There was something to be said for getting to watch the kids open their gifts—which wasn't something they usually got to do.

Alexandra looked forward to when she'd have her own kids and could savor the moment of watching them open gifts on Christmas.

Chapter Twenty-Nine

Catoctin Mountain, Maryland
Present

"Does the Christmas Eve event still happen? Do you still play Santa? Except, obviously, for tonight, I mean?" Lex asked as they set out on the path to pick out a tree, Gemma secure on JT's back and babbling excitedly as she grasped his hair like she was a rat trying to control a French chef.

Her breath puffed out in white wisps, making him hope Gemma was as snug as she'd looked in the hooded fleece footed jumpsuit he'd bought her. She wouldn't work up a sweat hiking uphill like he and Lex would.

"The party still happens, and I still buy all the presents, but they hire a Santa, and Lisa stopped running the event when she moved to Florida. Isabel—Senator Ravissant's wife—took over some aspects of the organizing when she worked for Talon & Drake, but she's pregnant now and busy with running a shelter for runaway teens, so I believe she's passed the torch to another politician's family."

"I met Isabel at Lee's wedding."

"Right. Sorry. I forgot the wedding was at the Ravissant estate. You were supposed to spend Christmas with them at Lee's too."

"And you said you were coming here for the holiday to escape being around kids." She reached up and tugged on Gemma's foot, which was kicking him in the shoulder. "Joke's on you."

He laughed. "I think this is going to be the best Christmas I've had in years."

He meant it. The last good Christmas he'd had was a year before the wedding that wasn't. There was nothing better than Christmas with Lex, except, possibly, Christmas with her and Gemma.

Snowflakes drifted lazily around them—this was the front edge of the storm that wouldn't hit with force until late afternoon. After getting a tree, JT would chop wood to ensure they'd have plenty of heat should the power go out.

Right now, he just enjoyed the fresh air, the weight of Gemma on his back, and having Lex by his side as they headed toward the patch of small evergreens he and his dad had planted several years ago, just for this purpose of someday having Christmas trees to harvest.

He still had a lot of anger at his father for the things he'd done, but one thing he'd worked on the last few years was remembering and honoring the man he'd loved. He and Lee had tackled that journey together.

Joseph Talon Sr. had many obvious faults and had made some horrific choices, but he also had been a good father and stepfather. Better than Lee's actual dad.

When Lee was in his teens, his relationship with his long-divorced birth parents had turned toxic, and he'd moved in with JT, who'd only been twenty-one at the time. Joe had stepped up as well, being the father figure sixteen-year-old Lee had needed.

Joe had loved both his sons, but he'd lost his way in politics, caring more about winning than how he did it.

But on days like today, a hike to harvest a tree JT had planted with his dad was a good way to honor the father he'd loved.

Lex began singing "Walking in a Winter Wonderland," and JT joined in, much to Gemma's delight as she made nonsense sounds that he assumed was her providing her own lyrics.

They reached the planted grove by the pond. JT waved his arm toward the trees that ranged from six to fourteen feet tall. "Take your pick. I can bring the snowmobile up to drag it down if it's big. Ceiling height at the peak in the living room is sixteen feet, but we'd have to trim to fit the stand if you want anything twelve feet or taller."

They walked through the grove, discussing the pros and cons of each, with Gemma weighing in based on criteria JT couldn't begin to understand.

The girl had an opinion, and it was fricking adorable.

In the end, Gemma chose a skinny nine-footer that he'd have no trouble dragging down the hillside. It had gaps in areas and was rather scraggly on one side, but it was the tree Gemma wanted, and that made it perfect.

He lowered the pack to the ground and Lex plucked her daughter from the seat. The girl didn't have snow boots. Her only protection from the cold was fleece footies. "You can head back while I cut it down. I know she'll get restless not being able to walk around."

"And miss watching you harvest a Christmas tree just for us? No way."

She bounced the girl on her hip and sang Christmas

songs to Gemma while JT stretched out on the ground and sawed at the trunk.

He hummed along, the tune providing rhythm to the sawing as wet snow soaked into his coat. The smell of mud and pine and cut wood filled his nostrils as bells on Bobtail rang as the horse dashed through the snow.

Gemma babbled in tune, and her giggle filled the copse of trees as the snowfall picked up momentum.

JT's heart swelled three sizes.

This was a Christmas unlike any other. He couldn't remember feeling such simple joy.

The power flickered while they decorated the tree, but it didn't go out. Alexandra knew JT had a generator if needed, but they'd only use it sparingly, as power could go out for days. Plus, the noise would be an insult to the quiet snowfall that made everything beautiful.

She'd thawed a small prime rib roast that she'd found in the chest freezer, and if she had to, she could cook it in a Dutch oven on the woodstove griddle tomorrow for Christmas dinner.

She almost hoped that would happen because there was nothing better than an improvised meal, and it would be that much sweeter for being Christmas. A gift for JT as a thank-you for his help. Cooking had always been her escape over the years, and the only real gift she could give to her millionaire boyfriend. Food made with love.

As they decorated the tree, there was a very simple—made with canned peaches—cobbler in the oven that made the kitchen and living room smell heavenly.

JT handed her a glass of white wine. Christmas music

played through the in-house speaker system. She said, "Thanks," and clinked glasses with him.

Gemma ever so carefully placed a plastic ornament ball on the lowest branches of the tree. "See, Mommy? Good?"

She smiled at her daughter and clapped her hands. "So good, baby!"

"She's amazing," JT whispered.

"Of course she is."

He laughed. "I never had any doubt."

She looked at her daughter and felt her heart ready to burst. After all the fear and horror, she had this moment to cherish. Having Gemma had been the best decision she'd ever made.

Chapter Thirty

Washington, DC
Christmas Eve
Sixteen years ago

The suite door closed behind JT. He leaned back against it as he watched Lex move deeper into the room.

He no longer had any doubt that Alexandra Vargas would bring him to his knees. She'd shown up at the event not because she wanted to ingratiate herself with his dad. Not because she wanted something from the CEO of Talon & Drake.

No. She wanted Jay and had decided to pay the price he'd set: her time and her name.

She turned to face him and said, "What does that grin mean?"

"You decided to buy the cow."

She smirked and shook her head. "I've never met a man who was so willing to call himself a cow."

"Pumpkin. Cow. I don't care what you call me, as long as

you call me." He took a step toward her.

"You were pretty confident I'd give in."

"I was. But I like that you did it on your terms instead of caving because you wanted sex in the moment." That was true. He'd fully expected to learn her name tonight. But he figured it would happen here, in bed.

"Getting the text from your stepmom about the Santa costume was too tempting to resist."

"So that's how it happened. I guess she didn't see my message with my new cell number. Fortuitous."

"You might want to message her again. If she keeps texting me thinking I'm you, it could get awkward."

"You can tell her. Or just keep pretending to be me."

"I feel like this relationship is too new for me to be fielding messages from your stepmother."

He grinned again. "So this is a relationship now?"

"No. It's a…holiday fling."

He'd slowly moved toward her, and now they were nearly chest to chest. He stroked her chin, running his thumb along her jaw. "Call it what you want. I figure I've got until January first to convince you this is more than a fling."

"What makes you so certain you'll still be interested in me tomorrow, let alone in a week? Maybe you only want me because I'm a challenge."

It was a good question. She was the first woman he'd dated who more than made it clear she wanted to use him for sex and walk away. That absolutely had secured his attention.

Before that, she had been the fierce woman who'd invited him to her hotel room to assert her bodily autonomy. But he knew that deep down, she simply hadn't wanted to be alone. She'd chosen him for that. And she'd let him comfort her. Without sex.

Tonight, however, the last thing he wanted was to remind her of the night they met, because this relationship, if it were to go anywhere, would be based on this good, wild energy they generated. The trauma that followed their first meeting would only be a footnote.

"You had me when you challenged me at the bar, assuming I thought you didn't work for Talon & Drake because you're blonde." He leaned in and ran his lips over her neck. "When you questioned whether or not I had a penis."

She tilted her head back as he kissed her neck. "Am I finally going to learn the truth?"

He wrapped an arm around her waist and pulled her tight against him. "You tell me." He was hard against her belly, his cock thickening by the second.

"I want to taste you."

His mouth found hers, and he kissed her deeply. Her arms circled his neck, and her fingers threaded through his hair.

She let out a soft moan as he explored her mouth with his tongue and stroked her ass, holding her firm against his erection.

He wanted to take her straight into the bedroom and bury himself inside her. It took a great deal of restraint to end the kiss. He raised his head, and her mouth moved to his neck. "Don't stop," she whispered as she kissed him, sliding her tongue across his collarbone.

"We need to order dinner before the kitchen closes. Santa needs to eat before his big night."

She stopped kissing him and muttered against his neck. "Crap. I suppose it's important to keep up your strength."

"Even elves need to eat."

"So, we order the food, then sex?" she asked hopefully.

"I'm not rushing the first time we're together because room service might interrupt."

"Promise you'll put out after the food arrives?"

"You make it sound like you only want me for my body."

"I said what I said."

He kissed her nose. "Sweetheart, tonight I'm going to give you everything you want and a few things you didn't even know you needed."

She laughed.

Damn, she was beautiful.

He placed their dinner order and was told they had a forty-five-minute wait.

To avoid temptation, he turned on the TV. TBS was showing *A Christmas Story* on repeat. He set the remote on the coffee table and settled back. "One of the greatest movies ever made. I, um, hope you like it. It *could* be a deal-breaker."

She laughed. "No worries. I love this one. I even remember seeing it in the theater. I was four, so my memories are vague. But it was still fun."

"I was ten—a year older than Ralphie. I had a BB gun that my new little stepbrother coveted."

"Aww. I bet you two were adorable together."

"Eh, he was already taller than me."

She snorted. "You must be joking."

"Yeah, but he *was* always tall, like his dad. He didn't pass me until he was fourteen or fifteen though."

Ralphie was still on his quest for the ultimate Red Ryder when the food was delivered. JT tipped the server, giving a hefty cash bonus as a thanks for working on Christmas Eve, then closed and locked the door.

"So, eat first?" he asked as he crossed to the laden table.

Lex gathered his dress shirt in a fist, then turned toward the bedroom, pulling him behind her.

Chapter Thirty-One

Catoctin Mountain, Maryland
Present

While Lex was upstairs putting Gemma to bed, JT pulled out the wrapped gifts from eleven years ago and placed them under the tree. He hoped it wasn't a mistake, reminding her of that Christmas, but if they were going to have a future, this was one of the things they needed to process.

More than anything, he wanted another shot at a future with Alexandra Vargas.

He'd never loved anyone more than Alexandra, and he'd never hurt anyone more either.

He hated himself for how rotten he'd been to the one person who gave his heart a reason to beat. That they were here together now was a Christmas gift he never dared to imagine, but still, he ached at the fear and danger that had made this moment possible.

Presents arranged, he picked up the remote and turned

on the TV. He let out a soft laugh at seeing *A Christmas Story* was on. This year's twenty-four-hour marathon had begun.

Ralphie's old man was weaving a tapestry of obscenities when he heard Lex's footsteps on the stairs. A rush of joy shot through him, just like it had that first Christmas Eve, when nothing between them was promised and he'd only just learned her name.

She entered the living room, and just like then, he caught his breath when he looked at her. Her face at forty-one was fuller, with faint lines that only added to her beauty.

The first time he saw her remained imprinted on his brain. The beautiful blonde sitting alone at a bar. Mad as hell. But it wasn't until he spoke to her that he was hooked. Looks were one thing. Sharp wit and sharper mind another. Alexandra had snared him before she'd invited him to her hotel room for a pumpkin muffin.

He rose from the couch as she entered the room. She startled at seeing the presents beneath the tree. "What? How…?"

"They were in the attic. Stored with the decorations."

"From that last Christmas. I forgot we never opened them."

"Same."

"I—I don't even remember what I got you that year. I know I didn't have time to bake, not with the wedding coming up. So at least we can be assured there won't be an extremely moldy dessert."

"No signs of rodents indulging either. But then, they were stored in a plastic box with a tight seal. To the best of my knowledge, the box wasn't opened in the eleven years since I packed them up."

"You packed them?"

"Yeah. It's how I spent New Year's Day."

"The day after what was supposed to be our wedding."

"Yeah. It sucked."

She took a step toward him. "I spent New Year's Day crying in bed. It was one of the worst days of my life."

He gave a sharp nod even as he felt his eyes burn.

"I didn't call it off because I didn't love you," she said. "I loved you deeply. You were everything I wanted."

He heard the past tense and felt the sting of it, but he had no one to blame for that but himself. "But you didn't love me enough."

She shook her head. "That's not it either. I called it off because I didn't *have* you. All of you. There was a massive power imbalance between us, and you had bigger priorities than our relationship. You kept it a secret that you intended to run for Congress and were starting your campaign within weeks. You didn't want to marry me for *me*. You wanted a campaign prop, just like Lisa was for your dad."

"You were never a *prop*. I loved you. I never stopped."

"Then why didn't you *tell* me? Why did I have to overhear your dad talking to you about it in this very room?"

He ran his hand over his face. "We didn't know the incumbent wasn't going to run until early December. I was still exploring options and wasn't a hundred percent decided. I knew you weren't happy about moving to New York, and I didn't want to freak you out before the wedding."

"So you left me out of the decision entirely. As your *wife*, I should have been part of it. Not an afterthought. Because hell yeah, I'd have had a problem with you making such a huge unilateral decision that would affect both of us right when we were finally moving in together full time. I should have had a say. But that was the power imbalance. Your money, your decisions."

She turned and faced the tree with the pile of presents, her spine stiff. "You'd already made it known you didn't want children. I had accepted that. I thought *you* would be enough. But then I realized I didn't really have you at all. Not if you shut me out of decisions like that. And it was only a matter of time before I would be like your stepmom. Only important when it was time to run charitable events. How long before you started bringing mistresses here just like your dad? Because if you didn't love me enough to give me a say in one of the biggest decisions of your life right before we married, it didn't feel like our marriage vows would be as sacred to you as they were to me."

His throat had gone dry. He'd known some of this, of course, but he'd never understood the depth of the damage he'd caused in keeping the potential campaign a secret. He cleared his throat and tried to talk around the tears that were clogged there. His words came out as a whisper. "I'm sorry. So deeply sorry."

A tear tracked down her cheek, and she swiped it away. "This is the first time you've ever apologized for that. At the time, you tried to convince me I was blowing everything out of proportion."

"I was a dumb fuck."

"You broke my heart. I still loved you, but I couldn't marry you. Not then."

Then they'd slowly slid back into a relationship when he chose not to run after all. But he'd never apologized. Never owned how he'd sabotaged their relationship. He'd finally been ready to step up and reconcile if she'd have him and had planned to propose again after Joe announced his candidacy for president.

But then his dad was arrested, and he fell apart. He couldn't turn to Lee, who was processing his own pain over what Joe did. Lee had Erica, and they both had their own trauma over what happened in the end.

So JT turned to Alexandra. She supported him. Loved him. She was the only thing holding him together. He moved to Maryland, and they finally, after all their years together, lived in the same area full time. Lex essentially moved in with him, but still officially shared an apartment with Kendall.

But he was angry and bitter over the pain of the canceled wedding. He'd treated her horribly instead of loving her like he should.

"I'm sorry. For what I did and didn't do. And for not owning my shit and apologizing then. For not loving you like you deserved when you were giving me everything. I hate myself for how I treated you. I was so awful, but you stayed by my side, and so in my head, I convinced myself you were only in it for the money. I'm so desperately sorry. You're the only woman I've ever loved. The only woman I ever will."

She took another step toward him. "Thank you. I spent a lot of years wishing we could figure out how to go back to who we were in the beginning. We were great together until the last months before the wedding."

"You knocked me off my feet." He glanced at the TV, still showing the movie they'd watched together that night. "Christmas Eve sixteen years ago was one of the best nights of my life. It was the night I learned your name."

She took the last step that separated them. "And I finally got to see you naked."

"You always wanted me for my body, not my money."

"Can you blame me? You have an excellent body."

"I've aged a bit."

"So have I. Plus I have stretch marks, and breastfeeding has made parts that were once firm quite soft."

"I like soft."

"That's *not* what she said."

He laughed.

She slid her arms around his waist and pulled him close for a hug he desperately needed. "Hold me?" she asked.

"Always." His arms surrounded her, and he held her tight against his chest. "I'm so sorry," he whispered again. "I've done a lot of work in the last few years, but I know I have more work to do."

The embrace continued, and JT felt whole for the first time in forever. If he could regain her friendship, it would be more than he deserved.

Lex tucked her forehead against his chest and let out a slow breath. "I needed this. The apology. The hug." She looked up and met his gaze. "And I'm sorry that I didn't look for a solution eleven years ago that included marrying you on New Year's Eve. I couldn't figure out another way to show you how deeply being left out of major choices hurt me. So I had to use the only power I had and make a choice without you."

He stroked her cheek. "Truth is, if we'd married, I *would* have gotten worse. All I had to go on was an awful example of marriage and politics. And Lisa was my dad's third wife. He was a lousy husband." He cocked his head. "I've learned a ton from Lee and Erica. And Curt and Mara. They were some of the first relationships based on equality I've ever had front-row seats to witness."

She leaned back in the circle of his arms. "Outside of Lee and Curt, you never had many friends."

"A product of never fraternizing with employees. I've only ever worked at one company, and it was the one place where I couldn't be anyone's friend. It complicated everything when I needed to make tough choices and got even worse after what Spaulding did."

On the TV, Ralphie was decoding a message from Little Orphan Annie.

"Is that why you're selling? Because you're tired of being on the outside?"

He tilted his head toward the couch. "Can we sit?"

She nodded.

He sat and was surprised when she chose to sit right next

to him. Not touching, but within easy reach when there was plenty of couch to go around.

He lifted the bottle of red wine, silently offering her another glass. She nodded, and he poured for both of them. He raised his glass and twirled it, staring into the swirl of red. "That might be part of it. But mostly I'm tired of living other people's plans for my life. Or trying to redeem people's opinion of me."

Her eyes widened. "But you love running T&D."

"I haven't loved it in years. Not since we learned what Drake and Dad were doing. I felt like I had to make things better. Prove that the company was good. That *I* was good. Not my father's son and not Drake's puppet."

"No one *ever* thought you were Drake's puppet."

"Sure they did. I was twenty-five when I took over. No one believed I was really running the company. I spent twelve years having to circumvent that asshole, working twice as hard because I had to work around him, not with him. Anyway. I'm done. I'm proud of the work I did. I'm selling for twice as much as it was worth when I started. It'll be someone else's headache."

"What are you going to do after the sale?"

"I've got six months of transition—they wanted two years, but I refuse to be on the hook that long. After that… who knows? Maybe I'll travel." He glanced around the living room. "Or move here and be a hermit. I've always wanted to be a hermit."

"Who's buying the company?"

"A competitor. Moss & Delano Architects and Engineers."

Lex was about to take a sip of wine, but she jolted. Red liquid sloshed from the glass and splattered over her and the sofa. "Shit! Sorry!"

"I don't care about the couch, what's wrong?"

She grabbed a napkin from the coffee table and patted at

the red drops on the cushion. "Russ Spaulding works for them."

"Not possible. I *checked*."

She shrugged. "That's what Kendall said the last time we talked."

"His direct employment is a deal-breaker." Spaulding had never paid a legal price for his attempt to assault Lex, but JT always made certain the man wasn't working for anyone he did business with.

"They hid it, then. He must be a contractor."

"Motherfucker." This workaround had been used more than once over the years, but there wasn't much JT could do after the subcontracts were signed.

"Another thing to have Raptor look into. I don't like that his name is crossing paths with Kendall's again. All this must be connected. It feels like, I don't know, Drake's ghost or something." She leaned toward him, her elbow on the couch cushion, her fist pressed just below her ear, supporting her head. "Drake hit on me, you know. One of the company parties—not a Christmas one—he said something pretty disgusting about if I ever got sick of you as my sugar daddy, he'd show me what a real man had to offer."

"What the *fuck*?"

"I kneed him in the balls and told him if he ever came near me again, I'd see to it that both you and Senator Talon knew he'd hit on me, and I'd make sure a call was put out through HR for women employees to come forward if he'd ever been inappropriate with them."

"Shit. Why didn't you tell me this then?"

"At the time, you were having enough problems with him, and a game of he said/she said with me wouldn't have made anything easier. Then later, when he was arrested…well, you were having a hard enough time. Confessing I hadn't told you something that you might have used to oust him sooner felt like a bad idea."

He heard what she didn't say. He might have blamed her instead of being horrified for her.

"I'm sorry you went through that and felt you couldn't share it with me."

"We were both bad at communication then."

"Fair."

She sighed. "I wonder if Officer Williams had a connection to Drake?"

"A solid question for Raptor's investigators."

She faced the TV. "But one that will wait until after Christmas. Tonight, let's see if Ralphie gets his BB gun." She surprised him by leaning into him, resting her head on his shoulder as she sipped her wine and watched the movie.

JT breathed deeply, unsure if this was the best Christmas Eve of his life, or second best.

Chapter Thirty-Two

Sitting snuggled next to JT watching *A Christmas Story* while her daughter slept upstairs was unimaginably sweet. Another fantasy she'd never dared to have.

She'd seen the movie so many times, she no longer laughed out loud, but she did smile at the familiar scenes that were like old friends. She understood the parents far better now than she had as a kid.

The Santa scene always made her think of JT in the Santa suit. JT's Santa was so very different, but he was a man not naturally comfortable around kids, and so the role had been a trial for him. But he'd done it because he loved giving gifts.

She'd forgotten that about him. His genuine joy at being able to bring light into the lives of children in need. She'd pretty much fallen in love with him the first night she'd watched him struggle in the role of Santa.

They watched in comfortable silence. The movie ended with a happy Ralphie, then started again. Alexandra reached for the remote and hit the Mute button.

"Should we look for something else to watch?" he asked.

She shook her head. "I don't want to watch TV."

"What do you want?"

"The same thing I wanted the first Christmas Eve we spent together."

He smiled. "My body."

"Can you blame me?"

"Nah. I'm pretty exceptional. But you know there's a price."

"How much you charging for milk these days?"

"Same thing I've always wanted from you. Your time. Your attention."

"I'm sort of trapped here, so I feel like you should up your ask."

He stroked her cheek. "I don't want more than you're comfortable giving."

She ran her fingers over his jaw, which had two days' worth of stubble. His beard was now peppered with gray, making him more handsome than ever.

JT aged like fine wine. He got better and better as time marched forward.

She ran a hand down his chest, pausing for a heartbeat at his belt, before moving down and feeling his erection through his jeans.

His body was so familiar and yet new again, given the years that had passed. She remembered that first Christmas Eve, when she'd practically dragged him into the bedroom, then stripped him down and taken him in her mouth. Her first touch. First taste. First time making love with the man who was destined to ruin her for other men.

Now here she was, sixteen years later, and still ruined.

Still desperate to see him. Touch him. Taste him.

Maybe even more so, because she knew exactly how he'd make her come apart. Beg for him. Come for him.

JT's hand covered hers as she stroked him through thick layers of denim. "Lex. God, how I've missed you."

She kissed him. Not with frantic fire and need, but with soft, languid hunger. This man had stirred this in her from the first night they met. It hadn't diminished with time or heartache.

He tasted of wine and peach cobbler and JT.

His hands slid beneath her shirt and cupped her breasts, and oh, how she'd missed that too. Her body had changed since the last time they did this, and Gemma had only been weaned for a few months. Her nipples were tougher than they'd been, and she wondered if his touch would trigger the sharp jolt of letdown.

She stiffened, and his hand stilled. "I'm sorry. I should have asked. Can I touch your breasts? Are you still nursing Gemma?"

She placed a hand over his on her breast and squeezed, letting him know what she liked. "You can touch. I'm not nursing anymore, but it's only been a few months, and sometimes I still have milk secretion. Letdown can be painful, so let's go with touching but no sucking."

His lips found her neck, and he kissed her as his hands explored the changes in her breasts. Softer, fuller, tougher. Did he find her as sexy as he used to? "What about you? Anything off-limits?"

"I'd say breaking my heart, but honestly, I'll take that too if it means I can be with you again."

His words struck home.

"Same," she whispered.

She was doing this. She was going to make love with the only man she'd ever loved, who was also the only man who'd ever broken her heart. Twice.

She went for his belt buckle. There was no point in taking

it slow. Not when she had years' worth of sexual frustration to make up for.

She opened his belt and then unbuttoned his fly. Her hand slid beneath the elastic band of his boxer briefs, and she had her very favorite cock in her hand once again. She stroked his hard length, and he groaned. She slowly scooted down his body until she was on the floor between his thighs as he sat on the couch. His beautiful penis was before her, and just as she'd done for the first time on Christmas Eve so many years ago, she swirled her tongue around the tip, tasting his precum as she teased him with light licks.

"Lex."

She remembered how he hadn't let her touch him the first night they were together. He'd given her his mouth and hands, but not the body part she wanted the most.

"I've missed you," she said to his penis.

He laughed. "Was that for me or my dick?"

She looked up at him and smiled. "You're a smart man. You know I've always only wanted you for one thing." She wrapped her hand around him and stroked the shaft. "And it was never your money."

He laughed again. And lord, she remembered how much fun they'd had. Sex with him had always been hot and passionate but also fun and even silly. They'd laughed so much in bed. Or on the table, counter, couch, in the shower, against a tree…

"Show me how much you missed me, and you'll get a demonstration of exactly how much I missed you."

"Challenge accepted." She took him into her mouth, and, as promised, his cock thickened even more. He was hot and hard against the roof of her mouth, and she sucked, then shifted so she could take him deeper into her throat.

He grew impossibly hard in her hand and mouth. She

sucked and stroked and slid her tongue down the shaft, then took him in her mouth again.

She loved this, being on her knees before him, his cock in her mouth, his hands in her hair. Giving him the same pleasure he'd given her more times than she could count.

They were both dressed. Only his cock was exposed.

She had him just how she wanted him.

Going down on him made her so hot. In more ways than one. She released him and pulled off the flannel shirt she'd borrowed from him. He found the front hook of her bra and freed her breasts.

"Fuck, you're beautiful."

She gazed up at him. "So are you. Lose the shirt."

He did as she instructed, and her gaze feasted on his muscular chest. Perhaps a little softer than he'd been years ago and lightly sprinkled with gray chest hair.

So beautiful.

She sucked on his cock and thoroughly enjoyed this unexpected reunion.

"Lex. I want inside you. Please."

She sucked on the tip, then popped off to say, "You are inside me."

"I want to fuck you. To feel your pussy clench tight around me as I make you come."

Well, when he put it that way, she wanted it too.

"I can't get you pregnant. And I haven't been with anyone in two years. My last round of tests were all negative."

She wasn't likely to get pregnant even if he didn't have a vasectomy, but that was a conversation for another time. "They test pregnant women for everything. All mine were negative."

She rose and pulled down her pants and panties, then

straddled him. He shifted his cock so he probed her opening and let out a low growl when he realized how wet she was.

She lowered herself onto him and groaned as he filled her. The sensation was an exquisite homecoming.

He moved his hips, his hands on her waist as he pulled her down in time with his thrusts.

Her breasts bounced in his face, and he licked her nipples—but didn't suck—and it was exactly what she wanted. Needed.

They moved in unison, starting slow as her body remembered his. The feel of him inside her was an intense pleasure she didn't know how she'd lived without for so long. The sensations built, and JT increased the tempo.

So good. Possibly better than ever before?

JT's thumb slid between their bodies and found her clit, and then he was stroking her with each bouncing thrust. There was no holding back or going slow at that point. His touch inside and out had pleasure coiling tight. It built impossibly until, with one deep thrust, she broke. His thumb continued stroking, his cock thrust again and again. She let out a groan as she climaxed, clenching tight on him as she came apart, the feeling more intense than she remembered.

She found his mouth and kissed him as she continued to clench around him. The kiss was deep and carnal.

This thing with JT, it had always been inevitable. Her love for him had never actually died. It had merely gone dormant.

She raised her head and looked deep into his beautiful brown eyes. Her heart pounded as she faced the fact that making love with JT had pulled her feelings from the depths of slumber. Awake now, her heart thrummed with emotion.

This JT was so much like the man she'd first fallen in love with. Before he began walling off sections of his heart. This man was everything she'd wanted since she was a twenty-five-year-old graduate student who'd played elf to his Santa.

She held her breath to keep from saying words that might destroy the moment. She would enjoy this time with the man she loved to the bottom of her soul.

Later, she'd figure out how she was going to recover from the coming heartbreak, because no way would she be with a man who couldn't love her daughter.

Chapter Thirty-Three

How many times had JT dreamed of this moment? The answer was higher than the number of days that had passed since the holiday party in which he destroyed the only good thing in his life.

Now, against all odds, Lex was in his arms. Spent. His cock still buried inside her. But it wasn't just sex with Lex. It never had been. From their first kiss, there had been so much more between them.

That initial kiss had been inspired by her need to claim autonomy and ownership of her body, and he'd walked a tightrope in giving her power while he made it clear he wasn't interested in being used and forgotten. He wanted more.

He'd always wanted more.

More, he'd discovered later, than he was willing to give her.

But those days were behind him. Now, he would give her everything. No holding back.

"I love you, Alexandra. Lex. Muffin. Elf… My former fiancée. My partner. My ex-girlfriend. My support. My heart. Through all the roles you've played in my life, I have loved you. Even when I was a beast and didn't deserve you. I have and always will love you, and nothing you say or do now can change that."

She sucked in a sharp breath but said nothing. He knew it was too much to hope she'd return the words. He didn't deserve it, and she had plenty of reason to be cautious.

He'd set fire to every bridge she'd built between them.

"You don't need to say anything. I just needed to let you know how I feel. I know I don't deserve another chance. You gave me too many, and I squandered every one."

She shifted so he was no longer inside her, but remained straddling his lap. She pressed her forehead to his. "It's not just me anymore, JT."

He inhaled deeply, taking in Lex's scent. "I love Gemma. More than I ever imagined I could love a child."

"Loving her isn't enough. You love your niece, don't you?"

"Sure. But Gemma is different. Because she's yours." He knew his mistake the moment he said the word.

She slid from his lap, grabbing the throw blanket and covering her naked body. He took the opportunity to tuck himself back in his pants and button the fly, leaving only the top button undone. He'd rather be stripping completely, but this conversation would go better clothed.

Lex must've done the same calculation because she set aside the blanket and pulled the flannel shirt back on. She slipped on her panties, then settled on the couch beside him. "Loving her because she's mine isn't enough either. You have to love her so much, you'd do anything for her. Sacrifice anything to protect her. You wouldn't be simply playing at dad. You'd have to *be* a dad. You'd have to love her like she's *yours*."

Unsaid was the simple truth: Gemma wasn't his. But he didn't care about that. "Gemma is absolutely perfect just the way she is. I don't care that she doesn't carry my DNA. If that mattered to me, I'd be a hypocritical asshole, wouldn't I?"

The look on Lex's face made his gut clench. But then, she had no reason to think he wouldn't be a hypocritical asshole on this point. He'd been horrible to her on this very topic—getting a vasectomy without telling her, then accusing her of wanting to trap him with pregnancy so she could get his bank account when he'd always known she wanted a child and had never been after his money.

He did not deserve the benefit of the doubt here.

"I couldn't love Gemma more if she were mine. It's not her biology that matters. She's her own special person and the piece you were missing that I wouldn't give you. I love her for bringing you joy. I love her for her. And I will sacrifice everything to keep you both safe. I would spend my last dime to keep you from prison. I will move overseas with you both if we have to."

"My daughter isn't going to live a life on the run for a crime I didn't commit. No. I need to know that if I go to prison, you'll be there for her. Raise her as your own daughter. That's the kind of love I need you to have for her. You'd have to love her even if I'm not part of the package."

Joe had always told Lee he was his son, that he loved him and would do anything for him. But JT had seen the video—over and over—of what Joseph Talon Sr. had done when his former stepson stepped in front of the gun Joe had pointed at Erica.

Joe would have pulled the trigger. Shot the man he'd helped raise and who loved him like a father.

With an example like that, it was no wonder Lex didn't trust his newfound parental feelings. The truth was, he'd loved Gemma even before he met her simply for the fact that she was Alexandra's child. What had surprised him this week was that he could love her for herself.

He cleared his throat. "Can I give you an early Christmas present?"

She glanced toward the pile of presents under the tree. "If it's jewelry, you've already gotten laid." She huffed out a breath and muttered, "Fuck. I shouldn't have said that."

He ran a hand over his face. "No. I deserved that and so much more. We both know how much I liked giving you jewelry back then and why, but I never should have said it at the party like I did. It was unforgivable. I am ashamed and deeply sorry."

She leaned her head on his shoulder. "If it makes you feel better, it made you look far worse than it did me. I'm fairly certain every person at that table was cheering me on when I left."

"Hundred percent. The only reason I survived the fallout is I sign all the paychecks. But human resources has a thick file on how uncomfortable I made everyone there. I wouldn't be surprised if even Lee filed a complaint."

She smiled. "He's a good egg."

"Erica lit into me, and she has yet to forgive—not that I ever expect her to. But I sabotaged more than our relationship that night."

She ran a finger down his leg, pinching the fabric of his jeans. He remembered this tick of hers. Rubbing cloth between her fingers as she considered her words. "You want to know what I did with all the jewelry you gave me?"

"I assumed you sold it. I hope you got what it was worth."

She gave him a soft smile. "I got so much more." Her hand left his thigh and landed on her belly. "I had trouble conceiving even with grade A sperm bank goods and tracking ovulation to the second. I turned to fertility treatment. I spent two years riding that roller coaster. IVF—when one finally gets to that point—isn't cheap, but it was thankfully a lot less expensive in Switzerland. I sold several pieces of jewelry to pay for treatment. It took three rounds before I was able to carry to term." She took a deep breath. "So. I have your gifts to thank for my Gemma. My Gem."

His breath left him in a rush. "Her name. She's named after the jewels that paid for her conception and birth."

She took his hand, threading her fingers between his. "I would never give my daughter a spiteful name. I love her with the weight of all the matter in the universe. I enjoyed your gifts. They made me feel pretty, sexy, and loved. The moments we shared with them were special to me. But then, when I was done with them, when they no longer brought me joy, I used them to buy myself the one thing I desperately wanted. I couldn't have you, but I could have her. I feel incredibly lucky that IVF worked for me. That I could afford it. I know people who've had the same struggle without success and who spent their life savings just for the attempt. I'm *happy*, JT, and so utterly thankful for your gifts that made her possible. Your gifts also covered a hefty downpayment on my house and financed my yearlong maternity leave. I'd be in a very different financial situation if it weren't for you."

His heart pounded as he took in her words. She'd taken the gifts he'd tainted with nasty words and turned them into something unbelievably beautiful.

A baby girl who told knock-knock jokes and had the sweetest giggle he'd ever heard.

He pulled Lex onto his lap again and buried his face in her neck. "Your daughter is amazing, and I'm so glad my gifts gave you her and the financial security you needed."

The knot that had held his heart in a tight grip for years loosened ever so slightly. He hadn't been a complete disaster for Lex. More important, if they'd stayed together, she wouldn't have Gemma, because he never would have changed his mind when it came to children.

Her lips touched his neck, then she snuggled against him. "We had to follow different paths. Where we were back then wasn't the place we were meant to be."

That sounded more woo than the theoretical physicist he once knew, but he guessed they'd both evolved from the people they were when they were younger.

"Why didn't you ever run for office?" she asked. "You could have overcome the senator's bad press. We've seen more shocking political comebacks."

"After you left, I started to question why I wanted it at all. And what it did to my dad. I know you won't believe it, but Joe was a good man."

"Oh, I believe it. I did get to *know* him after all. The man who cared about people and wanted to create change, who strove to make the world a better one than the one he grew up in."

"He was all that. And he got lost in the contest. The polling. Fixing the game. The broken system. He grew up in an utterly broken system, so he got it in his head that it was fine for him to work around the same system that would lock him out of power. He and I talked about it a lot in those last two years."

"You never told me that."

"I didn't know if you'd understand. He was never really kind to you, and after what he did to Erica, I worried you'd think I was making excuses for him. And maybe I am. But he was my dad. I loved him. Still do."

"I never would have held that against you. Nor would Erica. Lee's had his own struggles on that front."

"Yeah. We finally started talking about that before Gracie was born. Impending fatherhood will do that. Joe was the best father he'd ever had—and Lee had three."

"Is that…why you didn't want children?" She paused and shook her head. "Sorry. That's out of line. You don't have to justify your reasons any more than I would need to justify wanting children. We are who we are."

"That's true for a rando asking personal questions, but not for a woman who once agreed to marry me. And I don't have an easy answer. It just didn't feel like something I could go all in on. Hell, Lex, we both know I wasn't able to go all in on *you*. Think about how messed up it would have been to bring a kid into our world back then. My gut said it wasn't for me."

It was difficult to say the words because while he knew they were true, he also knew something had shifted inside him this week. Needing to step up for Gemma had changed him. His gut now felt very different about one child in particular.

It didn't mean his past self had been wrong. Hell, if anything, it confirmed that the man he'd been before hadn't been parent material. Still, Lex and Gemma could walk out of his life tomorrow and he wouldn't stop loving them. Just as he'd never stopped loving Lex. More surprising was that the idea didn't destroy him. Because it wasn't about *him*. It was about their happiness and what they needed.

He shifted on the couch. "I'm going to give you that present now."

She shook her head, letting out a small laugh. "I forgot that's where the conversation started. I'm afraid I don't have any gifts for you."

He kissed her nose. "You already gave me the greatest gift of all."

"Ahh. Just like our first Christmas Eve together."

"Why attempt to improve upon perfection? You will always be my favorite gift." He rose from the couch and grabbed the package he'd wrapped with paper he found in the attic. He'd stolen a bow from one of the old gifts to dress it up.

"Technically, this is for Gemma."

Her brow furrowed. "Okay, now I'm really baffled. How could there be a present for Gemma in the forgotten gift hoard?"

"Just open it."

He felt strangely nervous. Would his gift make her angry?

She wasn't a neat present opener. He'd always like that about her—she ripped with gusto. She frowned at the manila envelope revealed by torn paper.

She grinned. "Definitely exciting stuff for a toddler."

"She told me in the car on the way here she wanted to play 'home office' and needed files and a filing cabinet to make it work."

Lex snorted. "That's my girl." She flicked open the metal clasp and slid out the thick sheaf of papers.

She scanned the top sheet. Gemma Vargas was in all caps and not to be missed. She looked up sharply. "What is this?"

"A few things. College fund. Trust fund that will be hers at twenty-five."

The same age Lex had been when they first met. He'd wanted to give her everything then, but she wouldn't let him.

He cleared his throat. "The last one is my will, which I update every year. You've been my primary beneficiary since before we got engaged. I added Gemma to ensure that if anything happens to both of us, she'll be taken care of."

Alexandra was on her feet. "Taken care of? Like life insurance taken care of?"

"No. She gets everything not specifically willed to Lee and his family. Same thing you would get if you survive me."

"Lord, JT, I have never been certain I would survive you."

He pulled her into his arms. "Everything I have is yours. It always has been. I never changed the will except to add more assets and now Gemma as a beneficiary. Honestly, I'd give it all up if I could have you back. What's the point in having all the money in the world if I can't share it with you?"

"Buying Christmas presents for homeless kids?"

"I'll always do that. Hell, after I sell T&D, I'll have more time and money to devote to that and other charities. Maybe by the time I'm done, I'll have given it all away and Gemma will only get a nice college fund. But whatever I have when I leave this earth will go to you and Gemma. Outside of Lee, you're my only family. It doesn't matter that we're not married or that Gemma's not mine. You're the family I choose even if you won't choose me."

"I've always chosen you. But it's not just about me and what I want now. It's Gemma you need to win over, and you can't buy her off. You've got to *love* her. Change her diapers and put her in time out and…who knows how she'll be in the terrible twos, and we're not even talking about how difficult adolescence can be…"

"Will you let me try? Consider every day for the next ten years an audition, and if I pass, maybe consider marrying me? Eventually let me adopt her?"

She rose on her toes and pressed her lips to his. "Your audition started when you picked Gemma up from Lee's."

Chapter Thirty-Four

They made love again in the guest bed where JT had spent the previous night. They took their time with the second round. Alexandra feeling the promise in JT's touch that had been missing in the last year of their relationship. Afterward, when it came to deciding where to sleep, it was natural for her to invite him to share the large bed in the primary suite. Gemma was sound asleep in her crib, and she wouldn't understand the significance of seeing a man in her mother's bed.

Alexandra would be a fool not to accept JT's offer to audition for the role of father figure, not when it meant she could actually have everything she'd ever wanted. It was hard to believe he'd already claimed Gemma by making her his heir, but she'd seen the paperwork. Signed and notarized.

Could he really be a daddy to Gemma?

She'd never imagined he'd want the role.

It was midnight when they moved to the primary bedroom, and for the first time in seven years, she slept in the arms of the man she loved. They woke up together on

Christmas morning when her daughter started chattering to the stuffed panda and dinosaur that shared her crib.

"Huh," JT whispered. "When she woke up in the hotel room with me, she was always grouchy and hungry."

Alexandra snickered.

Gemma shot up in her crib, grasping the rail above her head, and said, "Hungy!"

JT laughed. "Ah. That's my girl."

His laugh rolled back the years. She remembered their first shared Christmas so many years ago and what it had been like to wake in his arms.

She brushed her lips over his. "Merry Christmas, Jay."

His eyes lit at her use of the private name. "Merry Christmas, Lex."

"Hungy!"

He rolled from the bed, circled around the foot, and lifted Gemma from the crib. Or rather, as JT called it, the baby jail. Then he climbed back into bed, depositing her daughter between them.

He kissed Gemma's round cheek. "Merry Christmas, Gemmy."

"Hungy!"

Alexandra laughed. "She doesn't really have the concept of Christmas yet."

He snickered. "I picked up on that."

He moved to lift Gemma, but Alexandra stopped him with a touch. She wanted to enjoy this moment a little longer. It was unfathomable to wake up on Christmas morning with the two people she loved the most—and this might well be the only holiday she'd get to have with both of them.

She grabbed her girl and pressed a raspberry kiss to her belly. Gemma grabbed Alexandra's hair and giggled. The girl then gave her a drooly kiss on the chin.

JT gave her the same raspberry kiss and received his own wet kiss in reply.

Gemma had more teeth coming in, and she was a drool monster. Thankfully, she had less teething pain this round, or she was better at self-soothing now that she was mobile and could talk.

"I was thinking I could make pancakes for Christmas breakfast. Is that something Gemmy can eat?"

"It's a soft food we can soak in cream. I bet she'll like it."

"Hungy!"

Alexandra laughed. "But I should probably give her Cheerios while she waits."

"Patience isn't really her thing." He winked at her. "Just like her mom."

She laughed. "Food is important!"

"I wasn't talking about food."

"You made me wait *days* before you put out. I was a paragon of patience."

He grinned. "Because I took care of your needs in other ways."

She kissed his chin. "You did, and it was mind-blowing. Now, let's head downstairs, because Gemma isn't the only Vargas who's hungry."

"Can't let my Vargas women go without." He scooped up Gemma and climbed from the bed, and Alexandra practically melted into a puddle of confused but happy emotions.

The text arrived just as JT poured a heavy stream of syrup over his short stack. Gemma, always hungry and impatient, was deep in her mess of scrambled eggs and milky pancakes that only had a touch of syrup.

LEE

Turn on the news. CBS local.

JT frowned at his phone. The text gave no hint as to whether the news was good or bad. But surely Lee would brace him for the worst?

It had to be big to interrupt Christmas morning. He met Lex's gaze and showed her his phone. Her brow furrowed with a tension that matched his own.

Phone in hand, he rose from the breakfast nook and crossed the room to grab the TV remote. He hit the power button, then punched in the number for the Maryland CBS affiliate.

Inset on the screen was a grainy video from what was probably a doorbell-type camera. Below the video, the chyron read: *BREAKING NEWS: Video of Maryland cop shooting obtained by Action News.*

The video showed gray-shaded night-vision camera footage of a swath of roadway. The front tire and hood of a small SUV were cut off on the left edge of the video. The gap between SUV and police cruiser was to the left of center. A short stretch of gravel shoulder was visible behind the cruiser.

Lex had followed him into the living room and now stood beside him, jaw open, eyes wide.

"This video is legit?"

"Yes." The word was breathy. He could only imagine the shock she must be feeling. "But the angle… That's…that's not his dashboard cam or body cam. I presume he'd turned both off."

"Looks like you pulled over across from a private driveway camera."

"There was a long driveway across the road. I pulled over

there because the shoulder was wider to accommodate the mailbox. Afterward, I considered running up the driveway for help, but it was utterly dark. I couldn't see the house at the end of the drive and couldn't trust anyone there would help me. So I opted to run back to Kendall's."

On the screen, the gray night-vision video showed Officer Williams reach into Lex's car, as the news anchor said, "Again, we must warn viewers about the violence you are about to see. This video was obtained from an anonymous source, but we have verified that it shows Officer Williams's traffic stop of Dr. Alexandra Vargas, a theoretical physics professor at the University of Maryland. Dr. Vargas has been missing since being pulled over by Officer Williams Monday evening. She was initially suspected of shooting the officer at the end of this traffic stop, but this video tells a different story."

Lex's hand covered her mouth. JT slipped an arm around her waist and held her tight against him as he watched the officer smash her cell phone and yank her from the SUV.

His body twisted with rage at watching the man assault her. He could only imagine the fear she'd felt. That she was here by his side was a miracle.

The camera caught it all, and he gave an internal cheer as she landed the blow that allowed her to escape the officer's hold.

"Good job, Muffin," he said through a tight throat.

"You taught me that," she whispered.

He nodded, remembering the hours they'd spent in the dojo he'd purchased after his sensei had passed. They'd made love after sparring more than once. He'd nearly proposed to her there before he caught himself and waited until they were someplace more romantic than a workout room with a rubber mat floor.

He was so thankful for all the terrible and wonderful moments that brought them together. If it hadn't been for the threat Russ Spaulding posed, he never would have insisted on teaching her the self-defense moves that had saved her Monday night.

He was even grateful for the twisted, painful path that gave her Gemma, because if JT had married Lex at any point in their timeline, she would never have had a child. Gemma wouldn't be here, demanding food, making jokes, and giving him drooly smiles.

JT would never know what it was like to fall in fierce love with a toddler.

On the screen, Lex dropped to her knees and touched the downed officer's tool belt. She removed the Taser from the holster, then abruptly glanced up, looking down the road. She sprang to her feet, nothing in her hands but the hard disk and coat as she darted for the ditch and shrubs on the side of the road.

A moment after she left the frame, the scene lit up. Headlights bathed the unconscious cop in white light. Dark black fluid dripped from the side of his head where he'd been hit with the hard disk.

"At this point, Dr. Vargas has left the scene," the newswoman said, "apparently because a car approached."

The light cut out, returning the scene to the artificial light of night video. The car must have parked behind the cruiser, out of the frame, because it never crossed the screen.

A person walked along the road shoulder, on the other side of the cruiser, only visible as movement within the frame. When the person reached the gap between Lex's car and the cruiser, they moved closer, revealing a head covered with a balaclava.

"Damn," JT said. It appeared the new arrival was a man,

but even that couldn't be certain given the long coat that obscured their frame.

The person nudged Officer Williams with a boot. JT figured they didn't bother to check for a pulse because that would require removing the dark gloves. The figure dropped to their knees, head bent over the officer's face.

Looking for signs of breathing?

A gloved hand pulled Williams's gun from the holster. The person stood and racked the slide, then pointed the barrel down toward the man on the pavement.

Without warning, the video ended.

The news anchor cleared her throat and said, "We will not air the rest of the video, but instead will state that the gun was fired at the unconscious officer. The shooter then searches the SUV and removes a box from the back. They then return to their vehicle and must've made a U-turn, as the third vehicle never passes before the camera. A few minutes later, Dr. Vargas returns, sees the dead officer, and leaves the scene on foot."

On the screen, a still frame taken from the video fills the space next to the anchorwoman who had been narrating the video. Alexandra's face is frozen with a shocked and terrified expression. "At this time, Maryland State Police have revised their APB for Dr. Vargas. She is wanted for questioning as a witness in the murder of Officer Williams. She remains a person of interest, but it is clear from the video that she did not fire the gun that killed him. If any of our viewers have information on the shooter, Dr. Vargas, or Officer Williams, please call or message this tip line." She gave the number, which also appeared in the chyron, and added, "Messaging charges may apply."

JT's phone vibrated in his hand, and he glanced down to see a new text.

LEE

Merry Christmas, big brother.

JT's throat squeezed. He had no doubt who'd leaked the video to the press. No way would the police have released it. He wouldn't be surprised to learn Lee had tracked down the video before the cops knew it existed. In cities, cops were always looking at private security camera footage, but the odds had been so slim that cameras were on that rural road, they might not have even checked for it.

Lee's specialty was finding signals in the air and isolating their source. Alexandra had called Erica the moment she was pulled over, so Lee had known exactly where and when to look.

JT

Thanks, Skippy.

Give Alexandra a hug from me.

Well shit, apparently, Lee knew exactly where Lex was now. But then, it was no longer an urgent secret. This video partially exonerated her.

Sure, the cops could believe she'd colluded in the officer's murder with the shooter, but the evidence she was simply a victim was compelling.

Lex took his phone from his hand and typed a message, then handed the phone back. He smiled as he read her message.

Lee, you beautiful giant. Thank you. xo A

Erica and I are so thankful you're safe. That video is terrifying.

Instead of giving the phone back to Lex, JT replied.

JT

Watching it took years off my life. Now enjoy your Christmas with your family. I need to call Raptor and see if they've lined up an attorney for Lex.

LEE

One more question. What did Alexandra hit the cop with? Looked like an old hard drive.

Yep. Kendall had Lex's old computer from when they lived together. It has photos and other old files Kendall wanted her to have.

Any chance that's what the shooter was after? He took a box from the trunk.

Could be. We think this relates to Spaulding and Forbes. The dead cop is one of the two who responded to Lex's 911 call the day Spaulding was released on bond after he attempted to drug her.

Yeah. I caught that. Trying to get cell numbers for Spaulding and Forbes so I can track them. I haven't broken down the video yet, but I think Spaulding is good for the shooter.

JT showed Lex the screen. It always came back to Russ Spaulding. She sucked in a deep breath as she read the string of texts.

Behind them, Gemma screamed to be released from her clip-on highchair, but in this moment, Lex looked too dazed to respond. He handed her the phone and went to get

Gemma, pausing to grab a soft washcloth to wipe her down first. She was coated in pancake goo.

He saw Lex tap the screen.

“What did you tell Lee?”

“That we don’t have a SATA cord to look at the hard drive, and that if it is, in fact, what the shooter was after, then the minute he sees this video, he’ll know I still have it.”

Chapter Thirty-Five

Two hours after the video aired, JT was behind the wheel of his SUV, driving Lex and Gemma south to Raptor's Virginia compound. Christmas had been put on hold because the detectives handling the investigation into the homicide had agreed to interview Lex with her attorney in Raptor's conference room.

"I feel guilty about disrupting everyone's holiday," Lex said as JT navigated the winding, snowy road down the mountain.

Light snow flurries dusted the windshield. In the backseat, Gemma talked to Panny in a singsong voice, content during this drive because her mom was in the vehicle and not some complete stranger who had zero experience with toddlers.

"I'll see to it everyone involved gets a massive holiday bonus from me."

JT had an on-call contract with Raptor to provide security for T&D's more dangerous contracts around the world. They no longer worked in Iraq, but they did have construction projects in other conflict zones. He'd have Keith invoice him personally for the holiday bonuses.

"I'm sure my attorney is going to add a hefty fee."

"Worth every penny. We can celebrate Christmas later tonight. Your place or mine?"

"It's hard to believe that's possible. Five days ago, I thought I might spend the rest of my life in prison or be killed by a cop bent on revenge."

JT took her hand and squeezed, then let her go as the road curved and he needed both hands on the wheel in these conditions.

"We'd have found a way to prove your innocence, but damn, that video is huge."

He'd called Lee while they packed. Lee had confirmed that he'd located the video before the cops, because the couple who lived in the farmhouse were out of town for the holidays. Lee had identified the signal and combed tax records to find the homeowners. He then paid for the public record dossier for the couple. When that failed to provide a phone number, he found them on social media and messaged them.

It turned out the couple had a camera on the mailbox because of stolen mail, plus more cameras along their long driveway and another at the house, because they'd suffered break-ins when they'd gone out of town in the past. They hadn't known about the incident in front of their driveaway until Lee reached out, but a quick check of their feed on their computer had revealed they'd caught the incident. They'd sent Lee the video at the same time they provided it to the police.

Lee had also encouraged them to release the video to the local news affiliate to expedite the verification process—and ensure the cops didn't bury the evidence of one of their own assaulting a woman he'd pulled over.

Shortly after the video's release, statements that other women had reached out to Maryland State Police within hours of his murder, claiming he'd pulled them over and assaulted them too, began to pour in on the broadcaster's tip line. MSP had never relayed those complaints in their briefings on the hunt for Alexandra.

Now the department spokesperson was claiming it was because they didn't report on ongoing investigations, which might be true, but it would have significantly changed the narrative regarding the hunt for Alexandra Vargas in her favor.

It remained to be revealed whether or not complaints had named Officer Corey Williams for abuse of power prior to Monday, December twenty-first, or if the reported assaults had never identified the officer involved. If the guy had been reported by name, and he'd been allowed to continue with MSP without charges or investigation, MSP would be facing significant lawsuits.

Just thinking about it had JT's fingers tightening on the steering wheel.

A lawsuit wouldn't change the trauma Lex had been through. Or that Gemma could have been used as a pawn and disappeared into foster care.

Still, they knew Lex hadn't been targeted at random. It had to be connected to Kendall, Brent, and Russ.

Someone had killed Williams for a reason.

Alexandra held Gemma on her hip with her right arm while JT held her left hand in a tight grip as she stepped into the conference room. Her breath caught when she spotted Erica, Lee, and their daughter, Grace.

Gemma started kicking and wriggling at the sight of her bestie. "Gase! Gase!"

Alexandra set down her squirming daughter, who shot

like a rocket around the table to see her friend and introduce her to her new T-Rex buddy.

The girls hugged and giggled, and Alexandra's eyes burned. She let go of JT and hugged Erica, full-on tears spilling down her cheeks. "Thank you for taking care of Gemma."

Erica held her in a fierce grip. "Of course. I was so terrified when you didn't call, and then I saw the news—I— I'm so sorry that happened to you."

Alexandra didn't have a choice when it came to not wearing makeup—she didn't have any with her—but now she was glad for the lack of mascara, which would be running down her face.

Erica's grip relaxed, and Alexandra would have pulled away, but then her arms tightened again and she whispered in her ear, "Don't think I didn't notice your hand in JT's. For what it's worth, he's changed over the last few years. He might finally be worthy of you and Gemma."

Erica's endorsement was probably the only one that could matter to Alexandra at this point. She'd only known JT through the worst times and was not inclined to give him the benefit of the doubt.

Alexandra pulled back and met her gaze. "You never said a word."

"At first I thought it might be performative, hoping to influence me to influence you. But he never tried to use my relationship with you. And then, when Gemma needed him, he stepped up without hesitation. If you could have seen the look of terror on his face the first time he laid eyes on her…"

"You know I can hear you, right?" JT said.

Erica grinned. She swiped at her tears as she released Alexandra and turned to JT, pulling him into her fierce grip. "You've always known how I felt. It's been a pleasure to see you become the man Lee always told me you were."

JT laughed. It was deep and rich and affectionate. "I will never be worthy of Lee's respect, but I'm deeply proud to have earned yours."

Erica's voice dropped to a stage whisper. "Don't fuck it up, because she can do way better than you."

He met Alexandra's gaze over Erica's shoulder. "I've known that from the day we met."

Alexandra turned to Lee and received a hug from him. From the beginning, he'd felt like the brother she'd always wanted, right down to moving her into his condo when her living situation with Kendall turned ugly.

As he held her, he whispered in her ear, "Is the hard drive in the diaper bag like I asked?"

She gave a slight nod.

He released her and scooped up his daughter. "Erica, why don't you grab Gemma and we'll watch the kids in the living quarters common area while Alexandra and JT confer with her attorney?" He picked up the diaper bag from where JT had set it on the table and headed through the door.

Erica smiled as she settled Gemma on her hip and followed Lee out the door.

Alexandra suppressed her own smile. Lee always had a narrow focus when he had a computer puzzle to solve, and she knew he was eager to copy the hard disk before she handed it over to the Maryland State Police.

No one wanted to take a chance that the drive would get lost or destroyed once it left her possession. After all, evidence against Russ Spaulding had gone missing sixteen years ago, allowing him to escape prosecution.

In this instance, the hard disk had been used as a weapon. The police had no reason to look at the files.

Lee promised to do his best to leave the blood evidence intact while he copied the contents of the drive.

Alexandra shook hands with her attorney, Anna Davidson, whom she'd spoken with on the phone before leaving the cabin this morning, officially hiring the woman so she could make arrangements for this interview with Maryland State Police investigators, and was introduced to Anna's assistant, Raul Peredes.

Next JT reintroduced her to Raptor CEO Keith Hatcher, who'd been instrumental in finding Alexandra a defense attorney and who'd coordinated all elements of Raptor's investigation since JT called him on the evening of the twenty-third.

"Thank you for everything you've done. I— I'm so sorry for disrupting your holiday."

Keith smiled. "JT's an honorary member of the Raptor family. So is Lee. Which makes you family too." He glanced toward the door. "And here's another cousin."

Alexandra turned as former US Attorney General Curt Dominick entered the room.

Once again, her eyes pricked with tears. She hadn't seen Curt since Erica and Lee's wedding over three and a half years ago, but still, he was here on Christmas Day, for *her*.

He gave her a hug and said, "I just wanted to let you know Mara and I are here. Keith invited everyone to move our Christmas dinner celebration here, since we were all going to be at Erica and Lee's anyway. Alec and Isabel will be arriving shortly."

She turned back to Keith. "I'm…speechless. Thank you."

"We've got your back," Keith said. "And it made sense to combine our holiday celebrations. Trina and I were hosting a dinner for the live-in operatives today. Now it will be a little larger and a little later, but a lot more fun. We'll all be in the common room when you're finished here. JT knows where it is."

Alone with JT and her legal counsel, Alexandra dropped into a seat at the table, overwhelmed with emotion.

"It was kind of Raptor to offer their offices for us to meet," Anna said as she and Raul settled in the seats across the table.

"Thank you so much for agreeing to meet on Christmas."

"My kids are with their dad this year, so it wasn't an issue for me." She nodded to her assistant. "And Raul assures me he's thrilled with the holiday bonus."

The man grinned. "Gonna upgrade my girlfriend's gift—February trip to Kauai—to first class."

Alexandra could see why that would be worth giving up a few hours on Christmas.

Before they began, Anna reiterated the legalities of her retainer and attorney/client privilege. Once that was done, JT kissed her cheek and left the room. If this went to trial, he would certainly be called to testify and anything she said in front of him was not protected by privilege.

Once the three of them were alone with the door closed, Alexandra gave her full account of the events Monday night, including the reason behind her decision to flee.

"There was no working phone at Kendall's house, so I couldn't call 9-1-1."

"But you could have used the police radio."

"I felt that would put me in danger from the police."

"You aren't wrong there, but that will be a sticking point. Really, that video is a godsend."

"If I had known there would be a recording, I would have used the police radio or tried harder to find a phone so I could make arrangements to safely turn myself in immediately."

From there, they discussed the officer's role in events that took place sixteen years ago. Anna took notes on a legal pad while Raul was on his computer, marking locations on maps and looking up dates and case numbers.

There was a knock on the door, and JT poked his head in.

"Lex, Lee found the hard drive in the diaper bag." He held up the drive, which was in the gallon-sized slider-topped bag she'd placed it in the night before last.

She rose and crossed to the door. They'd agreed not to lie and pretend it had been a mistake. They just wouldn't elaborate. "Thank you."

JT pressed a kiss to her lips as he handed her the bag with the drive, then he left, closing the door tight.

The slight smile on both Anna's and Raul's faces said they knew the drive being in the diaper bag was no accident but wouldn't make an issue of it. It wasn't about chain of custody when it came to this piece of evidence. The blood and video were verification enough.

"What's on the hard drive?" Anna asked.

"I'm not certain. A few days before her suicide, Kendall said she had my old computer—from when we lived together—but the motherboard was fried. She'd planned to attempt to rescue the files for me, but had accepted she'd never get around to it. She said if I didn't want the computer, she was going to recycle it, so I grabbed the drive when I was at her house sorting belongings with her sister. I assume it has old photos. Dissertation research. Stuff like that."

"You have those files elsewhere?"

She shrugged. "Maybe? It was so long ago, and I've had crashes with data loss since then, so there could be files I don't have copies of, but I didn't have a SATA cable at JT's cabin."

"I would imagine a place like Raptor would have everything you'd need to access the files."

"Yes. I imagine so. Would that be a problem?"

"I don't see one. It's obviously the same hard disk you had that night, unless that's someone else's blood."

"And hair. It ripped out a few strands of his hair."

"Even more DNA, then," Raul said.

"Why did you keep the drive when you ran?" Anna asked.

"I just reacted. It was in my hand. I shoved it in my coat pocket when I hid in the shrubs. I didn't really think about it."

Raul nodded. "That checks out. It's on the video." He pointed to the screen, and Anna nodded.

Alexandra was glad he didn't turn the computer around so she could see the screen. She assumed Lee had provided her legal team with the uncut version, including the gunshot, and she didn't want to see the full video.

At some point, she'd need to watch it—possibly even today with the detective observing her every emotion—but she'd be happy to avoid that as long as possible.

Another knock at the door came. This time, it was Keith informing them that the police were here.

Anna met Alexandra's gaze. "I'm ready. Are you?"

She braced herself as she nodded.

"Good. I want you to move to this side of the table. Don't answer any questions without my approval, and you'll do fine."

She moved as instructed, taking a deep breath as she settled into the seat. "Should I have kissed my daughter when she left the room?"

Anna's voice softened. "I can't make any promises, but with that video, you're in a very good position. And the fact that there have been several complaints filed against Officer Williams that went uninvestigated means you might have a case against the MSP. I have a feeling they're more interested in you as a witness now, but they need to clear you of complicity."

Alexandra knew better than most the mathematics behind the concept of it being impossible to prove a negative.

The only way to prove she wasn't complicit would be to identify the shooter and their motive.

Which, of course, she was desperate to do. She wouldn't feel safe until she had answers. But her innocence would not be proven until someone else's guilt was confirmed.

Two plain-clothed officers entered the room, and the interview began.

Chapter Thirty-Six

JT was relieved when it was his turn to be interviewed. His attorney was not available to be physically present for the interview, but Raptor was a haven of technology, and the man was present via secure video feed.

Twenty minutes later, he was done, and the officers left the compound. JT found Alexandra as she sat with Anna and Raul in the larger conference room. She rose to her feet, looking weary but not wary.

He pulled her into his arms, kissed her temple, and asked, "You okay?"

He felt her nod as she held him tight. After a long interval, her grip loosened, and she stepped back. "It was intense, but not awful. Lots of suspicious looks. But I'm not in handcuffs."

Anna and Raul were both on their feet, packing up computers and briefcases. "I'm certain they'll follow up—several times. Do not speak to them without me."

Lex nodded.

"This would be a lot easier for them if you're complicit.

If they can find a vendetta against Officer Williams after he failed to inform the prosecutor sixteen years ago, then Williams's assault would have a different context."

"I didn't even remember his name."

"And you're convincing on that point. I just want to warn you, that's where they'll start."

"Instead of looking for the actual shooter," JT said.

"Well, they're hoping to find that by investigating Alexandra."

JT nodded. He didn't like it, but it made sense. And odds were, the shooter *was* connected to Lex. And probably him.

"Thanks, Anna. Raul." JT shook each of their hands in turn. "We really appreciate your coming here today."

Anna smiled. "And now we will clock out and let you enjoy your holiday."

They left the conference room, and Lex reached for his hand, entwining her fingers with his. "Where's the common room? I really, really need to hug my girl."

"This way," he said, tugging her toward the open door. "She, Grace, and Colin are pretty damn adorable together."

"I haven't met Colin yet—Curt's son, right?"

"Yeah. He's ten months older than Gemma."

"That would make him ten months younger than Grace. Right in the middle. I was really looking forward to this—seeing Curt again and introducing our kids on Christmas at Erica and Lee's. Hard to believe it's actually happening after all."

She stopped short, her hand in his bringing him to a halt. "I never dared to dream you would be part of this Christmas. As terrifying as this all is, it's also incredible. Thank you."

He brushed her hair back, tucking it behind her ear. He'd loved this woman for sixteen years to the day. He'd woken up that Christmas morning after they'd made love for the first time the night before and known he was a goner. He hadn't said the words, but he'd known it was true.

That morning, he gave her jewelry for the first time. Gems which she later used to pay for the treatment that gave her Gemma.

And now it was Gemma who brought them back together.

"I want to marry you." The words escaped even though he knew he should hold them back. She had no reason to trust he'd really changed. "I want to protect you. Love you. Be Gemma's dad. I want the dream I destroyed for both of us. I want to be your family and for you and Gemma to be mine. I love you. I never stopped—the person I stopped loving was *me*, but I took it out on you."

He shook his head. Here he was, talking about himself when he should be asking what she wanted. "I—"

She placed a finger on his lips. "I know. I knew that then. It's why I tried as long as I did. I hoped to figure out how to get you to love yourself again. But it turned out that was something you had to do on your own."

She rose on her toes and kissed him. Her kiss was soft and deep and somehow different. Her lips trailed along his cheek as she whispered, "I see in you now both the man you once were—the one I fell hopelessly in love with—and the man you have become, a person who owns his mistakes and loves with his whole heart. I love this new JT even more than the man who swept me off my feet sixteen years ago. You're the only person I've ever wanted to marry. To share my life with. The only man I've ever wanted to be the father of my child. And so now, I'm asking, will you marry me and be Gemma's dad?"

He cupped the back of her head and pulled her in for a deep kiss as his heart pounded and his brain practically exploded with joy. He raised his head, "New Year's Eve ceremony?"

She grinned and nodded. "I'd say tonight, but we need a license."

"A week will give us time to do it right. We can get married right after the closing. I've even got a venue booked. Forget the T&D executives, although they can stay for the ceremony if they want. We'll invite friends. Make sure the people we care about most can be there." He nodded toward the door that led to the living quarters within the compound, and the great room where everyone who wasn't involved in meal prep was currently gathered. "My people are all in there. Will your parents be able to attend?"

"I'm not sure. They both have dementia and are in and out of lucidity. But I'll see what their caretakers think."

"Anyone else?"

"Kendall's sister, Tanya, I guess. A few colleagues at the university. But really, I'd be content with just the people who are here at Raptor today."

Chapter Thirty-Seven

Alexandra felt ready to burst when she entered the common room—which was basically a large living room and library that overflowed with people.

On one side of the room, couches and plush chairs had been arranged in a large rectangle. In the center, Grace, Colin, and Gemma played with toys that must have been brought by the other parents.

Grace was building with foam blocks, while Colin was pushing a green tank engine—she guessed it was Percy, but she was new to the train world—on a wooden Thomas the Tank Engine figure-eight track, while Gemma held a plastic dinosaur in one hand and Tee-Tee in the other and was using both to destroy train tracks and block towers. Her kid had discovered the joy of playing Godzilla, but neither Colin nor Grace was particularly happy about the dinosaur antics.

She covered her mouth to stifle her laughter as Grace—the oldest of the three—intervened when Colin got frustrated with dinosaur destruction. At six weeks shy of three years old, Grace sounded just like her mom as she attempted to settle the squabble in a toddler version of a maternal tone.

"I think I'm going to melt," Alexandra whispered as she gripped JT's hand.

Erica approached, a petite blonde woman—Curt's wife, Mara—at her side.

Mara pulled Alexandra into a hug. "Sorry. I realize we've only met once briefly, but I'm skipping the handshake because we've been so worried!"

Alexandra hugged the small woman back, feeling like a giant. Her mind reeled at the acceptance by this community she hadn't known she had.

From there she was introduced around the room to Raptor employees who lived in the compound and others who'd joined the holiday celebration with their significant others.

Some shared knowing looks as they glanced between her and JT. Most had entered JT's life after she had left it, but they all appeared to know at least some of their history.

Through all the introductions, Lee was in the back corner, head down as he stared at a laptop. His posture was so familiar, it could be fourteen years ago, except his previously boyish face finally showed his age.

She crossed the room and dropped down on the couch by his side. "Anything interesting?"

He nodded. "Very." He waved to JT. "You both need to hear this."

JT had picked up Gemma to redirect her from destroying Colin's trains, but catching Lee's summons, he passed her off to Isabel, wife of Raptor owner Senator Alec Ravissant.

Seeing JT make a beeline for Lee, Alec, Curt, and Keith followed him to Lee's corner.

"What's up?" JT asked.

Lee removed his headset. "There's an audio file on here you need to hear." He faced Alexandra. "A week before Kendall died, she recorded a conversation."

"Should we do this now?" JT asked, glancing back at the kids.

"Yeah, you don't want to wait. Plus, I'd like Tricia's thoughts as a former police officer and Curt's as a prosecutor."

Isabel had introduced Alexandra to Tricia a few minutes ago. She was glad to learn the Black operative was a former cop. Her take on the situation would be invaluable.

"I'll make sure the kids don't fuss," Mara said. "So Erica can listen too."

"Maybe put them in front of the TV," Lee said. "I don't want Grace learning any new words. I'm already in trouble for her delight in saying dammit."

They waited for Mara to get the kids settled on the far side of the room with *How the Grinch Stole Christmas* before listening. While Mara juggled toddlers, snacks, and sippy cups, Lee shared what he knew about the digital recording. "This was buried in a directory of very old files—grad school research notes of yours, Alexandra. It was nested three layers deep. But the date on the recording itself is from October of this year—a week before her death—so it was easy to find. Well, that and the file name gave it away."

"What was it?"

"GHB."

That came as a blow. She and Kendall never talked about that night, even though it undermined the rest of their friendship.

"How did Kendall die?" Tricia asked.

"It was ruled a suicide," Alexandra said. "She'd battled depression for more than a decade, so that part wasn't shocking. But according to her sister, she'd been in a good place the last few years. I hadn't seen her in the year since I returned from Switzerland, so I don't have firsthand knowledge of her general mental state, but Tanya said she was doing well."

"What was the method?"

Alexandra cleared her throat. She hated to think about Kendall's last moments, and it was worse now, with the knowledge her friend might have been murdered. "She died in her garage of carbon monoxide poisoning. She was leaning against the wall on the steps going into the house, not in the car. The Jetta's engine was running. The button to open the garage door was above her, next to the door."

Erica shuddered, and Alexandra remembered how close she'd come to dying from carbon monoxide nine years ago. That had been Drake's doing. But Edward Drake was dead and couldn't have anything to do with this.

Lee had also seen Erica's reaction. He patted the seat next to him, and she sat down and leaned against her husband as he wrapped an arm around her.

Alexandra glanced toward the kids. Grace giggled as the lyrics to "You're a Mean One, Mr. Grinch" played.

She turned back to Lee. "It's safe to start the audio now."

He nodded and hit Play.

"What are you going to do about it, stupid bitch?"

"That's Brent Forbes's voice," Alexandra said.

"Well, there's no denying I'm stupid. All those lies, and I believed every fucking one."

"And that, of course, is Kendall." It hurt to hear her voice, let alone the words.

"You can't tell. You're in this as deep as anyone. You're the one who signed off on the cost estimates that put money in Russ's hands."

"I was forced to do it. You know why."

Alexandra experienced a throat-clogging rage on Kendall's behalf. Brent and Russ had spent more than a decade gaslighting and belittling her. Brent's so-called *love* had turned Kendall into a shadow of her former self.

"I can ruin everything. I can end this sale. Make it impossible for

Calvin Moss to purchase T&D. But the best part is you'll go to prison for embezzling."

"If that were to happen, you'd be in prison right alongside me."

"Brent, I've lived in a prison of your creation for sixteen years. You think you scare me now?"

There was a long silence before Brent said, *"But there's your problem. You can't pin any of this on me. There is nothing—nothing at all—that connects me to any of the transactions. I never even got a payout. It was Russ who got the kickbacks from Drake. It was you who made sure the payouts continued after Drake was gone. I was just a midlevel guy working for a company that I've given my entire career to. I didn't even worry that Talon was never going to promote me. I put up with so much shit, and everything is documented by HR. I've got a sweet lawsuit against Talon in the works for smearing my reputation to the degree that I couldn't get a job elsewhere. I* had *to stay."*

"That's bullshit. You could have left at any point, and that's why HR never worried about you and your complaints. You were lucky you weren't fired. And you stayed because you knew that if you walked out the door, you'd lose everything, including that sweet little bank account in the Cayman Islands."

"What bank account? I already told you I got nothing."

"You know Uncle Sam doesn't like people who cheat on their taxes. Lee Scott can find your bank account and whatever you squirreled away. Bitcoin isn't worth anything if you can't access it. You must've turned it into cash at some point. Lee will find your money. See, he doesn't have to worry about it being an illegal search. He doesn't care about being able to present the evidence to a jury. But he does own one-third of T&D. And you can bet your ass that if he gets wind that you colluded with Russ and Drake"—the name was said with deep disdain—*"he will find proof."*

"And then, dear Kendall, he'll find out what you *did. Everyone will. Even your precious Alex. Everyone will know exactly why the false evidence against Russ disappeared."*

"That evidence wasn't false. The only fake was what you *planted.*

But don't you worry, I have it still. I held on to it all these years. Anything happens to me, and Alex will get it. She'll tell JT everything."

"Nice try. Everyone knows she hates him."

"Everyone is stupid, then. She's never hated him. The only person she hates is Russ. Well, and you."

"Are you prepared for her to hate you?"

Kendall's voice shook in her reply. *"I'm pretty sure she already does. I did nothing but betray her. For* you."

Chapter Thirty-Eight

"Are there other recent files on the hard drive?" Alexandra asked Lee.

"No. I'll do another scan in case I missed something, but…"

In spite of everything, she laughed. Lee didn't miss anything in this area. He could pull exonerating videos out of thin air.

"Looks like I've been tasked with going over Kendall's work in relation to Drake's projects that she managed after he was arrested," Lee said.

"Didn't Rob Anderson take over those?"

"He did, but when I left and he took over running the office, several of the projects went to Calvin Moss."

"Calvin, who is buying the company," Erica said.

"And Kendall mentioned him. When did he leave T&D?"

"A few months after you and JT split," Lee said. "He started his own firm with a partner. Took some clients with him. It wasn't pretty."

"Yet you're selling to him?" Alexandra asked.

JT shrugged. "I want out. He does good work. Hell, he was landing half the contracts we didn't get anyway."

Lee closed the laptop and stood. "That's all I found on the hard drive. Now, we have a holiday dinner to enjoy."

Alexandra let out a heavy sigh. For a moment, she'd forgotten what day it was. She'd forgotten the joy she'd felt earlier. She'd slipped into a painful past and knew there was more pain to come.

JT wrapped an arm around her and whispered, "Can we share our news?"

Warmth spread from her center. *Yes.* This was what she needed right now. A return to joy.

She nodded and turned to Erica. "Are you busy on New Year's Eve?"

Erica's brow furrowed. "Well, there's this whole closing party for the sale that JT insisted had to happen on that date, and Lee says I have to go."

"That's fine, because I'll be there too. But I asked because before—or maybe it will be after?—we haven't discussed how it will work, but I'll be in need of a matron of honor, and was wondering…"

Erica squealed and wrapped Alexandra in a tight hug.

Over Erica's shoulder, she watched as Lee embraced JT. "I'd better be best man."

"That's always been the plan."

JT turned to face the rest of the gathering. "You're all invited, of course. New Year's Eve wedding at the Mayflower."

Shock rippled through Alexandra. "You booked the Mayflower? For a *business* transaction? On New Year's Eve?"

It had been the venue for their canceled wedding all those years ago. It was also where she'd officially given him his ring back.

He held her gaze. "I booked one of the smaller ballrooms, Palm Court, because it also includes an office, which we needed for signing the closing documents. When I thought about where I wanted to be when I let go of the company that's directed the course of my life, it felt appropriate. For better or for worse. The Mayflower is the place where the best thing in my life began and ended."

"It's perfect." She smiled at Erica. "I think I'm going to need a dress that's Mayflower-worthy. You up for shopping this week?"

Christmas dinner was the most fun Alexandra had had on Christmas Day since the early years with JT, when it was just the two of them and they were crazy in love.

This was completely different—no fewer than thirty people including the three toddlers, several senior Raptor operatives and their partners—all of whom had worked with and were friends with JT or Lee—and at least ten operatives who lived in the compound all gathered in the compound's large dining hall, which had four tables arranged to form a rectangle large enough to accommodate everyone.

Alexandra had met some of the couples at Erica's wedding but there were several she was meeting for the first time. Not surprisingly, they all knew exactly who she was. A pretty psychology graduate student named Eden, who was the newest and youngest member of the group and engaged to a Raptor operative, said even she had been read in and knew JT had been pining for her *before* the news of the shooting had broken on Monday night.

To Alexandra's right were Leah and Nate. Leah was a drone engineer who lived with Nate, one of the senior operatives. To her left was Gemma, with JT flanking her on the other side.

Gemma made a mess of her mashed sweet potatoes and other ground foods. Grace and Colin sat across the table from Gemma. Her daughter made squeals of delight at her friends and generally enjoyed the noise and excitement of being surrounded by so many new people.

Gemma was a social girl, that was certain. Colin was less so, but he was comfortable with his friend Grace at his side, and he had his trains lined up around his plate *just so*.

Alexandra breathed deeply as her gaze wandered around the table filled with a few old friends and a lot of new ones. Laughter and teasing filled the room with a joyful buzz. It was unlike anything she'd experienced in so long. And she was here with her daughter and JT.

She was going to *marry* JT one week from tonight.

It was really going to happen this time.

Plus, JT was selling the company that had been an albatross around his neck since long before she met him. Who would JT be without T&D?

He'd be lighter, that was for sure.

She caught Erica's gaze from across the table. Erica's eyes flicked from JT, who was sharing his stuffing and gravy-covered mashed potatoes with Gemma now that she'd finished off the sweet potatoes. He spoke in a voice pitched to engage a toddler and was playing a word game with her, teaching her alternate words for "yes" and "no."

Gemma stubbornly refused to vary her language, sticking with the words that worked best.

Defeated, JT said, "Fine, then. Want a bite of mashed potatoes?"

"Okay." Gemma's grin was wide.

Erica pressed a hand to her chest as she laughed with the rest of them, then raised her hands beside her cheeks and made a noise as she moved her fingers in imitation of an explosion, showing her mind was blown.

Alexandra laughed with her. Her mind was blown too. She never would have believed JT would embrace the role of father. Even back when they'd been engaged and she'd hoped he'd change his mind about children, she'd been mentally prepared to be on her own when it came to caretaking.

She would have even accepted it as part of the deal back then. It was another reason why it was good that they'd broken up when they did. It would have been an unhappy marriage, with or without children.

They'd both had to grow and change.

She smiled at JT over Gemma's head. "Thank you. This is amazing."

His eyes shone with warmth. "I love you."

This time, she knew his love would be enough.

❋

It was after nine when they loaded a sleepy Gemma into JT's SUV and headed to Alexandra's house, which was closer to the Raptor compound than JT's Maryland estate. Considering she'd left the house for five days without planning to be away at all, she was eager to get home and make sure everything was fine.

The police had served a search warrant in her absence. The search had been conducted Tuesday afternoon. The warrant limited their search to looking for signs she'd been home or where she might have fled to, which meant they'd accessed her computer to view search history and recent emails, but they hadn't removed anything from the house.

Her financial and phone records had been released to MSP yesterday. As long as the investigation into the shooting remained open, she would remain a suspect. They would likely request more financial information, but unless they produced a new warrant, she wouldn't give them any more information.

She was braced for the worst as she unlocked the door using the spare key she'd given Erica. The police had her purse and keys along with her impounded vehicle. It was all evidence and unlikely to be released anytime soon. At least they'd used the keys to enter the house instead of breaking the door down. A reason to be glad she hadn't retrieved anything from her vehicle before running. She hadn't needed to because Kendall's house key had been in her coat pocket.

JT held a sleeping Gemma against his chest as she entered the dark foyer. The alarm had been disabled by the cops and didn't beep as she entered.

"Take Gemma. I want to search the place."

Knowing the police had been watching the house, she hadn't considered that the shooter could have been here too, but with the alarm off, there was always a chance someone could have slipped past the surveillance—which hadn't been constant.

Gemma let out an angry cry at being woken again for the handoff and remained angry that Alexandra held her tight instead of letting her roam while JT searched.

"Sorry, honeybun. You can't explore yet."

Little fists pummeled her, and Gemma's wail was earsplitting. The joys of having an overtired toddler.

The house was chilly. Someone must have turned off the heat pump, which ran on a schedule. Why would the police mess with her system?

JT returned after several minutes. He tucked a pistol into a holster—he must've gotten both from Keith at some point. They'd have to figure out ground rules for guns in the house with Gemma. She had a fireproof safe, but she suspected JT would want to keep it close while the shooter remained at large and unidentified.

He caught her gaze. "We'll talk about it. First, let's get Gemma in her crib so we can go through the house together. I think someone other than the cops has been here."

Gemma was *not* happy about being placed in baby jail before she got to re-explore the house she'd been away from for five days. She fought her diaper change, refused to sit with Alexandra in the rocking chair for a bottle and book, and, for an encore, threw Panny and Tee-Tee out of the crib.

Beyond overtired, she would not be soothed. Alexandra had no choice but to give her Panny and Tee-Tee again and tell her she was staying in bed until morning.

She turned her big, crying eyes to JT and raised her arms, a plea for him to spring her from jail. "Unky Tee! Up!"

"And so it begins," Alexandra murmured. "Trying to play us off each other."

She watched as he hesitated.

"Don't fall for it," she warned.

He gave a little half smile. "I won't. It's just… Would it be okay if she calls me Daddy, if not now, then at some point?"

Her heart did another little flip. "It would be easier to introduce that now." She picked up the bottle from the rocker and approached the crib. "Give Mommy a night-night kiss, and you can have your bottle with Daddy."

Gemma's face scrunched, but she eyed the bottle.

JT touched his chest. "Daddy Tee. Daddy."

She raised her arms to him. He took the bottle from Alexandra, then lifted Gemma from the crib.

Alexandra nodded toward the rocking chair. "I usually read her a few board books while she has her bottle. I'd limit it to one tonight because she's so overtired and doesn't need any kind of stimulation. If she doesn't settle down by the time the bottle is empty, just put her in the crib again and let her cry. But I think the novelty of you being the one to hold her might do the trick."

She kissed Gemma's cheek and left the room, quietly closing the door behind her.

This Christmas was full of gifts, and no price could be placed on the best ones.

Chapter Thirty-Nine

Ten minutes later, JT returned Gemma to her crib. She grumbled, but she was no longer a wailing banshee. He kissed her cheek before setting her down. "Daddy loves you, Gemmy."

To be honest, the title felt more than a little awkward, but not because he didn't feel it in his heart. It was just a term he'd never imagined using. In the last dozen years of his own father's life, he'd rarely used the word *dad*.

Joe had been the boss before JT took over the business, then he was the owner and the senator. Those roles overshadowed the father/son relationship, and the only time he appeared to act like a dad—and not a boss or political adviser—was when he gave mortifying advice about women lying about birth control.

JT would do better. Be better.

He would earn the title. It would be as comfortable as calling Lex his wife and being her husband. Gemma was his child. His family.

He closed the door quietly behind him, daring to hope that she had calmed enough to go back to sleep.

He found Lex in her home office. "The cops were really shit about watching over this place. My laptop was stolen."

He'd figured as much given that the search inventory had listed a MacBook Pro and a desktop computer in Lex's office. Only the desktop remained.

"We need to call the cops and file a complaint. We also need to tell your attorney."

"I'll do a quick search to make sure nothing else is missing. Then I'll email Anna if you call the detective?" She smiled at him. "I'm not supposed to talk to them without my attorney present."

It was also the more distasteful of the two chores, and she had a tidy excuse to pass it off to him. He kissed her nose. "Deal. As long as we get to enjoy eggnog by the fire afterward."

Thirty minutes later, they were settled on the couch. The gas fireplace heated up the room, which had been so cold, JT could see his breath. The detective was not thrilled with the late-night phone call, but he swore the investigators hadn't turned off the thermostat nor had they taken the computer.

"Tomorrow, I want to move to my place."

She nodded. "You have better security. I'd say let's go tonight, but it might break Gemma."

"Raptor has access to your security system, and they're monitoring it. Chase lives nearby and is outside already—he's taking a four-hour shift watching the house, then Raptor will send Tariq for the next four hours."

"I hate that they're being asked to work on Christmas."

"Chase volunteered because he lives so close and he has the next week off. He said he doesn't mind an extra shift now. Tariq was already scheduled to work nights this week—he likes the overtime."

"That's kind of them both. Eden is going to join us for

wedding dress shopping. She and Chase are getting married in the spring, so she's going to try on dresses too."

"That'll be fun. How many of you are going?"

"Most of the women who were there tonight. We'll be quite the entourage. Isabel is going to call and set up the appointments tomorrow. It's been a long time since I shopped at a place that requires appointments. I'm glad Isabel has connections."

Once upon a time, JT had set up accounts for her at all the DC couture shops. "I'll make some calls and add you to the accounts again. Actually, I'm pretty sure I never took you off them."

"It's okay, I can afford my own wedding dress. I mean, I won't be going designer, and Eden doesn't strike me as someone who wants to spend several thousand on a dress that will only be worn once." She tilted her head back and held his gaze. "I presume with the company being sold and your decision not to run for office that I won't *need* designer clothing moving forward."

"No. Only if you want them."

"I could see splurging here and there as I know you move in the kinds of circles where you get invited to black tie events, but I presume those will be fewer and farther between."

"Yeah." He paused, then broached the sensitive subject. "Will you…let me buy you jewelry?"

She stroked his cheek. "Only if you promise you're doing it for love. Because it makes *you* happy. No ulterior motive. No suspicion."

"Always. That was always why I gave you gems."

"And I loved the gifts and making love with you while wearing them. Your words that last night didn't change history or my memories of it."

He rose from the couch and went to his suitcase, which

he'd brought in from the car but had yet to bring upstairs to Alexandra's bedroom. He unzipped the top compartment and pulled out the wrapped gift.

He returned to the couch and presented it to her. "It's an hour before midnight. Still Christmas."

"This was in the attic?"

He nodded. "I'm not even sure what's in it."

She smiled and studied the square box. "You were fond of giving me necklaces. This is the right size box."

She tugged at the red ribbon and untied the bow. "I wish I had a gift for you."

"You gave me Gemma when you said she could call me Daddy. Whatever is in that box will pale in comparison to that."

She swiped at her eyes, then ripped open the gold wrapping paper. It was no surprise to see the box was Tiffany blue. She lifted the lid and pulled out the enclosed hinged jewelry box.

She gasped when she opened it, and the contents surprised JT too. He'd forgotten—possibly blocked out—that he'd commissioned this special piece just for her.

A galaxy made of colorless to blue diamonds for his theoretical physicist. The necklace was a spiral galaxy three inches in diameter at the widest point. One earring was a lenticular galaxy and the other a barred spiral.

"It's stunning," she said. "And it feels more *me* than most of the pieces you gave me." She held it to her chest. "I'm glad you never gave me this before because it would have been heartbreaking to sell it even though I'd never have a reason to wear it."

"Will you wear it with your wedding dress?"

She smiled. "Try and stop me."

"Put it on. We'll take a photo so you know what neckline will look best."

She slipped off the button-down shirt she'd borrowed from JT to wear to Christmas dinner and stood before him the same no-frills satin bra she'd worn all week. She could go upstairs and find a better shirt or a dress, but this was just a shopping aide and didn't need to be perfect. She lifted her hair, and JT draped the necklace around her and fastened the clasp.

She popped in the earrings and smiled. "How do I look?"

"You are the most beautiful woman I've ever seen. With or without the necklace."

He took her photo with his cell phone. "We can set up the phone Raptor gave you tomorrow, and I'll send this to you."

She nodded and took a step toward him. She placed her hand behind his neck and pulled his mouth down to hers. "Thank you for the jewelry."

She kissed him, and he was pulled back in time to when he first gave her a necklace on Christmas Day.

And just as she had then, she took his hand and led him to bed. They celebrated the holiday and the rush of feelings that engulfed them with each moment they spent together. As they made love, she wore nothing but the jewels he'd just given her.

Chapter Forty

Two days later, Alexandra met the others for dress shopping at Trina and Keith's house in Georgetown because it was closest to the boutiques where they had appointments lined up. The entourage consisted of the two brides along with Erica, Mara, Trina, Isabel, Tricia, and Leah.

Alexandra had to admit, this was so much more fun than dress shopping had been all those years ago, when Kendall had been her maid of honor but there remained so much friction between them.

Tanya had joined them on some of those shopping excursions, and the ache at thinking of Kendall triggered Alexandra's decision to send Tanya shopping photos.

They'd spent two hours on the phone yesterday, as Alexandra brought her up to date and shared her suspicion that Kendall had been murdered. When she asked if anyone knew they were going to sort Kendall's things that day, Tanya had replied that Brent had shown up at Kendall's two weeks before and was taken aback to find Tanya staying in the house. He was there to collect items of his that Kendall had held on to.

She'd turned him away, telling him she and Alexandra would be sorting Kendall's things at the start of winter break. If they found anything that might belong to him, they'd set it aside.

She'd never liked Brent and didn't trust him not to steal. Nor did she believe Kendall had anything that had belonged to him. She hadn't mentioned it to Alexandra when they were together because it was an emotional enough day without talking about the man who'd changed Kendall for the worse.

Alexandra didn't tell Tanya about the recording of the conversation with Brent that had been hidden on the old hard drive, but she did pick Tanya's brain for other hints Kendall might have left behind and if there was anything else she'd specifically mentioned wanting Alexandra to have.

Her words in the recording suggested there was more for her to find.

"That evidence wasn't false. The only fake was what you *planted. But don't you worry, I have it still. I held on to it all these years. Anything happens to me, and Alex will get it."*

She was taking a break from trying on dresses, letting Eden be the center of attention—she looked gorgeous in everything she tried on—when Tanya sent a text that had her full attention.

TANYA

The dress photo reminded me… I think Kendall said something about having your wedding dress in her attic.

Alexandra closed her eyes and tried to remember what had happened to that dress. She'd moved in with Kendall immediately after calling off the wedding. She and Kendall then remained roommates through the entire time she and JT were semi-reconciled.

They'd lived in Bethesda, not the same apartment they'd shared years before, but a larger place, affordable because Kendall had finished school, then a year after the breakup, Alexandra had her PhD.

She'd collected her things from JT's DC townhouse sometime after the New Year. Most everything in the townhouse had belonged to JT. Alexandra had taken her clothes, books, and the jewels he'd gifted her. That was it.

Later, her clothes had slowly drifted to JT's Maryland estate as they resumed living together when Joe was arrested and JT took possession of the family home. Her move had been glacially slow—she'd never fully committed and took only what she needed for social events or her teaching job.

The wedding dress had no reason to move out of the storage locker—if that was where it ended up—that was included with the apartment until Kendall moved into the house where she'd lived when she died. Alexandra was in Switzerland then, so Kendall must have moved the dress and put it in her attic.

ALEXANDRA

Oh, I should look for it. Maybe it will still fit?

TANYA

You should! It was a gorgeous dress.

Have the police said anything to you about entering the house?

Not a word. I don't think they're taking your suspicion about her death seriously. I called them after we talked yesterday and the detective was not happy to hear from me.

ALEXANDRA

They should be interviewing you! You know more about Kendall and her mental state than anyone.

TANYA

¯_(ツ)_/¯

You still have the key?

Yes.

Feel free to pick up the dress and anything else of yours you find. We can wait to do the furniture and the rest of the sorting until after the New Year.

Any chance you can come down for the wedding?

I wish I could, but I'm working NYE. So happy for you, though!

Alexandra responded with a heart, then tucked away the phone.

Eden stepped out of the dressing room in a simple silk dress with clean lines that was perfect for her outdoor spring wedding. The grin on her face said she'd found the gown she wanted. For her part, with each dress Alexandra tried on after that, she found herself thinking of the dress in Kendall's attic.

As she stood before her new friends in yet another gown that fell short, she finally spoke her thoughts aloud. "Eleven years ago, I was supposed to marry JT on New Year's Eve at the Mayflower. I had the perfect dress for the venue and holiday. Silver silk, lots of fabric with a full skirt and fitted bodice. It was gorgeous. Plus, it had the right neckline for the jewelry JT was sure to give me for Christmas that year, which, incidentally, he gave me *this* year. I didn't consider it for this because I didn't know where it had ended up—I forgot about it when I moved to Switzerland. But Tanya texted earlier and said it might be in Kendall's attic. Would it be wrong to wear it now?"

"Wrong to use a dress you've already paid for?" Mara said. "Definitely not."

"And it's not like you were going to marry someone else in it," Erica added. "Or even that you called off the wedding because you didn't love him or something else that sullied the original event."

"Well then, if Eden is done here," Isabel said, "I think we should take a little trip to Kendall's to retrieve Alexandra's dress." She turned to Tricia. "Do you see any problem with Alexandra going to Kendall's house from a former police officer's perspective?"

Tricia considered the question, then asked, "Is the house considered a crime scene?"

"According to Tanya—who inherited everything except the items that were mine—no. It doesn't sound like they're opening an investigation into her death, or if they have, they're being very quiet about it. They've placed no restrictions on entry."

"And not only do you have a key, but the homeowner has given you permission to use it."

"Yes."

"It's fine, then."

"Maybe we should get Chase, Keith, and Nate to meet us there?" Leah said. "Given that Raptor is providing security for Alexandra?" She grimaced and said to Tricia, "Not that you aren't an operative—"

The woman smiled. "I'm not offended. I wouldn't mind having them meet us there. I'm not armed today—we can only carry concealed in the city when we're working an event

—and I'd appreciate the backup given how many of you there are. The danger to Alexandra is real, and I don't want to give my boss a reason to think I let ego get in the way of my brains."

She touched the scar on her scalp, which wasn't hidden by her blue braids, reminding Alexandra of the story Erica had shared about the woman suffering a near-fatal injury last August at a security conference in Indonesia.

"I'll call Keith," Trina said. She paused before dialing. "Is there any reason to keep this a secret from JT? Do you want to surprise him with the dress?"

"He never saw it back then, so it wouldn't spoil any kind of surprise as far as what it looks like. He can tell him. But JT can't show up at the house. Not if I'm going to try it on there."

Eden spoke with the saleswoman who recorded the dress design and size she was interested in, and then they set off, eight women in three cars.

Alexandra rode in the backseat of Tricia's Raptor vehicle. Leah rode shotgun.

JT had told Alexandra a little about Leah after Christmas dinner, and she was glad to have a chance to chat with her now. "I went to Nationals Park last Christmas with some grad school friends—and Gemma in a baby pouch—for the drone show. It was amazing." She hesitated, then continued, "I was so sorry to hear about what happened to you afterward."

"Thank you. I was incredibly lucky to have just met Nate and to have Raptor's help through it all."

"I know the feeling," Alexandra said.

"What did Kendall do for T&D?" Leah asked.

"She worked in cost estimating—budgeting for massive engineering projects is a complicated business."

"It sounded like in the recording that she might have skewed some numbers."

"Lee's looking into it. I admit, I'm afraid of what he'll find. If she helped funnel money to Russ…it's unthinkable. That's not the Kendall I knew before Brent Forbes sank his fangs into her."

"Did she love him? In the recording, it sounded a lot like hate."

"I believe she loved him at first. Then…something happened, and I think…she *needed* to love him. To believe in him. It hurt how much she believed Brent over me, but she was fed a steady diet of JT-was-out-to-get-Russ. She thought I was as messed up by my relationship with JT as I thought she was by hers with Brent. We were quite a pair."

"But in the end, you were the one who was right."

"And I don't think she could forgive me for that."

Chapter Forty-One

College Park, Maryland
October
Sixteen years ago

Kendall would never be as pretty or smart as her roommate and best friend, but in the last five years, she'd learned to shine in her shadow. As undergrads, the hot guys had always come to attention when Alexandra Vargas entered the room. But Alex was too *everything* to be approachable, which is where Kendall came in. She was the friend they could talk to. An in with the genius blonde bombshell.

More than once, the guys gave up on trying to get Alex's attention and settled for Kendall.

They didn't know Alex was actually funny and approachable and not the cold, aloof beauty she appeared to be. She was so focused on her studies, she didn't much care what men thought of her. She maintained she didn't want to get seriously involved, and at this point, Kendall believed she meant it.

So Kendall did her part as gatekeeper, keeping the princess protected in the tower while getting laid by the unworthy suitors who wanted to storm the castle. But just once, she wanted to be the guy's first choice.

Now, as they stepped into the STEM job fair, she wished her beautiful friend had chosen to stay in her office on campus and let Kendall navigate this event alone. Alex was two years behind Kendall in grad school, having taken a break to work and save money. Kendall needed to line up an internship or entry-level job in the coming months or she was screwed.

It wouldn't help if the men working the booths drooled over her roommate and failed to notice Kendall. Not that this was a pickup bar, but men tended to get distracted by Alex.

She shook off her resentment. She was here to land a job. This required positivity. "God, I love the smell of science in the morning."

Alex laughed and glanced at her watch. "Eleven forty-five. Checks out."

"Literal Lex, you need to grant leeway for movie quotes."

"Alex. Or Alexandra."

Kendall rolled her eyes. "I know your preferences, but Literal Lex is alliterative. It plays better with single moms in the Midwest."

"Oh, are we polling in the Midwest now? Since we're being literal, why is it called Midwest, when it's middle with nothing west about it?"

"Once upon a time, before Schoolhouse Rock recorded their most egregious tune, 'Elbow Room,' about the glories of Manifest Destiny, the place that we now refer to as *Midwest* was the western edge of the United States and part of the Northwest Ordinance. You should study history sometime."

"Ah, but as a theoretical physicist, I'm actually focused on the past, the present, and the future of our vast, expanding universe all at once."

"Typical physicist copout. It's always unending everything with you people. You say you're studying everything when really, it's nothing."

"Not *nothing*. Dark matter."

"AKA *nothing*."

Alex smiled. "But also *everything* given that dark matter makes up most of the universe."

"Prove it."

She tilted her head back and laughed. "Someday, maybe I will."

Kendall smiled at her friend. Alex had a great laugh. Warm. Infectious. "I think you just might." She tilted her head to the vast room and dozens upon dozens of potential employers. "Now, let's find some internships."

"I wish CERN was here."

"They're still years away from the Large Hadron Collider being finished. You've got time."

"Time is relative."

"Sure, Einstein. Now, I'm going to the engineering section. I need a paid internship because twenty-four is too old to be subsisting on ramen noodles."

They went from booth to booth, taking trifold brochures and making polite chatter. Nothing looked promising until they reached the booth of an engineering firm that had an office just a few blocks from their apartment in Bethesda, which was a long commute to campus, but she leased it anyway because a family friend had cut her a great deal.

Being able to walk to work would be a huge bonus.

There were two men sitting in the booth, one a fisheries biologist, one a civil engineer. The biologist was young—probably only a few years older than her. The engineer had to be in his mid-thirties.

He spoke with confidence and authority. He had her dream job. And she couldn't help but notice he was handsome. Even better—probably her favorite thing about him—was that he didn't direct every statement to Alex. He barely even looked at her.

No. Brent Forbes only had eyes for Kendall, and it was a heady feeling. She wasn't second best.

Within minutes of introductions, Alex winked at her and wandered away. Kendall really loved Alex, but in that moment, her appreciation for her best friend might have been at the pinnacle. Alex played the dumb blonde at times purely for entertainment value, but she didn't have an unintelligent cell in her body.

Kendall turned her attention back to Brent, for once not wishing she had Alex's curves, hair, or brains. No. This handsome, successful engineer was interested in *her*.

Before she left the job fair, they had plans to meet at a bar in Bethesda for happy hour to talk about internships with Talon & Drake.

Brent Forbes could be the answer to her dreams. But the best part might be that she wouldn't have ramen for dinner that night.

Three weeks later, Kendall was certain she was in love. It didn't bother Brent that he was twelve years older than her, so why should it bother her? For once, she was dating a *man*. A man who wasn't trying to use her to get close to her gorgeous roommate.

The sex was exciting too. She'd had her share of lovers, but it had never been as good or exciting as it was supposed to be. Orgasms had been few and far between.

But with Brent, she'd finally found a man who knew how

a woman's body worked and cared enough to get her to the finish line every time. He pushed her boundaries in the best ways. She'd never imagined being so uninhibited.

It didn't hurt that he had a real job and took her out to dinner in restaurants that didn't give you a number to place on your table when you ordered at the counter.

It was wild to her that he spent hours in her apartment and didn't even seem to notice Alex. He only had eyes for Kendall.

She'd told Alex she was in love before, but Brent Forbes was *the one*.

Tonight, she faced an important relationship test. Brent's friend, another Talon & Drake employee—an *executive*—was coming over for pizza and a movie.

Russ Spaulding could make or break her shot at an internship. Plus, he was senior to Brent in the office hierarchy, so she needed to impress him. Brent was counting on her to be the kind of girlfriend who'd be an asset at dinner parties hosted by executives.

And someday, she wouldn't be just the girlfriend. She'd have her master's in civil engineering and a real job. She and Brent would host the dinner party, and the bigwigs would come to *her* house. Maybe the owner of the company, who was a US senator, would be among the guests.

Okay, the fantasy was over the top, but it was fun.

To impress Russ Spaulding, she'd opted to make a homemade pizza instead of having it delivered. She was busy kneading the dough when Alex got home and went straight to her room, mumbling something about black hole thermodynamics.

Kendall finished the dough, then set it aside and washed her hands as she rehearsed what she'd say to Alex.

After a cursory knock, she opened the door to see Alex

sitting on her bed reading a book. She glanced up, her nose and eyes visible above the hardback. "What's up?"

"Tonight is pizza night with Russ Spaulding—the Talon & Drake executive I mentioned. I was hoping you could join us? I really want to impress Mr. Spaul—*Russ*—because an internship at Talon & Drake would be amazing."

"I really need to study. I have a paper due—"

"You also need to eat. Just a half hour? Please? Everyone is always impressed when you start talking about black holes."

Alex laughed. "You mean it makes people shut down and tune me out. You know, I just string together random words to see if they're pretending to be interested."

"Of course they don't understand. No one understands. I've been your best friend for six years and I'm still not sure what theoretical physics is."

"We're really studying the angular displacement of anti-quarks and the gravity of Avogadro's number as it relates to the Big Bang."

"Uh-huh. Fool me once, shame on me, fool me twice, shame on Bose-Einstein condensates."

"You *do* understand this game."

"Live with you for six years, and a few random words are bound to osmosify with my brain."

"Now, now, osmosify isn't a word."

"And yet you knew exactly what I meant."

"I did. Point to Kendall."

She pumped her fist with victory. "A point! I'm redeeming it for your presence when we eat pizza, which is homemade."

"Will there be pineapple?"

Pineapple was Alex's favorite topping, but Kendall couldn't walk into that trap. "Too polarizing a topping when I don't know what Mr. Spaul—*Russ*—likes. I'm going basic—pepperoni mushroom for one, and the other is a veggie supreme, but with red peppers, not green." In this, at least, she could accommodate Alex's pepper preference. But then, it was her preference too.

"What if I bring my own pineapple?"

"Do you *have* pineapple?"

"Well, no. But I was sort of hoping you could lend me a can."

"Fresh out, but if you promise to join us, I'll make a pineapple-only pizza for you tomorrow."

"No sauce or cheese?"

"Hello, Literal Lex."

She dipped her head in a slight bow.

"Please, Alex? Just a half hour."

"What's the movie?"

"*The Mummy*."

"Why didn't you *lead* with that? Do you even *know* me?"

"My bad." She smiled. "So you'll join us?"

Alex nodded. "But thirty minutes is all I can spare."

She lunged forward and hugged her. "Thank you! You're the best."

Russ, mercifully, was incredibly charming. He was older than Brent, which put him around thirty-eight. Brent had told her he was the project manager for Talon & Drake's biggest East Coast contract—a bridge replacement and neighborhood revitalization project that was two years into the four it would take to complete.

He answered directly to Drake and was tight with the senator. He and Brent had been friends since Russ was hired four years ago. Russ was helping Brent move up the ranks.

With Russ's backing, she was sure to land an internship or even an entry-level part-time job. Talon & Drake didn't have rules around employees dating, but it would be easier to be taken seriously if she worked for someone like Russ and not Brent.

Her brain buzzed with excitement even as she asked

herself if it was wrong that she wanted her beautiful and brilliant roommate to catch Russ Spaulding's eye.

Hell, Alex would probably thank her. He was rich and moving up. Alex could use a sugar daddy. Not that she wanted one or would accept his money, but she could appreciate the free meals that came with dating a man who liked the finer things.

As promised, Alex emerged when the pizzas were ready. Kendall's heart thumped rapidly with the introductions, thrilled to see the spark of interest in Russ's eyes.

This was going to work splendidly.

Alex and Russ chatted for a bit. She played nice and didn't speak nonsense physics words. She seemed to enjoy chatting with him and even stayed for a whole hour before retreating back into her room to work.

After she left, Russ said, "You didn't tell me Kendall has such a gorgeous roommate."

Brent smiled, his arm tightening around Kendall's shoulder. "Is she? I didn't notice. Too blinded by Kendall."

She rolled her eyes, but laughed at the ridiculous statement. It was sweet even if over the top.

"Think Alexandra would let me take her to dinner?" Russ asked Kendall.

"Maybe, but probably not during the semester. She's got a heavy courseload and doesn't allow for much in the way of distractions."

"When does the semester end?"

"Finals start in two weeks."

He grinned. "Talon & Drake's holiday party is after that. What would you say to making it a double date?"

Kendall's belly fluttered. Brent had yet to ask her to be his plus one for the party, which was a formal event. "I can't answer for Alex, of course, but it might work for her schedule."

She tucked her hand between the cushions, hiding her crossed fingers, saying a silent prayer that Alex would say yes.

That night, long after Russ left and the glow of the light under Alex's bedroom door had disappeared, Kendall and Brent had sex, but it was hard for her to remain quiet. She wondered if she could convince Brent to buy Alex a pair of the new Bose headphones that canceled sounds. Of course, Alex wouldn't want to actually *sleep* in them, which was sort of key.

Afterward, she lay snuggled against him. "I wish we didn't both have roommates so we could be loud."

"When I get the promotion, I'll make enough to buy a house."

And now the fantasies of moving in with him would start. She really needed to rein in her expectations with this man.

The urge to tell him she loved him pushed against her chest. But no. She wouldn't be the first to say the words. Not again. Last time she'd been the only one who said it. She couldn't risk that.

His hand slipped between her legs and he played with her clit. This was his love language. She could live with that.

"I want you inside me again," she whispered.

He laughed. "I just came a few minutes ago. I'm down for the count." Then his lips found her neck as he slid two fingers inside her. "Unless…" His voice trailed off.

His fingers slid from her, and she felt empty. "Unless what?"

"Have you ever tried X?"

A ripple of excitement shot through her. She'd never been with someone she trusted enough for that. "No. You?"

"Yes."

"Did you like it?"

"I did."

"What's it like?"

He chuckled. "We agreed not to talk about past lovers." He slid his fingers between her legs again. "But if you're game, I can show you what it's like. We can create our own memories."

His teasing fingers stole her breath as the pleasure built. She finally managed to gasp, "Yes."

"Yes to X?"

"Yes!" She was so close, and this orgasm showed signs of being stronger than the one she'd had a few minutes ago. What would this be like with X to heighten her senses?

After she came, she curled up beside him again and said, "You can get some?"

He nodded. "It might take some time, but I can get it. Tell you what, if you convince Alexandra to join us for the holiday party, we could have this place to ourselves that night. After the party, we can try it, and you can be as loud as you want."

"What makes you so certain Alexandra will go home with Russ?"

"He and the other executives all get suites at the resort. But if she doesn't want to stay with Russ, we can still try it. We'll just need to be quiet." He kissed her neck as his hand caressed her breasts. "What do you say? Want to have the best sex of your life?"

The idea that he'd had better sex with someone else triggered a wave of insecurity. But she could replace that memory for him. She could be the only woman he thought of when he listed his best orgasms.

She smiled. "Okay. I'm in."

Chapter Forty-Two

The party was as magical as Kendall had imagined. Alex shone like a diamond, but Brent only had eyes for Kendall. And earlier, when he handed her the vial of X to tuck away in her nightstand—no way would he bring a club drug to a work party—he'd kissed her and whispered how excited he was to be taking this step.

She was certain he'd been about to say he loved her, when Alexandra knocked on the door to ask Kendall to zip up her dress.

Sometimes, having a roommate was so frustrating.

But now that they were at the party, all was forgiven. Immediately after the dinner plates were cleared, she and Brent were on the dance floor. The way he held her as they danced was heaven. This was by far the best party she'd ever attended.

She was practically giddy with excitement over the fun they'd have when they got home. But first, she needed to be certain Alex was settled. She'd disappeared into the casino with Russ, and Kendall hoped they were hitting it off.

After an hour of dancing, she was thirsty and eager to

head home. She returned to their table and sat down to rest her feet and drink water. Alex wasn't at the table, nor were she and Russ dancing.

Was it possible she'd gone to his hotel room already? Kendall had seen Russ slip her the room key earlier. But surely Alex would have said something before leaving? She didn't have a cell phone, and by rule, they kept tabs on each other, but admittedly, Kendall had been too wrapped up in Brent to pay attention.

A man Kendall hadn't met yet dropped into the chair next to Brent. "Forbes, messy business with Talon last week, but I'm glad to see you weathered it."

Beside her, Brent stiffened. She'd heard him griping about the company CEO with Russ a few days ago, but didn't know the details.

"Moss," Brent said in a clipped greeting. "It's fine. I'm sure Talon will come around."

"Ever the diplomat." He dropped his voice to a whisper. "But when JT is out and Russ is in, you can speak freely."

Kendall couldn't see Brent's face as he looked at the man, but his spine remained stiff.

The DJ announced a break, and the room quieted, allowing the man's voice to carry as he said, "Relax. I'm here to help."

Kendall placed a hand on Brent's back. "Sweetheart, I'd love another glass of wine."

A glance toward the nearest bar showed a line forming now that the music had stopped, but the bar on the far side of the room remained empty. Brent rose. "Of course, darling. Chardonnay?"

"Please."

"Moss, need anything?"

"Scotch. Neat."

"I'll bill it to your room." There was an edge to Brent's

tone. She'd overheard Russ tell him that even though he was an executive, JT Talon had refused to sign off on a room for him at the hotel. Russ had been forced to pay for his own room.

"That's not a problem. Talon & Drake is picking up the tab." Moss's tone was smug.

Okay, so some executives were getting comped rooms. Just not Russ. What was the deal between him and Talon?

Once Brent was gone, Kendall extended her hand over Brent's empty seat. "Kendall Gordon."

Moss smiled, took her hand, and brought it to his lips. "Calvin Moss. It's a pleasure to meet you, Ms. Gordon."

No man had ever kissed her hand before, and she felt strangely fluttery about it. He looked to be mid-thirties and had a chiseled jawline. Not as handsome as Brent, but not bad.

A noise on the other side of the dance floor caught her attention. It was hard to see with people in the way, but it looked like some sort of fight between two men in suits.

"What kind of company party is this?" Kendall muttered. The crowd shifted, revealing Russ was one of the men involved in the fight. And there was her roommate, right there in the middle.

Kendall bolted to her feet.

"Whoa," Calvin said. "Everyone knows Talon has it in for Russ, but this…"

Russ was seized from the other man's grasp by a uniformed police officer, who then cuffed and searched him.

Brent had stopped on his way to the bar and stood staring, open-mouthed. Kendall raced to his side. She wanted to approach Alex, but she was being questioned by police.

Suddenly, Alex let out a screech and said, "You put fucking *gamma*-Hydroxybutyric acid in my *drink*? So you could drag me to your hotel room and *RAPE ME*?"

And then her best friend kneed Russ Spaulding in the crotch.

She turned to Brent. “He drugged her drink? So he could rape her?”

“What? No. That’s insane. Talon must be setting him up. He hates Russ because Drake promoted him. The minute Drake left the party, Talon set him up.”

She glanced around, searching for the older engineer, but Brent was right, Edward Drake wasn’t here.

Regardless of what Brent believed, her best friend needed her. She ran to Alex, who glared at Brent. “Did you know about this?”

“No! Of course not!”

She faced Kendall. “You spent two weeks hounding me to be his date.”

“I had no idea! I swear.”

Did she believe her? But how could she think Kendall would have any part in this?

Alex’s attention returned to Brent. “You’re not welcome in our apartment ever again.”

Kendall was going to be sick. “No!” The word burst from her.

“It’s him or me, Kendall.”

Alex gave a few more instructions, then turned away.

With no other choice, Kendall left the party with Brent, the man she was in love with, who Alex had just banned from their apartment.

Chapter Forty-Three

Kendall paced the living room, waiting for Alex to leave. She needed to call Brent, but she didn't dare while Alex was home.

Police officers had been *here.* Alex had let them search *her room*. Because Brent and Russ had been here when she wasn't. Russ had assaulted Alex.

It was crazy. Impossible.

But that wasn't the reason she was ready to lose her mind. What had her freaked out was when she checked the nightstand, the vial of X wasn't there.

Worse, she'd looked it up online and learned that X—MDMA—was a pill, not a liquid. GHB—the drug Russ Spaulding had on him the night of the party—was usually available as a clear liquid. Just like the vial Brent gave her before the party.

Was it the same vial? How did Russ get it? Why did Brent get GHB not X? Both drugs could be dangerous, but GHB was more so. GHB was used as a date rape drug because when mixed with alcohol, it could cause blackouts, leaving sexual assault victims with no memories of their attacker.

Also when mixed with alcohol, even small doses could be fatal.

Had Russ really brought GHB to the party with the intention of drugging Alex? Or had the drugs been planted on him as he and Brent claimed, a ploy to get him fired?

Brent feared very much Russ would be fired. If that happened, Kendall could kiss her dream of a job at Talon & Drake goodbye. But that was a selfish thought considering her best friend could have been raped.

Or killed.

If Alex had died, it would've been Kendall's fault. She'd begged Alex to double date with them to the party. All because she'd wanted to impress Russ enough to get an internship and have a night alone with Brent.

She was the worst sort of best friend.

But she had a hard time believing Brent was involved.

No. Not her Brent. He loved her. He'd told her after the party, when they went back to the apartment, shell-shocked over the way the evening had ended.

Brent had taken her hand, held it to his lips, then whispered, *"I love you, Kendall. I was planning to say it tonight. I wanted it to be perfect. I have candles and flower petals in the trunk of my car. I was going to do it right. I don't understand how this could happen. Talon must have set Russ up. There's no way this could be real."*

Then they'd made love. They hadn't taken the X. The idea of taking it had turned her stomach.

But now the vial was gone.

Where was it?

The front door clicked closed. It wasn't like Alex to leave without saying goodbye, but she was beyond angry at Kendall.

Had Brent and Russ really been here when she got home?

Kendell left her bedroom and checked to be certain she was alone. Alex was gone.

She picked up the handset from the dock and pressed and held 3—which was Brent's shortcut. He answered immediately.

"What the hell, Brent? You were *here*?"

"Who told you that? You can't believe anything Alex told you."

"Why the fuck not? I've known her a helluva lot longer than you."

"She's fucking Talon. That's where she was last night, while Russ spent yet another night in the county jail."

"What?"

"She was gone last night, right?"

"Yes."

"Did she give you a number where she was?"

"Yes."

"Look it up. Use the reverse white pages."

Kendall tucked the phone into the crook of her neck and reached for the message book that made carbonless copies of everything written down. The original was torn away when the message was received; the copy stayed in the book. A permanent record that contained every number they had ever needed. Because the message had been for her, she'd left the original in the spiral-bound book.

Now she ripped out the sheet and went to the old desktop computer she and Alex were desperate to replace before they had a catastrophic crash. She typed the number into a reverse telephone directory.

She stared at the screen, not sure if she was surprised or not.

"Where was she?" Brent asked.

"She called me from the Mayflower."

"Did she give a room number?"

"Yes."

"Call the hotel. Ask to be connected to that room. It'll be Talon's. He's behind *everything*."

She did as Brent said—there was no reason not to—and a man answered the phone on the third ring. "Mr. Talon?" she said, thankful that caller ID wasn't available in hotel rooms.

"Yes?"

"Oh. Um. Will you be needing maid service today?"

"My room was already cleaned an hour ago."

"Right. Sorry. My mistake." She hung up as if the phone was on fire.

She took a deep breath. So. Alex had been with JT Talon last night. So what?

Sure, Talon had it in for Russ—and maybe even Brent—but that didn't mean he would frame Russ for drugging Alex. That was ludicrous. Alex had spent last night with the guy, and she was fine today.

Or was she?

Was there any chance JT Talon had drugged her? One side effect of GHB was hallucinations. It would explain her claiming Russ and Brent had been here today.

Brent had denied it.

She picked up the phone to call Brent back, but there was a knock on the door.

The Bethesda police officer was young. A year or two older than Kendall. His nameplate said WILLIAMS in all caps. "Can I help you, Officer?"

He gave her a smarmy grin that made her belly sink. This wasn't going to be good.

"Ms. Gordon, I presume?"

"Yes?" She didn't mean to make it a question, but her voice wouldn't cooperate.

He cocked his head, his gaze scanning her from head to foot. "May I come in?"

Years of watching *Law & Order* told her to close the door, but the foolish idea that she could clear this all up in an instant had her opening the door wider. "Of course."

He stepped into the apartment, then closed the door behind him, studying the lock. "New."

Kendall's throat was dry. "Yes. Alex changed the locks earlier today."

"I was here earlier."

"I presumed that. Why did you come back?"

The man gave an awful grin. "Because I saw the fingerprint results on the GHB vial taken from Russ Spaulding on Friday night."

She cleared her throat. "What…what are you talking about?"

"I think you know, Ms. Gordon." He reached for his belt. But instead of pulling a weapon, he unlatched it. "On your knees. Do a good job, and I can make this go away."

"*What?*"

"You're a smart woman. A graduate student in engineering. Don't play dumb with me. On. Your. Knees." He unzipped his fly.

"Whose fingerprints were on the vial?" she whispered.

"Yours."

"How do you know they're mine?" But she knew the answer. She'd been fingerprinted when she worked as a teacher aide at an elementary school years ago.

"Your prints are on file. We got more prints today when your roommate insisted we dust for prints after you gave your boyfriend a key without her permission."

She'd given Brent the key, but never in her wildest dreams had she imagined this. Were her fingerprints really on the vial? Was it the same one he'd given her Friday night?

Or was this cop setting her up?

Brent loved her. He'd said so. She believed him. He'd never met anyone who made him feel like she did. They were going to have fun together with some consensual enhanced sex. Other people took X and talked about it like it was ice cream on Christmas while watching the most beautiful sunset and riding a roller coaster.

She'd wanted the fun with her boyfriend. The man who loved her. But instead, she was facing down a creepy cop in her living room.

"Don't make me say it again. We can do this nice-like, or"—he grabbed her mouth and squeezed, making her jaw release—"I can make this less fun for you, but either way, if you don't suck me off, that evidence is going to the district attorney. Your choice if you want to face time for colluding to drug and rape your roommate. Word to the wise, there was enough drug in that drink to kill her. So you could go down for attempted murder."

She dropped to her knees.

Chapter Forty-Four

Kendall clung to the belief that Brent was innocent of Russ's scheme. He loved her. It was all some horrible mistake.

When she went to his apartment after being visited by Officer Williams, she didn't tell Brent what had happened or that she'd vomited and sobbed after. She felt guilty, as if she'd cheated on Brent, but she'd done the only thing she could in the moment.

A week passed before Russ was informed that the evidence against him had been lost and the prosecutor wasn't comfortable moving forward with charges based on JT Talon's testimony alone.

Kendall spent five days at Tanya's, too shell-shocked to enjoy the holiday they were supposed to be celebrating. She'd shared with her sister some of what had occurred, but the cop and the drugs and the forced blow job remained locked deep inside.

No one could know, or they'd hate her as much as she hated herself.

Russ invited her and Brent and a few other Talon & Drake employees over to celebrate the charges being dropped on New Year's Eve. Alex had barely talked to Kendall after she returned from her sister's, but she knew Alex was going to Senator Talon's New Year's Eve party at the family estate in Maryland and would be gone overnight.

She could finally have noisy sex with Brent in her own apartment, except she'd lost all interest in sex. Then there was the fact that Alex believed she and Brent had broken up.

He wasn't allowed in their apartment.

But it was Kendall's apartment too. Hell, hers was the only name on the lease because it was her connection that got them cheap rent. Still, she couldn't blame Alex.

"There was enough drug in that drink to kill her."

She dressed for Russ's party, glad Alex hadn't bothered to ask what her New Year's Eve plans were. On one level, she figured Alex knew she hadn't broken up with Brent, but she didn't want to push the issue.

Russ was full of bravado as the clock wound down to midnight. He planned to sue Talon & Drake to get his job back. He expected Ed Drake to support him.

Why he would want to work for a man who so clearly hated him made no sense to her, but one of the other employees in attendance—the biologist who'd been at the job fair—had responded to her whispered question.

"Drake runs the Bethesda office. Talon lives in New York. He's here about once a month, but that's all. And Russ was climbing fast once Drake handed him the Lewiston project. He was doing a good job—ahead of schedule, under budget. Talon & Drake is in the running to lead the redesign of the neighborhood in Southwest DC surrounding the baseball stadium that's going in near the Anacostia waterfront. With at least a year before construction on the stadium is set to begin, Spaulding was in a prime spot to lead the team if Talon &

Drake wins the project. Lewiston will be near completion just as the neighborhood refurbishment would be ramping up."

The biologist frowned. "Basically, Spaulding was on a meteoric path to success thanks to Drake's mentorship. But now he's job hunting. And Talon doesn't even have to bother with giving bad references. Russ's mugshot was shared all over industry emails. Someone hacked his LinkedIn and made it his profile picture. Hell, I bet even college kids were sharing it on MySpace and TheFacebook."

Kendall hadn't thought to check her MySpace and she wasn't signed up for LinkedIn or TheFacebook.

Why would someone with so much to lose bring a date rape drug to a company party?

It didn't make sense, which made it even more likely that JT Talon had set him up.

Alex's new boyfriend was the monster here. Not Russ Spaulding. Not Brent.

The cop… His role in the setup didn't make sense, though. Was it possible Alex was involved? Not before the party, obviously, but afterward? She'd spent the night with JT, then came home and claimed Russ had assaulted her and invited the cops to search Kendall's room.

The cop could have found the drugs in the nightstand during his search, then came back when she was alone, knowing she'd do what she had to.

Any woman who kept GHB in her nightstand would be an easy target for a crooked cop. And he might even assume she'd get off on it. Although in the moment, he'd known she hated it. Hated him. It was all she could do not to vomit all over him.

Officer Williams had kept up his end of the bargain, though. The evidence disappeared.

Her brain was spinning. She excused herself and stepped outside onto Russ's balcony. A chill wind snapped at her as she faced the Potomac River. Russ had a large condo on the Virginia side of the river. He was clearly quite wealthy, thanks to his executive salary.

"It boggles the mind, doesn't it?"

She startled. She hadn't realized she wasn't alone. She turned to see Calvin Moss standing in the darkest corner.

"Excuse me?"

"That Russ would risk all this." He swept out a hand to encompass the view, balcony, and condo behind them.

Could this man read her mind? Or was he just asking the same questions she was? How much did he know?

"I'm surprised you're here. Brent said most executives are too chicken to stand by Russ."

He gave her a pointed look. "If JT Talon finds out I'm here, I'll know who shared that detail. He's dating your roommate, after all. The woman Russ attempted to drug. What I'm wondering is why *you're* here."

She wished she could answer that. She shrugged. "Alex didn't get me an invite to the senator's party."

Moss laughed. "We're in the same boat, then." He cleared his throat. "Actually, I'm here because Drake asked me to come. We're keeping tabs on Russ. Making sure he doesn't do anything foolish as Drake tries to get him reinstated."

"It won't work." Kendall didn't know JT, but she knew Alex, and as long as Alex and JT were together, there was no way Russ was getting his job back.

"I agree. It makes one wonder why Drake doesn't distance himself too. What, do you think, does Russ have on him?"

She took a step back. "I'm afraid you're talking above my pay grade. I don't know Drake or Talon or even *you*. I'm a lowly graduate student who was hoping for an internship."

"Well, that's out as long as you've hooked your wagon to Forbes. JT will forever see him as Spaulding's crony."

"Is that why you're telling me this? To warn me?"

He shrugged. "You can do better than Forbes, and as the roommate of JT's girlfriend—for whom he's ridiculously ass over teakettle—you could definitely trade up."

What the hell? Was this man suggesting she use her roommate to spy? Was this industrial espionage? Was he trying to tell her *he* could get her an internship? Did he want a mole or a blow job—or both?

"It has been unpleasant chatting with you. Now, if you'll excuse me, it's almost midnight, and I have a boyfriend to kiss."

After the sad party wrapped, Kendall insisted they return to her apartment. She would start the year with her boyfriend in her bed. What Alex didn't know wouldn't hurt her.

They hadn't had sex since Officer Williams's assault—or was it blackmail?

Both, really.

She wanted to get the taste of the man out of her mouth, replace the nightmare of him in her mind.

Brent had a lot to drink, though—it was a good thing Kendall had been their designated driver—and he lost steam before she really got going. That was okay. They had backup. Brent had given her a vibrator for Christmas. This would be a perfect occasion for its inaugural run.

He kissed her as he fumbled with the nightstand drawer in the dark. Then she heard him knocking everything around as he searched for the toy. He made a surprised noise and turned on the light.

She blinked against the sudden brightness as Brent said, "Well damn. I forgot all about this."

Her vision cleared and she saw he held the small vial he'd given her on the night of the holiday party.

Was this false evidence, planted by Brent to exonerate him, or had the cop been the one with fake claims?

Chapter Forty-Five

Montgomery County, Maryland
Present

"In the recording, Kendall said Brent never quit his job at Talon & Drake," Leah said, "but why didn't JT fire him?"

"He was in a stalemate with HR. They could justify the lack of promotions, but unless JT had cause, he couldn't fire him. Brent made sure to color within the lines. He wasn't a great employee—no incentive to be that—but he did his job and no client or coworker ever filed a complaint."

"It makes sense he wouldn't quit," Leah said, "if money was being slid his way and all he had to do was the minimum to get by. I wonder where he's hiding his money. I wouldn't mind taking a crack at that if Lee fails."

Tricia snorted.

Leah laughed. "I know, I know. Lee is the greatest hacker of all time. But I'm pretty damn great too. I once saved Christmas, after all."

"I'm going to want to hear that story sometime," Alexandra said. She always liked women who weren't afraid to state their own worth and brains. Women in STEM weren't always vocal about their success. Academia often had a way of putting the best and brightest in their place.

"Nate and I will have you and JT over for dinner sometime, and I'll tell you all about it."

"It's a date."

"So tell us more about Kendall," Tricia said. "As a potential victim and likely collaborator, she's the one we need to figure out."

Tricia was right. They needed to focus on the crime. Whatever, exactly, the crime was.

"Why did she stay with Brent?" Leah asked.

It was a painful question. "Same reason as any victim of emotional abuse. There was so much gaslighting. And she did love Brent. I do believe that. She believed that. Every time I tried to tell her he was trouble, she was ready with ten reasons why JT had poisoned me against him. She truly believed JT had the cop plant the vial of drugs on him. The fact that the evidence went missing was just more proof it had been a setup."

"But now we know she turned the corner," Leah said. "In the recording, she'd switched sides to team Alexandra."

"She must've known she was in danger, or why would she have put the recording on my old computer? But I don't understand why she didn't just call me and tell me what she'd learned."

"She was trying to get evidence," Tricia said. "She couldn't find the money, and everything she had only implicated her."

"She was afraid enough to hide what she had—and made plans to give you the computer—but also, from what she said, there's more. Something you missed," Leah said. "She was *very* specific in mentioning Lee. She knew Lee could find it and was drawing him a map. She planned to give you something that you'd share with JT and Lee."

"She might have intended to give me more than the computer. I was supposed to see her, but had to cancel when Gemma got sick."

"One question: why was the hard drive not in the case?"

"She said the motherboard was fried. She intended to pull the drive and copy the files for me, but now that I was back and had my own place, she wanted to pass that task on to me. She was tired of storing it. I pulled the drive from the case before leaving her house that night. I figured it was better to leave the dead components with all the other parts that would be donated or recycled. There was a lot to sort through."

"Was the motherboard really fried?"

"I don't know. I didn't check."

"Clearly, she'd plugged the hard drive into a working motherboard in the days before her death. Was there anything else inside the case?"

"I was in such a hurry, I didn't look."

"If I wanted you to find something that needed to be kept hidden from everyone else, I would plant it in an old computer case and give the person—and only the one person I wanted to have it—a reason to open said case."

"Do Brent or Russ know about the internal hardware of computers?" Tricia asked.

"I don't know about Russ—I've worked hard to avoid him for sixteen years—but Brent knows how to use programs, not how to fix them. Kendall was his tech support."

"Do you mind if I skip the dress search in the attic and search through Kendall's old computer components?"

"I think that's a splendid idea."

"As long as Nate's with you," Tricia said. "We aren't going to Scooby-Doo this and have you go off alone in a house where a woman was likely murdered. And I need to stay close to my primary."

"Yes, Velma," Leah said.

"As long as I'm not Shaggy," Alexandra said.

Tricia laughed.

"Maybe whatever Kendall wanted me to have is with the—" She stopped abruptly as she realized how close they were to Kendall's house. "Slow down."

"Is that the spot?" Tricia asked.

Her throat was too dry to speak, so she just nodded, knowing Tricia couldn't see her response from the driver's seat.

"Want me to stop?"

"Yes." She had to force the word out as she wondered if she really wanted to do this.

They were the lead car. The other two pulled up behind them on the shoulder. They were about fifty feet from the driveway with the camera that made it possible for her to be here with these women today.

She looked at the lonely mailbox across the road. The reason for the camera.

"I should buy the homeowners a present," she said softly. "But I have no idea what."

"The night you went on the run, JT anonymously put out a reward for information," Tricia said. "It was paid through Raptor. If they haven't received it already, they will tomorrow when the deposit goes through."

Alexandra opened the door. She was practically in a daze as she approached the spot on the road where Officer Williams had been shot.

Tricia didn't say a word as she walked beside her.

Alexandra understood that Tricia didn't want her walking in the open like this, and she was thankful that she didn't try to stop her.

The other women climbed from the other vehicles, but only Erica approached.

Dear Erica, who'd been the friend she needed during the rough times.

She stared at the pavement. Rain had washed away the blood, but red bits of taillight remained.

Erica wrapped an arm around her as she studied the ground where Williams smashed her cell phone. She spotted tiny flecks of glass embedded in the pavement.

She leaned against Erica. "I've never been so terrified in my life."

"I know."

"It helped, knowing Gemma was with you. I knew she was safe."

"I'm glad I could do that for you."

"Promise me, if anything happens to me, or JT—"

"Of course. And I ask the same of you."

Alexandra nodded. "Thank you for agreeing to be my matron of honor. With everything—with Kendall… It's important to me to not be alone for the ceremony."

"I'm honored to be asked." She squeezed Alexandra's shoulder. "Remember the night we met?"

"Of course. I lied to you about Lee and later lectured you on how you were a fool not to forgive him, when I had no idea what he and JT had put you through. I was a smug brat."

"In your defense, I would have been a fool not to give him another chance. He's the best thing that ever happened to me."

"Lee has always been one of my very favorite people. The brother I wish I'd had."

"He and JT came to blows, you know, after what JT did. They fought in the dojo one night—but they definitely weren't sparring. I only know about it because I saw Lee's bruises. He wouldn't talk about it, but I suspect it was one of those things where JT wanted someone to kick his ass, and Lee was happy to oblige."

"I'm so sorry I came between them like that."

"*Someone* had to knock sense into JT. It was then that he realized he could lose Lee too. He finally started seeing a therapist."

"So that's what did it."

"I'm pretty sure Lee wishes he'd kicked his ass two, maybe three years earlier." She paused. "But that's not why I brought up the night we met. I wanted to share something. When we were in the limo, there was a moment when JT looked at you and…I realized how deeply in love with you he was. It was the first time I could relate to him. He was so intimidating—intentionally so, when it came to me—but when he was with you, he was different.

"The man I glimpsed that night disappeared when Joe was arrested. Over the last nine years—well, six, really—he came back, piece by piece. But Christmas dinner…that was a revelation. The way he looked at you and Gemma. I'm so glad you've found your way back to each other."

The words were a reason to smile as they stood on a roadside that would forever be inhabited by nightmarish memories.

"I'm finally getting my happily ever after. But it won't be complete until we know what happened here. I won't be free from worry or fear until the person who murdered Williams—and probably Kendall—is caught." She kicked at the flecks of destroyed cell phone. "Williams was awful and terrifying. But no one deserves to be executed like that. Even he deserves justice."

"Well, let's hope we find something at Kendall's. We were talking in Mara's car..."

"Oh no," Tricia said. "You are not Scooby-Dooing on me too."

"Scooby-Dooing? Is that a verb?"

"Everyone runs off separately to search Kendall's," Alexandra explained.

"What part are you searching?"

"Attic. Leah has called dibs on the dead computer closet."

"Only if Nate is with her," Tricia insisted.

"She's Velma," Alexandra said. "What room do you want to search?"

"No idea. But Kendall must've left a message for you somewhere. She was too deliberate with the recording. Didn't you say one of the couches is yours?"

"Convince Keith to babysit you," Tricia said. "Otherwise, you're in the attic with me."

"Trina, we're going to need you to give Keith sexual fav—"

Tricia covered her ears. "Stop. You are talking about my boss."

"Sorry, Trish," Isabel said. "I'll make sure they behave."

Tricia shook her head. "Right." But she was smiling. "C'mon. The sooner we get to the house, the sooner you meddling kids can start your crime solving."

A chill ran down Alexandra's spine as she approached the front door. The last time she'd been here, she'd been on the run and had only stopped to take Kendall's car, which was still up on Catoctin Mountain.

She and JT planned to drive north after the wedding to

enjoy a week up at the cabin with Gemma, and then she'd drive the Jetta back here, which was fine with Tanya.

Later, she and JT would take a real honeymoon, leaving Gemma with Lee and Erica for a few days.

But first, she had to cross this threshold.

"I want to search the house first," Keith said. He, Chase, and Nate had been waiting in the driveway when they arrived.

She handed him the key and stepped back. Three operatives searched the house while Chase stood guard over the rest of them outside.

After the house was cleared, Tricia led Erica, Mara, and Alexandra to the attic. Nate and Leah headed for the home office with a closetful of old components. Trina and Isabel went with Keith to search the upstairs bedrooms, while Eden and Chase took the living room and kitchen.

The attic ceiling was low and pitched, requiring Alexandra to hunch over even in the very center. It contained a daunting number of boxes even though Kendall had only lived here for five years. But of course, she was storing more than her own lifetime in this attic. She'd been generous and held on to Alexandra's forgotten items.

Penance for the little betrayals of letting Russ show up in their apartment periodically?

Deep down, she must have known there was more truth on Alexandra's side.

"Will you recognize the box?" Erica asked hopefully.

"No. Honestly, I don't remember packing it up. It's entirely possible Kendall did it and didn't tell me. I might have told her to donate it. Or throw it away. I was a bit of a wreck."

"Let's hope Kendall liked labeling things, then."

Sadly, Kendall was *not* a labeler, and the first several boxes were a bust. They were several boxes in when they found one that held textbooks and papers from graduate school—and some of the papers were Alexandra's.

"The box will be large—the skirt of the gown is *big*—and lighter. The heavy ones are almost certainly school papers and books."

They lifted and sorted. Some boxes were plastic, some cardboard. They had to move heavy ones to the side to reveal stacked boxes in the next row.

"This plastic one is light for its size," Tricia said as she lifted a hinged storage box that looked to be four feet long, two feet wide, and eighteen inches high.

Alexandra set aside a small but lighter box and joined Tricia. "That does look promising. It's sealed tight with plastic wrap." Most boxes were taped shut, not wrapped with cling wrap. "Let's move this downstairs where the light is better, and it'll be easier to cut off the wrapping when we aren't hunched over."

"I would not mind getting out of this attic," Mara murmured.

"Same," Erica said.

Mara descended first, followed by Erica, then Alexandra. When she was halfway down the attic ladder, Tricia handed down the box, which Alexandra then passed to Erica below.

They all sported a fine layer of dust and cobwebs as they carried the box to the living room, where Eden and Chase were searching the bookshelves.

"Any luck?" Eden asked.

"We hope so."

Mara grabbed four knives from the kitchen and passed them out. They each took a side and made quick work of the layers of wrap. Hearing the commotion, the others left their search areas to watch as Alexandra flipped the latches on the plastic trunk and raised the lid.

Her heart surged as she lifted the pile of silver silk fabric from the airtight container. The gown was more beautiful than she remembered.

She held it to her chest, and there was a collective gasp along with more than a few cheers.

"Wow," Trina said. "That's stunning."

"Perfect for New Year's Eve," Isabel said.

"I hope it still fits. Eleven years and one baby later, my body has changed."

"Dresses—especially ones with that much fabric—can be altered," Trina said.

Leah cleared her throat. "This trip was successful in more ways than one."

Alexandra's gaze jerked in her direction. "What did you find?"

"First, I found two things inside the case, taped to the side. A Post-it Note with a file name for a Word doc, and this." She held up a plastic bag with the note and what looked to be a small vial with some kind of liquid in it.

"Last," Leah continued, "I found something jammed in the CD ROM slot, which is where I'd hide something if I didn't have time to open the case where I'd already hidden other items." The bag contained a small memory card—the kind used in digital cameras. "It holds a terabyte."

"Not something I'd have used with that old computer. It's been at least ten years since it was used regularly. I don't think terabyte storage disks were even available back then."

Leah nodded. "They were not—not in this format, anyway. I'd ask if anyone has a camera so we can view the contents," Leah said, "but I think this is something we should do at the compound. Mothman can make sure the files aren't damaged or contain a trojan or virus."

"We should check out the other old computers and drives before we go," Keith said.

"Nate and I already started. We'll finish while Alexandra tries on the dress."

Tricia looked to her boss. "You want to call Rav, Dominick, and the investigative team while I call the operatives?"

Keith nodded. "Tell everyone to meet at the compound in two hours."

Chapter Forty-Six

Mothman queued up a video. They'd all gathered in the big conference room with the large screen. JT's focus should be on the screen, but Alexandra had all his attention.

Erica had texted to give him the heads-up that they'd visited the spot by the side of the road where she'd been assaulted by Williams. This was before they'd searched Kendall's house for clues. That she'd found her old wedding dress was a nice surprise, but the rest, he knew, had a high emotional cost.

They were once again traveling through the most painful parts of their past, but this time, it was also their present, and Kendall Gordon wasn't holding her peace.

She was present, almost life-sized, on the big screen. A voice from the grave.

This was the Kendall he'd last seen at the office in October. She'd always been lovely. Pretty face, with a warm smile, dark hair. Their first meeting had been fraught, and he acknowledged she'd never had a chance with him.

His protectiveness of Lex, combined with his loathing of

Brent Forbes, meant he'd never looked at Kendall and seen Lex's best friend. The woman she loved, even now, when she knew they were going to learn some painful truths today.

She hadn't given up on Kendall.

JT took Lex's hand, cupping it between both of his.

Kendall's first words were a wrench in the works. "Whoever is watching this, and I hope it's you, Alex, I really need you to read my diary first. Before watching the rest."

"The diary must be the file on the computer," Keith said. "Lee, how are we doing with that?"

"I think we should let Alexandra read it first."

"Do we really have time for that?" Curt's question wasn't unsympathetic. JT understood his urgency.

"In this instance, I think so. The diary begins sixteen years ago, but there are only a half dozen entries over the next eight years."

Lee closed his laptop and slid it across the table to her.

Keith's voice was kind as he said, "You can use my office. JT will show you the way."

JT was glad for the offer. He hoped she'd allow him to read it with her.

Before they left the room, Alexandra turned to face everyone gathered around the table. "While I read this in privacy with JT, the rest of you should read it here. Lee, you have another copy?"

He nodded. "The entire drive is on a secure Raptor server."

"Good. We can watch the videos when I get back."

JT led her down the hall to Keith's office. They settled on the couch side by side. "Thank you for letting me be here with you."

"Of course. I wouldn't want to face this alone."

He kissed her temple, and she opened the laptop. The diary began on New Year's Day, sixteen years ago.

Alexandra was going to be sick. Reading the horror that Kendall went through at the hands of Officer Williams… It was grotesque.

"Do you think this is what Williams was after?" she asked. "Her diary?"

"It's possible. I'm not sure how admissible it would be in a court of law, but given that it's on an old hard drive and the last save of the file was eight years ago, maybe?"

"But hasn't the statute of limitations run out?"

"Maryland has no statute of limitation on felony sex crimes," JT said. "I looked it up a few days ago, when we realized this was probably connected to Spaulding."

"But he didn't rape me."

"Thank god," JT said. "Still, I wanted to know, in case there were other women he abused around the same time."

"Still, in Kendall's case, obviously there's coercion, but it was blackmail, and a defense attorney would argue she performed oral sex willingly. What an ugly mess."

"Given the other complaints against Williams that MSP might or might not have been investigating, this could've been a problem for him even if it's not felony rape. A history of using his badge to force sex. Destruction of evidence. And the fact that he was obviously lying to Kendall. He never would have been able to intercept fingerprint results. He worked in a different county, and it's not like the results wouldn't have been in a system with multiple backups."

"But she was so terrified that she believed him in the moment." Alexandra could imagine her terror. Williams had been intimidating then and now. "Later, when the evidence against Spaulding disappeared, she had to think that confirmed his claim. She was convinced her fingerprints were on the vial taken from Russ that night."

"And they might have been, although I don't understand why Spaulding and Forbes would have implicated her ahead of time. What was the point? You'd never believe she played a part in your rape."

Alexandra scrolled up and reread Kendall's confession, including Williams's threats about the GHB. She tapped the screen. "There were enough drugs in the drink to kill me. But they couldn't know that. Half the drink spilled." Cold dread hit her in the gut. "What if the plan wasn't to rape me that night, but to kill me?"

"If you turned up dead in Spaulding's hotel room, the only person implicated would have been him."

"But Spaulding wasn't the only one with a hotel room. All the executives had them. He was resentful that his wasn't being comped as promised."

"They weren't all being comped, just the ones for executives who worked over fifty miles away."

"And Drake."

"Yes, but he was one-third owner."

"And he hated your guts but couldn't fire you."

"Shit," JT said, his voice cracking as he added, "But if a woman was found dead in *my* hotel room…"

"Could Russ have gotten your room key?"

"I'm sure Drake could have gotten it, since our rooms were booked in the same block. Claim a mix-up with the room numbers. Easy."

"In the audio recording, Kendall said Drake funneled Talon & Drake money to Russ Spaulding. This could be Russ's extortion. Drake asked him to remove you from the picture. I was chosen as the victim for no other reason than I was Kendall's roommate and could be convinced to attend.

But Russ had no real interest in me. He even went off and played blackjack instead of spending time with me."

"I'm not sure if it means he had a conscience and didn't want to get to know you, or if he was just a cold motherfucker who had better things to do before committing murder."

Alexandra felt the air thicken. Once upon a time, she'd thought the worst thing that would have happened to her that night was a horrific rape.

"So how does Williams play in? He was involved somehow. He responded to my 9-1-1 call, then coerced Kendall and destroyed evidence. Kendall was fully locked in at that point. Complicit in the crime Russ had tried to commit."

"Until the GHB vial showed up again in her nightstand, forcing her to question everything. Brent could be innocent. So could Russ—they always claimed *I* had the cops plant the vial on Russ. And then there was another cop, with another vial."

"But the vial in the nightstand was GHB, not X."

JT tapped the screen. "Which Brent explained away as a mistake."

She nodded. Kendall's diary gave Brent's embarrassed admission that he'd never tried X, so when he was sold GHB instead, he didn't realize he'd been tricked.

Kendall had been so desperate to believe him, to believe she wasn't complicit in a *real* crime, that she'd accepted his explanation. She'd clung to the idea that Russ really was innocent, because then it meant she hadn't caused the charges to be dropped against a guilty man just to save herself.

The diary entries that followed over the years were written at times when she struggled with her guilt and belief in Brent. She was haunted by nightmares of Williams and terrified Russ was a monster.

She saved the diary file without a password on the desktop computer they shared, not the personal laptop she used for school most of the time.

Alexandra was convinced Kendall wanted her to find it. Wanted to confess. She probably even wanted JT investigated, because she was sure he was guilty of something. Alexandra's uneven relationship with him didn't help Kendall's opinion of him.

But Alexandra had never looked at Kendall's files. It honestly had never occurred to her.

So Kendall suffered in silence. Complicit in crimes she couldn't begin to understand.

Chapter Forty-Seven

When JT and Alexandra joined the others in the main conference room, Erica jumped to her feet and wrapped Alexandra in a tight hug.

Somehow, she and JT had made it through reading the diary and discussing what it meant without tears, but this hug was her undoing.

This was the hug of a friend, not a lover. Erica had also known Kendall. Not well, but they'd met several times.

Next came Lee, who had been there from the very start. The brother she never had, and she was afraid her sobs might become audible.

She held her breath to keep the sounds inside. Finally under control, she tilted her head back so she could meet his gaze. His eyes were watery too. "I think you and JT might have saved my life that night."

He nodded. "I've shared with the others the details of what I knew. We came to the same conclusion. It always seemed odd that a man who was on the rise like that would risk everything, and at the company party, no less. Especially since there was no evidence he was a serial predator."

She pulled back from his embrace and faced the room. "Kendall said she and Calvin Moss pondered the same question that first New Year's Eve. For her, it was her reason to believe JT must've set him up. But it was really Russ setting JT up. Whether I died or not, if I was found drugged in JT's bed after a company event, he'd have been out at T&D. Plus, being a company party, Russ could get access to JT's hotel room, which he'd never have at another time or place."

"Why drug your drink right there in the ballroom?" Mara asked.

"By that point, he knew there was no way he was getting me up to his hotel room, where he could have drugged my drink in private. I was ready to leave. It was his last shot."

"And he had to kill a certain amount of time first," JT said. "Too early, and I had dozens of alibis, not the least of which was Lee. The effects of GHB take fifteen to thirty minutes to appear, and it peaks within twenty to sixty minutes. Not a lot of time. He would have needed to get her in my room before I left the party. Brent's job might have been to alert him when I left."

Alexandra circled the table and resumed her earlier seat. JT settled in beside her. "Someone else might have been at the ready to delay you if needed. Even to spike your drink. Make it look like consensual use of a club drug gone wrong."

"I think we're all on the same page with this," Keith said. "Shall we start the video?"

"Just to be clear," JT said, "we think Drake set Spaulding to the task of ensuring I was removed from Talon & Drake in a way that my father couldn't object to. Facing trial for rape and possibly murder... Dad would have believed my innocence, but he would have been equally focused on the scandal. He'd just been reelected by a wide margin, so it was a good window for his reputation to take a hit and have plenty of time to mend."

"Shrewd of Drake."

"He was an excellent engineer—the ultimate planner. Very good at seeing the structural flaw in any design." He glanced at Erica. "He was only brought down when faced with something he couldn't anticipate when Erica zealously researched Thermo-Con. And in this instance, his hands didn't get close to dirty. It was all on Spaulding to take the risks. All Drake had to do was get my room key, which would have gone unnoticed in the aftermath."

"Spaulding must've had proof of Drake's involvement," Alec said. "That was his blackmail."

"When Drake was arrested and I took over the Bethesda office," Lee said, "I looked deep into Brent Forbes, figuring if Drake had an accomplice in the office we didn't know about, it would be him. I never found anything conclusive."

"Brent had to keep his nose clean, or he was out," JT said. "Any involvement he had in the artifact and money smuggling would have been through Spaulding."

"We still don't know how the cop—Williams—is connected to all this," Lee said. "I looked for a link to Spaulding and Forbes but came up empty."

"Could he be connected to Drake?" Alexandra asked, then she shook her head. "Instead of speculating, we should see what Kendall has to say."

She braced herself as Keith tapped the Play button on the computer.

The video restarted with the warning about reading the diary. She paused long enough to allow the viewer to do the same, then resumed speaking. There was a date and time stamp on the video, several days before her death. "Okay, so now you know how this all started." She closed her eyes and took a deep breath. "And how I spent sixteen years as an unwilling and sometimes unwitting accomplice to two horrible men. One of whom professed to love me. He lied.

He manipulated. Gaslit. You name it. But still, I did what I did, and I *was* complicit."

She swiped at her eye. "I'm so sorry, Alex. You were like my other sister. I loved you as much as I love Tanya, and I fucked it all up. I destroyed our friendship and my life." She shook her head. "I felt like if I believed Russ was guilty and Brent colluded, it would make what I did so much worse. So I stood by my man. Accepted his lies as truth."

The camera was probably on a tripod. Kendall rose from her seat and paced in front of the lens. "Nine years ago, Lee Scott hired me to work as a cost estimator at the Bethesda office." She gave a bitter laugh. "I finally got my dream job, but it only added to my nightmare."

Alexandra remembered calling Lee and begging him to give Kendall a chance. She and Brent were broken up, and the project she'd been hired to work on for another engineering firm was wrapping up. She was being laid off.

Kendall had been so grateful. She'd hugged Alexandra tight and thanked her profusely. But Alexandra had brushed it off because she knew Kendall would be great for the job and Lee likely would have hired her without the nudge. The part Alexandra had really played was letting Lee know she and Brent had broken up.

She'd really thought it was over that time. But then, working in the same office, he clawed his way back into her life.

"Within a few months of taking the job," Kendall continued, "I noticed some discrepancies in the budget allocation on some of Drake's long-running projects. I was tasked with auditing the projects and updating the projections. When I noticed the issue, I put a pause on one of the payments, requesting the invoice number and budget code. A message popped up, overriding my actions. It was locked tight. So naturally, I started digging and documenting. I set up a meeting with Rob Anderson—he'd taken over from Lee at that point—to show him what I'd found.

"But that night, I received a visitor at my apartment. Alex, you were pretty much living with JT at that point, although lord knows why. He was being a raging dick."

"That's fair," JT muttered.

On the screen, Kendall continued. "My visitor was Officer Williams."

Alexandra jolted. JT sat at attention.

Someone whispered, "Motherfucker," which was exactly the word Alexandra had been thinking.

Kendall's head dropped into her hands. "Williams told me I was to let the transactions go through, or my role in getting the charges dropped would be revealed to JT and Lee. I would lose everything. My job. My best friend. Face legal charges."

She raised her head again. "I'm no dummy. I knew Williams couldn't implicate me without revealing his part. But he…" She dropped her head again. "Oh god. I can't believe I'm saying this. *Fuck!*"

She slammed her fist on the table. "After…after the vial showed up again in my nightstand, I found out where Williams lived and showed up at *his* house. With a crowbar."

"Oh fuck," Alexandra said on a sharp exhale.

"Yes, I'm stupid. I was so angry and broken. That fucker made me give him a blow job, but he had to be lying about everything. I don't know what I wanted to happen. He wasn't home, so I smashed his windows. It was winter, and I was wearing a hat and scarf and gloves. But…"

Alexandra thought she was going to lose it in the pause that followed the *but*.

"I cut my arm on a shard of glass. Badly. I fled, but I had to go to the emergency room to get stitches. A week later, I received a police report from an anonymous email address. It listed the evidence collected from the vandalism, which included coat fibers and blood. DNA would be run when a suspect was identified."

Again, she faced the camera. "I fucked myself."

She took a deep breath and continued, "And so I let the money flow. I told myself actively stealing from the company and letting embezzling that had been going on for years to continue were two different things. Most days, I believed it. Some of the projects ended, and the amount of money being stolen dwindled. Then, about five years ago, I received new instructions. Anonymously this time. I was told to phase out the remaining payments. I was so thrilled! My nightmare was ending."

She huffed out a breath. Then she dropped back in her seat, took off her shoes, and dropped one, waited a moment, then slammed the second shoe on the coffee table. "That, of course, is the other shoe dropping. My next instruction was to do two cost estimates on some of my new proposals—one for T&D with slightly inflated numbers. Nothing noticeable, but *just enough*, and the other more accurate with specific specs. It took me months to figure out who I was working for—it usually takes months for projects to be awarded. A pattern emerged. Not all the projects I did two estimates for went to the same company if T&D didn't win, but the majority went to one company."

"Moss & Delano Architects and Engineers," JT said at the same time Kendall did.

Alexandra gripped his hand. There was still a chance Calvin Moss wasn't complicit and JT could move forward with the sale.

Kendall looked wryly at the camera. "Of course, I dug into MDAE and learned that Russ was working for them. Buried under sixteen layers of subcontracts so JT would never know. It was well known among A&E firms that JT wouldn't hire any sub that employed Russ. So Russ had to hide. He worked for a bunch of companies that had subcontracts with T&D, but his part was always small and hidden. With MDAE, his role wasn't small, but it was deeply hidden.

"Honestly, it was a relief when I was told MDAE was buying T&D. I couldn't be blackmailed anymore. I would be *free*. I was fairly certain Russ would move out of the woodwork and into the official executive branch, but *I* wouldn't need to hide that from my employer. No more double estimates. No more nightmares. Hell, I'd learned that Officer Williams had moved to Maryland State Police a few years ago. We no longer lived in the same town or even the same county.

"I was going to be free." She picked up a shoe and studied it and set it down. "It wasn't so much a shoe drop as a wakeup call. I ended things with Brent for good at the same time I was forced to do double estimates. I was no longer able to fool myself into thinking he was ignorant of what was going on. I mean, I still *wanted* to believe he was ignorant, but I was done lying to myself. Honestly, I've felt nothing but hate for him for the last five years. If we stood at a crosswalk and a bus was coming, I don't think I'd hesitate to push him in its path. I mean, I might get away with it.

"I never left work at the same time he did. Too much temptation. Think of the possibilities of a crowded Metro station..." Her voice sounded dreamy, then she sighed. "For the last eighteen months, I've been seeing someone new. Not an engineer. He doesn't work for Talon & Drake. He's an event photographer and the nicest guy." She nodded to the camera. "Mark Kaufman. He gave me the camera that's recording this and taught me how to use it. It's got different lenses. Zooms and stuff, which has come in handy these last few weeks. So now we're going to do a little slide show. I'm going to splice in the photos into the video. I'm not great at this, so bear with me."

The screen went black, but Kendall kept talking. "Pausing for dramatic effect, but let me set the scene. A month ago, my boyfriend and I met for lunch in Bethesda because it was one of my in-office days. We were sitting in the front of the restaurant near the window, and he'd just given me a new zoom lens, which I was testing out. I raised the viewer window to my eye—I really prefer that to the screen—and zoomed in to a restaurant across the street. I nearly dropped the camera at what I saw."

The screen flashed, and an image appeared. There, in crystal-clear HD, was a plain-clothed Officer Corey Williams seated across from Calvin Moss.

Alexandra slapped a hand over her mouth. Around the table, others gasped and cursed.

"Now, like me, you might be wondering why my worst fucking nightmare is having lunch with my very near future boss. Lucky for us, the information that a tech savvy person can find on the internet is a lot more detailed than it was sixteen years ago, when I first started searching for information on Williams. It's even better than it was five years ago, the last time I checked. The other difference between then and now is I added Moss to the searches."

The screen changed to show a graphic with a family tree. "As you can see, they're second cousins."

JT shot to his feet. "Goddammit."

Kendall continued speaking from the grave. "Once I had that, the pieces came together. I still don't know how Williams and his partner ended up taking the initial 9-1-1 call, but I'm guessing they were waiting in the wings after Brent and Russ showed up to threaten Alex.

"Remember, everyone was scrambling because Russ royally fucked up and was caught drugging Alex's drink.

There was video of him trying to convince her to take a sip—that didn't go missing, by the way, just the vial and glass. Anyway, they're in a panic. Russ shows it by assaulting Alex. Brent knows he fucked up for letting him in the apartment. They probably just planned to scare her. I'm guessing Brent took the vial from the nightstand while they were there and replaced it on New Years. Williams used the missing vial to terrify me. I don't know if Brent knew what he made me do. I think Williams made his own rules.

"I was a puppet, all my strings being pulled by different men. One who claimed to love me. One who raped me. One who manipulated me into providing him with a victim for a scheme I'm only just beginning to understand, and one who pretended to be a voice of wisdom but hinted at how useful I'd be as a spy as long as Alex was with JT. I was thoroughly trapped. But now…now that the last pieces of the jigsaw have come together, I look at the picture and I have no fucking proof."

She shook her head. "Nothing but a stupid vial that could contain anything and doesn't connect to Russ at all. Just me and Brent."

She held up her arm to show the scar that she'd told Alexandra she'd gotten when she slipped on icy steps outside their apartment building and was cut by a jagged piece of metal on the old iron railing. "The evidence only implicates *me*. I'm the one who kept the money flowing to Russ's slush account. I'm the one who gave Calvin the specs to win the projects. I'm the one who was on my knees.

"The only way for me to win is to kill the deal. And so I will. But if I fail because Moss and Williams figure out what I'm doing, well, I'm going to document what I *do* know. Proof or not, the truth matters. I'm doing this for Alex. For Gemma. I love you both. Gemma, I hope I get to meet you. I'm going to do my best to compile everything and hand it to

Alex on Saturday. The files on this disk include everything I've gathered so far. I'll keep updating until I give this to the police, stop the sale, or am found out and silenced."

The video ended without fanfare, but the next video was an addendum. "Oh! I broke up with Mark because I didn't want to drag him down with me if this got ugly. And I figured I might have to have sex with Brent to get him to talk and couldn't bear the idea of cheating on Mark. Which I did. You have the recording of the fun conversation I had with Brent after sex saved to the hard drive along with my diary.

"Mark doesn't know anything, but…I really hope he can learn why I did what I did. He was the best thing to happen to me in a long time and for the first time, I think I get how Alex felt about JT when he wasn't being a raging ass. Here is his website. Tell him I loved him."

"She knew she was going to die," Isabel said.

"She did," Alexandra said, "but she tried to pretend otherwise."

The next files on the disk—they were numbered—included a series of photos of the four men she appeared to have followed over the last weeks of her life. None of the photos showed any of the four together with the others. The one lunch at the start was the exception, but then, she'd only had three weeks to spy.

There was a series of videos of her with Brent. Making out in her garage before they stumbled into the house. They were picked up by a camera in the laundry room followed by the living room, where they had sex. Thankfully, Kendall had blurred the image, and they didn't have to watch Brent's bare ass as their skin slapped together.

As she'd said, after they had sex, she confronted him, threatened him with killing the deal, trying desperately to get him to say something on camera that could be used against him.

Now the cameras in the house made sense. Brent was the weak link, but he also had the least to lose. On paper, he was innocent of everything. But with their history, he had the best chance of cracking. He was also the only one she could get easy access to.

But it was the last video that made bile rise in Alexandra's throat and the hair on the back of her neck stand up. There was no tripod this time. It was a selfie with Kendall holding up the camera to her face. But unlike a phone, there was no selfie screen. Her face was cut off as she ran through the house. "Oh fuck oh fuck oh FUCK. He's here. That coward Brent. He must've run to Daddy when he searched my office and knew I was close to crushing the sale. Fuck. I expected to have more time while he tried to figure out how to use me to his advantage again."

She turned the camera away from her face and pointed it out the window to the woods behind her house. She hit the zoom and dialed way in. And there he was, a closeup on Corey Williams as he approached the house, dodging from tree to tree.

He was coming for her.

She turned the camera back on her face. "I'll get him to talk. Fuck him if I have to. Or maybe I'll cut his dick off. I won't go down easily. This isn't over."

The video ended.

Leah cleared her throat. "I'd guess this is when she pried open the CD ROM drive and taped the camera disk to the tray. She had a few minutes, but not enough to open the case."

"Goddamn. I wish she'd kept the camera rolling, but if she did, we never would have found this video," Chase said. "Williams would have taken it." He turned to Nate. "You and Leah searched her office. Did you find a camera?"

"No. But her sister might have it."

"I'll ask Tanya," Alexandra said. "But she never said anything about Kendall taking up photography or having a new camera—and we spent hours looking at photos that day."

"Williams probably took the camera," Keith said. "Figuring he was getting the evidence Kendall had collected."

"Williams probably killed her," Nate said, "but we still don't know who killed Williams."

"Wait," Eden said. "Keith, go back to the video that was spliced together of her with Forbes."

Everyone groaned. No one wanted to see that horrific sex show again, even if the worst parts were blurred. Still, Keith complied.

They watched the video at double speed.

"Stop," Eden said when they were making out in the garage.

The image froze on the couple as Kendall straddled him on the steps to the side door. "That's a good angle," Eden said. "It captures most of the garage. Too high for a tripod, but of course, Forbes would have spotted a tripod. I'd bet the camera was mounted high. Probably attached to an air duct or the garage door mechanism, but hidden."

"A doorbell camera?"

"No way," Eden said. "Far better quality. But probably motion sensitive. It clicks on when they're already in the frame, and this wasn't a professional edit. That's raw footage."

Eden knew cameras from her previous work as a camgirl, for which, Alexandra assumed, she'd done a fair amount of filming using remote cameras.

"She didn't have cameras hooked up to her Wi-Fi," Lee said. "I checked. No signals. No streaming. Her killer would have had to remove all traces, and from the number of angles we saw in some of the videos, she must have at least a half dozen cameras hidden in the house and garage."

"What if," Eden said, "she wasn't streaming at all? What if it was all cameras with disks on a motion detection setting? Far better images, and she didn't have to worry about signals giving her away. Power isn't an issue when outlets can be screwed into a lightbulb slot so she's not burning precious camera batteries. To save disk space, she could change the setting from video to stills."

"What you're saying is the cameras could still be in the house, with their storage disks intact."

"Yes," Eden said. "And she had a camera in the garage. Where she died."

Chapter Forty-Eight

It was one thing to enter Kendall's house and take what already belonged to Alexandra, and quite another to dismantle hidden cameras to view the contents. It took an hour to arrange for Alexandra's attorney and the MSP investigators to agree to meet at the Raptor compound.

Aside from Alexandra and her attorney, the meeting with the police included Keith to provide context for Raptor's role, and Lee and JT as owners of T&D.

They went over the diary—pointing out the original file was on the hard disk currently in MSP evidence. Alexandra, JT, and Lee verified the dates given in the diary were accurate to their recollections.

Next came the videos, which was where Lee came in. "In the days immediately following Drake's arrest, I made a backup of the entire Bethesda network and archived it, in addition to handing everything over to the FBI, who did their own vetting separate from my own audit. With JT's permission, I will give you the files that pertain to the projects through which Drake funneled subcontract money to Russ Spaulding."

"But this isn't actual evidence of embezzling by Spaulding or Forbes?"

"Unfortunately, no. We can't prove extortion or that Spaulding didn't fulfill the contracts—although it was doubling up on work T&D did in-house. But too many years have passed, and Drake is dead."

"Did the payment structure change when Kendall took over?" one of the investigators asked.

"It appears so. But I'm afraid the only person implicated in the embezzling there is Kendall."

"She was solidly trapped," Alexandra said. "But Russ and Brent must be hiding the money somewhere."

"Neither of them killed Kendall Gordon," the detective said. "They have alibis for the day she died—yes, we checked. *If* she was murdered. In the video, only Williams approached her house."

"Well, he was the man who scared her the most. Makes sense they'd send him in." Alexandra would never forget the terror in Kendall's voice as the camera zoomed in. Her own terror at Williams's unwavering viciousness also remained vivid.

"Okay, then," the detective said. "We'll send a forensic team to the house to do a thorough search and collect the cameras if they're there. Do *not* enter the house again."

"Any chance you'll share the videos with us?" Lee asked.

"Right, as if we'd give them to Mr. Leaky," the officer muttered.

Alexandra snickered.

"I didn't leak it. The homeowners did."

"*This* time."

Clearly, this officer was versed in Lee's past indiscretions.

"We'll be in touch if there's a change in status in Ms. Gordon's death."

"As Ms. Vargas's attorney, I have the right to see any videos you may find in Ms. Gordon's house."

"Only if the prosecutor files charges. Depending on what we find, we may decide to close the investigation into Ms. Vargas's role in the shooting of Officer Corey Williams."

They were no closer to having proof for who killed Williams, but Alexandra was close to being in the clear.

After a long day of Gemma being babysat by a Raptor employee, Alexandra was more than ready for a quiet evening with her newly complete family.

Gemma was out of sorts due to the long day with a stranger babysitting her at the compound and was extra clingy and grumpy. She rejected JT's attention, wanting only her mom, which was fair considering how much the toddler's world had been upended for the last week. Even her house had changed, as they'd moved to JT's better-secured estate the day after Christmas.

It was too soon to try to enforce JT as parent when Alexandra was the only one she'd ever known, so JT retreated to his office while Alexandra and Gemma built with blocks and read books in the library, which they'd set up as a temporary playroom.

For ninety minutes, she gave all her attention to her daughter. She didn't think about the past or the future. She simply joined Gemma in living in the moment.

Peace settled over her. In all of the vast universe, composed of supermassive blackholes and subatomic quarks with hundreds of billions of galaxies, this was the very best place and time to be.

Two nights before the wedding, JT's daily call with the investigators produced results. Kendall's death had very quietly been deemed a homicide. The detective did not say if the killer's face was visible on camera, but the fact that no arrests were immediately made meant either no one was identifiable or it was Officer Corey Williams.

In spite of this, the detective's request had JT grinning.

He hung up and turned to Alexandra, who was feeding Gemma an early dinner. The toddler was strapped into her highchair and making a huge mess of homemade mashed yellow goo and pureed meat of some kind.

"The police think they have enough to get a warrant to search Calvin Moss's house and offices. They should get it tomorrow. New Year's Eve at the latest."

"Interesting timing, given the sale."

JT had told the police of his intention to appear to move forward with the sale. The last thing he wanted was to tip off Calvin Moss. He'd even sign papers and had his attorney working on language that could nullify the sale in the event of Moss's arrest. In the meantime, it would serve to tie up Moss's funding. He had a lot of investors on the hook and would be destroyed financially, which wasn't justice, but still offered a small amount of satisfaction.

"Yeah. I said that. And we can use it. They wouldn't mind serving the warrant while they *know* he's not at the office or home."

"Interestingly enough, you have a very important meeting scheduled with him before close of business on New Year's Eve."

"Exactly. The paperwork on this kind of thing takes a

while, which is why we're doing it at two p.m., hours before the party."

"So they'll serve the warrant while you keep him occupied?"

"Yep. And then we'll get married—and if all goes well, he won't be among the guests."

"If they find anything in his home or office, they'll serve the warrant for his arrest at the Mayflower?"

"Yes."

"What a fabulous wedding gift."

"I aim to please."

"This gives me an idea. Tomorrow, I'm meeting with Mark to make a video for the wedding reception. What do you say we make a special version for Calvin to preview?"

Kendall's photographer boyfriend, Mark, had been hired to photograph the ceremony, but this was the first JT had heard of any kind of video.

She grinned. "It was going to be a surprise. Lee's been helping me find photos—some are on that old hard drive, some in T&D archives."

JT returned the smile. "I think it sounds great. And I love the idea of fu—" He glanced toward Gemma. "Messing with Calvin while we have his attention."

"Oh, we'll have his attention, all right."

He kissed her forehead. "Rip him a new black hole, Muffin."

Chapter Forty-Nine

"Thanks for meeting earlier than we'd scheduled, Calvin. Sorry I hijacked our original plans for the night." JT gave him his very best grin, eager to get this over with, but also ready to savor every moment of watching this guy squirm.

"No worries, JT. This was always your show. I've never been big into the holiday spectacle. Too much opportunity to fuck it all up." He grinned at the obvious reference to what JT had done at the party years ago. "By the way, big congrats on getting her to forgive you."

"I'm a lucky man," he said with absolute sincerity.

This sort of transaction was usually completed at a title company or other neutral office, with the seller signing first, but given the scope of this sale, they'd all—even the attorneys involved—agreed to do this in the office attached to the ballroom at the Mayflower, just prior to the start of the New Year's Eve party.

JT had bumped up the timeline for the closing, but the party for T&D employees was still on if they wanted to attend. It also just so happened to now be a wedding reception.

In a few hours, JT would marry Alexandra, right after appearing to sell the company that had been his dad's life work. He was sad his dad wasn't here for this. Joe might not be pleased that JT intended to sell—not to Moss, but he'd find another buyer—but his dad had come to respect Alexandra. In their last conversation, Joe had urged him to repair the relationship.

Instead, the next day, within an hour of his father's death, he'd torched it.

Life had given him one more shot, and he wouldn't waste it.

The paperwork was endless, which was just what they needed to buy time. An hour and twenty minutes into the process, Alexandra entered the conference room.

"Are you supposed to be here?" Calvin said. "Shouldn't you be hiding behind a veil or something?"

"No time for superstitions when you plan a wedding at the last minute like this."

JT was glad for that. Waking up with Alexandra this morning had helped steel him to face the more difficult aspects of today, while feeding Gemma her breakfast had grounded him. He wasn't in this for the big party. He was in it for the life.

He smiled at his bride. "What's up, beautiful?"

"I hate to interrupt—I know how important this is. But the video we're going to show during the reception was just finalized. JT, I really want you to see it in case we need to make any tweaks. We won't have time later. Do you all mind taking a little break? You're welcome to watch."

"How long is it?" Calvin asked.

"Ohh, about fifteen minutes? It was really hard with so

many years' worth of photos to decide what to put in, but we really managed to pare it down. You'll like it, Calvin. You're even in a few of the pictures."

"I am?"

"All those company events."

"It's fine with me," he said. He turned to the attorneys. "You can take a break if you want."

"I could use some food."

"We've got snacks in the suite," Alexandra said, giving them the room number for the suite they'd reserved for wedding prep.

She sat at the table next to JT and plugged a USB drive into his laptop. There was a frilly graphic with their names and the date in a script font popular for weddings.

The first image in the slideshow had been taken the night of the holiday party when they first met. An event photographer had taken candid shots during dinner, and there was a photo of JT with Drake and Calvin and a few other executives. The next image was Alexandra, laughing at a table with Brent, Russ, and Kendall. JT had never seen that photo before, but wasn't surprised Lee had managed to find it in the archives.

"I get why you're including photos from that night," Calvin said, "but I can't help but wonder if you really want photos of Drake, Russ, and even Brent to be shown at the reception?"

"JT and I discussed that, and we agreed everything is part of our journey. And let's face it, if it weren't for Russ, Brent, and Kendall, we never would have met. Besides, Calvin, you're in there too."

He chuckled. "Well, I'm not some high school senior scouring the yearbook for pictures of myself instead of seeing the shared moments with my classmates."

"It's only on the first pass that you look for photos of yourself," she replied. "And I get your point, but the thing is, Kendall was and will always be my friend. We had our rough moments, but I'll never have another friend like her. With her death so recent—which I don't know if you heard about? It's all so raw and recent, and I really want her to be part of this ceremony."

"I ran into Brent Forbes a few weeks ago. He mentioned his ex-girlfriend had died. I remember Kendall from when I worked at T&D. I'm sorry she's gone."

Yeah. JT knew exactly how familiar Calvin was with Kendall's work for T&D.

Alexandra rewound to the photo that included Kendall and hit Pause. "I went to her house a week and a half ago. It was…*the* night. I'm sure you saw the news… Anyway, I took some things that she'd left for me. Important mementos. But they were stolen from my car. I'd give anything to get those back."

"I'm sorry," Calvin said, "that's terrible. They didn't show that part of the video on the news but mentioned a box had been taken. That's what it was?"

She nodded. JT rubbed her shoulder in a show of sympathy.

It was that exact box the cops were searching for in his house. JT hoped to hell the man felt so secure that no one had a clue of his involvement that he'd hidden the box rather than getting rid of it when it didn't contain what he was looking for.

Alexandra let out a soft sigh. "Yes. The box didn't have anything important except to me. Framed photos. My mom's copy of *The Joy of Cooking*. Mom wrote notes in the margins of the cookbook, adjusting the recipes. She has dementia now, and I want more than anything to make my daughter

Grandma's snickerdoodles. That might be the loss that hurts the most."

"I forgot about your mother's snickerdoodles," JT said. "Those things were insanely good."

"They tasted like love."

Alexandra was good at this. JT didn't see the act in her words. She was stringing Calvin right along.

"I won't give up hope it will turn up. In the meantime, I went back to Kendall's house a few days ago to get my wedding dress—which is *amazing*, by the way." She laughed, her chuckle soft and fun, showing none of the strain that she must be feeling. "While I was in the house, I searched for anything that would offer a clue as to why a police officer would pull me over and then another person would kill the officer and steal a box that I'd taken from her house."

"Did you find anything?"

She smiled. "Actually, I did. But we had to turn it over to the police. I didn't even really get to look at it. I hope someday to get it back."

She hit Play on the video. The next slide made JT laugh. It was a photo of him in a Santa suit with a grimacing kid on his lap. The girl clutched a present in one hand and Alexandra—crouched down in an elf costume—in the other.

He remembered that moment when she'd swooped in like Rudolph to save Santa. He'd been such a goner.

There were more photos from more holiday parties over the years. Photos of him and his father along with Alexandra and Lisa. So many political and charity events.

Then there was the engagement portrait that was taken years ago. There was a gap in time, and the next photo was taken the night his father had announced he was running for president. A newspaper with a front-page photo of Lee and Erica taken the same night.

Even a headline about Joe's arrest side by side with the

revelation that Ed Drake had murdered JT's grandmother when his father was four years old.

Any time JT questioned whether or not Drake would have paid Spaulding to put a drugged woman in his bed, he reminded himself the man had committed murder at the age of sixteen.

"Edgy," Calvin said.

"It's kind of like a New Year's Eve rewatch of *It's a Wonderful Life*—but different in that no one gets wings," Alexandra said.

"Oh, if we didn't have plans tonight, I'd totally do a rewatch," JT said.

She laughed and kissed him. "Then that's how we'll celebrate our first anniversary."

They'd moved on to the last holiday party that both Alexandra and Calvin had attended. JT had been braced for it, knowing it was coming. He only felt a twinge of shame instead of the boatload that usually accompanied thoughts of that night.

If Alexandra could let it go, so could he.

There had been more photos of Kendall throughout, and now the screen showed one of her and Brent at that same holiday party, followed by photos from when Alexandra lived with Kendall full time again.

A handful of photos showed Alexandra in Switzerland. Pregnant in some, in the last, she held a newborn. Her return to the US was documented with a photo of her with Lee and Erica and their daughters.

Next up was a photo of Kendall taken by her photographer boyfriend and one with him by her side. It was followed by the photo of Calvin with Officer Corey Williams that Kendall had taken from the restaurant across the street. The image slowly zoomed in, using the Ken Burns effect.

"*What?* What...what... What's *that* doing there?"

Alexandra hit Pause, freezing on Calvin in a relaxed posture, smiling at his second cousin. "Kendall's boyfriend, Mark, had that in his photos. He said it was important to her. He'd forgotten about it until we started working on this. Imagine his surprise when he realized one of the men in the photo was murdered just a few weeks after this was taken."

Calvin started to rise. "I think…I think that should do it. We really need to wrap up signing the docs."

She pressed down on his shoulder, nudging him back into his seat. "But wait, there's more!" Her voice had taken on the tone of an infomercial. She hit Play again, and there was the video of Kendall kissing Brent in the garage.

"I think that the best part of this video is the voiceover that plays next." She hit the Volume button that had been playing generic wedding slideshow music until now. Kendall's recorded conversation with Brent played. The conversation that mentioned Calvin Moss.

Calvin looked ready to crawl out of his skin. Had he recognized the same thing Eden had about the angle of the camera in the garage? He had to know that was where Kendall died. Corey Williams would have told him exactly how he'd killed her.

"What's this about?" Calvin asked.

"It's a wonderful life, isn't it, Calvin?" Lex's voice was silky smooth.

"Best of luck to you both." He rose. "We can finish the signing later."

"But we need to do it now," JT said, "while the numbers are settled to the day. Before the end of the year. Close of business is in an hour."

"I'll get the attorneys, then." Calvin took a step toward the door.

Alexandra was closer and blocked him. "Sit. Stay. I'll get them for you."

"I'm not a fucking dog." His voice was low and menacing.

"Careful there, Calvin, or someone might think you have something to be afraid of." She smiled innocently.

JT took a position behind Calvin. "Yeah. Very, very careful. Unlike the others, she hasn't been drugged into submission. And I will *never* let you lay a fucking finger on her." JT wasn't armed, but he had thirty years of martial arts training on his side. "Now, do as she said. Sit. Stay. Alexandra will fetch your attorney."

Calvin lunged for Alexandra. She pressed the bar on the door with her hip and stepped backward into the promenade, a wide, ornate hall just off the hotel lobby.

Calvin stumbled forward, still reaching for Lex. She evaded his grasping hand as JT caught him and spun him around. "Fight me, not her, asshole."

This began sixteen years ago with Lex as the victim, but the target had always been JT. Kendall had suffered and paid the ultimate price because of this man's greed and Edward Drake's need for power.

JT threw a punch that bloodied Calvin's nose.

The man grinned through the blood. "You've got nothing on me, JT. But my attorneys will be thrilled to hear you assaulted me."

"Why did you kill your cousin, Moss?"

"Who?"

"Stupid to lie about things that are a matter of public record. Suspicious that you didn't mention your connection to Officer Williams to Lex when you had the chance."

"Of course I didn't say anything. I'm in the middle of buying your company. What my distant cousin did has nothing to do with me."

"Second cousin isn't so distant," Lex said. "Did you kill him because he fucked up when I knocked him out and escaped?"

"You're out of your mind."

"Did you order Williams to kill Kendall," she continued, "or was he acting on his own?"

Moss opened his mouth to answer but he saw the trap and snapped his jaw closed.

"Forbes is talking," JT said. "You and Spaulding are going down for murder."

"Bullshit."

Lex stood in the promenade behind Calvin, who faced JT standing in the office doorway. She glanced toward the lobby and grinned. "Oh, good. They're here."

Calvin turned and saw the approaching officers. He blanched and twisted, grabbing Lex and holding her in front of him before JT could stop him.

He pulled a gun from the inside pocket of his jacket. Before he could bring it up, Lex swung out with her right arm, shoving the gun up. She pivoted to face him and kneed him in the balls. JT made his move, grabbing Calvin's gun hand and twisting his arm behind his back.

Then the cops were upon them, completing the takedown. Moss was cuffed and patted down as his rights were read. Carrying concealed in the District of Columbia would be added to the charges that included murder, extortion, embezzlement, industrial espionage, and accessory to murder.

Kendall's camera had been found in Moss's home, as had Alexandra's laptop and a box of memorabilia that included her mother's copy of *The Joy of Cooking*.

Moss's business attorney, who had been present for the signing, made it more than clear he didn't handle criminal law, but he agreed to accompany the man to the police station for booking and advised his client to say nothing until he found an attorney who could give him proper representation.

Good luck finding a defense attorney on New Year's Eve.

Next week, JT would begin the search for a new, far better, buyer. He would make sure his employees were taken care of. And then he would bow out.

But for now, the only thing on his agenda was getting ready for their wedding.

Chapter Fifty

Erica fastened the necklace around Alexandra's neck, then stepped back. "Now that's a spectacular something blue."

She laughed, touching the blue diamonds at the center of the galaxy. She studied her reflection, running her hands over the fitted bodice and voluminous skirt of the silver gown. She'd forgotten how much she loved this dress. Had blocked it out.

"This is really happening," she murmured.

"You look fabulous. Ready to head down?"

"Yes."

"I'll text Lee and make sure JT's in the ballroom and not out on the promenade."

They left the suite's primary bedroom and knocked on the other bedroom door, where Curt and Mara waited with Gemma and Grace. "Ready when you are."

Curt opened the door to reveal Gemma and Grace in silver flower girl dresses.

Alexandra and Erica both squealed at seeing them. "Utterly adorable," Erica said.

"I'm a princess, Mama." Grace twirled, letting her skirt flare.

"Yes, you are, baby."

The plan was for Mara to accompany the two flower girls down the aisle because it was unlikely they would successfully navigate the distance on their own. They would be followed by Erica as matron of honor. Colin was already with best man Lee, acting as ring bearer.

Alexandra would be escorted down the aisle by Curt. Her parents would be seated in the front row, but neither was truly cognizant of the occasion. It was enough that they were there.

They took the elevator to the lobby and Alexandra enjoyed the oohs and ahhs that greeted them from hotel guests. They were all princesses today.

They took their spot outside the side door for the ballroom, where Trina had been waiting. She darted inside and let the officiant know they were ready to begin.

Alexandra kissed Gemma and repeated the instructions for walking with Mara and Grace. Erica handed both girls baskets of flower petals, but they all knew the odds of any being sprinkled were slim at best, just as Colin was too young to take ring bearer duties seriously.

But neither Alexandra nor JT cared if the kids performed their roles or if they chose to sit or stand. They just wanted their friends present, and she wanted her daughter as close as possible.

She smiled at her assembled attendants. "Let's roll."

Mara and the girls entered, and she heard laughter as the two underage flower girls stole the show.

"I hope Mark is getting video."

"If he's not, I know at least half a dozen others are," Erica said. The laughter subsided. "Sounds like I'm up." She kissed Alexandra's cheek. "See you on the other side."

She went through the door. Curt held out his arm, and Alexandra took it. "Thank you for doing this."

"It is my absolute honor." He kissed her temple, and the bridal march started.

It was so strange how the song struck her in the heart at that moment. But before she could take it in, they were stepping through the door, and her gaze traveled the aisle and landed on the tuxedoed man on the other end of it. He was devastatingly handsome. His eyes were fixed on hers with an intensity that took her breath away.

The love of her life was finally and completely hers. No holding back.

Alexandra had mesmerized him from their first meeting, but JT had never guessed it was possible for her to be even more beautiful than the twenty-five-year-old he'd wooed and won, or even the thirty-year-old he'd foolishly lost. But here she was, sparkling in a lush silver gown and glittering with a diamond galaxy around her neck.

This incredible woman was his. Now and forever.

Not once during the ceremony did he think of Moss or anything that could mar the moment. He only had eyes for Alexandra and the life they were forging together, again, and for the first time.

Gemma had made it almost all the way through his vows before squealing and attempting to break free of Mara's hold. Alexandra asked JT with her eyes how he wanted to handle it, and he nodded.

She gestured for Gemma to join them, and he finished his part while Gemma played with the voluminous silk fabric that made up Alexandra's skirt. He then scooped the girl up and held her on his hip while Alexandra said her vows.

With Gemma between them, the kiss was chaste and brief, and the little girl then demanded her own kiss, giving them each a wet smack in return.

And then it was done. On what would have been their eleventh anniversary, Alexandra Vargas was his wife at long last.

For an impromptu wedding, it was surprisingly organized. For what was supposed to be a company party, it was surprisingly fun.

After a five-course dinner, JT danced with his wife, holding their daughter between them. They danced and visited with guests for at least an hour before they both escaped into the suite to put an exhausted Gemma to bed. Thankfully, she was too tired to fight the new setting and being left with a sitter, and they were able to return to the party twenty minutes later.

They were greeted with the news that both Russ and Brent had been arrested—the vial that had been found inside the computer had indeed held GHB and had Brent's fingerprints on it. It might not be admissible given the broken chain of evidence, but between that, the diary, the recording, and other conversations Kendall had caught with her hidden cameras, they had enough to bring them in and hope one or both would turn on Calvin.

Brent was their best bet. He had the most direct tie to Kendall and would be eager to distance himself from her murder. The video of them together prevented him from claiming he hadn't spoken with her in the weeks before her death.

The search for the money had only just begun.

They drank champagne, toasting to arrests in addition to

the usual wedding speeches, then they danced until it was time for cake.

They'd been unable to order a tiered cake at the last minute, but JT had promised he'd find something special and was gratified by Lex's laugh when she saw the plate of fancy muffins next to several eight-inch cakes in different flavors.

Instead of cutting a piece from one of the cakes, she plucked a pumpkin muffin from the plate and held it up to him. He took a bite from the top, just like he had that first night.

"You are the very best thing that ever happened to me," she whispered. "You even gave me Gemma, in your own way."

He cleared his throat of emotion and said, "And now you're sharing her with me and I can't believe how incredibly lucky I am."

He turned the muffin to her, and she took a bite. "Do you want a slice of cake?"

She shook her head, grabbed his hand, and pulled him back toward the dance floor. "Let's shake the rust off your ballroom."

He laughed and took her into his arms as "The Way You Look Tonight" came on. He stared down into her beautiful face. "I think it's time I sell the Lotus."

She stopped swaying, eyes wide with surprise. "Seriously?"

"Yeah. I see a minivan in my future."

She grinned. "Just when I think you can't surprise me any more."

The joy in her eyes stole his breath. He kissed her, then tightened his hold, and they swayed to the music. This was one of the most content moments of his life.

"This is better," she said.

"Better?"

"Than if we'd done this before. Sure, the wedding would have been just as pretty. I'd have worn the same dress and necklace—and I love both so much, I might not let you take them off me tonight."

He grinned. "I can work with that." Oh yeah, that silver fabric did things to him.

She laughed. "But even so, if we'd done this eleven years ago, the marriage would have failed because it's not about the wedding. It's about what comes tomorrow and the day after that."

He gazed into her eyes, which were so full of joy and warmth, he might burst. "I am so excited for tomorrow and the day after that. I'm excited for all our tomorrows."

"How attached are you to staying here until midnight?" she asked.

"Not even a little."

"Then let's say our goodbyes and ring in the New Year right."

He scooped her up and carried her toward the double doors that opened to the promenade, pausing so she could grab a bottle of champagne from one of the servers. "We'll need that for midnight."

She took the bottle and said, "No goodbyes?"

"They just take precious time. After wasting so many years, I'm ready to start enjoying our tomorrows now."

Author's Note

Readers have been asking me to write this book since the day after *Concrete Evidence* was published on April 16, 2013. It made the work challenging, knowing the expectations readers have for JT & Alexandra. I will be honest and say that without the relentless campaign by readers begging for this book, I would not have written it. I was content with leaving them be, but around the time I was writing *Silent Evidence*, something about the excitement and enthusiasm made me curious to explore these characters more.

Still, it was daunting when the time came, and I must thank Gwen Hayes for her wise counsel in helping me find my path into these characters and the joy they could find in the midst of trauma and after heartbreak.

Concrete Evidence was my first published novel. *False Evidence* is my twenty-fifth. I began drafting *Concrete Evidence* in 2005. Now, nineteen years later, I've finished the final book in the twelve book series, a book that itself spans sixteen years—less time than it took me to start and end this series. It's been quite a journey and I can't think of a better finish than to end with a direct sequel to the first book. It's like I planned it or something. (I did not. Not even a little bit.)

Never fear, the series is done, but the Evidence world continues in Evidence: Under Fire, which merges the

Evidence and Flashpoint worlds. Look for book four in that series sometime in 2025.

Gemma's verbal skills are based my children, who both started speaking before they were ten months old, but knock-knock joke credit goes solely to my son, who, at fifteen months old, made up the world's funniest and cutest joke, which Gemma tells in the story.

About the Author

USA Today bestselling author Rachel Grant also writes thrillers as R.S. Grant. She worked for over a decade as a professional archaeologist and mines her experiences for storylines and settings, which are as diverse as excavating a cemetery underneath an historic art museum in San Francisco, survey and excavation of many prehistoric Native American sites in the Pacific Northwest, researching an historic concrete house in Virginia (inspiration for her debut novel, CONCRETE EVIDENCE), and mapping a seventeenth century Spanish and Dutch fort on the island of Sint Maarten in the Caribbean (which provided inspiration for the island and fort described in CRASH SITE).

She lives in the Pacific Northwest with her husband and children.

For more information:
www.Rachel-Grant.net
contact@rachel-grant.net

www.ingramcontent.com/pod-product-compliance
Lightning Source LLC
Chambersburg PA
CBHW071357261224
19522CB00028BA/300